This Time Around

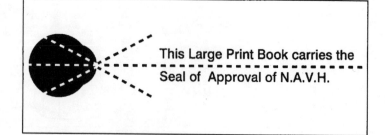

Debra White Smith

Thorndike Press • Waterville, Maine

Published in 2006 by arrangement with
Harvest House Publishers

Thorndike Press® Large Print Christian Fiction.

The tree indicium is a trademark of Thorndike Press.

The text of this Large Print edition is unabridged.
Other aspects of the book may vary from the original edition.

Set in 16 pt. Plantin by Ramona Watson.

Printed in the United States on permanent paper.

Library of Congress Cataloging-in-Publication Data

Smith, Debra White.
    This time around / by Debra White Smith.
       p. cm. — (Thorndike Press large print Christian fiction)
    ISBN 0-7862-8300-9 (lg. print : hc : alk. paper)
    1. Single mothers — Fiction. 2. Abused wives —
Fiction. 3. Widows — Fiction. I. Title. II. Thorndike
Press large print Christian fiction series.
  PS3569.M5178T48 2006
   813'.54—dc22
                                     2005029578

To my wonderful children
Brooke and Brett Smith

While I have been writing *The Seven Sisters*, Brett (now 8) and Brooke (nearly 6) turned my life and my heart upside down. They spread staples around my office. They distributed my pens all over the house. (If you want to know what my house looks like, check out Samantha Jones' in the following pages.) They vigorously participated in sibling rivalry when I was trying to wrap up "one more chapter."

I have gotten up with them in the middle of the night more times than I can remember, then after only a few hours sleep continued writing the series. I have sat with my laptop beside the bed and written when Brett made frequent trips to the bathroom due to a stomach virus. I have sat with Brooke on my lap and, while she put her head on my shoulder and went to sleep, I have written like the wind.

It's been nothing short of a miracle of God that I got one word written! But I wouldn't change a thing. Every difficult moment is always washed away by the joy in Brett's eyes when he's mastered another task, the thrill of discovery on Brooke's face when she shares a beautiful rock, and their smiles that reach deep into my heart.

And, as you can guess, my wonderful children have filled my heart and life with a love that leaves me breathless. They have taught me what it means to be loved beyond words by a heavenly Father who adores me. And now that they are getting old enough to handle some responsibilities, they help during my speaking engagements by helping set up my book table and even singing with my husband and me when we minister together. God is so good to give us precious gifts in our children then teach us through their presence. I absolutely adore my two kids.

Now I'm off to the store to buy more tape for my office. . . . Yesterday the kids made off with what I had for one of their art projects.

Acknowledgments

A special thanks to Dr. Grady Ellis, DVM, for his continual help as I consult him for details regarding animals. Dr. Ellis is a tremendous source of information.

As the Founder/CEO of NAVH, the only national health agency solely devoted to those who, although not totally blind, have an eye disease which could lead to serious visual impairment, I am pleased to recognize Thorndike Press* as one of the leading publishers in the large print field.

Founded in 1954 in San Francisco to prepare large print textbooks for partially seeing children, NAVH became the pioneer and standard setting agency in the preparation of large type.

Today, those publishers who meet our standards carry the prestigious "Seal of Approval" indicating high quality large print. We are delighted that Thorndike Press is one of the publishers whose titles meet these standards. We are also pleased to recognize the significant contribution Thorndike Press is making in this important and growing field.

Lorraine H. Marchi, L.H.D.
Founder/CEO
NAVH

* Thorndike Press encompasses the following imprints: Thorndike, Wheeler, Walker and Large Print Press.

The Seven Sisters

Sonsee LeBlanc Delaney: A passionate veterinarian known for her wit, Sonsee grew up in a Southern mansion outside of New Orleans. She and Taylor, a Texas rancher, have recently given birth to their first child.

Jacquelyn Lightfoot Franklin: An expert in martial arts, Jac has seen plenty of action in her work as a private detective. Jac is married to Lawton Franklin (Melissa's brother-in-law), and they reside in Denver, Colorado.

Kim Lan Lowery O'Donnel: Tall, lithe, and half Vietnamese/half Caucasian, Kim is a much-sought-after supermodel. She and her missions-coordinator husband, Mick, adopted a son with special needs from an orphanage in Vietnam.

Marilyn Douglas Langham: Joshua and Marilyn, along with Marilyn's daughter, Brooke, live in Arkansas. Marilyn works as an office manager for a veterinarian; Joshua is a minister.

Melissa Moore Franklin: After a stormy reconciliation and an eventful Mediterranean cruise, Melissa married Kinkaide, a well-known Christian musician. An M.D., Melissa runs a small medical clinic in Nashville.

Sammie Jones: An award-winning writer/editor for *Romantic Living* magazine, Sammie also is building a writing career as a Christian novelist. Her husband, Adam, was killed in a car accident. Sammie and her son, Brett, live in Dallas.

Victoria Roberts: A charming, soft-spoken domestic "genius" who loves to cook, work on crafts, and sew, Victoria is married to Tony and lives in Destin, Florida.

This Time Around Cast

Barry Cox: Terrence Blackwood's brother-in-law. Barry is a veterinarian who loves dogs but doesn't care that his dealing cocaine is affecting the lives of humans.

Brett Jones: Sammie's three-year-old son, who keeps her life turned upside down.

Colleen Butler: R.J. Butler's mother and co-owner of *Romantic Living* magazine. She and her husband, Tom, are enjoying an extended season of travel.

Larry Tently: R.J. Butler's partner who shares responsibilities at their boys ranch in Mena, Arkansas.

Mallory Cox Blackwood: Terrence Blackwood's deceased wife and Barry Cox's sister. Mallory has been dead for years, yet her presence in Terrence's confused mind robs him of any chances of peace.

Mara O'Connor: Sammie Jones' estranged mother. Mara lives in east Texas.

R.J. Butler: Sammie Jones' first love and former fiancé. R.J. is the family rebel with a heart of gold. He owns a ranch for troubled boys in Mena, Arkansas. R.J. loves motorcycles and, most of all, Sammie.

Terrence Blackwood: Barry Cox's brother-in-law. Terrence is a deranged dog breeder whose past absorbs his future. He and Barry Cox are actively involved in distributing cocaine across the U.S.

11

Tom Butler: R.J. Butler's father and co-owner of *Romantic Living* magazine. He and his wife, Colleen, are enjoying an extended season of travel.

Wanda Martin: The managing force behind *Romantic Living* magazine.

One

Adam's going to kill me! He is . . . he is! I know he is. He's going to kill me!

Her heart hammering, Sammie Jones raced across the cluttered living room and up the hallway. The short corridor stretched forth like a warped mirrored maze at a carnival. As Adam's footfalls slammed behind her, a wail burst from her lungs. His ragged breathing raked along her spine; her lips quivered. She swiped at the sea of tears streaming down her face.

"You better stop, woman, and take what's comin' to ya." Adam's slurred threat sent a rush of cold sweat from her forehead to her feet.

Sammie coughed and sucked a panicked breath into heated lungs — a breath that seemed to pierce the ribs bearing her husband's brutal bruises. *Adam's going to kill me this time. I know he is. What's going to happen to Brett?*

Adam's fingernails scraped along her shoulder leaving a fiery trail in their wake.

Sam screamed, slammed through the bathroom door, and tried to close it. But she wasn't fast enough. The door smashed against the bathroom wall as Adam lunged inside. Samantha stumbled backward, and a shriek surged from her soul and ricocheted off the tile. It was the cry of an animal hunted and wounded. Wounded and desperate. Desperate and hopeless.

"Oh, God, no . . . don't let him! Not again! Oh please . . . please stop him. . . ." Sam gasped as she stumbled into the wall and the towel rack stabbed her sore spine.

Adam's fiendish eyes sparked with a devilish glint that promised another round of torment. He dashed stringy bangs from a forehead beaded with sweat and lifted a lean arm.

"I tol' you, woman! I tol' you not to run from me in the ga–garage! I told you I wouldn' hurt you if you'd cooperate."

The rancid odor of whiskey mingled with the smell of deodorant soap. Sam's stomach threatened to unload the Mexican food she'd consumed for supper.

"But you aren't interested in me, are ya?" He grabbed her upper arms and lowered his face to inches from hers. *"No!"* he bellowed, and his hot breath stung her cheeks like the winds off a merciless desert. "You aren' interested! If I didn't know a–any better, I'd say you've been snugglin' up ta that ol' boyfriend of yours."

He paused and peered into her soul. His wicked eyes glistened with an insight that pierced Sam's conscience. Trembling, she wanted to look away but couldn't muster the strength. Her wobbling knees collapsed, and Adam hauled her up and slammed her into a towel rack. A scream tore from her throat as her back arched.

"*R.J. Butler!* Why haven't you tol' me about him be–before now, Sammie!" Adam screeched.

"How — how did you know about — about —"

"Mamma! Mamma!" Brett's voice echoed up the hallway.

A broken sob from a mother's anguished heart exploded from Sam.

"*Stop, Adam!* Don't do this! Not in front of Brett!"

"Brett! Brett! Brett! That's all I ever 'ear from ya!" Adam slapped his palm against Sam's face with the crack of perspiring skin against a tear-stained cheek. Samantha groaned. Her head snapped back into the wall as scalding tingles erupted from her cheek and raced down her neck.

"I hate Brett! Do ya hear me! I hate him!"

"Mamma!" The soft patter of child's feet moved toward Sammie.

Adam doubled his fist, and Sam slid down the wall, a choking cry upon her breath. "Oh, Jesus, help me! Help Brett! Oh, God, get us out of this!"

The bathroom floor opened beneath Sam, and she plummeted into a tunnel, long and dark. Her moan mingled with Brett's panicked calls, and she clawed against the slick walls to no avail. Without warning, Sammie plopped onto a plot of ground, familiar and cold. Cold and hard. Hard and uninviting. The barren trees swirled around her like angry ghosts with bony fingers ready to claw out her eyes.

"Help!" she cried and covered her face. "Somebody help me!"

"Mamma!" Brett's voice now accompanied a ringing noise, and Sam fought the bonds that held her on the ground.

Yet all the thrashing availed was her toppling forward. Sam fell headlong into a stone that bit into her forehead. She uncovered her face and stared at the stone standing midst a sea of other grave markers. This headstone bore the name of the man who had promised to cherish her . . .

16

Adam Jones
1962–2001
May He Rest in Peace

A chorus of sniffling moved Sam's gaze up from the stone and into the sympathetic eyes of her friends. Sam looked for her sister. As usual, Rana wasn't to be found. Instead, her mother stood at a distance, her face barely discernible in the heated mist.

Sam's college friends gathered around her and offered bucketfuls of encouragement and support. Victoria Roberts, Jacquelyn Franklin, Marilyn Langham, Kim Lan O'Donnel, Melissa Franklin, and Sonsee Delaney — these six women were her true sisters. Together they reached down and tugged Sam upward. She floated on a cloud of their support. Gradually the vast cemetery detached from her senses and the distant ringing halted. She turned and moved away from the grave, away from the past, away from the violence.

"Mamma!" A pair of tiny hands tugged on her arm. Sam struggled from side to side as she attempted to merge the phantoms of her mind with reality.

"Mamma! Aunt Victoria is on the phone. She needs talk to you."

Like a dash of icy water, the present reality crashed upon Sam. She sat straight up in bed and stared at her little boy. The apparitions fled in the face of the dim morning light. Only the sweat along her hairline remained as testimony to her turbulent journey. Sam tugged on the damp neck of her flannel gown, and then she touched her cheek. Heated but not harmed. She glanced at her scarred alarm clock that proudly proclaimed three a.m. was soon approaching. Sam's eyes bugged; then she grabbed her wristwatch from the nightstand. "Seven forty-five!" she shrieked. "We should have been up an hour ago, Brett!"

Sam shoved aside the covers and glowered at the brass clock that had been her companion for more than 20 years. "You're history," she snarled. "I should have replaced you with a digital a year ago." But the clock was a link to her family, to the years before her mother left them for another man.

"Mamma!" Brett insisted as he shoved the cordless phone into Sam's hands. "Aunt Victoria is on phone." His blue eyes peered up at her as if he were bearing the most important news of the century.

"Okay . . . okay . . ." Sammie muttered. "Thank you. You're such a good helper," she added as a drowsy afterthought. Stifling a yawn, she rumpled the three-year-old's carrot-colored hair and placed the receiver next to her ear.

"Oversleep did we?" Victoria's soft voice floated across the line.

Sam grimaced against the pasty taste in her mouth. "You better believe we did," she replied as she stood and traipsed toward her closet. "I've got 30 minutes to get Brett and myself dressed, do *something* about breakfast, and then leave for the office. Can I call you back . . . uh . . ." Sam eyed Brett trotting toward the bathroom. His chubby legs churned beneath the bulge of Pull-Ups, and she wondered if he would make it in time.

"Call me back whenever," Victoria said. "It's not anything urgent. Just wanted to chat. Thought maybe you'd have a minute this morning. Oh — have any of the other sisters filled you in on the latest?"

Samantha snatched a teal blazer from the closet and the hanger danced on the rod. "No, what's up?" She reached for a pair of khaki pants.

"I'm pregnant."

With a gasp, Sam stopped.

"Toodles!" Victoria chimed, and the line went dead.

"Aahhh!" She looked at the phone, pressed the off button, and racked her mind for Victoria's number.

"Mamma, I need you!" Brett wailed.

With a grunt, Sam tossed the cordless amid her rumpled sheets, quickly dressed, and trotted toward the bathroom. No sooner had she stepped into the hallway than a tweeting parakeet, the color of the sky, flapped past her ear. The chirping bird landed on the bathroom's door frame and glared down at Sam as if it were a king awaiting homage.

"Oh, no," Sam groaned. "Brett, did you let the parakeets out again?" she asked as a yellow parakeet flapped right over Sam's head and ascended to a lofty ledge near its companion. The two birds joined in a chorus of high-pitched chirping that underscored Brett's guilty silence.

"I was out of my mind when I even thought about stepping into that pet shop," Sam muttered. *I should just leave them out for the day.* Her Siamese, Miss Kitty, trotted from Brett's room but stopped midstride when she spotted the two delectable birds sitting near the ceiling. Her ears twitched, and so did her tail. Sam had a swift vision of parakeet feathers hanging out of the cat's mouth. She thought about tossing Miss Kitty out for the day, but the image of the neighbor's Great Dane crushed that idea. Sam had declawed Miss Kitty a year ago. She'd be no match for a large canine with filet of feline on the brain.

"Mamma, I *neeeeeeeed* you!" Brett screamed. "I went tee-tee on the floor."

"Oh, nuts!" Sam spat out as she trudged toward the bathroom. *This is going to be a crazy morning!*

"What!" R.J. Butler said in disbelief as he stood. His eyes bugged; his fingers clutched the receiver. He placed his hand, palm down, in the middle of the lacquered desk and shut his eyes tight. R.J. closed out his mother's ornate executive office and blocked the responsibilities he had assumed at his parents' Dallas magazine. Only one thing bore upon his mind. His partner, Larry Tently, had just reported that three boys — three of *their* boys — had crawled on top of the church they attended in Mena, Arkansas, and nailed three female mannequins to the roof. The figures were each dressed in lacy underwear that, according to Larry, would make the most outlandish hussy blush.

"How did they get up there?" R.J. asked

as he stared at the brass-trimmed ceiling fan hanging in the center of the office.

"Beats me," Larry said.

"Are you sure it was our guys?"

"Yep. They confessed 'bout an hour ago."

"Which ones?"

"Dave. Jake. Carlos."

Groaning, R.J. lowered himself back into the chair. "Oh, great. Not Carlos again. That kid . . ."

"Well, look at it on the bright side. At least it doesn't involve drugs or theft or anything seriously illegal. Actually, this sounds more like something from *my* church camp days." A soft chuckle escaped Larry.

"Where did they get the mannequins and underwear?" R.J. asked, shaking his head.

"Goodwill."

"Will the Ingrams press charges?"

"Don't think so. I just spoke to them on the other line." Larry hesitated, and R.J. imagined the tall biker's gray eyes dancing in revelry. "It would seem that the ladies' mission auxiliary was meeting this morning. They were the ones who first spotted the wanton mannequins. Word has it that old Mrs. Belomy might near fainted." A snicker teetered over the line, and R.J. was hard-pressed to resist an impish urge to join in. "I'll just say the Ingrams are not happy campers."

"It wouldn't be half as bad if this congregation hadn't already bent over backward to help us." R.J. swiveled to gaze out the window behind his desk. A collection of majestic skyscrapers, clothed in Dallas mist, closed in for a claustrophobic squeeze. "The youth group just got through paying for those three to go to the winter retreat, didn't they?"

"Yep. Who knows, they may have cooked up the idea there."

"Maybe." R.J. sighed and rubbed his knuckles along the side of his short beard. When he agreed to take over *Romantic Living* magazine, R.J. had debated how well he could manage a full-time job in Dallas along with his small boys ranch in Arkansas. If not for his trusted partner and their new assistant, Steve, the undertaking would have been a fiasco. Still, Carlos was not adjusting to the situation well. R.J. wondered once again if taking the *Romantic Living* job was such a good idea.

"Do you have any suggestions about what we should do with these three adventurous boys?" Larry asked.

23

"Boil 'em in oil," R.J. growled. He reached past his tie to unbutton his shirt's collar. He picked up the end of the striped silk tie and frowned.

"I was thinking about making them wear women's underwear for a week," Larry quipped.

R.J. guffawed and slammed his palm against his forehead. "That's brilliant!"

"No, seriously, I'm going to make them formally apologize to the Ingrams," Larry continued.

"Why not also have them 'volunteer' to clean the church from top to bottom."

"Yes, that's nice," Larry purred. "We are good, now, aren't we."

"Actually, maybe my suggestion was more from experience. I had to clean the church once myself." R.J. eyed the pleat in the pants of his charcoal-colored suit and wondered why he had let his mother talk him into wearing suits in the first place.

"Uh . . . *I* had to take care of the church lawn for a month," Larry admitted.

"Ouch! You must have been *really* bad."

"I usually refer to those days as . . . creative," Larry said with a sly edge.

"Well, it looks like our guys are in good company then," R.J. said.

"Actually, this is rather refreshing when

24

you consider what they've been through and what they could have done. At least they didn't steal money or set the church on fire or —"

"Did you explain all that to the Ingrams?"

"Yep. Considering the fact that the bishop was also visiting this morning, I think the Ingrams would've preferred a nice, quiet theft that went unnoticed for a few days. Mrs. Ingram wasn't happy when she explained that the bishop had just asked her and her husband to do a seminar on husband-wife team ministries. Let's just say their team ministry didn't look so peachy this morning."

R.J. rested his head against the high-backed chair and sighed. "Do you think I need to come up?"

"No, that's okay. I think Steve and I are going to handle it all just fine. I just called to let you know the latest and get your input on punishment."

"Well, thanks," R.J. said dryly. "Good news is always welcome."

"Speaking of which, what's up with Sam and you? Married her yet?"

"Not since you asked last week." R.J. eyed the to-do list lying near his computer printer. Every morning, he printed out his list for the day. His gaze skimmed down to the last item — the item he had placed at the bottom of his list every day since last fall: *Marry Samantha Jones.*

"Well, hurry up, will you? I'm not sure all that time in the big city won't ruin you. 'Fore you know it, you'll be sippin' tea with your pinky in the air, wearing suits, and we'll be calling you Rhett," Larry snickered.

R.J. stood. "You start calling me Rhett, and I'll dress *you* in ladies' underwear and tie you to the *church steeple!*"

Larry's raucous laughter bounded over the line, and R.J. imagined his friend slapping his jeans-clad knee as he did any time he scored a point. R.J. ripped at the tie's knot and succeeded in a swift, one-handed removal. He slammed the menace in the center of his desk and glanced at his mother's elegant crystal clock sitting near a silver-plated bowl of potpourri — gardenia, to be exact. R.J. had 30 minutes to go upstairs to his parents' penthouse and change into his jeans and boots and T-shirt. *I have worn a suit to this office for the last time,* he vowed.

"Listen, if you think you can stop your laughing, I gotta go," R.J. said. "If you change your mind and need me to come up there this weekend to talk some sense into those three, call me. Otherwise, I'll stick to plan A and see you in two weeks."

"Sounds like a winner, *Rhett!*"

"I'm going to get you good, Larry Tently. You are *dead meat!*" R.J. dropped the receiver into its cradle and frowned at the phone for several seconds. Then he grabbed the tie and stomped toward the office door. For the millionth time he wondered what in the name of common sense had possessed his mother to name him Rhett Butler.

"I hate that name," he muttered, as if he were a rebellious ten-year-old. "I *hate* Dallas, too," he continued. "I hate suits. I hate being cooped up in an office. I want my bike . . . and the road . . . and my freedom."

But you also want Sammie. The thought stopped him in his tracks.

R.J. gripped the doorknob as long-cherished memories of Samantha Jones danced through his mind. He had known of Sam most of his life because his father and hers had been best friends from childhood. But only when the Joneses moved back to Dallas and started attending the same church did R.J. really get to know Samantha. She'd been all of 17, with long,

27

red hair, freckles, and a set of baby-blues that would stop traffic. R.J. had told himself over and over again that she was way too young. He was 23; she was 17. He had kept his distance for months, but when she was 18 *she* asked him to a church banquet. R.J. had decided to turn her down, but then he heard himself agree.

"And I could kick myself for not marrying her that summer," R.J. whispered. He exited the office and strode up the deserted hallway toward the back exit. The old guilt scurried from beneath a row of desks and enveloped him in what-might-have-beens.

If I had married Sam instead of riding off and leaving her, she would have never married Adam Jones or had to endure all that abuse. R.J. opened the heavy door that led to a narrow elevator. *But you did try to get her to marry you before she married Adam — and she wouldn't.*

With a sigh, R.J. relived that heated conversation the week before her wedding. He had done everything but sit in Sam's lap and sob. Yet Sam had refused his offer — coldly refused. She made no attempts to hide the fact that she didn't trust him not to ride off and leave her again. "Besides, I'm in love with Adam," she had claimed, and the look in her eyes said she believed Adam was everything R.J. could never be.

With a wince R.J. pressed the elevator button, and the doors bumped open. He stepped inside, jabbed the up button, and the doors slid shut. "Truth is, Sam, Adam *was* everything I could never be," he muttered. "I'd *never* hit a woman. *Never!*" The elevator began the brief upward glide, and a cold knot formed in R.J.'s stomach as he contemplated the horrors Sam endured at the hands of that jerk. A warm wash started at the base of R.J.'s throat and crept under his beard. His fist tightened around the tie, and his toes curled inside his glossy leather shoes. "It's a really good thing you're dead, you creep," R.J. whispered. "Otherwise . . ."

The elevator hummed to a halt, and the doors hissed open. R.J. stepped out and forced himself to take several deep breaths. *I need some anger management here,* he thought and began talking to himself in a steady, calming voice. "There's no sense in majoring on the past. There's nothing I can do about water that's gone under the bridge. All I can do is hang in there for the present and future. Bottom line is, Sam needs a husband — whether she'll admit it or not. And Brett . . . that little guy needs a father, a *real* father."

As he approached the penthouse door, R.J. imagined the little redheaded tyke motoring into his office and crawling onto his lap, just as he had yesterday evening before Samantha left for the day. Brett had thrown his arms around his "Uncle R.J.," kissed him soundly on the cheek, and said, "See you 'morrow!"

R.J. smiled. The bottom of his to-do list said he was supposed to marry Sam today. And maybe, just maybe, this would be the day.

Two

Subject: Sammie's phone number
On Monday, 15 Jan 2002 8:58:46 -0800
Mara O'Connor
<mara@oconnor.hhp> writes:

Colleen,
   Hi! I haven't heard from you since Adam's funeral. I hope all is well. It seems I've either lost my daughter's address and phone number or she's had her number changed or she's moved. Would you be so kind to send them to me? I am sorry to bother you, but I haven't seen or talked with her since Adam's funeral, and I wanted to get in touch.
   At the funeral, you mentioned that you and Tom were going to retire and try to get R.J. to manage *Romantic Living*. Did he agree? Is Sam still there as well? I'm hoping that Sam and R.J. might reignite the old flame since they're working together. I do think he would be so good for

31

her and Brett now. Hope to hear from you soon, dear!

Your friend,
Mara

Subject: Sammie's phone number
*On Monday, 15 Jan 2002 9:58:22
Colleen Butler
<candt@butler.hhp> writes:*

Hi, Mara!
   Great to hear from you. Yes, we are finally taking a break from work! I am sitting on the couch of our travel trailer and e-mailing you with my Pocket PC while Tom is whizzing along the freeway. We're in New Mexico right now. What a riot! I love all these new technological advances.
   Re: Sammie and Rhett. *Whew!* Now there's a toughie! I don't think Rhett suspects that we're really not all the way retired. Actually . . . *ssshhhh* . . . if you repeat this I'll have to hunt you down and feed you cat livers or something . . . we are viewing this "retirement" as an extended vacation. Tom wanted to taste the freedom of the road, and I wanted to see what would happen if Rhett and Sam

were forced to work together for awhile. Tee hee. I know my son too well to think he'll stay cooped up in that office for more than a few months. Actually, I'm dead certain the only reason he agreed to manage the magazine was because Sammie is there. I think it almost killed him when she married Adam, and I, too, wanted to sob the day of her wedding. But there was nothing I could do about it. I mean, she was all grown up, and she made her own decision. I've always considered her like a second daughter, and I'm hoping and praying nature will take its course and she and Rhett will reconcile. If you could have been around the mag the last few months — the undercurrents between those two are enough to take down a saint. At times, I didn't know whether it was good or bad!

Anyway, I'm babbling along here. Sam moved last fall. Her new address is 1012 Elmwood Lane, Plano, TX. Her phone number is (214) 555-9972. And it's supposed to be unlisted — *again*. I know I have said this in the past, Mara, but *please* don't tell her I'm the one who gave you the number. I wouldn't breach her confidence like this, but I can't bear the thought of a mother being estranged from her daughter. I know the past has been hard on both of you, but I am praying that someday you and Sam will be able to reconcile the past and move on to a better relationship. Here I am babbling on again. I certainly didn't mean to drag up the past. Please forgive me.

I hope everything is going well for you in east Texas. I will be praying for you and Sam.

Blessings!
Colleen

"Okay, okay, if I have everyone's attention, let's get started." R.J. Butler's voice boomed from the executive office and Samantha jumped.

"Late, late again," she mumbled and hoped her new boss would be as understanding as his parents — maybe even more so, if the adoration in his eyes was anything to go by. Sam dropped her purse and cloth tote on the edge of her desk, and a tower of papers toppled to the floor with a swish and plop.

"Nuts!" she whispered as she dropped down to scoop together the rough draft of her latest novella.

Brett crawled into her rolling chair and placed his knee on the desk's edge.

"Mamma! Where my doughnut?" he demanded.

Sam glanced up in time to see the chair rolling back. Brett's crystal-blue eyes rounded, and he teetered between the desk and the chair.

"No, Brett!" Sam dropped the manuscript and lunged up. The desk's edge cracked her forehead, and she lurched backward with a grunt and a stab of pain that felt like one of Adam's punches.

Her nightmare phantoms rushed from hiding and hurled the gruesome dream to the forefront of her mind. Her hand flew to her forehead. Her watering eyes squeezed shut. She bit her lips and forced herself not to release the rush of stinging tears. The chair clattering against the bookcase behind Sam's desk suggested the worst. In a breath, she anticipated Brett's pain-filled wails, and her eyes popped open.

The three-year-old crouched in the middle of the cluttered desk and peered at Sam as if *he* were the parent. "Mamma okay?" he asked.

Sam rubbed her throbbing forehead and eased her knees onto the steel-blue carpet. "Okay, I think." She sighed and rested a hand against her khaki slacks as the corn plant near the spacious window tilted at an odd angle. Sam shook her head, gripped the desk's edge, and felt as if the floor were going to suck her into the dark tunnel from her dream. With another shake of her head, her equilibrium gradually returned. Sam rose to her full height. *That was only a dream,* she reminded herself. *It's all over. Adam's dead. He is dead.*

Brett rocked back on his heels, and then plopped onto his knees as if he were a gold miner staking his claim.

"Baby, you don't need to be crawling on top of Mamma's —"

"*I* not a baby!" Brett exclaimed. He puckered cherry-colored lips, raised himself onto his knees, and placed his hands on his hips. "I a big boy! Uncle R.J. *say* I a big boy. I *not* a baby," he reiterated with an indignant glare.

"Come on, tiger," Sam said through a weary chuckle. She lugged her son into her arms and lodged him on her hip. Her lower back protested against the added weight, and Sam grimaced. She tried to ignore the stab that shot from her back to the front of her thigh, but it wouldn't be denied. She wondered how long Adam would be gone before she fully recuperated from his blows.

"As you all know, this is my first day to

solo here," R.J.'s voice continued from the adjacent office. "Last I heard from mom and dad, they were driving across New Mexico."

"They didn't waste any time, did they?" a male voice called, and a collection of chuckles underscored the claim.

Sam glanced over her shoulder, out her office door, and through the six-inch crack in R.J.'s doorway. The limited view of the mammoth office offered a glimpse of innumerable shoulders and heads. *Everyone else must already be there.*

"I want you to know that I'm really looking forward to working with all of you. From what I have gathered so far, you are an efficient group of people who do your jobs so well that, well, mom seemed to think I wouldn't be needed all that much."

"Sounds like you've been hornswoggled," Vice President Wanda Martin teased, and raucous laughter exploded from the room.

Sam smiled. She recalled the first time she and R.J. had really gotten to know each other. She had been a mere teenager, innocent and trusting and impressionable. Her mind began a fanciful journey, tracing the infatuation that gradually grew into something far more serious, something her father would have frowned upon because of

R.J.'s age and rough appearance had he not been the son of Tom and Colleen Butler. Nevertheless, what promised to be true love turned sour, and Sam was forced to taste bitter betrayal for the second time in her life. The first time came when her mother abandoned the family. The second was when R.J. broke their engagement. *And Adam was betrayal number three,* Sam thought. *The third time was it. I'm through trusting R.J. or anyone else. I'm through.*

Sam gritted her teeth and admonished herself to whisk aside the what-might-have-beens. But they haunted her as she snatched the bag of doughnuts from her stained canvas bag. Sam scrounged through the bag and its collection of Pull-Ups, snack crackers, and baby wipes in search of the cup of milk she thought she put in that morning. She unearthed a cold can of soda she had dropped in for herself. With a grimace, Sam set the Dr Pepper aside and dumped the bag's contents onto the desk. No milk toppled out. She eyed the soda and looked at her son.

"Well, I guess it's better than nothing." She tousled Brett's carrot-colored hair, so like her own. "Let's get you into your room, young man," she said, grabbing the pop. "Mamma's got a meeting to attend, and I'm late!"

"I want ta watch Winnie Pooh!" Brett declared.

"That's fine." Sam stepped into the modest playroom that once functioned as an oversized closet. She peered past the scattering of toys and the mini jungle gym to the videos sprawled across the TV stand. A sour, musty smell invaded her senses and announced that she had forgotten to empty the room's trash the previous evening. She kicked aside a pile of picture books, deposited Brett in the center of the brightly lit room, plopped the doughnut bag and Dr Pepper in front of him, and reached for the trash can that contained a used Pull-Up. Some days Samantha wished she had never insisted on being responsible for the janitorial duties in this room. When the Butlers had graciously agreed to her bringing Brett to work and even provided a playroom, she had wanted to do all she could to cause as little trouble as possible.

R.J.'s good-humored address penetrated her mind, urging her to hasten.

"I'm sure some of you thought my parents had lost their minds when they announced they were turning the magazine over to me." His claim preceded a new round of guffaws.

"I want Uncle R.J. to watch Winnie Pooh with me," Brett said, the rattle of the paper bag punctuating his words.

"No way, little guy. Not right now. Uncle R.J. is busy in a meeting, and I've got to go, too." Sam deposited a kiss on the top of her son's head and hovered close to relish the scent of baby shampoo. With a rush of love that minimized her throbbing forehead, she stroked his cherub cheek and tapped him on the end of his pug nose. "You're such a good little trooper," she crooned, but the endearment was lost on the child.

With a determined frown, Brett reached into the doughnut bag and pulled out his prize. Sam, shoving aside a strand of her wayward hair, tried to remember where she'd put her headband. Trash can in hand, she plopped in Brett's favorite video and hit the fast forward button until the featured presentation appeared on the screen.

"Mamma will be standing right there." She crouched beside her son and noticed that his cobalt-blue sweat suit intensified the hue of his eyes. Sam hesitated and searched for any sign of her husband in her son's freckled face. As always, all she saw was herself. She hoped little Brett would soon forget the abuse they had endured . . . and that he wouldn't resort to violence once grown. Sam pointed toward R.J.'s office as the boss' voice mingled with the cheerful music floating from the TV. "You'll be able to see me all the time. I'll be right back. But now you need to be a good boy and watch Winnie the Pooh for me."

"Okay, Mamma."

I wonder if R.J. even misses me in there, she mused.

"Looks like everybody is here except Sam." R.J.'s comment hit Sam right between the eyes. She raced from the playroom, dropped the trash can beside her desk, and snatched the headband, lying near the disheveled manuscript still on the floor. She shoved the band onto her head while striding toward the meeting room. With a last glance over her shoulder, Sam eased into the executive office and hovered at the entry. The smells of freshly brewed coffee and gardenia potpourri invited her to relax.

R.J. stood behind what used to be his mother's desk and peered down at a sheet of paper. With his black T-shirt, faded blue jeans, and short beard, he looked as out of place in the ultramodern office as a peasant at a king's banquet. *Well, I guess you couldn't take the suit another day, you rebel,* she mused.

"Ah, there she is." R.J.'s drawl suggested he should be out on a ranch rounding up cattle rather than heading up a magazine called *Romantic Living.* He reached for a pair of black-rimmed reading glasses and nudged them onto his nose. Every head turned her way.

With an apologetic smile, Sam wiggled her fingers in R.J.'s direction and shrugged. He peered at her over the reading glasses, and Sam suppressed the urge to laugh out loud. The sprinkle of gray in his short, dark beard, the trace of silver in the braid hanging across his shoulder, the heart-shaped tattoo peeking from beneath his shirt sleeve mingled together to create an image of a middle-aged renegade.

Who'd have thought R.J. Butler would ever settle down enough to hold a regular job? she wondered.

"Glad you could make it, Sam," he said with a quirk of one brow, yet his words held an undeniable nuance that suggested he was much more than glad.

Sam's fist clenched against her slacks,

and she would have sworn that the 30-plus magazine employees inhaled a collective gasp. The staccato rain upon the massive window behind R.J. announced that the threatening clouds had finally released their burden. A flash of lightning and a clap and rumble of thunder proclaimed that Dallas was in for a rouser of a January storm. The weather forecasters warned that this storm was ushering in a wicked cold spell that might bring snow and ice.

"And even the heavens applaud her entry." R.J.'s chocolate-brown eyes narrowed, and a glimmer of revelry sparkled from his soul. Revelry and ardent admiration. Admiration and unbridled love.

A clammy rush assaulted Sam's palms and her gaze faltered. *So why don't you crawl on top of the skyscraper and tell the whole world you're in love with me while you're at it?* She scrutinized the steel-blue carpet in front of her loafers. As a curtain of rain slammed into the window, she wondered for the thousandth time if she were crazy to keep her job. When R.J.'s parents had offered her the job seven years ago, Sam had jumped at it. But R.J. had been out of the picture — riding his Harley who knew where. Somebody shoved a cup of steaming coffee into her hand, and Sam compulsively gulped the hot, black liquid. The brew scalded her tongue and stung the back of her throat. Samantha winced, yet swallowed another mouthful. She glanced at the person who proffered the needed boost and received a candid wink from Erica Rodriguez, who had joined the staff last week as receptionist.

"Thanks," Sam whispered.

"You bet," she replied as R.J. picked up where he left off. Erica reached forth and snagged something from the edge of Sam's ear, then extended a parakeet feather to her friend. Her dark brows rose over almond-shaped eyes the color of teak.

Sam grabbed the turquoise feather and relived the mad bird chase less than an hour ago. During that ruckus, Sam had decided to see if The Pet Shoppe would let her return the birds for a puppy — maybe a cocker spaniel. Anything would be better than the commotion she had endured the last three days. No matter where she placed the cage, Brett somehow managed to free the birds.

"Been plucking chickens again?" Erica whispered with a hint of mirth dancing at the corners of her mouth.

"You know me, always the farm girl," Sam said.

44

"Yeah, right," Erica giggled. "I'd like to see you try to pluck chickens!"

"Oh yeah? Well at least I know what a live chicken looks like!" Sam shot back. "A city girl like you probably thinks they're wrapped in Styrofoam and cellophane! And what if you broke one of your fingernails. Oh, my . . ." Sam draped the back of her hand across her forehead.

Erica fanned her fingers between them — fingers that usually sported an elegant French manicure. But three of her sculptured nails were chipped, one nail was completely gone, and the rest looked like a food processor had chopped at them.

Sam gasped. "What happened?"

"I've been helping my parents redo their farmhouse," Erica claimed with a smug air. "*Their* chickens are arriving today." She flipped her waist-length braid over one shoulder with a swagger and swerve as if she were an accomplished farmhand. The two new friends burst into a round of snickers.

"Is there something you'd like to share with the rest of us back there?" R.J. asked.

Sam looked into his impassive face. This time his eyes lacked revelry. Sam groaned. She had hit her stressed boss on a raw nerve. She gazed into her steaming coffee and saw Adam's fiendish glare. A rush of chills raced up her neck, and she barely stopped herself from glancing behind to see if Adam were watching. Her shoulders hunched and she winced.

"No . . . uh, no sir, Mr. Butler," Sam squeaked out.

Someone produced an uncomfortable cough. From the corner of her eye, Sam noticed several employees casting speculative glances toward her. She blinked against a rush of tears — tears that made no sense whatsoever and heightened the tension of her hectic morning. *Whatever possessed me to call him Mr. Butler?* she wanted to wail.

A choked hiss sputtered from R.J., and she dashed a watery glance back at him. He slammed his glasses onto the desk and rubbed his jaw. Sam swallowed another mouthful of coffee. She stared past him to the droplets of rain slithering down the glass, which was surrounded by sheaths of polished cotton the color of gunmetal. In spite of his crazy faults, R.J. Butler made a point of never interrupting others or talking when he was supposed to be listening. He expected the same of others and considered any infraction a blatant affront to the interrupted party.

But you certainly didn't mind riding off on that Harley of yours and leaving me to deal with the leftovers 16 years ago, did you? Sam accused. *If you want to talk disrespect, then let's talk disrespect.*

After a weighty pause, R.J.'s voice began playing upon the edges of her mind as she reflected over the last three months. During that time her former fiancé had received a crash course from his parents on the basics of running a magazine. In those frenzied weeks, R.J. had been so busy that he barely acknowledged Sam, although he had certainly taken the time to charm Brett. Sam had breathed easier when she thought he only vaguely noticed her. She had assumed that maybe — just maybe — the past wouldn't forever fill their every second together at the office.

I'm still not ready to get involved with someone, and I don't know if I'll ever be. She sighed. *This is going to be one long, long day.*

A loud commotion from her office validated her claim, and Sam's shoulders stiffened. She swiveled toward the slightly ajar door and gazed the short distance into her office and the playroom. Brett sat perched in the middle of her desk. Her office caddie's contents were scattered across the top of her papers, and her toddler was in the process of blissfully dismantling her stapler while Winnie the Pooh's voice gurgled from the playroom.

Oh great! Sam thought. She gingerly rubbed the bump on her forehead. *Whoever said the twos were terrible must have forgotten about the threes.* Sammie glanced across the room, pressed her lips together, and started to ease out of the office with as little stir as possible.

". . . which leads me to the reason for this meeting." R.J.'s voice crowded into the forefront of Sam's mind. "I wanted you all here so I could announce the person who'll replace Valerie Sadler as vice president. We're going to miss Val, but I think the time has come to go ahead and line up a new partner in crime for Wanda Martin."

"Ah, Wanda could run this rag with her hands tied behind her back," a male voice claimed.

"Hel–lo!" Wanda's rich voice reverberated around the room, and another round of companionable laughter heightened the camaraderie.

Sam's gaze shifted from Brett to R.J. Everything in the room melted into a blur — everything except R.J. His brown gaze

48

snared hers, and Sam's fingers flexed against the coffee cup.

Oh no, she thought. *He can't be thinking of making* me *the new vice president! Not now! Is he nuts? Can't he see I'm so pressed for time I barely have room to breathe!*

"I've chosen someone who has been with the magazine seven years and has proven loyal as well as highly talented." He paused for a dry grin. "She's also known for whispering when she's supposed to be listening and yelling when she's supposed to be talking."

Erica's hand covered Sam's forearm.

"If you haven't figured out by now, Samantha Jones will hold the official title of editorial vice president." R.J. waved toward Sam as if he were announcing royalty, and a polite round of applause crescendoed into a rumble of approval that mingled with a new clap of thunder. Every employee in the room stood and turned beaming smiles toward Sam. They never once faltered in the applause. This group of people had been more than kind after Adam's death. Indeed, they had been her champions. Sam couldn't claim one enemy from the midst of them. Yet the very applause, meant to encourage and uplift, stifled her every breath. The coffee cup shook. Hot liquid splashed onto her fingers. Every ounce of blood seemed to drain into her feet.

"That's it!" R.J. declared. "Let's go out there and put the latest issue to bed."

Sam ducked into the hallway just as R.J. called her name. She never broke stride. She stepped into her office, closed the door, dumped the coffee cup into the trashcan with the smelly Pull-Up, and scooped her child from her desk.

"No, no!" she admonished while prying the stapler from Brett's chubby grip.

Brett promptly arched his back and released a shriek powerful enough to bring six grown men to their knees. The scream slammed into the back of Sam's neck and slithered down her spinal cord. She gritted her teeth, dropped the stapler onto the desk, and hauled Brett into the playroom to muffle the sound. She forced herself not to give in to Brett's wailing. Anything seemed better than the kicking and screaming, but a voice of caution reminded her that rewarding a fit only invited more negative behavior.

"You're supposed to be watching Winnie the Pooh!" Sam snapped, wishing she could feign a calm aura. "I told you not to get up on my desk!" she scolded. The child thrashed more and slammed his doubled fist against her chest. How many times had he seen his father perform similar tactics? Samantha could no longer deny that Brett was exhibiting the early signs of emotional turmoil. On a choked sob she continued, "And if you don't stop this fit, I'm going to put you in time out."

"Here, let me have him." R.J.'s voice calmly floated from the doorway. Brett hurled himself toward his hero.

Three

Samantha pivoted as R.J. reached for Brett. The child ceased screaming and embraced R.J., who avoided eye contact with Sam. R.J. was sorely pressed to keep from hauling Sam into his arms as well. She had looked nothing less than shattered in that meeting only minutes ago. He could have ripped out his own tongue for snapping at her and Erica, but his stress level the last few weeks had been enough to make him testy at best. *I have no earthly idea what possessed me to agree to take over this magazine. I must be in the early stages of losing my mind.* But deep inside R.J. knew what had possessed him. At this point in his life he was willing to do anything — *anything* — to get into Sam's life and stay there . . . even if it meant giving up his beloved Arkansas hills. The whimpering child nestled his head against R.J.'s neck, and the biker stroked his little buddy's silky hair.

"Hey, what's got you so upset, chum?" R.J. asked as he eyed the half-eaten chocolate doughnut and can of Dr Pepper in the center of the room. He frowned at the sight of the sugar-laden snacks as a foul odor made his stomach churn. "Is that doughnut and soda all Brett's had for breakfast?" R.J. continued. "And what *is* that odor?"

Without a word, Sam swept past him and snapped the door shut. R.J. eyed her through the narrow window beside the door. She knelt near her desk, snatched a disheveled stack of papers from the floor and deposited them onto the desk. Her mane of shiny red hair and fresh freckled face coupled with the classic loafers and stylish teal blazer suggested a woman who had it all together. Yet R.J. knew from the moment he stepped back into her life last summer that the Samantha Jones he'd once begged to marry him was only a shell of her former self.

Oh, dear Lord, he groaned inwardly, *if you'd only make her see that she should marry me. . . . I would provide for her and Brett, and she'd never have to work again. I could make everything right. If only she'd let me . . .*

But her "no" to his proposal last fall had been firm — firm and final. So R.J. had silently pledged to do the next best thing to provide for her — and give her a promotion as soon as he had the authority. "Mamma take away my stampler," Brett whimpered.

"Ah," R.J. said. "Well, now we're getting to the bottom of this." He opened the door and eyed a stapler lying in the center of the cluttered desk. For the first time, he noticed the office caddie contents strewn all over the floor. Never once did Sam acknowledge his presence. Instead, she snatched up a trash can topped with a used Pull-Up and marched up the hallway toward the bathroom.

Okay, R.J. thought. *It doesn't take a genius to figure out she's mad at me. I gave her a major promotion that she must know involves a nice raise — and she's mad at me!* His jaw muscles clenching, R.J. strode into his office and closed the door. He set Brett down on his desk. The faint smell of his mother's gardenia potpourri blotted out the vestiges of the souring diaper. With determination, R.J. reached for the silver-plated dish on the desk's edge and emptied the potpourri into the marble trash can near the computer.

"The first thing I've got to do is get this office in shape — in *my* shape," he groused while glowering at the floral painting beside the bookshelf. "I wonder if there's an

54

artist who does Road Kings?" he mused. He took Brett into his arms and planted a firm kiss on his forehead.

"Look, Uncle R.J. has some yummy almonds and granola. Doesn't that sound good? I think you need something to counteract all that sugar and caffeine," he continued under his breath. "Somebody's going to want to put you on medication for being hyper if I don't get that mother of yours to stop giving you so much junk food."

"Coke!" Brett exclaimed with a determined frown. "Brett want Coke."

"Why am I not surprised?" R.J. chided and rolled his eyes. "You're outta luck, champ. All I've got is apple juice — *organic* apple juice at that," he added as he neared the small refrigerator in the room's corner.

His office door opened then clapped shut with a resounding slam. Sam's strained voice ricocheted off the mauve walls. "How could you?!"

Brett jumped. R.J. tightened his hold on the child and pivoted to face the woman he loved. "Excuse me?"

"How in the name of Horace McDugal do you expect me to take on the responsibilities of a vice president? Have you lost your ever-lovin' mind?" She hurled her hand upward. Her cheeks flamed crimson. Her crystal-blue eyes flashed with the fire of diamonds. R.J.'s momentary exasperation vanished. Samantha Jones was obviously stressed beyond reason.

"Who, pray tell, is Horace McDugal?" R.J. asked with an attempt at light humor.

"Don't try to change the subject on me, mister," Sam said as she lowered her index finger toward his nose. "I'm not going to take that vice presidency, and you can't make me!"

"Okay, okay." He jiggled Brett who suddenly became fascinated with the rubber band on the end of R.J.'s braid. "I was just trying to help, Sam, for cryin' out loud. I figured you could use the raise."

"I'm doing fine." She crossed her arms and set her face in stony resolve. She might as well have erected a wall of steel between them. "I a–appreciate everything you've done, R.J.," she rushed on as her cheeks gradually lost their scarlet intensity. "*Really*. But — but you have not — not taken on Brett and me as dependents." The edge came back into her voice. "Just because I work here, a–and you're my boss now, that doesn't mean —"

"That you're any more interested in

marrying me than you were last fall . . . or almost six years ago, for that matter." The acrid words hung in the air, and he could have once again ripped out his own tongue.

Sam's eyes sparked, and she stomped her foot. "Don't do this, R.J. I can't work here if this is the way it's going to be. We've got to put our past behind us and — and —"

"Yes, I know." R.J. stroked Brett's tear-dampened cheek and marveled at the paternal love that had stormed his entire heart. At the ripe old age of 40, R.J. felt more like a doting grandfather than a father. "Problem is, Sammie, putting the past behind us is easier said than done."

"Implying?" she asked, and one finely penciled brow arched in a way that suggested she understood his meaning.

His mind raced back 17 years, to the first time he'd ever felt Sam's lips against his. She had been so innocent and trusting and full of blatant hero-worship. R.J.'s gut tightened, and a tremor zipped straight to his knees. He strode toward the fridge and forced himself to emit a calm aura. "Believe me, I'm not implying a thing, babe," he said with a placid nuance that masked the effect she had on him. "Putting the past behind us is going to be easier said than done. End of discussion."

"Don't call me babe!" she snarled.

"Like son, like mother," R.J. muttered.

"I not baby either!" Brett said, his eyes round.

"So I've heard . . . so I've heard," he said on a laugh. R.J. nudged open the refrigerator with the toe of his snake-skin boot and snagged a bottle of icy apple juice. "Here, hold this." He thrust the juice into Brett's ready hands, kicked shut the refrigerator door, and grabbed the bags of almonds and granola on a nearby table. Never once glancing at Sam, he shoved a mountain of papers to the center of his desk and placed Brett on the smooth surface. He set the two plastic bags in front of the child and pointed to each as he spoke. "Now, this bag is granola. This one's almonds. Eat all you want." R.J. popped the top off the apple juice, and Brett gulped several swallows.

"You know, Sam," R.J. said, never taking his attention from Brett, "you really should watch his sugar and caffeine intake a little more closely. I think part of the reason he's so hyped at times is because —"

"Now you think you're an expert on children?"

Silence reigned as R.J. clamped his lips together and forced himself to remain calm and watch Brett eat. *She's just stressed out,* he reminded himself.

"Not in my wildest imagination, did I ever dream you'd *ever* act like this." Sam's voice had lost all traces of irritation. Instead, she sounded as if a miracle had taken place.

"Excuse me?" R.J. leveled a steady gaze at her.

Sam crossed her arms, and her baby-blues reflected her fascination. She slowly shook her head, and her fiery locks swished around her shoulders. R.J. swallowed hard as the memory of her hair beneath his touch broke into his concentration. *What if she had agreed to marry me instead of that jerk?*

"It's as if there's been some kind of invasion of the body snatchers going on here," Sam said. "What has gotten into you? Granola? Almonds? A real job? Sugar intake? Caffeine? Would you listen to the man?" Sam raised her hand and faced the stereo system, as if she were talking to a companion. "He's worried about *sugar intake?* He used to smoke cigarettes and who knows what else, and nobody knew from one week to the next where he was or if he'd eaten a decent meal all week and —"

R.J. covered Brett's ears and gasped as if

he were offended. "Hold your tongue, you brazen woman. You are in the presence of tender ears. This is not the time or place to drag up my sordid past." He fluttered his eyelashes, and Sam burst into a guffaw.

"Oh, what *am* I going to do?" she exclaimed and covered her face with slender fingers. "I've got Martha Stewart for a boss, and she's disguised as a Hell's Angel."

R.J. clutched his chest, feigned another offended gasp, and placed his hands over Brett's ears once more.

"*Puullllease,* madam." This time he tried his dead-level best to sound like some rich woman's snobbish butler. "Not in the presence of the baby!"

"I *not* baby!" Brett hollered, and granola sputtered from his lips.

Sam rested her hands on her cheeks and observed R.J. in contemplative silence. "You have gotten *so* weird," she finally said.

There's so much you don't know about me now, Sam. You think I'm the same person I was all those years ago, but I've grown. If you'd only give me a chance, you'd find out it's for the better, too. Instead of voicing his thoughts, R.J. conjured his best Elvis impression and said, "Thank you. Thank you very much."

The impersonation was lost on Sam.

"Your mom told me awhile back that you were a big name in the Christian Motorcyclists Association." Sam's forehead wrinkled. "At the time, I had my doubts, but . . ."

"Whatza matter, Sammie? Did you think I was so low that even God couldn't reach me?" R.J.'s challenge floated across the room like a ripple on the surface of deep, deep waters.

Sam pressed the ends of her fingers against her lips and looked past him. "I'm sorry, I didn't mean it that way." She darted a glance his way, looked down, and tugged on the edge of her blazer. "I also regret slamming in here and yelling at you," she mumbled as a red flush colored her cheek.

"Well, I'm sorry a–about snapping at you and Erica in the meeting," he stuttered and stifled a grimace. Apologizing had never been one of his strong points. Abruptly, he helped Brett invade the bag of almonds and didn't dare glance at Sam. "And if you ever call me Mr. Butler again, I think I'll barf on the spot," he said with a hint of a grin.

"You always did have a way with words, Butler," Sam chided.

"Hmph," he grunted. R.J. wanted to say more but didn't quite know how. He wished he could tell her that he feared his impatience had made her relive some of the abuse or that he would rather lose his own life than intentionally hurt her. The patter of rain against the window filled a silence that stretched several seconds, a silence that was finally broken by the door's click. R.J. looked up and Sam was gone.

He expelled a slow breath and lowered himself into the rolling chair. "Well, champ, looks like it's just you and me for awhile." He patted Brett's leg then followed through with a gentle squeeze. The telephone rang, and R.J. snatched up the receiver. Before he could utter the usual greeting, Sam's determined voice came over the line. "If Brett starts getting in the way, send him back in here. He can watch a video."

"Okay. No problemo." R.J. patted the child's leg again. "We're doing just fine right now."

"Also, I'd like to leave a little early today, around four or so. I bought a couple of parakeets three days ago, and they are not working out. I'm going to see if I can exchange them for a dog — maybe a cocker spaniel," she added.

"Okay," R.J. said.

"Part of the reason I was late this morning is because Brett keeps letting the birds out of their cage, and I have to chase them down," she continued in a breathless staccato. "I can't leave the birds out all day because my cat will eat them. I can't put the cat outside because she's been declawed and the dog next door would eat her."

"That's fine, Sammie. I understand," R.J. said, not hiding the indulgent smile that laced his words.

"I'm not sure how long The Pet Shoppe stays open," she explained. "If I leave early, I can probably go home, get the birds, and make the exchange —"

"Sam," R.J. said, "it's okay. Go ahead and exchange —"

"Don't say the 'b' word in front of Brett right now," she quickly interrupted. "I don't want him to know about the birds yet. He'll drive me nuts about it all day."

R.J. laughed out loud.

"This is not funny," she snapped. "I overslept in the first place. Then I had to chase down those squawking monsters, and —"

"And then I announced that you would be the new vice president on top of all that," R.J. added in a reflective voice.

"Exactly!" Sam exclaimed. With a quick goodbye, she hung up.

R.J. pulled the receiver from his face and stared at the ebony phone. "Your mom is stressed out, little guy," he said, simultaneously brainstorming ways he might relieve some of her load.

"Mamma sad," Brett said, his three-year-old eyes full of an uncanny intensity.

"Oh?" R.J. hung up the phone and pressed the button that would boot up his computer.

"She cry," Brett continued as if he were announcing new information.

R.J. swiveled to face Brett, and his hand quivered on the keyboard.

Brett picked up the juice with both hands and slurped down several swallows before depositing the beverage on the desk and plunging his chubby fist into the granola bag. "My daddy mean. He hit Mamma. He died in car wreck. I not see him anymore."

"Yes, I know," R.J. said, and his eyes stung. "I know." *You've told me a dozen times,* he wanted to add. Instead, R.J. lifted the toddler onto his lap, wrapped his arms around him, and stared at the floral painting he had thought of replacing only minutes before. This time the painting blurred into the image of a family portrait; a family of three.

I'm not going to take no for an answer this time, Sam. I don't care what I have to do. I don't care if it takes me five years, I'm not going to let you and this little guy get away from me. So just get ready, woman. I took this position to be close to you. Every time you turn around, I'm going to be there. I'm going to charm you senseless, and mark my words you'll be saying "I do" before you ever know what hit you.

Despite his conviction, a nagging doubt clouded R.J.'s claims, a doubt that reflected the cold glint in Sam's azure eyes.

Four

Terrence Blackwood steered his truck to the back of the shopping strip and counted the doors until he came to the sixth one. The Ford's tires ground against wet pavement and crunched to a stop outside The Pet Shoppe's door. He put the truck in park, turned off the engine, and reached in the passenger seat for the cage holding six cocker spaniels. He grimaced at the musty smell of wet puppies; he'd had little choice but to put these in the cab with him. The truck bed was full. Terrence glanced in the rearview mirror and caught sight of numerous cages just like this one, holding three breeds of puppies. Shrill yelps announced the tiny pups' despair.

"Hush now," he ordered as he scrambled from the vehicle into the fine mist, cold and clinging. Terrence whipped off his glasses and shoved them into his shirt pocket. He headed toward the door, a blurry mar against gray brick. "At least the downpour has stopped," he muttered, pushing the red service button beside the door.

The knob rattled; the door swung outward. A young man with skin the color of rich coffee smiled a warm welcome. "Terrence! Great to see you." his voice rang with a heavy British accent.

"Hello, Demitrius," Blackwood said and stepped into the supply room that smelled of pet food and cedar shavings. Out of habit he glanced around the shadowed room to verify they were indeed alone and unwatched.

"Believe it or not, I just got a call from a man requesting a cocker spaniel. I'll be right with you! Let me finish this call." Demitrius strode to the threshold of the store and turned to face Blackwood. "Come on into the store, if you like."

A whimper erupted from the cage, and a round of puppy grunts followed. "No, that's perfectly fine. I prefer waiting here. I don't have much time," Blackwood said and feigned a polite smile.

"Yes, of course." Demitrius nodded with understanding. "I will be but a minute!" The owner rushed into the brightly lit store and left the door open. A slice of light cut into the shadowed room.

Terrence set the cage on the concrete

floor, then pulled his glasses from his pocket. He shoved them onto his nose, stepped toward the doorway, and glanced past gurgling fish tanks, up the aisle to his left, then his right. No one. A knot of tension uncoiled in his gut. He eased the door closed and eyed the bags of dry dog food piled against the far wall. Without another thought, he whipped off his glasses once more, shoved them back into his pocket, and grabbed a 40-pound bag. He wasted no time loading the food into his truck cab, then scurrying back into the storage room. When the door sighed to a close behind him, Demitrius arrived, check in hand.

Perfect timing! Blackwood thought and bestowed a smile upon the trusting buffoon. Over the years Terrence had lost count of the supplies he had lifted from Texas pet store owners just like Demitrius Youngblood.

The youthful man beamed back as if they were the best of friends. "Do we have six here, like I ordered?" he asked, picking up the cage and peering inside.

"Yes, six," Terrence said. The Pet Shoppe was a new account, and Blackwood had only met Demitrius once before. Today's collection of puppies looked healthy, but in this case appearances were misleading. Terrence hoped they sold quickly because they might not make it to week's end. Two of the pups from this litter were already dead from some intestinal ailment. Barry Cox had dosed them all with high-powered antibiotics, but who knew how effective that would be. Cox said the disease was contagious. Terrence hoped none of the other dogs had been infected.

"They look good," Demitrius said. "Two-fifty each you said?" he asked, extending the check.

"Yes. Exactly." Blackwood glanced at the check, verified the amount, and nodded. He pulled a bundle of papers from his leather jacket's inside pocket and extended them to the owner. "Now, if you'll just empty the cage, I'll be on my way."

"Oh, of course," Demitrius said and accepted the documents. "There's a cardboard box right here." He reached beside a stack of parrot food and produced a small box. "We can put them in here, and you won't have to wait on me to put them in the display cage."

Within seconds Terrence completed the exchange and folded his six-foot-four frame into the pickup cab. He looked at the check, thought of his impending debts, and frowned. Even with all the corners he was cutting, Terrence was still coming up short. He eyed the dingy deck of cards lying in the middle of the seat. His habits were getting more and more costly at every turn. He pondered the possibility of cutting back but the option appeared impossible. When his wife, Mallory, died, his gambling gradually became his mistress. During the height of his fervor, Terrence could forget that he had been married. His eye twitched. He scrubbed rough fingers over a face tense and thick as leather. He shook his head and wished he could kill the phantoms that continually appeared . . . and sometimes insisted he tell Mallory's brother the truth.

With a decisive jerk he cranked the engine. Terrence glanced over his shoulder to observe the cages crammed into the truck's bed. His gaze wandered to the chilling mist that some forecasters said was going to turn into sleet and snow. Terrence shook his head, and the corners of his mouth turned down. "I don't think so," he claimed. Numerous stores from Dallas to east Texas awaited his deliveries this evening, and he wasn't going to let a few wild-eyed meteorologists stop his business.

Blackwood mentally calculated the night's haul and came up with a figure close to $12,000. That should help him break even this month. His thoughts moved to his new business and the wealth it would bring.

He bit the inside of his cheek, clenched the steering wheel, and hoped the new distribution routes would be more profitable. He and Barry Cox had partnered together on various adventures, including smuggling wildlife to foreign zoos where legalities weren't a top priority. But when the latest gorilla venture turned nasty and almost cost them their lives, they decided to change their avenue of raising funds.

Recently, the two brothers-in-law had broken into a new market that proved much more lucrative. So far, they had arranged six airline shipments of cocaine without a hitch. Their methods were ingenious and nearly risk-free. They packaged the fine white powder in plastic bags then secured the stuff inside emptied silicon breast implants. With Terrence as assistant, Barry inserted the sealed-off bags into the intestinal wall of large-breed dogs they acquired through newspaper ads or animal shelters. A few times they had used a dog or two that had outlived its usefulness in Terrence's dog breeding business.

A week after the surgery, Barry removed the dogs' sutures. Then they bought a spot on an airplane for the animals and shipped them to their customers. The clients killed the animals, cut open their bellies, and retrieved the goods. At that point they electronically transferred funds to an account Barry had set up.

The method had been Barry's idea, and it worked beautifully because the dogs' bodies didn't reject the breast implant material. How Barry had managed to talk the implant supplier into selling to him was anybody's guess. Terrence had stopped worrying about unnecessary details long ago. All he cared was that Barry did his part and did it well.

Their next shipment would be the last small one, consisting of a couple kilos that should net them more than $50,000 dollars. After this shipment, they would be entering the big leagues. A stiff grin tugged on the corners of Terrence's mouth. The cocaine deals were proving to be less time-consuming and turned a better profit margin than smuggling exotic animals.

As soon as he had enough money, Terrence planned to sell his dog breeding business and be free to spend his time at casinos enjoying the "good" life. Then, perhaps, Mallory would leave him alone.

"The Pet Shoppe. How may I help you?" a deep, British voice proclaimed.

Sam gripped the telephone's receiver and tapped the end of a pencil against her desk calendar. "Is this Mr. Youngblood?" she asked, gazing out the window toward the blanket of gray clouds that hung above the Dallas skyscrapers.

"At your service," he replied with a smile in his voice.

"I was in your store a few days ago and bought two parakeets, a cage, some seed — the whole nine yards." She stared at the tip of the pencil then tapped it a few more times.

"Yes?"

Sammie placed the pencil on her desk and rolled it with the tips of her fingers. "Well, the birds are just not working out, Mr. Youngblood. I was wondering if you might consider trading them for a cocker spaniel puppy? You see, my little boy is just three, and he keeps letting the birds out of their cage and —"

"Yes, that would be fine," the store owner declared.

"It would?"

"Of course. You still have your receipt, I assume?"

"Oh yes, I have all that!"

"Great! There shouldn't be a problem. I just got a new litter of cocker spaniels not half an hour ago."

Sammie tossed the pencil across her desk, smiled, and leaned back in her chair. She had owned a cocker spaniel as a child, and the dog had been her loyal companion during a time in her life when she doubted human constancy. Sam breathed in deeply, and the faint smell of stale coffee attested to the staff's affinity for the brew.

"How much are cocker spaniels now?" she asked unable to hide the glee. *The bird chasing is over!* she wanted to cheer.

"Five-fifty."

"What?" Sam's spine stiffened, and she sat straight up in her chair. "As in 550 dollars?"

"Yes," Mr. Youngblood answered, and his words held the undertow of a chuckle. "But you'll be getting a full-blooded, registered dog with an excellent pedigree."

"I had a cocker as a child, and it was free!"

"Was it registered?" the proprietor asked, a slight stiffness in his tone.

"No, she was a half-breed."

"Ah, well, you get what you pay for," he said, and a smile softened his voice once more. "Look, if you like, I can come down to 500 dollars. And I'll give you a full refund on the birds."

"Okay, okay," Sammie mused, doing the math in her head. "I'll wind up owing about 425."

"Now that's a steal," Mr. Youngblood claimed.

Sam chewed the inside of her bottom lip and assessed her financial situation. Adam's life insurance policy had allowed her to pay cash for their current home and still stash away a significant nest egg. She had also gained respectable equity from the sale of her former home. While Sam wasn't independently wealthy by any means, she and Brett were a long way from starvation. Still, 425 dollars for a dog was a chunk of money. She thought about skimming the newspaper for a free puppy but wondered how long it would take to find a breed she liked. She could tap into the emergency fund she'd put in a money market account a few weeks ago. Images of those birds flapping all over the room swooped upon Sam. She pondered the bird feather Erica plucked from her hair. *This qualifies as an emergency!* she asserted.

Before Sam knew it, she was blurting her acceptance. "Okay, I'll be there in just over an hour!"

"Great! I'm open until seven o'clock," he said with flourish.

"Yes. I'll be there sooner. I want to get home before dark in case it snows." She bid her final adieu.

Sam hung up the desk phone and checked her watch. "Four," she whispered and calculated the time it would take to drive all the way home, get the parakeets, and take them back to The Pet Shoppe.

I hope Brett is as gracious as the store owner when he realizes the birds are no longer going to be with us. Sam shut down her computer and grabbed her handbag from beneath the desk. *I'm not even going to think about Miss Kitty and the puppy. I'll worry about her when we get home.*

Wasting no time, she rounded the desk but stopped when she noticed the disheveled novella manuscript, scattered across the edge of her desk, right where she'd left it that morning. "Oh great," she groaned and glanced at her desk calendar. The manuscript was due at her publisher next week, and she hadn't so much as read through the first draft. *Well, at least I have a first draft!* As she shuffled the pages together into a manageable pile, Sam pondered her editor's latest remarks. *Your novels keep getting better, Samantha. We don't know how you do it!*

She bent toward the floor and pulled the rumpled canvas tote from underneath a pile of reference books. "I don't know how I do it, either," Sam mumbled as the stack of books snapped together then toppled over. "I had a horrible marriage that was anything *but* romantic, and getting myself involved in another romance is the last thing on my 'to do' list. But here I am writing romantic fiction like I believe in it." She rolled her eyes, shook her head, and stuffed the manuscript inside the tote, amid a collection of rumpled Pull-Ups.

Sam glanced out the window. The morning storm had finally settled into a day-long mist. According to the radio forecast, the thermometer had dropped to freezing, and the mist was supposed to turn to snow tonight or tomorrow morning.

You never know with Dallas. The snow of the century could start at six. Then again, we might not see one flake. "All the more reason to get out of here now," she mumbled, casting a cursory glance into the playroom. As with yesterday evening, the trash can was stuffed. Movies were spread willy-nilly across the TV stand, and a Happy Meal bag claimed the center of the room.

"Rats!" Sam gritted her teeth and snapped off the light. The playroom could wait until tomorrow.

After the tumult in the morning, the day had ticked along at remarkable speed. Sam had put the finishing touches on her serialized novel that appeared every month in *Romantic Living*. Then she had previewed several ideas for travel pieces and sorted through a pile of unsolicited manuscripts. Brett had toddled between her office and R.J.'s until about two hours ago when he disappeared into R.J.'s office and didn't return. Samantha figured R.J. had probably made a pallet for him on the floor.

She approached R.J.'s office and noticed a scrawled "Do Not Disturb" sign that hung crookedly from a snatch of tape. Sam hesitated then lightly tapped the door. When no answer came, she turned the knob, stepped into the office, and strained through the shadows to detect some sign of R.J. or her son. A quick scan of the room revealed that the polished cotton drapes were tightly closed. As her eyes adjusted to the shadows, Sam took a few cautious steps and finally noticed somebody lying on the floor near the stereo system — *two* somebody's to be exact. With a sigh, Sam walked across spongy carpet toward the floor lamp that regally stood between a couple of wing chairs. She flipped the light on low and eyed the pair whose steady breathing filled the room. R.J. lay flat on his back with Brett's head resting on his arm.

"And here we have the new president of *Romantic Living*, folks," she whispered through a smile. "Asleep in his office with . . ." Sam hesitated and lowered herself into one of the upholstered chairs, ". . . with my son." The final words wobbled out. Sam bit her lower lip and recalled another day last summer when she had stumbled upon the two in a similar pose. She had just left Adam, and she and Brett had landed at Colleen and Tom Butler's home as a transitional hiding place. . . .

Laptop case in hand, Sammie opened the penthouse door and stepped into the shadowed haven. The afternoon sunshine squeezed through the lowered blinds to create razor-thin strips of light across the pale carpet. The faint hum of the air conditioner mingled with the sound of soft snoring, and Sammie scanned the living room. At last her gaze rested upon a pair of partners stretched out in the leather recliner. Brett, his head snuggled against R.J.'s shoulder, slept in the crook of the biker's arm. The child's snoring mingled with R.J.'s steady breathing.

Sammie, her eyes pooling with warm tears, stood in the open doorway. The barely discernible tick of the cherry grandfather clock seemed to count the years that had elapsed since Sam and R.J. first fell in love. Years that almost stretched to eternity. The man always had been rough around the edges, and Sammie attributed that to his mother's trying to make him into something he wasn't. Despite his insistence that his leather and jeans stayed, despite his ever-present need of a good shave, R.J. Butler would have made a dynamite father.

"Going home now?" R.J.'s drowsy call broke into Sam's memories, and she blinked in an attempt to focus on the present.

"Yes. And there's a snowstorm threatening, in case you haven't heard."

"I've heard," he said and placed his free arm under his head. "But I'd bet my Road King we don't see one flake."

"Oh ye of little faith."

"Oh me of great experience," he retorted. "Sometimes I think these Dallas weather forecasters are being paid by the grocery store owners to make outrageous predictions. Every time they threaten a snowstorm people rush to the grocery store like they think we live in Alaska and we're going to be snowed in for weeks."

Brett rolled closer to R.J. and mumbled a long line of protests that involved a ball and a bird. R.J. patted Brett on the back then waved at Sam. "Go ahead," he whispered. "I'm sure you can use the time alone. I'll feed him dinner and bring him home later."

Sam immediately conjured images of R.J. driving Brett around the wet Dallas streets on one of his Harleys. She opened her mouth to refuse, but R.J. beat her to the mark.

"Don't argue." He held up his hand. "He'll be perfectly safe with me. I traded in my Fat Boy for a truck last month."

Her mouth fell open. "You traded in one of your Harleys? No way!"

"Yes way. I did." His dark eyes dared her to comment.

"You really are losing it, aren't you?" she muttered and shook her head.

R.J. rolled his eyes. "Just go, will ya? You're wastin' time here."

"But you don't have a car seat," she hedged.

"There's a store just around the corner. Brett and I will walk over and buy one as soon as we are ready to leave."

Sam's visit to The Pet Shoppe loomed in her thoughts. For the first time she seriously considered R.J.'s offer. Maybe she could pull off the whole bird/dog switcharoo without Brett, thus avoiding a big scene. With the distraction of a new puppy, days could pass before he realized the birds were missing. On the other hand, allowing R.J. to keep Brett for the evening would mean he would arrive at her house and perhaps want to stay for a cozy chat. Sam's fingers tightened on her purse strap. She snagged her bottom lip between her teeth and teetered on the precipice of decision.

"Go on," R.J. insisted. Never once did his silky brown eyes leave hers.

Sam felt as if she were drowning in a pool of adoration, warm and promising. He might as well have wrapped her in his arms and pledged that he would make all her troubles vanish. *What would happen if you allowed him to embrace you?* a lonely voice whispered. *Just once. What would once hurt?* A chill raced across her shoulders and prickled down her arms. R.J.'s eye narrowed a fraction, as if he were reading her mind.

If I ever allow you that close — even once — you won't stop until you have a wedding band on my finger. Sam tore her gaze from R.J.'s and stood. "You don't understand, R.J." she croaked, as if her thoughts had been said aloud. "There's nothing left of me. There's *nothing* I can give you," she choked out. Sam dashed toward the door. "G–go ahead and bring Brett home l–later. There's a bag of ex–extra training pants in his playroom if you n–need them," she wrapped her fingers around the cold doorknob but hesitated as an unexpected current bade her to turn around and fling herself into R.J.'s arms. As if rooted to the spot, she stiffened her back and battled the allure of beautiful brown eyes full of promise.

"Sam?" R.J.'s drowsy voice crept to the edges of her soul.

With a frown, Sam shoved aside the inviting appeal. She opened the door and stepped out of the room.

Five

Subject: phone call to Sam
On Monday, 15 Jan 2002 4:33:35
Mara O'Connor
<mara@oconnor.hhp> writes:

Hi, Colleen!

It's me again. Sorry to bother you, but I just left a message on Sam's answering machine. I hope she returns my call. I have toyed with calling her at the magazine, but the last time I tried, she was so busy – she was running out the door for a meeting. I'd hate to disturb her again.

I've been trying for years now to get close to Sammie, and it's just not working. This time I've decided not to be rebuffed by her lack of response. It's going to be difficult since I'm not very assertive. But, by the same token, I just can't go on year in and year out like this. What I did was wrong, Colleen. I know that now. At the time, I was so blinded by that man that I duped myself into believing my daughters would understand. Now I'm staring at my senior years and I'm really alone. Last I talked to my ex-husband, and he didn't even know where Rana was. I gave him my number and made him promise to give it to her if she ever contacts him. I know I've shared this with you before, but I wonder if she would have been lured into the drug culture if I had been there . . .

I'm starting to cry now, so I've got to stop. I'm sorry to share such a downer on your vacation.

All I want to know is what time Sammie gets off. I want to know what time she'll receive my message so I will be home when she returns my call.

Bye, now!
Mara

Subject: phone call to Sam
On Monday, 15 Jan 2002 3:46:21
Colleen Butler
<candt@butler.hhp> writes:

Oh, Mara, don't worry about ruining my vacation. I'm glad you've gotten back in touch! As I've told you in the past, you need a friend — we all do. Looking back on my life there was a time or two when I could have fallen into temptation myself. I think all husbands and wives, regardless of how dedicated they are to Christ, have those moments of weakness when they are attracted to someone other than their spouse. I'm just sorry for your sake and Sam and Rana's that I didn't make myself available as your confidante before it all happened. And I don't fault you one bit for pursuing Sammie. I would do the same. She is your daughter no matter what. I will be praying that your attempts will at last melt the wall of ice she has built around herself. But be patient with her. She has been through so much that I wonder sometimes how she is holding up. She keeps producing quality work at the magazine and writing novels like her life depends on it. And maybe it does. I don't know. The writing might be the outlet that helps her keep balance. As I said, I will be praying for you and her.

The mag office usually closes at 4:30. Sammie has been known to stay until 5:30 many days, especially if she arrives late. Did I tell you that Tom and I arranged for her to bring Brett to work with her? I think it's really helped her financially.

Oh, one more thing, I don't think I mentioned that Wanda Martin is serving as my "top-secret" contact while Tom and I are out. Wanda is one of the vice presidents at the mag. Anyway, I plan to check with her every day or so to make sure everything is going well. You know, she can run that mag better than Tom and me put together. She's carrying a lot of the weight, as always. All that is to say that we just chatted an hour ago. She says that Rhett offered Sammie the other vice presidency and that by noon the whole office knew she turned it down. Sigh! I guess she thinks she's too busy. I was hoping she'd take it. That would have put her working even closer to Rhett, although her office is just down the hall from his now.

Enough of my gossip. Smiles. Tom says we're about to stop and stretch our legs. We're just entering Arizona. I'll be glad for the break. Let me know if Sam calls you back.

Blessings!
Colleen

Terrence's cell phone's peal pierced the rhythmic beat of country music spilling from the radio. He groped in the pocket of his leather jacket until he produced the phone. Keeping his eye on the traffic zooming along the freeway, he pressed the answer button and bit out a greeting.

"Barry here," Cox replied.

"Did you find four good dogs?" As Terrence came up on a diesel, he pressed the brake, checked his sideview mirror, then sped into the next lane.

"Yes. A German shepherd that's a beaut and three that are the Heinz 57 variety. We can go ahead with the surgeries tomorrow evening as planned."

"Good work," Terrence said.

"The only thing I hate about all this is that they kill these poor buggers once they get them," Barry complained.

As the vet continued to dwell on the German shepherd that caught his fancy, Terrence squinted. He didn't even try to wrap his mind around the contradictions in Barry's values. The veterinarian didn't seem to care that they were dealing an illegal substance that sometimes caused the untimely deaths of some unsuspecting teenagers. Cox's only hesitation involved the treatment of the dogs. With a shrug, Terrence decided not to analyze Barry's psyche. Cox's connections in the animal kingdom had lined their pockets more than not. Terrence didn't intend to shake the setup. For years now he had remained silent regarding his partner's varied inconsistencies. He would continue in silence. Silence and avarice. Avarice and the duplicity. *I don't care about the drug users, much less the dogs,* he thought as Barry brought his diatribe to an end. *As long as I get my money, those idiots can do what they want with the coke.*

"Are we doing okay on all our supplies?" Terrence asked. "Do I need to buy more plastic bags or anything?"

"No, we're fine," Barry affirmed.

Terrence imagined his brother-in-law's flushed cheeks, dimpling with each word.

"I double-checked. We've still got a box full. Right now, we're set with half a pound each for four dogs. That's two pounds this time." His bass voice gurgled with greed, and his concern for the welfare of the animals vanished.

"Have you made arrangements for us to pick up the next batch?"

"Yes. We're scheduled in the Gulf of Mexico next Thursday."

"Great!" Terrence nearly exploded in glee.

The Cuban connection was proving valuable and dependable. And since the brothers-in-law were receiving the drugs straight from the manufacturer, they were able to turn a sizable profit. Posing as deep-sea fishermen out on their rig, Barry and Terrence went out the night before the meeting and fished until they caught sizable groupers, amberjacks, cobias, or red snappers. They killed the fish and iced him down. Once the carrier, or "mule," arrived, they paid for the coke, double bagged it in thick plastic, and shoved it down the throat of the fish. When they docked, no one gave them so much as a second glance. Soon their shipments would increase, and they would retrieve the product via shrimp boats.

Terrence imagined the stacks of money that would soon be his. He glanced toward the deck of cards nestled against his thigh and smiled. The country music's seductive beat invoked him to stroke the top of the leather-covered steering wheel. He could almost smell the cash. Barry's voice cut into his musings, and the music that once pleased now proved a distraction. Terrence needed to think — and think clearly. He and Barry couldn't afford one mistake.

"Just a minute." Terrence laid the cell phone on the seat, clicked off the blaring music, and regripped the phone. The sound of tires whirring against damp pavement replaced the thumping tempo and urged him to greater heights in his new business endeavors. The green road sign announcing I-20 unexpectedly loomed ahead, and he swerved in front of the diesel before moving into the far right lane. The semi's horn blasted a protest into the cold gray mist. Terrence yelled at the driver; then he pressed the cell phone against his ear.

"I'm back," he stated.

"Where are you anyway?" Cox asked.

"I'm about to merge onto I-20, heading for Tyler. I've got several stops between here and there."

"Delivering puppies?"

"Yep." He squinted against the increasing mist accumulating on his windshield, then upped the speed of the wipers.

"How are they?"

"Right now, they all look fine — best I can tell." Blackwood peered into his rearview mirror at the sea of cages in the back of his truck. "But this cold front can't be too good on them."

"Poor guys."

"All I care is that they don't die on me before I get them sold," Terrence asserted callously. The exit sign for I-20 appeared, and he gripped the steering wheel in the crook of his thumb while flipping up the blinker switch with his third and fourth fingers. After maneuvering his Ford onto the off ramp, he continued the checklist planning.

"So, what about the plane reservations next week for the dogs? Are they taken care of?"

"Yes. Two are going to Chicago on the 8:34 flight next Wednesday. The other two are going to L.A. on the 9:10 the same evening. I booked them at Dallas/Fort Worth, both on Delta this time."

"Good." At the beginning of their endeavors, the two had decided to rotate airlines and airports so no one would become suspicious with their frequent dog shipping.

"I guess you'll be here tomorrow afternoon?"

"Yes, I will — as planned." The purr of the truck's engine vibrated the bench seat and Terrence's eyes began to droop. The day had been a long one.

"Good. Oh . . ." Cox began, ". . . how is the litter of cocker spaniels doing?"

"I just delivered them. They were fine. As fast as those usually sell, I doubt the store owner will even notice they've been sick."

Out of nowhere an economy car loomed

in front of him. Startled, Terrence jerked the steering wheel to the left and avoided the vehicle by inches.

"Look," he shot out, "I better get off this phone before I kill myself. That was my second near miss. I'll see you late tomorrow afternoon."

"Okay, that works," Barry agreed and a click announced the end of the call.

Terrence disconnected the phone and plopped it onto the seat near the cards. "Another day, another deal," he mumbled and snapped the country music back on. The hard-beat rhythm had been replaced with the classic ballad "Lady" sung by Kenny Rogers. The song was one Mallory had always enjoyed. With a frown he punched a radio button and switched stations. *No sense in inviting her into this,* he thought with a quiver in his gut. A prickle raced up his back, and an involuntary shimmer racked his body. Terrence gazed hard toward the passenger seat — a seat that remained empty. His shoulders dropped a fraction then he shifted his attention back to the road.

Too bad I didn't get along with Mallory as well as I do with her brother . . . too bad for Mal, anyway. From the day Terrence and Mallory were married almost

20 years ago, they fought like two gladiators. Seven years into their marriage, Terrence had taken all he could stand of his wife's perpetual nagging. After a particularly nasty fight, Mal came up "missing." When the police questioned Terrence, Mallory's family vouched for his innocence with fierce loyalty. Not one of them ever suspected Terrence was involved.

The next time Terrence saw Mallory was in his dreams — dreams in which she demanded he tell Barry the truth. Initially, Terrence was able to dash aside the nightmares, but when he decided to find himself another woman, the dreams merged with reality. Through the years Mallory paid spontaneous visits at the most inopportune times. The last time she showed up, about seven months ago, she had acted like her usual self and pestered him to confess to her murder. Terrence had screamed at her and demanded that she not return. Fortunately, the screaming had worked. The resurrected nightmares had stopped, and so had the daytime visions. A chill danced along Terrence's nerves. A tiny doubt sprouted in its wake — a doubt that Mallory would ever stay away for good.

Months had passed since Terrence had been visited by Mallory, months since he experienced the prickly knowing. Months that he had not sensed her hovering nearby. When she did show up, sometimes she wouldn't even talk. She just looked at him with accusing brown eyes. Eyes the size of saucers. Eyes that brought back that cold night when he buried her lifeless form in their barn. That evening had started much like this one. Another shiver seized Terrence, and he adjusted the heater blower until it shot hot streams of air throughout the cab.

The last time Mallory visited Terrence had been at the July Fourth family picnic — seven months before. Nobody else saw her. *Nobody.* Not even his date. And that was the last time Terrence saw another woman socially. Mallory never failed to make an appearance on March twelfth — even if Terrence was alone. *Never.* The date of her death was the worst day of the year for him. She usually showed up in the wee hours of the morning and hounded him to tell all until he was ready to rip his hair out.

March twelfth is only eight weeks off, he thought. His stomach churned; his eye twitched. Terrence peered into the thickening mist. Biting the tip of his tongue, he glared straight ahead and wondered if she might show up on his truck cab. "You better stay away from me, woman," he snarled. His fingers ate into the steering wheel. "Just stay away!"

Six

Samantha pulled her Honda into her driveway, put the vehicle in park, and expended a heavy sigh. She switched off the wipers and watched unblinking as thousands of plump snowflakes assaulted her vehicle. Amid the silent fluff, a steady peppering of ice slammed into her windshield. A weatherman's alarmed voice floated from the radio, "This is looking really nasty really fast, folks. Everyone who can should stay at home. This is looking worse than we originally thought. We might be in this one for the long haul!"

With a groan Sam pressed her fingers against her temples and wondered if R.J. had tried to call her. The snow had started while she was in The Pet Shoppe exchanging the birds for the puppy. Even though the road accumulation wasn't drastic yet, Sam had taken her time getting home.

She turned off the engine. A worried whimper drifted out of the plastic dog carrier, nestled in the passenger seat.

"Hey, little gal," Sam crooned and reached for the cage. "We're home. You don't have to worry." She held up the carrier and peered through plastic bars at the tiny cocker spaniel. The dashlights cast a warm glow upon the forlorn creature, whose ears and feet appeared too big for its body. The puppy yapped then wailed, and Sam chuckled. Figuring the robust pups would find quick homes, Sam had picked out the smallest and weakest looking — the runt. The kind pet store owner had suggested she take the biggest and best since she was getting first choice, but the runt snared her heart in an instant. The dog grunted and sniffed the bottom of the cage as if looking for food.

"Come on," Sam said and turned off the vehicle's lights. "Let's get you inside. I've got some milk we can warm up in the microwave, and you'll be full as a tick before either of us can say 'scat.' "

Sammie bustled from the car and raced into her small, frame home in a cozy Plano neighborhood. As she twisted the front door's deadbolt lock behind her, the telephone rang. Sam kicked off her wet loafers and rushed across the braided rug toward the answering machine sitting on an oak end table.

"R.J.?" she blurted into the phone and deposited the dog, purse, and canvas bag onto the southwest-striped sofa.

"In the flesh," he said. "Looks like I was dead wrong 'bout the weather."

Sam eased onto the sofa's arm, rubbed her lower back, and winced while the cocker spaniel released a high-pitched howl. She absently noticed a Sippee cup of milk sitting in the middle of a stack of old cable guides on the coffee table — the same cup she'd thought she placed in her canvas tote that morning.

"Hel-lo!" R.J. called. "Are you trying to decide how to tell me I'm weird again or what?"

The puppy howled then crescendoed into a round of ear-piercing yaps.

"Now she's started howling on me!" R.J. teased, and Sam imagined the revelry dancing in his eyes. "Miss me that bad, darlin'?" he drawled.

"No!" Sam exclaimed with more fervor than she intended. "Um, I mean it's — it's the puppy, you doofus. And no, I wasn't trying to think of a different way to tell you you're weird. Weird is weird. You've gotten there — all the way. That's it. There's no other way to say it. Now, how's my boy?"

"Your boy is sitting in front of the TV eating —"

"Bean sprouts and water chestnuts, right?"

"No, it's much better than that. I fixed him pizza, and he's got a carbonated drink with it."

Sam gasped. "Pizza and soda? You would let something so rotten touch his lips?"

"Think again. I got them at the health-food grocery store where I buy all my food. The pizza is made with organic ingredients and soy cheese. The drink is carbonated fruit juice. Quite healthy."

"You'd probably faint if you could see what's in my refrigerator." Sam gazed into the open kitchen toward her small fridge cluttered with magnets and Brett's "art."

"Why? Because you're as big a junk food junkie as ever or are you actually inviting me over?" His deep voice weaved its way across the miles to caress her troubled soul.

She fixed her gaze on her answering machine's blinking light, rubbed her forehead, and tried her best to deny the pleasurable memories his teasing evoked — memories of picnics and love notes, promises and expectations, kisses and sighs. Memories of being the senior girl with the eldest boy-friend . . . of R.J. taking her to the senior prom on his motorcycle . . . of the tiny diamond he placed on her ring finger that night.

The recollections fluttered through her heart like frolicking fairies, but they soon took on a dingy hue and grew forbidding. By late June R.J. didn't show up for a date. Then he failed to return a few calls. Sam's sister reported she had seen R.J. at the theater . . . with another girl. One night in early August, Sam hurled the diamond ring across her bedroom and sobbed all night.

She swallowed hard and curled her fingers through the phone's cord. "Has Brett cried for me?" she asked, her voice strained.

"No, but I —" R.J. cut off his sentence and cleared his throat.

The word he didn't speak blazed through Sam's mind and turned into a chant. *I have. I have. I have.*

"Uh," he continued, "I was wondering what you thought about Brett just spending the night with me. I'm not really interested in driving in this mess — especially not with him."

"Weren't you the guy who used to do

stunt jumps on your motorcycle?" Sam asked, shaking her head.

"That guy grew up, Sam," R.J. snapped.

"Missing the stunts are you?" she taunted, not questioning the urge to needle him.

"I'm 40 years old, for cryin' out loud!"

"But you still dress like you did when you were 25 and as wild as a March Hare." She stood. The urge to apologize and move closer to R.J. overwhelmed Sam. Her legs stiffened. Instead of an apology, Sam spewed forth another barb. "And you expect me to believe you've undergone some sort of metamorphosis?"

"When are you going to stop living in the —" R.J. rushed, and then he halted. "Never mind. This won't get us anywhere. Let's just drop it, shall we?"

Sam was almost certain that a thread of pain laced his words. Torn between regret and the need to protect her heart, she remained silent. Instead of responding, she eyed her Siamese cat, Miss Kitty, as she trotted from the tiny kitchen toward the whimpering puppy. *This could get interesting,* she thought as she welcomed the distraction.

"Look," R.J. continued, his voice a little too steady, "is it okay for Brett to stay here with me for the night? Because of the storm I'm going to notify everyone that the magazine won't be open tomorrow. We'll just ride the weather out and see what happens. The city workers will probably have the roads cleared by tomorrow evening anyway. This stuff doesn't usually last more than a day around here."

"I don't know," Sam hedged. "I might be able to make it over there. I could pack a bag, and Brett and I could check into a hotel downtown."

"I'd drive Brett to your house and check into a hotel before I let you do that." R.J.'s decisive voice invited no argument.

"Let me talk to Brett," Sam replied without acknowledging his claim.

"Okay. Let me get him."

Actually, she saw precious little choice but to go along with R.J.'s original suggestion. Brett's staying at R.J.'s was by far the safest measure, but she would feel much better about it if her son showed no hesitancy.

She peered toward the front yard through the half-opened drapes. The streetlights illuminated the cascade of snow that fell like feathers upon the freezing ground. The occasional "ping" against her wood-burning stove's aluminum chimney revealed the occasional presence of sleet. Sam shivered and noticed the three sticks of wood in the cedar box in the corner — all the wood she had. *So much for a cozy fire,* she thought.

A series of shuffles on the phone preceded Brett's voice.

"Hewo."

"Hi, bab— uh — honey," Sam said. She glanced toward the puppy's cage and, after quick consideration, decided not to tell Brett about the dog. He might cry to come home if he knew about the new pet. "How are you doing?" Sam imagined his short, red hair curling around shell-shaped ears and she smiled.

"Fine."

"Are you enjoying being at Uncle R.J.'s?"

"Yes — uh-huh."

"Would you like to spend the night with Uncle R.J.?" Sam held her breath and observed the dishes from last night's dinner still scattered across the dining room table. If Brett started crying she just might risk the trip to go get him.

"Yes, mamma. I stay here. We're gonna make cookies," he said with so much enthusiasm that Sam didn't know whether to feel left out or jubilant.

"Oh, well then, it sounds like you're going to be busy."

"Yes. I stay with Uncle R.J. a whole bunch a nights!"

"Oh no, little tiger," Sam said through a chuckle. "You'll be back with me to-morrow night."

"I through!" Brett replied and the phone clicked in Sam's ear.

She held the receiver away from her face and stared at it. "Well, that's that." She hung up the phone. "And I didn't get a chance to apologize." The stray thought sent a pang of regret through her heart. The truth was that she didn't detest the way R.J. dressed . . . and never had. And she *liked* his braid.

Sam eyed the blinking message light. The dog yapped, and she glanced toward her. "Just a minute. You're next." Sam pressed the button to retrieve her messages. Only two messages awaited her.

"Hey, Sammie! This is Victoria. Just trying to reach you tonight. The sisters are going to have a gab session tomorrow night at 7:30. I'm arranging the conference call this time. Hope you're going to be home!"

Sam's eyes bugged. "Oh no! I forgot all about Victoria!" she exclaimed, pressing the heel of her palm against her forehead. "And she's pregnant!" Sam glanced at her watch. It was barely six. *I should call her back tonight,* she mused.

The next message obliterated all thoughts of Victoria.

"Hi, Sam. This is your mother." Sam went rigid. *"Please* call me." Mara O'Connor began reciting her number, but Sam hit the delete button before she was halfway through. A thin film of tears clouded her eyes and her knees trembled. Mara hadn't tried to contact Sammie since she had her number changed. That was shortly after Adam's funeral. Through the years Mara had occasionally attempted to maintain a relationship with her daughter, but Sam had usually not responded. After Mara left their family with *that man* and moved to Australia, she had written and sent some presents on special occasions. However, Sam had been so full of fury and feelings of betrayal she had never replied. The times Mara had connected with Sam by phone, she had either not returned the calls or kept the conversation to a brief encounter. In the last few years, her mom had occasionally dedicated seasons of time to trying to reach Sam. She did participate in Sam's wedding and was at Adam's funeral; but both occasions had proven awkward. It seemed that no matter where Sam landed or what important events were occurring, Mara somehow managed to track her down and learn the necessary details. Sammie had yet to determine who always leaked her unlisted phone number and the other information. At times, she suspected her father, but she wasn't sure. Whatever the source of her contact, Samantha hoped her mom would back off this time.

"You left us 22 years ago," Sam rasped at the phone. "Y–you moved off to Australia with that — *that man* and let me down when I needed you most. You left me to cook for myself, to shop for myself, and to do the best I could to make it." Tears seeped from the corners of Sam's eyes. "Then . . . more than a decade later when 'Mr. Wonderful' turned out not to be s–so wonderful, y–you moved back to Texas and acted like you c–could just pick up where you left off. But it doesn't w–work that way." She reached for the puppy's carrier. "It just doesn't work that way!" she said through her sobs.

Seven

Subject: Great News!
On Tuesday, 16 Jan 2002 3:14:11
Colleen Butler
<candt@butler.hhp> writes:

Mara!
Are you there? I just got off the phone with Rhett! They had a snowstorm in Dallas! Did you get any of it in east Texas?
Brett wound up spending the night with Rhett — I'm not really clear how all that happened, but that's not the point. The point is that Rhett is leaving soon to take Brett home to Sammie. He mentioned offering to cook dinner for the three of them.
Quick! Pray that she'll let him cook and that sparks will fly!

Later Gator!
Colleen

On Tuesday, 16 Jan 2002 4:03:21
Mara O'Connor
<mara@oconnor.hhp> writes:

Dear Gator,
   Praying . . . and add a few words for me as well, will you? Sam hasn't returned my call from yesterday. I'm wondering if I should try to call her again tonight or give it a few days. I'll keep you posted on what I decide.

Yours,
Mara

   R.J. pulled his truck into Sam's driveway and put the vehicle in park. The snow blanketed the small home in a cozy hug that made it look like a Swedish bungalow. *All you need is a big mountain in the background, Sammie,* R.J. thought. Yet a horn's toot witnessed that this was an urban neighborhood, not a mountainous haven. R.J. eyed the red birds leaving their prints in the front yard snow as they gobbled up a scattering of seed. *Sam always did enjoy feeding birds,* he mused.
   The snow had lasted until the morning's wee hours, and then it sped away as

quickly as it arrived. By noon the sun had blazed upon the city enough that the streets began to thaw. Although a cloak of snow still covered the buildings and terrain, by four o'clock the streets were clear enough to drive without hazard. "And that's what you call a Dallas snowstorm," R.J. commented aloud with a smirk. "The whole thing is over in less than 24 hours." He glanced over at Brett whose head rested against the side of a new car seat. With a smile R.J. stroked a strand of hair from his freckled face and caressed the child's cheek with the backs of his fingers. With a flutter of regret, R.J. glanced toward the front door then back at the child. "I'm going to miss you," he whispered. "You brought some life to that apartment last night." R.J. wondered what it would be like to have Brett around every evening.

He narrowed his eyes as his mind traveled in other directions — in wanderings that conjured images of a wife named Sam who was around every night as well. He thought about her laughter filling the living room, her latest manuscript scattered over their computer desk, her lingerie in their bathroom. R.J. ran calloused fingers through his beard, opened the truck door, and got out before his mind got him into more trouble than he could get out of. He crunched through the snow around the new vehicle and popped open Brett's door. After releasing the safety belt, he snuggled the boy into his arms and snagged the sack of groceries from the floorboard. As he wrapped his arm around the brown paper bag, a long loaf of French bread flopped against his nose. R.J. nudged aside the fragrant bread and managed to slam the door with his boot before hitting the lock button on his key chain. He hoped Sam still liked spaghetti.

The smell of smoke hung in the air as R.J. thumped onto her tiny porch. A pair of wicker rockers claimed each side of an old milk can, and R.J. imagined sitting with Sam on a summer night, soaking up the ambiance of a southern evening. He sucked in a lungful of the cold, damp air and muttered a desperate prayer for divine guidance. His stomach tense, R.J. contemplated the best way to invite himself to dinner. Brett stirred against his neck. R.J. shrugged and pushed the doorbell.

Within seconds the door opened and Sam's eyes, alert and marred by dark circles, darted to her son. Without a word she reached for Brett, and R.J. transferred his burden to her. "Come here, li'l tiger," Sam crooned as the child's eyes slid open and he yawned. "I missed you."

She bestowed a tender kiss on Brett's forehead, and R.J. was tempted to raise his hand and request a turn. Instead, he shoved his keys into his pocket and shifted the bag of groceries. "He is worn out. We played hard today. I had barely left the parking garage when he was sound asleep."

"Thanks," Sam said with an uncertain smile. "I hope he wasn't too much trouble."

"No trouble at all," R.J. answered and produced the most charming grin he could muster. While he had never tried to convince himself he was devastatingly handsome, R.J. had been told his smile could influence the coldest of hearts. He shamelessly upped the warmth of the grin and dared to hold Sam's gaze.

A vague spark glistened from the depths of her soul, and R.J. nearly fell to his knees as he shouted a silent *Yes!* Yet her gaze faltered to the bag of groceries, and she cleared her throat as if she were uncertain of the next conversational vein.

"Oh . . . I, uh, I . . . was wondering if you'd mind if I hung around and cooked dinner for you and Brett." R.J. hooked his thumb through his jeans belt loop and did his dead-level best to feign nonchalance.

Samantha's brow wrinkled.

"I didn't know you could cook."

"Of course I can. How do you think I've survived all these years on my own, woman? I'm a lean, mean cookin' machine."

Sam snagged the corner of her lip between her teeth, and R.J. was almost certain he detected a faint smile. But then she looked away and fidgeted with the neck of her powder blue sweat suit. "I don't think . . ."

"No pressure I promise." R.J. raised his hand, palm facing toward her. "I just thought you might enjoy having the evening off. And, well," he shrugged, "I've got cabin fever. I could use some company." He tossed her another outrageous grin and was almost certain a faint blush tinged her cheeks.

A puppy's shrill yap echoed from behind her, and Brett raised his head. The child craned his neck to look as he said, "Doggie?"

"Yes, mamma got you a new doggie," Sam said. "He's in a box by the sunroom."

Brett squirmed against her hold, and Sammie deposited him upon taupe-colored carpet. He wasted no time trotting across the living room and straight toward the sunroom that branched off the open dining area.

R.J. chuckled and shook his head.

"So whataya say, Sam?" he prompted. "Wanta give some company to a lonely ol' bachelor?"

Her mouth hardened into a firm line. "I really don't think —"

"Please?" R.J. interrupted.

"Uncle R.J.! Uncle R.J.! I've gotta doggie!" Brett squealed. "Come see!"

Sam glanced over her shoulder, sighed, then looked back at R.J.

"Looks like you've been outvoted," R.J. quipped.

"I guess so," she said, her gaze lowered in defeat.

"You don't have to sound so enthusiastic, ya know," he muttered on his way past her. "If you keep this up, I might get a complex."

"I've already got a complex," she mumbled. "You'll be in good company."

"Oh, I'm in good company." R.J. paused then pivoted to face her. "Complex or not, you are good company." He produced a sly wink, and Sam stiffened.

"You said no pressure," she challenged.

"Okay, okay. I'm sorry." R.J. shifted the

bag of groceries as Brett raced forward to tug on his arm.

"Come see!" the child bellowed.

"Let me have this," Sam said, reaching for the grocery bag. "You go see about the puppy. She kept me awake most the night." She rubbed a weary hand over her eyes, and R.J. understood the reason for the dark circles. "It's like having a newborn."

R.J. released the bag and was delighted by a faint whiff of sweet fragrance that reminded him of a wide-open Arkansas field. The scent tempted him to move closer to Sam. Instead, he walked across the southwest-style living room and into the open dining area where Brett hovered near a cardboard box. R.J. lowered himself to the tile floor between the dining table and the sunroom. A squirming cocker spaniel placed twin paws over the side of the box, just tall enough to keep him from escaping. It lifted its nose into the air and howled then yapped. Brett, all vestiges of sleep erased, squealed with laughter and reached out to touch the puppy, who playfully nipped the ends of his fingers.

With a gasp the child retracted his hand and turned horrified eyes toward R.J. "Puppy bite me!" he squeaked, and his eyes brimmed with tears.

"Oh, it's okay," R.J. assured. "The puppy is just trying to play." He reached for Brett's fingers. "Like this." With a playful growl, R.J. inserted the ends of the child's fingers into his mouth and pretended to be a gobbling monster.

A gurgle of laughter bubbled from Brett as the puppy wagged its whole body and barked. R.J. scooped up the dog, held him close, and began to soothe it with endearments. The pup immediately snuggled down and licked R.J.'s hand.

"Now try to scratch his ears, little buddy," R.J. said. "Right here." He directed Brett's hand to the soft spot behind the puppy's ears. As Brett caressed his new pet, the dog closed its eyes and produced a round of contented grunts. "See? He was just excited. He didn't mean to hurt you."

"He wikes me." Brett's blue eyes sparkled, erasing the shadow of pain usually present.

"Yes, of course he does. Who wouldn't like you, champ. You're the greatest!"

Brett, glowing in the praise, turned an adoring gaze upon R.J. as his chubby cheeks dimpled.

R.J. leaned forward and bestowed a kiss upon the boy's forehead.

"Want to hold your new pal?"

Brett shook his head, wrinkled his brow, and retracted his hand.

"No. Puppy bite."

An indulgent chuckle erupted from R.J.

"Okay, okay, maybe I'll just hold him awhile then." The dog squirmed into the front of R.J.'s leather jacket and tried to crawl up his chest. "Oh no you don't," he admonished and leaned back in order to get a better grip on the dog.

Yet his new angle proffered him a glimpse of Sammie standing on the other side of the dining table, still holding the bag of groceries. R.J. glanced up to encounter her solemn gaze leveled straight at him. He raised his brows to prompt her to speak, but Sam remained silent. Silent and watchful. Watchful and pensive. As the gaze lengthened, R.J. was nearly certain he detected a glimmer of admiration stirring her features. Indeed, a trace of awe scampered through the admiration. Sammie looked as if she were seeing him for the first time. Something warm and inviting and luscious swirled in the pit of his stomach. R.J. was reminded of the way she looked at him when he and Brett were lying in his office. His grip on the puppy tightened. R.J. forced himself not to march across the room, grab Sam, and lay a kiss on her she wouldn't forget in a million years. He yanked together every scrap of self-constraint he could muster and stayed on the tile floor. Still, his eyes narrowed of their own volition, and he bit down on his bottom lip.

Sam's gaze faltered. She cleared her throat and deposited the grocery bag on the table.

"It's a she," Sam commented.

"Excuse me?"

"The puppy. He's a she. I mean, it's a girl. You keep calling her a him. It's a female."

"Oh!" R.J. rubbed the pup's head with the ends of his fingers. "Sorry li'l lady," he rumbled. "Didn't mean to insult your girl-hood."

"She's perked up a little, now that you guys are here. She's been acting a little weak the last couple of hours. I wondered if I might have to take her to the vet in the morning."

"Really?" R.J. queried.

"I hungry!" Brett proclaimed. "I want a cookie!" He eyed the dog. "Puppy want a cookie. She say so," he added with a nod.

"Oh, she does, does she?" R.J. asked. "Well, I brought some of the cookies you and I made last night, but you've got to eat your spaghetti first."

"I guess I'll start dinner," Sam stated.

"Not on your life." R.J. deposited the pup back into her box. "I'm the cook tonight. You go soak your feet or play with the boy or something." He stood, shrugged out of his leather jacket, dropped it over the back of a dining chair, and nabbed the bag of groceries.

"But . . ." Sam protested.

"No buts." R.J. raised his hand for added emphasis, and then pivoted to face the kitchen. "If you'll just show me where you keep your pots and pans . . ." He scanned the tiny kitchen's cabinets.

"Look up," Sam said.

R.J. obeyed and encountered a collection of pots and pans hanging from a rack attached to the ceiling.

"Oh, I see," he said through a laugh. "They're all right out in the open — right where I won't ever see them." He shook his head. "Some days I think I need glasses *all* the time."

"Well, when I moved in last fall it was really the only option." Sam walked to the rack, took down two of the pots, and set them on the stovetop. "I had more room in my other house."

Not long after her husband's death, Sam had sold her home in Richardson and bought this place. R.J. had applauded her attempts to put the past behind her, but frowned for a week when she refused his help. She had insisted that her father, her close friends, and the movers could handle the task.

"Wish you would've let me help with the move," R.J. complained under his breath.

"I know." Sam shrugged, then reached for a skillet, just the right size for browning ground meat. "But you'd already done so much when you followed me all the way to Arkansas for that visit with Marilyn, and I just hated to impose any more."

"It would have been far from an imposition, Sammie," R.J. insisted with soft restraint.

"We've already had this discussion once." She plopped the skillet on a third burner with a clang that announced the conversation was closed.

R.J. raised his brows, then shrugged off the rebuttal. He deposited the bag of groceries on the kitchen counter and removed the pasta, prepackaged salad, and French bread. "So, how do you feel about ground turkey?" With a flourish and snap he pulled an oversized apron out of the bag and slipped the top loop over his head.

"I feel like I like ground beef better."

Her voice held the hint of a smile as she glanced over the front of his apron that featured a disheveled duck wearing a chef's hat and an apron with a spatula in one hand and a skillet in the other. *All tips appreciated* was scrawled across an array of chopped vegetables at the duck's feet.

R.J. returned the smile. "I have to protect my 'drobe," he quipped.

"Your 'drobe?"

"Yeah. My wardrobe." R.J. tugged on the collar of his worn T-shirt. "Once you get one of these babies worn to the comfort zone you don't want to stain it with meat juices or anything."

A soft giggle escaped Sam before she purposefully turned her back on him and watered the wilted ivy sitting in the kitchen window.

A companionable silence settled between them, and R.J. observed his former fiancée from behind. Her glossy hair gracing her shoulders was the same hue as the copper-colored pots hanging over her head. The absence of makeup made her look less polished than she usually did in the office, and R.J. enjoyed seeing this side of her. She looked comfortable. Comfortable and relaxed. Relaxed and inviting. His gaze moved to her hands now resting on the edge of the sink. She shifted her feet and remained with her back to him, as if she were afraid to face him.

Clearing his throat, R.J. removed a pound each of turkey and beef from the bottom of the bag. "Mind if I mix ground turkey and ground beef? It makes a lower-fat sauce."

She pivoted to face him, leaned against the sink, and propped her hands on the counter behind. R.J. wasn't certain whether she was settling in for another chat or preparing to shove off and bolt.

"Don't tell me you've started eating ground turkey now." A mischievous light swirled through her eyes, and R.J. warmed. She continued, "Nuts, granola, low-fat meats, juice . . . what's next — carrot tops or something?"

She's teasing me! he thought as her lips tilted upward. *This is a good sign — a really good sign.* "Actually . . ." R.J. laid the meat aside and reached back into the bag.

"I was only joking," Sam gasped. "You haven't really started eating carrot tops have you?" her voice rose on an incredulous shriek.

"No, no, no," R.J. sighed then pulled out a jar of bright-orange juice. "But I *do* juice

my own carrots. I brought this for Brett."
He shoved a stack of opened mail against
crockery canisters and deposited the jar on
the yellow counter. "He loves the stuff. Do
you know how high in antioxidants fresh
carrot juice is?" R.J. raised his hand. "Out
the ceiling!"

Without a word, Sam stepped to the refrigerator, opened it, and pulled out a Dr
Pepper. "But it doesn't fizz," she said, her
blue eyes wide with conviction. She clutched
her chest and closed her eyes. "Give me fizz
or give me death!" Sam snapped the door
shut before popping the tab on the soda.
The drink produced a hiss that applauded
her dedication to the effervescent liquid.

R.J. laughed out loud. "Ah well, you're
quite a few years younger than me, Sam.
At some point all of us have to start
watching vitamin intake and cholesterol
levels and all that. Besides, you haven't
smoked some of the stuff I did when I was
younger, either. I'm doing my best to make
up for some of the damage that weed ad-
diction did."

"You were addicted?" she asked.

"Yes," R.J. leaned against the kitchen
counter, crossed his arms, and squinted.
"It had me for 'bout ten years, I'd say. I
thought you knew."

"I suspected right before we split up that —" she scrutinized her navy-blue socks, "— that you smoked some mari-juana, but I didn't know you were actually hooked." She slowly shook her head and peered into his eyes.

R.J. broke eye contact and stared at the burgundy tile to observe a moth fluttering along one of the veins in the floor. "Yep," he said. "Some people think pot isn't habit-forming, but it is. It does bad things to a person. Makes you act like a bonehead mostly, especially when you're 25 and actin' like you're 13. I'd say I've had my share of boneheaded moments, wouldn't you?" R.J. didn't look at Sam; he didn't dare. Yet he hoped that the heartfelt words revealed his deep regret for breaking their engagement those many years ago. Even though he had apologized when he tried to get her to marry him nearly six years ago, R.J. figured another apology wouldn't hurt — not by a long shot. "It seems that some of us take a little longer to grow up than others," he added.

"Now look at me." R.J. shoved his braid over his shoulder. "I'm just an old guy who's trying to combat the lasting effects from my more stupid era." He smiled at the moth and stopped himself just short of leveling a lighthearted wink at Sam. "Before you know it, I'll be buying electric blankets and eating pureed food."

"Humph," Sam said under her breath as she turned to leave the room. "If you're an old guy, I'll eat my ink jet cartridge."

"Excuse me?" R.J. asked through a chuckle, even though he'd heard every syllable.

"Never mind, Butler," Sam shot over her shoulder. "Just stop it with the syrupy speeches. You never have been good at them anyway. Make your spaghetti however you like it. I'll choke it down somehow."

"Oh, you will, will you?" A naughty temptation rushed upon R.J. — a temptation to twirl Sam into his arms and tickle her neck with kisses until she begged him to stop. R.J. took a step toward her retreating form then halted. His eyes narrowed, and he crammed his hands into his jeans pockets. *You're going to get yourself into more trouble than you can get out of in two years,* he admonished himself. *Get a grip!*

Sammie glanced at Brett, who was still distracted by his new pal. With a relieved sigh, she strolled down the hallway to her bathroom. She kicked aside the towel she had left on the floor that morning, stepped inside, shut the door, leaned against it, and took three deep, cleansing breaths. She turned toward her image in the mirror, deposited the Dr Pepper on the tile counter, gripped the edge of the sink, and observed a woman whose hair had flopped. Her bangs were so straight they looked like they had never seen a bottle of mousse. When R.J. called to say he was bringing Brett home, Sam had yet to bother with makeup for the day. After his call she decided not to put on any. Samantha didn't want to send the message that she had dressed up for R.J. Fresh makeup would certainly have spoken for itself. The dark circles under her eyes made her look haggard. Sam sighed and shook her head.

But he still looks at me like I'm some beauty queen, she thought. She quickly covered her lips with unsteady fingers.

A clank resonated up the hallway. The sound of sizzling meat followed. Sam closed her eyes and imagined that hulk of a man beating around her kitchen like a buffalo in a house of glass. *The wild part is, I actually got a kick out of seeing him in there — especially when he put on that crazy apron!*

"What a hunk," she whispered. "And . . .

I still love that braid." Sam's eyes popped open and she stared into the depths of her own gaze. "I'm slipping," she gasped. *He's finally getting to me, and I'm letting him!*

"He used your own son to worm his way in for dinner, and you didn't have the guts to stop him. Go in there and tell him to go home. *Now!*" Sammie insisted to herself. But she didn't move. She just kept staring at herself.

"Okay," she breathed. "I don't have what it takes to tell him to go home — especially since Brett enjoys him so much. But I don't have to flirt with him, for pity's sake. Or dwell on all his good points, for that matter. I am not ready for another marriage, and I probably won't ever be!" Images from that recurring nightmare swam into her mind, and Sam winced. She snapped up the Dr Pepper and took a long, tingling swallow.

"I wouldn't have teased him," she argued with her reflection, "but he is too good with Brett. I almost let myself get a little too impressed there for awhile." Sam looked at herself a bit longer then hesitated. "Okay, it's more than just how good he is with Brett. I'm just not ready . . ."

Without another breath she continued, "You're finally going nuts! You've started talking to yourself!

"But Brett needs a father so bad," she whispered as if she'd never interrupted her monologue. Sam turned to lean against the counter. "He's never really known what having a loving father is like." She relived those moments when R.J. told Brett he was the greatest. Sam thought her son was going to glow in the dark, and she wanted to sink to the floor in appreciation of the man who was willing to get involved and love her son like his own.

"But I can't get married for Brett," Sam asserted, as memories of Adam's sexual forcefulness stomped across her wounded spirit. She gulped another mouthful of soda, then coughed against a droplet that took a wrong turn. Her eyes burned, and the poster-sized floral photo hanging crooked on the wall blurred in a wash of tears. Sam reached forth to right the photo — a gift from her "sister" Melissa. As she focused on the splendid dew that cascaded across tiger lilies, Sam recalled what she had told R.J. yesterday evening, "There's nothing left of me. There's nothing I can give you." Was that the truth? Regardless of the answer, thoughts of being a wife in every measure of the word jabbed a spear of dread through the internal scars.

One of her six "sisters," Jac Lightfoot,

had also experienced sexual abuse, only hers happened during childhood. Jac, still a newlywed, recently told Sam that every day she seemed to be moving closer and closer to complete freedom from the past. But Sam's past was so recent that she was still in survival mode. She was living one day to the next, praying to move past those horrid dreams that tormented her nights.

"Okay, Jesus, You've already gotten me through a lot . . ." Sam recalled the lonely nights after her mother had deserted their family. Sam had lain awake and cried until she wondered if her bed would float away, yet God had remained steadfast. Sam relived those destitute days when R.J. had betrayed her faith in him, when she found herself face-down on the carpet, wretched and undone. Still the Lord had never forsaken her. Her mind traveled to the years of abuse Adam had hammered into her. She sensed that Christ had taken the abuse with her. She even pondered the church that she and Adam attended. That church had inflicted another kind of pain upon Sam by insisting she remain a demeaned subordinate in her marriage, regardless of her husband's ill-treatment. Nevertheless, Sam could sense Jesus standing beside her, giving her the strength not to go back to that church, the strength to ignore Adam's threats and the pastor's disapproval. By standing firm, she had discovered the courage to leave Adam. And the Lord had sent Jac Lightfoot as a direct answer to prayer. Jac had stepped in, used her martial arts training to defend her friend from Adam's abuse, and had broken Sam out of her cage of terror.

"Oh, Lord, you've already gotten me through a lot," Sam repeated with a nod. "Please get me through this evening. And somehow help R.J. see that I don't need to be pushed right now or ever."

She rubbed her cheeks and observed her sock-clad feet until they blurred into a navy-blue mist. "Okay," she whispered. "I'm going back out there. I'm going to play with my son. I'm going to eat R.J.'s spaghetti, and I'm going to hint that he make a swift exit." She squared her shoulders, grabbed the doorknob, and steadily opened the door.

And you will not look into those silky-brown eyes again, she added.

Yet she had barely taken one step down the hallway when the telephone rang. Sam stopped in her tracks and gazed down the short passageway, toward her answering machine in the living room. Sam had screened her calls all day because she didn't want to encounter her mother on the other end. So far, her mom hadn't attempted to call after yesterday's message. Hopefully, she wasn't trying again now.

Eight

Victoria Roberts waited until Sam's answering machine picked up before replacing the receiver on its cradle. With a sigh she turned from the telephone and stared at the immaculate beach home ensconced in windows that proffered a breathtaking view of the Destin, Florida coastline. The sun inched toward the western horizon — a giant ball of fire that looked as if it would be extinguished by the vast ocean. Yet the scenery that often inspired left Victoria empty.

When her pregnancy test came back positive two days ago, Victoria had longed for Tony to cancel his deep-sea fishing trip and focus on her for a few days. After all, her goal in life was to be a great wife and mom. For six years of marriage, being a mom seemed to forever elude her. Yet now that her life's goal was at last growing inside her, she had hoped her husband would be more understanding of her need to savor and share the event. But after the initial celebration, Tony went on with his plans as usual. Nothing came in the way of this hallowed annual event. Nothing. *Not even me,* Victoria thought bitterly. She stroked her abdomen. *Not even our baby.* She stifled the twist of resentment that threatened to uncoil in the pit of her stomach. Another sigh escaped her.

Victoria eyed the half-read novel lying open on the end table, then checked her dainty watch, encircled in tiny diamonds. "Five of five," she mumbled. "Still more than two hours until the sister conference call." She lowered herself into the corner of the overstuffed couch and reached for the book. But her hand moved to the framed snapshot sitting near the brass lamp.

The shot had been taken right after she and Tony first got married. The two of them stood side-by-side near a yacht. He held up a swordfish nearly as long as he was tall. At six feet three inches, Tony wasn't a small man by any means. With blond hair and pale gray eyes, he looked like he belonged on a surfboard rather than in a fireman's uniform. Indeed, he was as comfortable in the water as out. Victoria, always petite, barely reached his shoulder. Both of them were squinting against the

133

afternoon sunshine. Her light-brown hair, naturally soft and a bit frizzy, curled around her face, and her red nose attested to too many hours in the sun. When she first met Tony, Victoria had never dreamed the two of them would get together. While he would never have modeling scouts after him, Tony still turned a few heads. And Victoria had always considered herself quite mousy, especially when she was without her rouge and lipstick. Tony was always so boisterous and charming, while Victoria preferred the quieter life. She stroked Tony's image and the urge to resent him melted into a dull ache, the protest of a lonely heart.

Victoria set the photo down, and then frowned at the book. She glanced toward the kitchen and eyed the cabinet that held her recipes. Her brows rose a fraction, and she stood and stepped toward the kitchen. Victoria had been meaning to try out a new taco soup recipe that a church friend had passed on. Every Friday Victoria cohosted a home-and-garden show on a local TV station, and she was the one responsible for the recipes they featured.

As she stepped inside the kitchen, the doorbell rang. She pivoted and padded across the Italian tile toward the front door, wondering if her new curtains were finally arriving from Spiegel. She eyed the taupe checked drapes that claimed her front window. The pattern that had been refreshing and matched her decor two years ago now left her cold. As far as Victoria was concerned, checks were now out — all the way out — and flowers were in.

Before opening the bevel-glassed door she peered out the peephole, fully expecting to see a young delivery man dressed in a brown uniform. Instead she encountered a familiar man wearing a sports coat and slacks. Ricky Christopher, the new choir director, stared at her door and fidgeted with the zipper on his organizer. His arresting features, shocking blue eyes, dark hair, and light tan jolted Victoria into admitting that if she weren't married she could be interested in this man — despite the fact that he was five years her junior. He'd arrived at their mid-sized church a few months ago. From the start, the married choir ladies teased him about arranging his marriage. The gentlemen members usually protested with warnings about the woes of being in the snares of a woman. From there, the choir usually went into a playful session that left Ricky blushing and insisting they move on to the reason they came — practice.

With a soft smile Victoria tugged open the door. "Ricky, how nice to see you," she said and swept the door wide. "Won't you come in?"

The young choir director obeyed her prompting and entered the home. As Victoria closed the door against the tepid coastal air, he gazed around the living room. "Wow! This place is gorgeous!" he exclaimed.

"Thanks," Victoria said, and her heart warmed as she took in the blend of pastels from sky-blue to sea-foam to the palest of taupe. "We bought this house about two years ago. It was in need of repair, and I've put a lot of work into it."

"You've done a *great* job!"

"Thanks! It's my gift, I guess. I love homemaking and entertaining and all that."

"You're like my mom," he said and turned an appreciative grin toward her. "She can pull stuff out of a junkyard, recreate it, and decorate a whole house."

"Actually, I did find this chair in a Dumpster." Victoria walked toward an antique claw-footed chair covered in polished blue cotton. "I refinished it and recovered it myself."

"See what I mean?" Ricky raised his hand. "Women like you — it's amazing." He snapped his fingers. "You people could turn a rusty dog food can into art in 30 minutes flat!"

A gentle giggle flowed from Victoria. "Well, I wouldn't go *that* far," she said, "but I have pulled off a few feats." She pointed toward the brass lamp near the photo of Tony and her. "I bought that lamp at a garage sale last year — two dollars! All it needed was some polish and a new shade. I got the shade at a discount craft store in Pensacola."

"No kidding?" Ricky walked toward the lamp, and his leather-soled loafers tapped along the tile. "I didn't know they sold hand-painted lamp shades." He held up his hand. "Wait — don't tell me! *You* painted the sea scene on it, right?" He observed her with eyes the color of a sapphire sky at sunset.

Warm pleasure sprouted in Victoria's midsection.

"Of course. I bought the smooth shade, so I could paint the scene. Do you like it?"

"Like it? I *love* it!" He deposited his organizer on the table, strode around the lamp, shook his head, and soaked in Victoria's creation.

The longer Ricky examined the lamp shade, the longer Victoria admired him. Part of the reason why the older choir women teased him was because he was so attractive. And his simple, enthusiastic personality lent him a certain boyish appeal that made them wonder how he had escaped matrimony. *He has to be nearly 30 by now,* Victoria thought. *If I weren't married . . .* The recurring thought shoved itself upon her mind, and Victoria stared at the couch cushion, the color of the Destin ocean on a clear summer's day. Her stare soon turned inward, and she reminded herself that she *was* a married woman.

Victoria touched her abdomen. She glanced down at her perfectly manicured toenails and shapely feet strapped in low-heeled sandals. *Why isn't Tony ever pleased with any of my endeavors?* Years had passed since he'd done more than state a monotone "that's nice," when Victoria had done the domestic equivalent of turning the water into wine. *He used to think my homemaking was incredible,* she mused. *But now . . .* Her gaze wandered back to the snapshot near the brass lamp. *Now he'd rather go fishing.*

An exclamation from Ricky snatched Victoria from the pensive realm. He raced to the strip of wall that connected two sections of the massive windows. She had placed one of her oversized paintings in that exact spot in hopes that it would serve as a mere reflection of the majestic view she enjoyed every day.

"I can't believe this!" Ricky exclaimed as he stopped in front of the painting. "This scene matches the one on the lamp!"

"You noticed," Victoria said. She slowly approached him from behind.

"Of course! Look! There's the lighthouse." He pointed toward the white building, perched upon a sandbar in the midst of the sea. "Oh, I don't believe this!" he whispered as his gaze trailed out the window toward a lighthouse. "You've painted your own view, haven't you?"

"That's exactly what I did." Victoria slipped her hands into the pocket of her linen shorts. This time she didn't bother to stifle the feelings of gratitude Ricky's kudos spawned within her. Earlier she had felt so needy — desperately needy — that any praise, no matter the source, was a welcome reprise to her lonely spirit.

Ricky spun from the painting, and his hungry gaze took in the interior once more. "Victoria, would there be any way you'd come over to my place and make some suggestions?" He turned to face her, and a desperate light gleamed in his eyes. "I've only been in my house about four months, as you know, and it just doesn't have it."

Victoria imagined herself strolling around Ricky's home, putting her touches here and there. The image was a bit too inviting. She broke eye contact and tried her best to stop the warmth from creeping up her neck. "I don't think —" she began.

"No, listen." Ricky touched her forearm. "I've got a big problem. M–my dad died when I was just ten. My mom and I are very, very close. Anyway, she's finally met somebody, and I think they're going to get married. She's bringing him for a visit, and I'd really like to make a good impression — for Mom's sake. I'd do anything for her. All week, I kept thinking that I needed to do something to spruce up my house, but I really can't afford to hire a professional, and I'm clueless about what to do myself." He dropped his hand and shrugged. "I have 500 dollars I can use . . . and if I hit pay dirt at some Dumpsters . . ."

Victoria raised her gaze to meet his. A sparkle of expectation lighted his eyes. She imagined him dressed in his sports jacket and slacks and digging around Dumpsters all over Destin and Pensacola. A chortle gurgled up her throat. "Don't count on the Dumpsters. I'm notorious for checking them, but I can go nearly a year before finding anything that's salvageable."

"Then I'll hit some garage sales. Goodwill. Wherever! Just tell me what I need, and I'll do my best to find it!" He raised his hands.

A flicker of caution flashed through Victoria. She peered deeply into Ricky's eyes, searching for any signs of an ulterior motive. His guileless gaze held no hint of anything but childlike hope that she would help him. Victoria felt like a wanton woman. The poor guy had no idea the effect he had on her. *None*. And she was half crazy to even think he would find her attractive. She was married, and Ricky Christopher was a man of God.

"Okay," she heard herself say. "I'll help you. I really don't have much on my agenda right now anyway — except the TV show on Fridays," she said. "Since I got this place shipshape, I've been feeling a little bored. Except . . ." she hesitated and wondered if she should mention her pregnancy. She decided he'd find out through the grapevine soon enough. "Oh nothing. I'll help you," she repeated. "Name the day."

"Thank you *so much!*" Ricky gripped her hands. "Can you stop by tomorrow morning? My mom and her friend are flying in from California in a month. I don't have much time."

"Yes, tomorrow morning is fine, just fine."

"Does 9:30 work for you?"

"That's fine with me." Victoria's attention trailed to the photo again. "My husband is out of town and won't be back for a few days. I'm at loose ends right now, so this will give me something to do."

"*Great!* This is an answer to prayer." He placed the heel of his hand between his eyes. "Oh, man, I almost forgot the reason I came!" A carefree laugh escaped him as a set of twin dimples claimed his cheeks. "We missed you last night at practice. I was in the neighborhood and thought I'd stop by and tell you. I also brought the schedule of choir practices through February." He walked to the end table, where his organizer still lay. Ricky unzipped it, extracted the schedule, and extended it to Victoria.

The textured paper connected with her fingertips, and the schedule's neat layout reflected both professionalism and thought.

"If you'll look right here," he stepped to her side, and the smell of sporty aftershave heightened Victoria's need for distance, "the second week of February, we're having a Valentine's party. Feel free to bring your husband," he encouraged.

"Okay," Victoria agreed and stepped out of the sphere of the masculine scent.

"Great! Well, thanks again." Ricky extended his hand for a warm shake. "You have no idea how much I appreciate your help."

Victoria smiled, nodded, and felt as if she were toppling into a blue ocean the exact color of Ricky's eyes.

"No problem," she choked out. She tried to remember the last time she had felt such warmth toward Tony.

"I'll see you tomorrow."

"Excuse me?" she queried and groped for the reason she'd see him so soon.

"For your consultation at my house," he prompted. "Tomorrow at 9:30."

"Oh yes! That will be just fine," Victoria agreed. "Why not e-mail me your address and directions."

"My address is in the new choir directory."

"Oh duh!" Victoria shook her head. "I guess it would be, wouldn't it."

Accompanied by companionable laughter, Ricky hastened toward the front door. Before leaving, he gripped the doorknob and pivoted to face the home once more. His gaze roved the expanse of the room and a hopeful smile tilted his full lips.

Victoria clasped her hands behind her back, twined her fingers, and squeezed until they ached. *Well, I may be married,* she thought, *but I'm not dead.* As her toes curled, the cliché rang too true for comfort.

After Ricky stepped outside and bid a final farewell, Victoria closed the door. She watched out the window as he stepped off the white deck and headed around the house. His carefree gait and light whistle testified to the sparkling personality that could probably charm the teeth out of a shark. She squeezed her eyes tight. *Taco soup,* she thought with fervor. *I was going to make taco soup!* Her eyes snapped open, and she rushed toward the kitchen.

Before stepping into her favorite room, Victoria glanced toward the hallway. Across from the living room entryway hung a poster-sized photo of the seven "sisters": Samantha Jones, Jacquelyn Franklin, Marilyn Langham, Kim Lan O'Donnel, Melissa Franklin, Sonsee Delaney, and herself. Each of the sisters' joyful demeanors seemed to take on an accusing glare.

Sammie's azure eyes burned with blue flames. Jac's full lips, tilted in a smile, appeared firm and disapproving. Marilyn's light-brown brows looked drawn as if she were about to say, "How could you!" Victoria gulped as she imagined Kim Lan, that oriental beauty, shaking her finger in sisterly censure. And she could almost hear "mouth of the south" Melissa sharing with a scandalized Sonsee about "the latest" concerning Victoria. She turned away from the photo, and decided she'd be better off if her friends didn't know about Ricky Christopher.

Nine

Terrence pulled his pickup into the driveway of Cox Veterinarian Clinic, put the vehicle into park, and turned off the engine. The setting sun glowed upon the blanket of snow covering the classic frame home Barry had renovated as his clinic. The snow glistened in the veil of light like a million tiny diamonds. Terrence squinted against the annoying sheen.

"Stupid snow," he groused. At least he had gotten out of Dallas before the storm set in. He never saw more than a flurry as long as he traveled east. But by the time he turned around and headed back west, he knew he wouldn't make it home. Terrence spent the night and most of the day in a hotel — the hotel Mallory used to frequent.

"Why are you bothering me *now?*" he growled under his breath. *It's not March, and I'm not with another woman!*

Terrence opened the truck door and stepped out of the cab. He darted a glance across a parking lot that was occupied by only one Cadillac — Barry's sporty black number that fit the portly vet as well as a mink coat fits a coon hound. Terrence clenched his teeth and glared at the collection of busy fast-food joints, the ever-present traffic, the strategically placed traffic lights. No Mallory peered at him from inside a restaurant. She didn't materialize behind the wheel of a car. Neither was she a pedestrian, scrutinizing him in wide-eyed accusation over six lanes of traffic. Mallory was nowhere in sight. His jaw relaxed. *Maybe she won't be back for awhile.*

After slamming the truck's door, he strode toward the back of the vehicle. Terrence's cowboy boots crunched upon the chilled parking lot, and every crackle raked along his spine. He rubbed his eyes, gritty and weary, and counted the hours until he could drive to his farmhouse, east of Plano, and crawl into his own bed. He never had slept well in hotel rooms, and especially with uninvited guests who sat on the end of his bed and glared at him all night. But at least this time Mallory didn't talk. The perpetual badgering to tell Barry about the murder was, at times, almost enough to make Terrence blurt out the truth. By the time Mallory got through with her verbal warfare, Terrence was often ready to do anything to get relief. *Anything.* A few times he had even contemplated suicide. A horn blasted nearby, and he jumped. The skin along his shoulders squirmed like the epidermis of a molting python. His left eye twitched.

He reached into the back of the truck and pulled out one of the cages. A lone bichon frise pup lay in the bottom, now nothing more than a stiff, white puff. The rascal had been a reject at a pet store, which didn't surprise Terrence. It had been sickly from the start. Conveniently forgotten when Terrence checked into the hotel, the five-and-a-half-week-old animal had been too frail to survive all-night exposure to the arctic temperatures that burst upon Texas. As Blackwood strode toward the animal clinic, the cage's icy handle pivoted back and forth against his callused palm. Barry would dispose of the beast. For the last 13 years, Terrence shoveled dirt only when absolutely necessary.

Blackwood marched past the renovated home's front door that sported a "closed" sign. He rounded the clinic, stopped at the back door, inserted his key, and let himself in. As the door clicked shut behind him, the smell of fur and pet food enveloped his senses. Terrence strode up the narrow hallway, past the restrooms, toward Barry's office. He knocked on the half-open door and shoved it open as Cox hollered, "Come in."

Terrence deposited the cage on the mound of papers scattered across Cox's desk and observed his former brother-in-law, ensconced in a cloud of cigar smoke. "I lost another one. Would you take care of it for me?"

Barry nodded then leaned forward to observe the dead canine. Thankfully the man looked nothing like his sister. Where Mallory's eyes had been brown, Barry's were pale green. Her hair had been the color of flames; Barry's was mostly missing. What mousy-brown hair wasn't missing had turned gray. Mallory's form, slender as a cane, probably weighed one-third of Barry's oversized body that looked like a collection of balls, soft and rotund, pressing upon each other.

As Barry inspected the dog his cheeks sagged. "Poor joker," he muttered before taking a long draw on the cigar.

Terrence stopped himself from rolling his eyes in scorn of Barry's emotional weakness. Terrence grimaced at the cigar smoke and swallowed the compulsive

149

cough rising in his throat. The only thing he hated more than the smell of his dog barn was tobacco smoke — the one negative in his casino lifestyle.

As Barry focused on the mutt, Terrence's attention wandered to the huge tiger print hanging behind the desk. His gaze trailed toward an updated arrangement of what looked like family photos of Cox's extended family — Mallory included. Terrence stopped breathing. He peered at one photo of Mallory standing in a wide-open field next to a horse. Her horse. The horse Terrence sold shortly after her death. A quiver started in the pit of his stomach. He gripped the front of his leather jacket and released a slow breath as a thin film of sweat seeped from his palms and forehead.

And Mallory . . . Mallory reached to pet the horse then stared straight at Terrence. This time her brown orbs glowed red. Her neck took on crimson streaks that testified to the cause of death. Her lips moved, forming words that he, at first, could not decipher. Finally the message became clear: *Murderer. You're a murderer. You strangled me. You killed me. Killer!* The silent accusations became an onslaught of icy pricks that drove into his mind like shards of glass. The blood drained to

Terrence's feet. His face went cold. The room began a slow spin, and he lowered himself into the chair across from the desk.

"Terrence?" Cox's voice boomed in a concerned echo. "Are you okay?"

Even though Terrence knew he should answer his brother-in-law, he couldn't tear his gaze from the photo. Mallory's eyes glowed brighter and branded the memory of their final fight into the fabric of his brain. She had been angry — so angry — about his gambling.

Barry stopped between Terrence and the photo, took it off the wall, dropped it into the top drawer of his desk, and eyed toward his brother-in-law with a trace of sympathy. Cox sucked on the cigar stuck between his teeth, and the smoke billowed from his mouth as he spoke. "Audry just came in and hung these up yesterday," he bit out. "I told her to leave 'em at home, but she wouldn't listen. I'll take this one back."

Terrence gripped the arms of the leather chair. "That's — that's a good idea," he stammered as he mopped his forehead with the back of his hand. *She isn't real,* he told himself. *She can't be. She's dead. This isn't real. I've got to get a grip. It's just — just like having a dream, but I'm — I'm awake. This has got to stop!* he reasoned once more. *She shouldn't be doing this to me.* Terrence drew his brows together and stared at the desk phone until his vision blurred. At last he arrived at the only logical conclusion he could conjure up: *I'm just tired. I'm tired — that's the problem. I'm stressed. The last week has been tough. Once I get some sleep, she'll leave me alone.*

"Well, we've got a job to do. You ready?" Barry bent over to cram the end of the cigar into a shell-shaped ashtray.

"Yes, but I'm exhausted." Terrence stifled a yawn. "Didn't sleep well last night." He stood and stretched. "I never have been able to sleep in hotel rooms much." He shrugged out of his jacket and draped it across the back of the chair.

After standing, Barry wobbled side to side in a gait that resembled a football bouncing on grass. With labored breathing he crossed the floor and stopped beside a six-foot metal cabinet. He pulled a wad of keys from his pants pocket and inserted one into the lock. The door squeaked open, and Barry reached inside. When he turned around he held a cardboard box taped shut. His pale eyes sparkling with fiendish glee hinted at the box's contents. Terrence returned Barry's smile.

"Let's go!" Barry looked like a fat serpent ready to swallow a satisfying meal. "The carriers are in the cages. If we don't waste time, we can be out of here by ten."

With a nod Terrence rolled up the sleeves of his corduroy shirt and followed his brother-in-law down the hallway into an examination room.

"I filled eight bags last night. I think I left the box cutter and tape in the drawer."

Another monumental yawn crawled up Terrence's throat as Barry plopped the box near the stainless steel sink. He yanked open a drawer, extracted the cutter, and slit the box open. Barry dug inside, pulled out one of the half-pound bags, and held it up. "Isn't it great that white powder can be so valuable?" he mused with a wicked tilt to his lips. He replaced the bag, peered inside the box, then pivoted to face Terrence, his baggy eyes bugging.

Blackwood, taken aback, held Barry's gaze for several seconds as the hair along the back of his neck prickled. "What is it?" he demanded.

"One of the bags is missing," Cox rasped.

An ominous silence shrouded the room — a silence pierced only by the faint whine of a canine, the yowl of a feline, and low-pitched growls from other animals.

"What?" Terrence felt as if he were doused by a tub of icy water. The desire to sleep vanished. He curled his fists.

"I prepared eight last night. *I know I did!* Two for each dog."

"Well, do you think — do you think you maybe dropped one or . . ."

"No, I couldn't have!" Barry leaned toward the box and pored over the contents. "They were here. Every one of them —"

"How late was it? Maybe you were just tired or–or —"

"No!" Cox slammed his canvas shoe against the tile floor and whirled to face his brother-in-law. "They were all here! I know it!"

"Had you been —" Terrence stopped himself from saying the final word — "drinking." Whether he wanted to admit it or not, Barry delved into his whiskey on too regular a basis. Terrence had always prided himself on avoiding that habit.

The flourescent lights cast shadows on Barry's pudgy cheeks as he stepped around the table. The ever-present flush darkened, and his cheeks took on a bluish hue. Barry's mouth hardened. His nostrils widened. His pale eyes narrowed. His brows drew together like two bushy caterpillars attempting to meet above his nose. A pillar of something cold and ugly and imperious flashed between the partners — a dreadfulness Terrence had never endured from Barry, even after Mallory's death. Terrence stepped back. His blunt fingernails dug into his palms. His legs grew rigid.

"I didn't touch the stuff," he snarled. "How dare you assume I would —"

"I'm not assuming a thing that isn't a possibility," Cox shot back.

"What's the matter with you!?" Terrence raised his fist and slammed it against the wooden examination table.

"All I know is that I put *eight* packets in this box last night at seven o'clock. Now, there are only seven!" The vet's coarse voice became a roaring crescendo. "You're the only person who has a key to the clinic *and* a key to that cabinet!" A tinge of scarlet tipped Barry's ears. His gaze pierced into Terrence with the same intensity he felt when Mallory hounded him.

"I was in a hotel room off I-20 because the roads were so covered up in that — that stinkin' snow that nobody in Dallas was driving anywhere!" Terrence croaked. He stepped toward Barry and thrust his index finger at his chubby nose. "I couldn't have come in here and taken one of those bags even if I had *wanted* to!"

Another shroud of silence permeated the air. Again, distant meows and woofs invaded the room. The smell of Barry's breath soon obliterated all traces of the pet smells, and Terrence was forced to inhale the rancid odor of whiskey. "You've been drinking today!" he accused.

"So what!"

Barry always had been able to hold his alcohol without much evidence of imbibing, usually because he stopped one step before the substance took him under. Terrence had only seen him debilitated half a dozen times in 20 years. And while Barry seldom allowed himself to get fully drunk, the alcohol *always* inserted a splinter of paranoia smack into the middle of his psyche.

"Were you also drinking last night?" Terrence finally challenged. He answered his own question. "You were! Why am I even asking?" He didn't bother to hide his disdain. "You know what I think, Barry? I don't think there was an eighth bag. I think you miscounted because you let yourself get too close to the edge." Raw fury raced from Terrence's gut. Gooseflesh attacked his shoulders. Flames of perspiration licked his neck then leaped upon his upper lip and cheeks. He grabbed the front of the vet's rumpled scrubs and wadded it in his fist, hot and hard. "I oughtta . . ." He lowered his face to within inches of Barry's. A flicker of something unexpected glistened in the depths of Barry's eyes — fear. Fear and doubt. Doubt and regret.

With a disgusted grunt Terrence released his brother-in-law and snatched the box. "Let's just get this over with!" he demanded. "I'm too tired to put up with much more of you tonight! We'll do the best we can with what we have and tell the buyer you misfigured. We'll ship another bag next week if we have to."

Terrence stalked into the hallway and moved straight toward the boarding room. The woofs and howls mingled with the slap of his boots against tile. He struggled to control the urge to strangle Barry . . . just as he had strangled Mallory.

Ten

The phone rang and Sammie jumped. After R.J.'s delicious dinner, he had insisted she relax in the living room. Eventually Sam stretched out on the couch. Brett soon joined her. Now his head rested in the crook of her arm, and she was crowded against the back of the couch. The telephone continued to ring, and Sam gazed around the room, trying to remember where the phone actually was. A hulking figure approached from the kitchen, and his solid footfalls stopped at the end of the couch. Just about the time Sam decided she needed to find the phone, R.J. picked up the receiver and whispered, "Hello."

As the fog of sleep began to seep away, Sam's eyes flew open and she checked her wristwatch. *Seven-thirty on the money. It's the conference call.*

R.J. eyed her with a mild flicker of mischief as he said, "Yes, she's here. I fed her dinner. Her stomach is full so she flopped out on the couch. They just don't make women like they used to," he drawled and softly laughed.

"Ouch!" R.J. winced. "You people don't take teasing very well, do you?"

Rolling her eyes, Sam could only imagine what her six friends must be thinking or saying. Not one of them would hesitate to give R.J. ample grief over his joking. "I can't believe I conked out on the couch," she muttered before raising herself up on her elbow. Something warm and fuzzy stirred near her feet, and Sam noted that the puppy had opted for a nap as well. "That figures. She stayed awake most of the night — and will probably do the same tonight."

"Looks like Sammie is rising from the dead," R.J. continued; then he watched Brett, who stirred and mumbled, "Puppy." The biker extended the cordless receiver to Sam. She took it, swung her feet over the dog, and sat up. R.J. moved to Brett's side, gently scooted him further into the couch, and placed a couple of throw pillows next to him. "Poor little guy," R.J. rumbled. "He played so hard today. His catnap just wasn't enough."

Sam peered into R.J.'s face, ablaze with blatant adoration for her child. Her mind raced to yesterday evening when she found him and Brett asleep in his office. As R.J.'s gaze roved to her, she didn't break contact despite her decision to avoid looking in his gentle brown eyes. Sam had somehow managed to eat a whole meal with only a couple of direct glimpses at R.J., but the aftermath of sleep left her vulnerable. Vulnerable and unsuspecting. Unsuspecting and unprepared.

His eyes took on the flames of ardor; flames that burned with a love that had never died. Sam's cheeks heated, and a voice deep within warned her to flee. But she couldn't. An odd unity bound them together using memories that would not be erased . . . motorcycle rides at sunset . . . watching the late show on TV . . . the first time they had kissed.

Without a word he bent and brushed her forehead with a brief yet potent kiss that tickled because of his beard. He straightened, turned, and strode back toward the kitchen as if nothing had happened. A warm wash cascaded from the place where his lips brushed her skin, and Sam sat in stunned silence. Her mind skipped back to their first kiss. At the ripe old age of 17 she had dared to ask R.J. to the church banquet. He accepted. That night he walked her home, only three houses from the church. Standing on her front porch, he gripped her upper arms and planted a chaste kiss on her forehead. Sam had been elated and disappointed. Deep in her youthful heart she had hoped for a kiss on the lips . . . yet that innocent kiss had begun the courtship that lead to R.J.'s proposal.

As he moved into the kitchen a round of faint whistles pierced the silence. Sammie stared at the cordless phone as if it were a foreign object from outer space. She gulped and was tempted to hang the thing up. No telling what teasing her friends were going to force her to endure. The wolf whistles now floating from the receiver were evidence enough that she would be given the fifth degree.

Her reminiscent musings soured. She touched her forehead and stared at R.J., who stood at the kitchen sink with his back to her. When he invited himself to dinner, he had promised no pressure, no advances. As needles of irritation stabbed her cheeks, Sam decided that taking advantage of her sleepy state certainly qualified as breaking his word. After she got off the phone with her friends, she would politely ask R.J. to leave. She also figured he hadn't forgotten their first kiss any more than she had. And there was a chance that his repeating the gesture signified a new courtship was beginning.

Sam placed the receiver to her ear and barked out an irritable, "Hello." The pup whined faintly, and Brett turned onto his side. As her sisters began the expected mischief, Sam stood and walked toward her bedroom. She closed the door behind her, flipped on the light, and settled into the center of her unmade brass bed.

"Cat got your tongue, Sammie?" Melissa finally asked, and she imagined the pediatrician's intelligent eyes sparkling behind her glasses.

Funny you should be teasing me, Samantha thought. *Kinkaide jilted you just like R.J. did me. I at least expected some respect from your corner.* As the banter continued, Sammie's ire gradually rose. *Why does this bunch always think they have the right to torment me like this?* A soft voice deflated her irritation. *You know they don't mean any harm. They love you.* Sammie sighed as she recalled Adam's funeral and their support. Three of the sisters — Victoria, Kim Lan, and Marilyn — were able to make it to Richardson. Sonsee had been put to bed by her obstetrician, and Jac and Mel were maintaining a bedside vigil for Melissa's brother-in-law, Lawton. Nevertheless, the sisters who couldn't make it were just as supportive as those who could. Even in those horrid nightmares, they made repeated appearances, standing firm during some of the darkest days of Sam's life.

Kim Lan's teasing broke into Sam's mental meanderings. "Sometimes the guilty dog stays silent."

"We're on the verge of voting about whether or not you and R.J. secretly got married over the weekend," Sonsee said. "Are you going to clue us in or not?"

"Not!" Sam claimed while rolling her eyes. Her gaze landed on a spider spinning a web in the upper corner of her ceiling. "Okay, okay, guys. Here's what happened. I decided to trade my birds in on a cocker spaniel puppy. R.J. offered to keep Brett while I did the exchange. Meanwhile, a snowstorm set in —"

"I heard about that little flurry you guys had over there," Jac chided. "It looked like dust compared to what we get in Colorado. All Lawton does is gripe about the snow. He's an ol' Okie and not quite adjusted yet."

"I'd probably whine just as much," Sam replied. "A day off is kind of nice, but then

it gets old after awhile. And we're not prepared for snow like you guys are. Anyway,
Brett wound up spending the night with
R.J. Then, when R.J. brought Brett home
this afternoon, he invited himself in to
cook dinner for us."

"And you didn't turn him down?" Marilyn asked.

"Sounds to me like she didn't," Victoria
chimed in.

"I tried," Sam said on a sigh. She peered
across the room and into her dresser
mirror. Her straight hair now had the
"plastered to my head" look. She suppressed a groan. "But just about the time I
was going to turn him down, Brett wanted
to show R.J. his new puppy, and well . . ."

"Well, well, well," Kim Lan drawled, and
the tone of her voice reminded Sam of the
shampoo advertisement the Vietnamese
supermodel starred in. "Looks like *I* win!"

"Win what?" Sam observed the brass
alarm clock on her nightstand and noticed
the second hand ticking away. *The thing
has hauled off and started working again!*

"I said R.J. would soften you up by Valentine's Day. The rest of our hardheaded
friends all thought it would at least take
until summer."

"Some of us didn't think he'd *ever* pull

it off," Jac said, and Sam was reminded of the recent courtship between the private detective and her husband, Lawton. Lawton certainly met his share of obstacles when trying to woo Jac. Although she was tough-minded and independent to a fault, she had to overcome serious childhood pain before making marital commitments.

"Everybody out there isn't as ornery as you are, Jac." Victoria's soft voice floated across the line, and Sam smiled. Victoria was the epitome of the consummate lady. Sam had always admired her graceful demeanor and charm. In her presence, Sammie sometimes felt gangly and awkward. And she never failed to writhe in embarrassment if Victoria came to her home. Clutter seemed to crawl out of Sam's cabinets and hurl itself across her home. Victoria's house usually looked like it came straight from the pages of *Better Homes and Gardens.* Indeed, Sam had even written an article in *Romantic Living* about the home Victoria and her husband had remodeled in Destin.

As Sam eyed the pile of clothes draped across the rocking chair in the corner, a series of faint clangs floated up the hallway reminding her of the man in her kitchen. She stroked her forehead and soon lost track of the conversational volley — until the word "pregnant" crackled across the line.

"Oh, Victoria!" Sam breathed and covered her mouth with her fingertips. "I am *so sorry!* I never did call you back yesterday."

"That's quite all right," Victoria soothed. "I called and talked to all the sisters, and I just wanted to make sure you were in on the news. *I am so excited!* I've already started decorating the nursery — and I'm only about six weeks along!"

"Oh, girlfriend," Sonsee groaned, "just wait a few more weeks. You'll be throwing up your toenails." As the newest mother of the crew, veterinarian Sonsee Delaney often spoke up when the subject of child-birth arose.

"Thanks for the encouragement," Victoria said dryly.

"Actually, I didn't have any problems at all when I was carrying Brooke," Marilyn chimed in. "I felt great the whole time except for the delivery. That's what was so bad for me."

"I'm voting for another adoption," Kim Lan claimed, referring to the child they adopted last year from Vietnam. "This pregnancy thing sounds a little stressful to me."

All the biological mothers — Marilyn, Sonsee, Sammie, and Victoria — simultaneously cried, "Chicken!" A round of raucous laughter followed.

"Actually, Josh and I have been talking about adoption as well, Kim," Marilyn added. Sam smiled when she thought of Marilyn's vow never to get married again after her minister husband divorced her and married the "other" woman. Amazingly, Marilyn *did* remarry — and to another minister at that. "Even though we can have children," Marilyn continued, "we think the Lord is leading us to adopt."

"You go, girl!" Kim Lan cheered. "Just give me and Mick a nod, and we'll arrange a connection." A pensive pause followed. "I happen to know somebody very close to you who has decided she needs to fund some adoptions for Christian couples."

As a companionable silence seized the moment, a warm appreciation for the wealthy supermodel sprouted in Sammie's midsection. She shifted in the bed, snuggled her toes beneath a flap of the comforter, and recalled the season of Kim Lan's life when God began asking her for a deeper commitment — for a willingness to direct her vast fortune toward the things of the Lord. During that time Kim had gone on a mission trip to Vietnam with Melissa and Sonsee as companions — and the model had met her husband, missions coordinator Mick O'Donnel. Now the two worked as a team, using Kim's money to promote innumerable causes for Christ.

As the sisters continued their companionable banter, a demanding beep pierced Sam's ear. "I'm stepping out for a minute guys," Sam said. "I've got another call." But as Sam pressed the button, a flash of panic zipped through her midsection. *What if the caller is mom?* All day Sam had expected her mom to try to call again. *I wonder if she's the one who called earlier but never left a message.*

A rope of tension twisted around her and squeezed. Sam gripped a wad of the striped green comforter in her fist and produced a raspy, "Hello."

"Hello?" a man's unfamiliar voice prompted. "Who am I speaking with please?"

"This is the Jones' residence," Sam replied, fully expecting the admission of a wrong number.

"Uh . . ." the man hesitated. "I'm looking for R.J. Butler. Is he there?"

Samantha's brow wrinkled. "Yes, he is," she said, her voice oozing with puzzlement.

"Can you hold a second? I have a call on the other line."

"Sure."

Sam pressed the button once more. "Listen, girlfriends," she said, "somebody's on the other line for R.J. I'm going to sign off. Y'all try to stay out of trouble."

"Oh, baby!" Melissa howled. "Now he's taking his calls at your house!"

"Give it a break, will ya?" Sammie chided. "You people need to get a life!" She snickered and disconnected the call before any of them could tease her further.

"Just a minute," Sam said into the receiver while padding across the room.

"Sure," the man said as Sam opened the door. "Is this Samantha Jones?" he added.

"Yes, it is," she replied, striding down the short hallway toward the kitchen. The smell of dish detergent mingled with the leftover smell of spaghetti, and the click of a dishwasher dial preceded the roar of water.

"Hi! Nice to meet you. I'm Larry Tently," he chatted. "I'm sure R.J. must have mentioned me to you."

"Uh, no." Sam rounded the corner and stopped at the edge of the kitchen.

R.J., still dressed in that duck apron, held a broom in one hand and a dustpan in the other.

"Oh," Larry said blankly. "Maybe he's just mentioned me as his partner."

"Actually . . ." Sam shook her head, and the tenor of her voice attested to another denial.

"That rat!" Larry quipped.

"The rat's right here," Sammie said. She covered the mouthpiece and extended the phone to R.J. "Somebody named Larry Tently. Says he's your partner. Did you give him my number?" she asked, an accusing edge to her voice. "It's unlisted!"

"Actually, no. I have call forwarding on my phone, and I set it to forward my calls to here." He propped the broom against the cabinet, deposited the dustpan on the floor, retrieved the phone from Sam, and started to place it against his ear.

"You must have been awful sure I'd let you stay for dinner," she challenged. Once again the memories of their very first kiss leaped from years past. Images tender and precious. Precious and poignant. Poignant and haunting.

R.J.'s eyes widened, and he covered the phone with his callused fingers. The kitchen's flourescent light cast a dull sheen upon his features.

"Well . . ." he hedged, "I . . ."

Feeling manipulated, Sam's anger rose.

"If you ever kiss me again, R.J. Butler," she snapped, "I'll — I'll call my friend Jac Lightfoot and have her knock you flat. She already took care of one man for me, and she can do it again!" Her voice rose on an emotional squeak, and a rational voice deep inside suggested that she was over reacting. Yet Sam could do nothing to stop the emotional explosion.

"Hey, Sam," R.J. cooed, "don't stress out on me, now. I'm sorry. It was just . . ." he shrugged, ". . . just an impulse. That's all, okay?"

Sam's eyes narrowed as R.J.'s gaze caressed her. Despite his obvious feelings and his understanding words regarding her past, a tremor raced across Sam's body as she recalled that pivotal night when Jac had facilitated her leaving Adam. A black belt in TaeKwonDo, Jac had wasted no time defending Sam when Adam had arrived home drunk and out of control. Jac kicked Adam flat on his back. Then she drove Sam straight to the police station where she pressed charges and filed a restraining order.

A shroud of concern cloaked R.J.'s features. Speaking to Larry he said, "I'll call you back later. . . . Sure." The off button beeped with the pressure of R.J.'s fingers.

Samantha swayed. Those horrid days before she left Adam unexpectedly swirled from her nightmares like rancid waters full of bitter bile. The feel of hard, cutting lips biting into hers. The bruising hands that prowled her body like a groping bear. The selfish taking of tender flesh. The hateful blows that usually preceded Adam's sexual brutality. And those sickening flowers he sent every time he physically hurt her. The "I'll do betters," the promises, the vows . . . were always followed by more abuse, including death threats if she ever left him.

"Sam?" R.J. settled a steadying hand on her shoulder. "You're going pale on me. Are you okay?"

With an abstract nod she stumbled away. "J–just don't kiss me again, R.J.," Sam cried. "You promised no pressure!" she declared, then glared at the broom. "What are you doing with that broom?" her voice rose in accusation as she pointed toward the broom propped against the counter. Sammie's face flamed hot, and a sane side of her suggested that she was stepping over the precipice of rational behavior.

"I thought I'd sweep," R.J. answered, his voice steady, his face impassive. R.J. set the receiver on the cabinet and approached Sam. "Hey," he soothed and loosely placed his hands on her upper arms. "I'm *really* sorry. I didn't mean to —"

"I think it's t–time for you to g–go home," Sam stammered.

R.J.'s brow wrinkled as his lips drooped.

"I need to be alone," Sam stated before she spun on her heel and stomped from the kitchen. She neared her son, fast asleep on the sofa. Sam gently scooped him up, and he snuggled his head into the crook of her arm. With an ache in her heart, Sam placed trembling lips upon Brett's head. Although she marched toward his bedroom, out of the corner of her eye she caught a glimpse of R.J. standing on the kitchen threshold. Sam kept her face forward and continued her trek up the hallway. Once inside Brett's room, decked with Barney decor, Sam shoved aside an oversized Baby Bop lying on his bed pillow, then nestled Brett amid the unmade covers. She tugged the comforter up to his chin, brushed aside his bangs, and bestowed another kiss upon his cheek.

"I don't know if we'll ever completely get over it all, little guy," Sammie whispered. She lowered herself to the floor, propped her arms on the mattress, and placed her forehead on her arms. The tears, her continual silent companions, streamed her cheeks in hot rivulets. Deep within a voice assured her that she had never once deserved the treatment Adam had dealt. But her emotions drowned out that voice, insisting that she had deserved what she got because she was a worthless vessel.

Jesus, she pleaded, *help me!*

Blindly, Sam reached toward Brett's nightstand and groped for one of the numerous Bibles she kept around the house. This one, worn and dog-eared, served her purposes the nights she crawled into bed with Brett to comfort him or help him go to sleep. Sammie would wait until her son's steady breathing indicated he was sleeping before snapping on the lamp, propping herself up in bed, and poring over God's Word.

One good thing that had come from her marital betrayal was that, in the aftermath of emotional, physical, and spiritual abuse, she had scoured Scripture for the truth — the *whole* truth — on marriage and God's view of women. For the first time in her life, Sammie had dared to question the superficial Bible reading that produced the demeaning doctrine that women are less valued than men, that women can't make sound decisions and need someone to keep them "in line." During her searching, Sammie concluded that a Savior who washed feet, embraced women in unconditional love, proclaimed such truths as "do to others what you would have them do to you," and willingly stretched Himself out on the cross to die would never approve the subservient message Adam and his pastor had insisted was truth. Samantha had finally seen that the very passages Pastor Laurel had used to ascertain that Adam had been Sam's superior really were calls for husbands to adopt a servant heart, to wash their wives' feet, to lay down their lives for their wives. A person with a servant's heart, whether male or female, would never ask more than to pour oneself out for the other. A man who was willing to die for his wife wouldn't ask, "How can I rule you?" but rather, "How can I make your life better?" The type of "love" that insisted on a pecking-order marriage ignored the Bible's complete teachings on marriage and relationships.

Sam hugged the Holy Scriptures close to her chest and prayed that the truths she had intellectually embraced and the healing balm of unconditional love Jesus Christ offered would trickle from her head all the way to the bottom of her heart.

"Not that I ever want to get married again, Lord," she whispered. Her thoughts moved to R.J., standing in her kitchen with that broom. Sam glanced over her shoulder and peered down the empty hallway. She figured he had left and tried to whisk away memories of that evening . . . of R.J. pretending to gobble up Brett's fingers . . . of the man claiming he didn't want to mess up his 'drobe, his crestfallen face when she told him to leave. Yet her effort failed as even more memories crashed into her thoughts. Sammie reflected on R.J.'s supportiveness after she left Adam. He had been in town for a brief visit and had been willing and available to help with Brett, to offer a hug or two, and to follow Samantha all the way to Marilyn's house in Arkansas just in case Adam showed up. At the time, Samantha had been so distraught she couldn't remember if she thanked him. She hadn't thanked him tonight, either. Guilt consumed her soul like a ravenous inferno.

But if I thank him will he take it as an encouragement? I'm afraid that if I show appreciation, the next thing I know I'll be marching down the aisle wearing lace. Sam's thumb wandered to the base of her ring finger and a jolt of panic burned her palms. "I'm not ready for that — at all." *I'm a long way from being free of the effects of what Adam and his belief system did to me.*

Sammie bit her lips as a heaven-bound plea burst from her soul. "Lord, those awful flashbacks won't stop, and the dreams are driving me crazy . . . *please,*" she begged, "will you please stop the dreams?"

She squeezed her eyes tight and sniffled against the salty tears that trickled down the side of her nose and pooled in the corners of her mouth. "Oh, Jesus, I need help with so much. I still feel so beaten up. I know in my head that you don't value men more than women — or women more than men. But I still *feel* so inferior much of the time."

You're not the only one. The thought entered her mind, and Sammie opened her eyes to observe the splatter of tears marring her sweat pants. "No, I'm really not the only one, am I?" she said quietly. With the eyes of her soul, Sammie caught a glimpse of a sea of women that stretched as far as the eye could see. Women, young and old, black and white, Asian and Hispanic who walked into holy sanctuaries, expecting to be uplifted and embraced in love, only to be restricted and told that, in God's eyes, women are "lesser" than men.

Sammie blinked and held her breath as she pictured Pastor Laurel behind his pulpit, addressing the congregation. The short, thin minister with gray hair and wire-rimmed glasses plucked the spectacles off in a gesture Sam had observed numerous times. Snatches from his messages on the roles of women reverberated through her mind — messages he had conveniently begun after Sam went to him for help with her abusive husband.

"Women will never hold the same influence in church and their homes as men."

"But my mother left us," Sammie squeaked out as the remembrance of those lonely nights after her mother's desertion scraped a desolate path through her ravaged heart. "Her influence was so great that I thought I would die without her. I questioned whether I could go on." Through her tears she argued, "So, how can you say her influence wasn't as great as my dad's? If your mother ever walked out on you, you'd *never* say something like that!"

She imagined Pastor Laurel's assertive pose as he raised his hand to continue his message.

"The man is king of his home. If the wife disagrees with him on any decision, she is to always comply to his wishes. Scripture says the wife is ruled by the husband. Her role is to follow him. Anything less is a spirit of rebellion."

"But I thought *Jesus Christ* was supposed to be on the throne of our hearts and home and be the center of all we do," she rasped aloud, as if the preacher were in front of her. "That's what Adam and I said the day we got married — that we would cherish and respect each other and put Christ at the center of all we do and that we would follow Him *side by side*. Isn't it impossible to really cherish somebody when you make her walk behind you? How many men would want their wives to rule over them? And how many men would attend churches that demean their leadership abilities? The apostle Paul, himself, commended women in spiritual leadership."

Sammie wiped her eyes. "Jesus, am I — am I off here? Doesn't this setup go against Your command that we are to submit to each other and treat others how we want to be treated?"

Pastor Laurel's message reverberated through her mind, and Sam recalled the

179

ever-present, condescending glint in his eyes.

"If a husband tells his wife to sin and go against the Word of God, she is to do what her husband says."

"Lord, isn't this idolatry?" Sam's fingernails dug into her palms as another sob broke free.

Eleven

R.J. placed the broom and dustpan back into the narrow closet beside the refrigerator. He retrieved his jacket from the dining chair and tiptoed halfway down the hallway — far enough to catch a glimpse of Sam kneeling beside Brett's bed. R.J. stroked his beard and could have kicked himself for kissing her. But she had been sitting on the couch, her hair mussed from sleep, her eyes droopy, and he had given in to the desire to move closer. Almost before he knew what he was doing his lips were upon her forehead. In that instant he remembered the first time he had kissed her. She had been so young and innocent. Her freshly washed hair smelled of apples. Her skin felt like satin. As time wore on, he found he couldn't get Samantha Jones off his mind. Their age difference didn't matter to him. In the beginning of their courtship, R.J. had expected her dad's disapproval, but after a short while R.J. sensed that her father trusted him. R.J. made certain he never broke that faith.

With a sigh he settled his jacket over his shoulder and teetered between silently leaving or staying to say goodbye. Finally, he decided to obey Sam's bidding and leave. With a boulder-sized weight in his stomach, R.J. shoved his arms into his jacket, pivoted, and strode up the hallway. He yawned then eyed the puppy. *No sense in leaving her out and giving her the opportunity to mess up the floor,* he decided. R.J. scooped the dog into his palm, and the tiny creature fit loosely into the curve of his hand. He placed the dog back into the box and frowned as she barely stirred. Throughout the evening the puppy had seemed to gradually lose her zest. *Sam mentioned taking her to the vet — perhaps that's not such a bad idea.* He continued to appraise the animal then thought, *Maybe I should volunteer to take her,* but he dismissed the notion. *Looks like Sam needs some space. I need to back off.*

As he turned for the front door, R.J. stopped in his tracks and frowned. *I kept the woman's child all night. I cooked enough spaghetti for her to have four meals. I even cleaned up the kitchen. And I* hate *doing dishes. And then she told me to leave.* R.J. compressed his lips and stared down the hallway. *She never once even said thank you!*

"Darn right I'm going to let her take her own dog to the vet," he growled under his breath. He went to the front door, twisted the deadbolt lock, flung open the door, and stepped into the cold, velvet night still cloaked in white. He closed the door behind him and turned to leave, only to realize the door didn't lock. With a disgruntled sigh, R.J. opened the front door once more and fidgeted with the lock. It could only be set if the door was shut. *Oh great!* he groused as a car's headlights illuminated the yard seconds before the vehicle purred by. He thought about leaving, but he couldn't. The last thing he wanted was for Sam and Brett to become a late-night statistic on the local news.

R.J. pondered his possibilities. *I could go get Sam and tell her to lock the door behind me,* he thought. But he wasn't in the mood to face more rejection. Even if Samantha never spoke a word, her steely appraisal would stab him in the heart. Another yawn descended upon him, and R.J.'s eyes sagged. He rubbed the back of his tense neck and sucked in a lungful of cold air.

The smell of chimney smoke filled the

air. R.J. had noticed that Sam didn't have a fire going and wondered if all the wood she possessed were the three scraggly logs in the brass holder. The crunch of footsteps on concrete prompted a backward glance. A masculine, shadowed figure huddled inside an overcoat jogged by Sam's home. The image reinforced R.J.'s determination not to leave her unprotected.

A new idea seized him, and R.J. peered around the house for a place where Sam might have hidden a key. After lifting the doormat and checking under the pot of an artificial fern, he tilted up the oversized milk can sitting between the two rocking chairs. Sure enough, a house key appeared. With a relieved sigh, R.J. retrieved the key, clicked the deadbolt lock into place, and replaced the key. As the milk can settled back into place with the clang of metal against concrete, a new aggravation grabbed R.J. by the throat. *She shouldn't leave a key hidden out here like this. Anybody with half a brain could find it.* R.J. glanced over his shoulder to catch a glimpse of the pedestrian, now trotting back from the corner, three houses down.

What if he saw me? R.J. lifted the milk can and snatched the key. He'd give it to Sam in the morning and ask her to find a more ingenious place to hide it. He rubbed his gritty eyes with forefinger and thumb, shoved his hands into his jacket pockets, and crunched through the crusty snow to his truck. If anybody ever told him that taking care of a three-year-old wouldn't wear a person out, he'd laugh them to scorn. R.J. had played just as hard as Brett, and he was ready for an early bedtime.

He crawled into the cab of his Ford, snapped the door shut, and savored the smell of leather. Thankful for the pickup, R.J. decided he'd rather be riding in the warm confines of a cab tonight than be on his Harley with the icy wind slapping his face. The seat seeped its leather chill through his jeans, and R.J. cranked the engine. He reached to pull the headlight knob, yet a movement at Sam's curtain halted his fingers. A glimpse of her pale face preceded the porch light's termination by seconds.

"Yeah, I'm gone, woman," he mumbled. "Just like you wanted." He yanked on the light knob, and the snow reflected the bold beams. R.J. put the vehicle into reverse, nudged the gas pedal, and the truck rolled out of the driveway. Soon he was cruising up the street. R.J. propped his elbow on the door ledge and pressed his index finger against his temple. *She's going to put me into an early grave, that's all there is to it.*

As he arrived at the end of her street, Sammie's haunted expression in the kitchen swam into the forefront of his mind. *She actually had the audacity to threaten me with her friend, Jac Lightfoot! What did she say? Oh yeah, she said "Jac has taken down one man for me and she can do it again." Sam sure has spunk.* R.J.'s fingers flexed against the wheel as he recalled the brief meeting he had with Jac in his parents' kitchen late last summer. His bet was that the martial arts expert probably liked him too much to hurt him. *But she probably could take down Godzilla if she set her mind to it.* She certainly hadn't blinked when the need arose to knock Adam Jones flat, orchestrate Sam's escape, and help her press charges.

When Samantha and Jacquelyn arrived at his parents' flat in the middle of the night, R.J. had been in the midst of a brief visit home. He had also been sound asleep. He awoke the next morning to the sound of Brett's laughter and his father's gentle admonishment not to wake up Sammie. When Sam entered the kitchen that morning, R.J.'s stomach had nearly unloaded his breakfast. A shadow near her eye was all the evidence he needed that Adam Jones was the lowest jerk of the century.

He gulped more icy air then snapped on the heater knob, illuminated by a thin strip of green dashlights. He maneuvered the vehicle out of the cozy neighborhood and onto the thoroughfare that would lead him to the loop.

With the whiz and rush of vehicles surrounding him, R.J. reached to turn down the heat as he steered his vehicle toward downtown Dallas. He pondered the days after Adam's death. R.J. had made himself available to Sam's beck and call, yet when marriage was hinted at she had done the emotional equivalent of shoving him to the other side of the planet. Even when he'd shown up after her friend's wedding, Sammie was distantly polite — heavy on the distantly. R.J. had talked more with the new bride and groom, Jacquelyn and Lawton Franklin, than with Sammie.

She used me as long as she needed me and then dropped me like a hot potato, he thought with a grimace. "I don't even know why I'm still here, for cryin' out loud!" he complained. The smell of spaghetti, still clinging to his clothing, heightened his exasperation. *She didn't even say thank you!* he fumed again.

The majestic skyline loomed like lighted sentinels overseeing the thousands of cars that zipped along the freeway. R.J. rubbed his beard and wondered if he'd lost his mind. *Here I am in the big fat middle of a city I don't like. I'm chasing a woman who refuses to be caught, and running a magazine I have no idea how to run.*

In a wink his mind went back to his college days. He wondered what his parents would think if they knew that not only had his "B" grade average not measured up to his elder, "perfect" sister's straight A's, but he had paid to have his college term papers written for him! That bachelor's degree in journalism his parents made him get was just a bought piece of paper. He rubbed his callused hand along his leg as a burst of regret ignited in his spirit. "Oh well, nothing I can do about it now," he mumbled. "They'll be proud of my recent accomplishment of earning a B.A. in biblical studies — if I ever get around to telling them." He squinted and eyed the towering hulk of a building that housed the magazine and his parents' penthouse. "Hopefully the staff at the magazine will be patient." He raised his hand then flopped it back onto the steering wheel. *As soon as I get Sam to agree to marry me, I'm going back to Arkansas.* He thought of his parents and a hope flared that perhaps their retirement might turn into just an elongated leave of absence. At least his first day to solo at the magazine had been much less hectic than he'd imagined. "I suspect that Wanda Martin could run the magazine with both hands tied behind her back," he commented aloud.

Yet a basketful of doubts toppled inside him and spilled a thousand tiny questions onto the fitful sea of his troubled heart. *What if Wanda leaves and I get stuck in the top of that Dallas skyscraper for the rest of my life? What if Sam never comes around? Or what if she* does *agree to marry me but doesn't want to live in Arkansas? What if she wants no part of my work with troubled boys?*

R.J. braked his vehicle, turned into the parking garage, and stopped at the automated ticket vendor. He inserted his coded plastic card into the appropriate slot, and the striped arm lifted to permit his entry. R.J. began the slow drive to the top floor and pondered his calling. In the three years he and Larry had been operating the boys ranch, they had helped approximately 30 kids. Most of them passed through for a year or so then went back to their former behaviors. But six boys had done a complete turnaround. All six left the ranch to go to college; they still kept in touch. *Three even call me dad since their own fathers failed miserably.*

The connection R.J. felt with God when he was at the scenic ranch was beyond any realms of human understanding. And knowing he was a catalyst to introducing wayward teens to Jesus and seeing their lives truly changed brought him a joy beyond compare.

But what if I have to choose between Sam and my calling? Dread settled in the pit of his stomach. R.J. wanted Sam more than anything in the world. A sudden bolt of insight, like a flash of lightning upon a crest of sooty clouds, made him shake in his boots. *Perhaps I want Sam too much.* He tightened his jaw and resisted the possibility. *Marrying her has to be God's will,* he insisted. *It just* has *to be. I love her too much.* The overhead lights illuminated the garage in a pale glow that seeped a lonely aura into R.J.'s bones. *I love Brett, too!* He slowly nodded his head. *And Brett . . . Brett loves me. He needs a father.*

Twelve

Subject: Changing Plans
On Wednesday, 17 Jan 2002 6:14:30
Mara O'Connor
<mara@oconnor.hhp> writes:

Colleen,
   Sammie hasn't returned my call. It's been two days now. I think I'm going to live dangerously and drive to the magazine today. It's only a little more than two hours from here. If I leave by eleven, I could be there by one-thirty. That way Samantha will probably be done with lunch and back at her desk. Do you think anyone on the staff will mind if I just pop in? I'd really like to see Brett. I got brave and called my ex-husband's house on Christmas. Sure enough, they were there, so I talked to them briefly.
   Do you think it would be okay if I visited the magazine's office? I know I'm vacillating like crazy. Yesterday I didn't want to call the magazine because I didn't want to interrupt Sam's work, but today I'm des-

perate for some way to break through to her.

Any news from the dinner party last night?

Hugs,
Mara

Subject: Changing Plans
On Wednesday, 17 Jan 2002 7:45:12
Colleen Butler
<candt@butler.hhp> writes:

Mara,

Go, baby! And I say more power to you! As the official founder and current owner of that magazine, you have my seal of approval and my applause. Go see Sam. Let me know what happens. Maybe Sam will even invite you home for dinner.

Re: the dinner last night with Rhett and Sam: I e-mailed Rhett late last night and asked him how it went. His response was, "I'd rather not talk about it." Sigh! Those two are going to put me into an early grave. Here's hoping your visit with Sam will go better. Have a safe trip.

Happy trails . . . (literally) ;-)
Colleen

Sam turned into the driveway of Cox Veterinarian Clinic, which was several blocks from her home. She'd chosen the clinic because it was close and on her way to work. With some reserve, she eyed the aging home-turned-clinic and hoped the service matched the prominent ad in the yellow pages. She put the Honda into park, turned off the engine, and observed the listless puppy lying in the bottom of the dog carrier that claimed the passenger seat. Last night Sam had thought about calling to consult with her "sister," veterinarian Sonsee Delaney, about the dog's ailments but decided not to bother her. Sonsee was now the mother of a four-month-old and still adjusting to the demands of motherhood. Sam understood all too well the dramatic changes babies bring. Besides, even if Sonsee could have come up with a diagnosis, Sam was sure the pup would need medication.

"Miss Puppy sick," Brett said from his car seat in the back. He drank from his Sippee cup then continued, "I spend the night with Uncle R.J. and come home and see puppy. Now she sick."

"Yes, that's right, bab— uh, honey." Sam nodded and gazed over her seat into her son's sparkling eyes. The indulgent smile that sprang upon her wouldn't be denied. "We're going to take her in to the doggie doctor and see if she can get all better."

"Will the doctor give shot to Miss Puppy?" Brett's lips puckered as if a sudden thought assaulted him. "Will I get shot?"

"Oh no," Sammie protested and shook her head for added emphasis. She never knew what might be going through Brett's three-year-old brain. She reached down to grab her purse from the passenger floor-board. A strand of hair, damp and fragrant, plopped across her cheek, and Sam extracted a headband, the color of tortoise shells, from the folds of her purse and shoved it across her hair. She glanced in the mirror. *Two bad hair days in a row — but at least I managed to slap on makeup this morning!*

Sam glanced over the seat again, and Brett inserted the cup spout into his mouth. Never taking his worried gaze from Sam's, he sipped on the liquid and the spout produced a light wheezing sound with every draw. He had thrown down his bottle at the ripe old age of ten months and picked up a cup. That had been the extent of her efforts in weaning him from the bottle. But some days Sam wondered if he might go to college with a Sippee cup in hand.

"Come on," she said. "Let's get Miss Puppy doctored, and then we need to go to work."

"Can we take Miss Puppy with us?" Brett asked, tossing aside the cup. It flopped from seat to floorboard with the ease of an empty container.

"I don't know if we're going to have a choice." Sam eyed the limp dog. "She looks like she needs all-day care. I'm afraid that if I leave her by herself —" Sam cut off her fateful words. "Maybe Uncle R.J. won't mind if we bring her to work," she said. The corners of her mouth turned down. She imagined the dubious expressions of R.J. and the staff when she hauled in the latest addition to her family. *Oh well. Sometimes it's easier to ask forgiveness than permission.*

She checked her Timex and groaned. The vet appointment was ten minutes ago — the exact time Samantha was supposed to be at work. She still hadn't called the office to tell them she would be late.

"All systems go, li'l tiger," Sam declared and stepped out of the car into the frigid morning air. Yesterday's meltdown had di-

195

minished the snow by about half the initial volume, but enough of the white stuff remained to produce the winter wonderland appeal — if you could dub a metropolis teeming with traffic a wonderland. Sam slammed the door, and her breath came out in jagged, white clouds. Accompanied by the whir and jostle of traffic, she slung her oversized bag onto her shoulder. Soon she managed to maneuver Brett and the puppy into the two-story vet's office. As Sam signed in the patient and answered the receptionist's pertinent questions, the smells of pets, medication, and a thread of cigar smoke mingled with the light floral scent of her body lotion.

"If you'll just have a seat, Dr. Cox will be right with you," the middle-aged woman advised in a hoarse voice.

Sammie settled herself, Brett, and the dog into the waiting room. While Brett peered at the puppy and conversed with her, Sammie dug her cell phone from her bag, removed it from the vinyl case, and punched in the numbers for *Romantic Living*. The phone rang twice before a voice boomed over the line.

"R.J. Butler."

"R.J.?" Sam yelped, and her eyes popped open.

"Sammie? What's up?" he asked, a worried twist to his words.

"Everything's fine. The dog needed a trip to the vet. That's where I am now. I'm going to be late. I thought I dialed the main number, but I must have punched in the direct line to your office."

"Actually, you *did* dial the main number — not my office."

"Where's Erica?"

"Not here. She's running late. Had a flat. I volunteered to fill in. It's the least I could do," he said with a sarcastic twist. "I certainly don't want to get in Wanda's way."

"Well, I was going to leave a message with Erica and ask her to pass it along to you," Sam said, hoping to avoid chitchat.

"How's the dog?"

"She's barely responding. I just hope . . ." Samantha glanced at Brett and didn't state the obvious. For the thousandth time that morning she blasted herself for paying so much for a puppy. She didn't know what, if any, kind of guarantee The Pet Shoppe offered, but she figured her chances of recompense were nominal since she had traded in the birds. Still, one good thing *had* come of the puppy acquisition. Brett hadn't uttered one word about the winged squawkers that flew their prison every chance they got.

"How are you feeling this morning?" R.J. continued, a stiff edge to his voice. An edge that ushered in memories of the former evening. An evening that haunted Sam's dreams. Last night she had traded in her nightmares for fantasies of R.J. Butler — R.J. and Sam and Brett all together, all happy.

She swallowed hard. "I'm doing okay," she said with an evasive undertone. While the nocturnal illusions had tantalized her imaginative juices, the morning's light uncovered the brutal truth — the gaping, infected wound Adam had pounded into her spirit refused to heal. The probabilities of forming a happy union in real life were nearly nonexistent. While Sam figured Brett and R.J. would fall into homelife without a hitch, she wasn't hitch-free — not by a long shot.

In an attempt to block out the events of the former evening, she observed the selection of dog food stashed on a wooden shelf and wondered if she should buy a special brand for the pup. A black Persian cat, perched atop one bag of food, shifted its paws and stared back at Sam, daring her to touch the bagged food.

"I never told you that I halved the left-over spaghetti," R.J. continued as if speaking to a business associate. "I put half in the freezer in a plastic container. The other half is in the blue bowl on the bottom shelf. You should have enough for dinner tonight, and then for a couple of meals next week, too."

"Thanks," Sam said, the word flopping out like an ungracious blob.

"Glad to help," R.J. snapped.

Sammie started to snap right back then caught herself. A genuine wave of gratitude had washed over her that morning when she stepped into a spotless kitchen. But if she expressed her appreciation too fervently, R.J. would interpret her warmth as encouragement. She wasn't so sure that last night's flirtatious conversation about that blasted spaghetti hadn't been the provocation for the kiss. She touched the center of her forehead and decided that encouragement was the last thing R.J. Butler needed.

"I'll be there as soon as I get through here," Sam said, her voice devoid of emotion.

"No problemo. I've got Larry holding on the other line, so I need to go," he said abruptly. "We've had an emergency."

"Okay," Sam commented. She disconnected the call without another word, placed her phone in its holder, and dropped it into her purse. Even though Butler had grown since his earlier years, he obviously hadn't lost his moody streak.

A new thought descended upon her. *I wonder who Larry is.* Last night he'd said he was R.J.'s partner. Sam tried to piece together any clues R.J. might have dropped to indicate what endeavors he and Larry were involved in. No hint posed itself. *Oh well,* she thought, *probably something to do with motorcycles.*

"Mrs. Jones?" a feminine voice called from the edge of the hallway. Sam looked up into the eyes of a smiling young blonde dressed in a blue smock along with the typical Texas attire of jeans and boots.

"Yes, that's me," Sam replied.

"Great. You can wait for Dr. Cox in the first room on the right." The woman turned and pointed toward a room about six feet behind her. "He'll be with you shortly."

After nodding, Sam faced her son. "Come on, Brett. Let's go take Miss Puppy in to the doctor. You can be a big helper with the cage if you want."

"*I do it!*" Brett claimed with vigor and

assurance as he gripped the port-a-pet that was half his size.

Sam allowed the child to pull the cage a few inches on his own before suggesting that they carry Miss Puppy together. As Brett reluctantly agreed, Samantha hoped they weren't on the verge of a canine funeral. The two of them maneuvered the carrier into the tiny examination room. And, as usual, Sammie had so much help from Brett it took her twice as long to accomplish the task. *But that's okay,* she thought and rumpled his bright hair. *Some things are worth the extra effort.*

"Let's go ahead and get Miss Puppy out of her cage," the bubbly assistant said as she entered the room. Cloaked in a cloud of exotic perfume, she placed the dog carrier onto the wooden examination table, her ponytail swishing with every move.

The aging exam table featured drawers along the bottom, reminding Sam of a dresser without a mirror. She moved to the assistant's side in case the puppy proved more of a handful than she thought. As she stepped forward, a sharp edge jabbed into her shin. Wincing, Sam glanced down to see that one of the drawers was ajar.

"Mind if I shut this?" she asked and gave the drawer a shove when the assistant approved the request. As if it were a well-oiled silverware drawer, the repository freely rolled into the cavity, tapped the frame, then bounced back to its former position. Sam bent back down and attempted to shut the drawer. This time she kept her fingers against the front until it completely closed and remained that way. As she rose from the task, her mind replayed the brief glimpse of the drawer's contents. On top of an array of bandages and medical tape had lain a clear Ziploc bag full of white powder. The first word that jumped into Sam's mind was "cocaine." She immediately dismissed the thought. Obviously, the vivid imagination that enabled her to write novels was getting the best of her.

She recalled her recent drugstore purchase when she'd picked up Brett's vitamins. On her way to the medicine aisle she had stumbled onto a display of fine carpet fresheners in a variety of designer scents. They were packaged in clear bags much like the one she had glimpsed — only smaller. Sammie had opted for the one that smelled like Obsession and planned to use it in Brett's playroom. Perhaps someone in the veterinarian office had made a purchase from a similar display to freshen up the carpets. *And maybe you can get it in the jumbo size somewhere,* she thought. *I could probably use that much myself.*

She glanced at the slick floor, covered in faux wood tile. *Tile doesn't require carpet freshener. But there might be a room somewhere that* does *have carpet.* She dismissed her mental meanderings; the possibility of that bag holding cocaine was slim to none. *Why waste any more of my brain power on it?* Sam focused on the task at hand and observed the young woman who coaxed Miss Puppy from her cage and cuddled the dog close. Her slender build and fine-boned features reminded Sam of a Barbie doll, causing a blight on her day. Sam pondered the cellulite that began attacking her thighs several years back. With a wistful sigh she watched the assistant. Too many years had passed since Sam could slip neatly into a pair of size seven jeans.

"Ooo, this little one doesn't look like it's feeling well," the assistant crooned.

"What's your puppy's name?" As the lady knelt beside Brett, Sam noted that her name tag said "Audry Cox." She figured the young woman must be related to the veterinarian.

"Miss Puppy," Brett said and gripped the side of Sam's slacks. "Are you going to shot her?" he queried and leaned closer to his mom.

"I don't know." Audry shook her head. "We'll just have to see. My dad will look at her and decide."

Brett puckered his lips. "We don't want your daddy. We want the *dog doctor*."

An indulgent smile exploded from Sam.

"My daddy *is* the dog doctor," Audry said through laughter. "And what about *your* daddy," she asked, caressing the child's hand. "Where does he work?" Her pale-green gaze glittered with the same fancy Brett repeatedly invoked.

"My daddy died. He was mean 'cause he hit mamma. He died in car wreck. I not see him anymore."

About the time Sam decided she should clamp her hand over Brett's mouth, he ceased the rote flow of information.

"Oh," Audry said as a silence, awkward and tense, descended upon the room. The assistant stood, cut Sam a compassionate glance, then busied herself with the puppy's care.

Sammie's headband crept forward. She shoved it back into place, and began a nervous chatter regarding the puppy. When she finished describing the various symptoms, a portly gentleman in his early fifties waddled into the room.

"Hello," he said to the accompaniment of a desperate chorus of dog yapping filtering from somewhere down the hallway. "Having trouble with a cocker, I hear." He pointed a general smile toward Sam, glanced at the dog, then back to Sam. He shoved the door shut with a snap, and the canine yapping was no longer detectable.

"Yes, I was just describing her symptoms to Audry," Sam responded as the doctor's appraisal lengthened. Eventually a tendril of something warm yet perverted wormed into his pale gaze. Sam focused on Audry and the pup. She had seen that look in Adam's eyes more than she wanted to remember, and a nauseous root sprouted in her midsection.

The doctor ignored Brett and scooted toward the exam table. Sam, lowering her gaze, preferred to watch his canvas shoes rather than spend another second looking upon the man's countenance. With a shiver she picked up her child and edged as far away as possible. She stopped near a glass cabinet stocked with various bottles and compounds. As Audry briefed her father about the puppy, Samantha kept her ear tuned for pertinent details but tried to look anywhere other than catch the doctor's eye. Brett, usually committed to squirming when Sam held him, rested in his mother's arms without protest. His focus upon the limp puppy, the child was too mesmerized to wiggle. Sam brushed a kiss against his cherub cheek before glancing back at the doctor, whose subtle cigar odor mixed with Audry's perfume. Sam's nausea increased. Soon the father-daughter team extracted a feces sample from the puppy, who voiced a series of traumatized yelps.

Whimpering, Brett reached for his pet. "They hurt Miss Puppy!" he exclaimed, lurching from side-to-side in an attempt to break Sam's grip.

"No, no," Sam admonished quietly. "Miss Puppy is just fine. They just have to see what's wrong with her."

The dog burst forth with a final screech, and Brett joined in with a wail of his own. He pounded at Sammie's arms. As her headband slipped onto her forehead, she struggled to maintain her grip.

"Miss Puppy! They hurt Miss Puppy!" Brett screamed. From his extreme reaction, Sam wondered if he was having a flashback to nights when she thought he was asleep — nights when Adam's cruelty resulted in Sam's own tears.

As Dr. Cox lumbered out with the sample, Audry cradled the dog close to her chest and approached Brett. "Look, honey," she crooned, "your doggie is fine." The listless animal rested her head against Audry's arm and turned soulful eyes toward her new family.

Brett stilled as quickly as he had begun the desperate struggle. Sam gave her headband a hard upward shove. Huffing in shallow pants, Brett observed his pet then reached toward the dog's oversized ears. The cocker spaniel whined and tried to lick Brett's fingers. With a gasp, the child yanked his hand to his chest. "Puppy bite," he worried.

"Oh, she's just trying to say she loves you," Audry purred. "I'm going to have to step out a minute. My dad will be right back — just as soon as he looks at the sample under a microscope. Do you want to hold the puppy or should I put him back in the cage?"

This time Sam's headband inched backward then toppled to the floor with the click of plastic against tile. A stray string of bangs flopped forward. Shoving her hair out of her eyes, Sam wondered why she even bothered to get up some days. She peered into the blonde's guileless green gaze and noted that her eye shadow perfectly matched the hue of her eyes. Sam decided her ego had just about had all it could take of the Barbie doll. *Nobody in real life should ever look that perfect. She probably doesn't even have cellulite,* Sam thought bitterly as she lowered Brett onto the tile floor. She reached for her headband at her feet and figured the quicker the blonde dispensed with the puppy the sooner she would leave and take her high-pitched, bubbly voice with her.

"I'll take her," Sam declared and reached for the animal. "She'll give Brett a distraction and keep him from climbing the walls."

"Oh, I'm sure this little angel wouldn't do that." Audry bent down to Brett, and Sam listed her exotic perfume as one more reason she needed some distance from the doll. The last time Sam even remembered to spray perfume was the week before Brett was born.

"Bye now!" Audry said with a white-toothed grin. Sam thought of the tiny chip in her front teeth. "You take care of your puppy. We'll be back soon," the assistant claimed and turned for the door.

Sam knelt beside her son and stroked a tear from the corner of his eye. "If I put the puppy right here, will you take care of her while I brush my hair?"

"Yes, mamma." Brett gave a solemn nod, and Sam gingerly placed the puppy at his feet. The child squatted and stared at the animal with wide-eyed awe while a mixture of fear and fascination claimed his features. He was a long way from forgetting that first playful nip, but at least he wasn't traumatized for life.

Sam stood, removed her handbag from her shoulder, and plopped it upon the counter near a stainless steel sink. She dug out her brush, stroked it through her drying hair, and shoved the headband back into place. In the aftermath of the Barbie encounter, Sammie grabbed her compact and stared at her features in a mirror smeared with powder. A smudge of mascara dotted the corner of her left eye, a strip of lip gloss had somehow slid off her bottom lip, and she had sketched in one fair eyebrow higher than the other. *So much for eyebrow art,* she thought. Sam sighed when she noted that her concealer did little to hide the dark circles under her eyes or the zit on her chin. *It's no use. I just don't have it today.* She stretched her lips away from her teeth and held the mirror close. Yes, the chip was still there.

For the first time in ages, a reminiscent wisp of hope whispered in her spirit. Sam was tired of looking haggard. Oh how wonderful it would be to dress up and feel beautiful — even for half a day! Years had passed since Sam had felt remotely attractive or cherished.

Lowering the compact, Sammie stared into the sink. The faucet released one droplet at a time in a steady rhythm that echoed the tempo of the gradual breakdown of her self-esteem. And while Adam's abuse within itself was enough to destroy her, their pastor's taking her husband's side had dug the pit of her despair deeper. An image of Adam's contorted face flashed through her mind, and a scenario that repeatedly haunted Sam rose its ugly head once more.

Months before his death Adam had met Samantha in their hallway and slammed his fist into her midsection. Sammie, astonished by the sudden attack, doubled over then fell to her knees as aching bands diffused from the fist-sized agony in her gut.

"That's what you get for going to Pastor Laurel!" Adam screamed. "I just got off the phone with him. He told me you went to him yesterday and told him I was beating you. *He doesn't believe you, Samantha!*" Her name ricocheted up and down the hallway — a mocking mantra that wouldn't die. "Don't even think he's ever going to believe your lying, manipulative ways any more than I do. If you *ever* try something like that again, I'll kill you! Got it?"

Sammie, reduced to a trembling huddle, gasped for breath as scorching tears spilled down her cheeks. While the physical abuse was destructive in its own right, her spirit took an equally brutal blow — a blow no one witnessed. Even though she had sensed Pastor Laurel harbored his share of doubts about her story, he had posed himself as her confidant to pull forth myriad details about her situation. At the time, she thought the pastor was being supportive. Obviously it was just to report to Adam. Betrayal struck hard.

"Got it?" Adam yelled again and drew his leg back to kick her.

"G–got it," she rasped. His foot settled against the spongy carpet.

Adam convinced Pastor Laurel that Sam was a rebellious and undisciplined wife who refused to bow to her husband. By the looks of Pastor Laurel's wife, Sam figured that living with him probably wasn't much different than living with Adam. Shortly after Sam confided in Laurel, he started that series of sermons that "put women in their place."

When Sammie had finally scraped together the courage to stop attending church with Adam, Pastor Laurel was even more convinced that she was in the wrong. He even called to remind her of her subservient position within her own home by firmly explicating the biblical concept regarding wifely submission. He conveniently avoided the numerous passages that focused on mutual submission within marriage. Eventually Sammie hung up on him. That day she resigned herself to Adam's public charm continuing to dupe Laurel and the church leaders.

Like most abusers, male or female, Adam had manifested the "Dr. Jekyll and Mr. Hyde" syndrome. In public he was the smoothest, most humble man you could ever meet. He had even been voted favorite high school teacher by his students two years in a row! And his Dr. Jekyll persona was so powerful that when Sammie filed a restraining order against her husband, the pastor thought she was seeking attention and trying to sully Adam's good name. He refused to believe Sammie was anything but what Adam said she was — crazy and vindictive. Even at Adam's funeral the pastor had peered at Sam with a scorn that at one time would have bruised and cut her. Sam reminded herself that she would most likely never see the man again. So far that assumption had proven true.

The clinic's water spout continued its steady dripping into the sink. Sammie snapped the powder compact shut then stared at the green, plastic disc as the dark memories faded in the face of the potential for her present health. With each pulse of the dripping water a slow realization began in the deep recess of Sam's heart then radiated a balmy glow that manifested itself as warm pools in her eyes. The sink blurred, and Sammie clutched the compact. Today was the first time in ages she had longed to feel attractive — and didn't question she could.

The sound of a drawer rolling open penetrated her reverie. Sam jumped and her mother's instinct kicked in. She had been too distracted for too long. She whipped around and spotted her son, who had forgotten about the wobbly pup and decided to explore the exam table's drawers. He stuck his hand inside the very drawer Sam had recently closed and pulled out the bag of powder.

"Look, mamma!" he exclaimed. "They got carpet fesh'ner, too."

"Brett, put that back," Sam admonished as the room's door swished open and Dr. Cox stepped inside.

"Well, it looks like this little lady has a really nasty intestinal infection," the doctor began. When he glanced at Brett, Cox stopped short . . .

Thirteen

Victoria Roberts stood on the porch of Ricky Christopher's tiny brick house. The languid melody of a Kenny G saxophone solo floated from inside the home, and Victoria recalled the solo Ricky had played during the Sunday evening service. Her stomach lurched with a delicious, delightful quiver as she pondered his dark hair and striking blue eyes gleaming beneath the sanctuary's lighting.

The minister of music was awaiting Victoria's arrival, expecting her to share her domestic expertise. She reached for the illuminated doorbell then stopped and contemplated her motives — motives that weren't exactly pure. A seagull's distant call seemed to echo a truth Victoria was trying to avoid: *You're married! You're married! You're married!*

The ocean breeze lifted wispy tendrils of hair that escaped the saggy bun into which she had twisted her wavy locks. The smells of sea and salt tugged at her senses even though the Destin shoreline was blocks away. She shifted her feet, swallowed, and gazed toward the southern horizon where a band of dark clouds promised a squall was blowing in. Victoria glanced down at her ankle-length denim dress and laid her palm against her lower abdomen. The decent thing to do was make this visit quick. Quick and professional. Professional and instructive. Nothing more; nothing less.

She straightened her shoulders and pressed the doorbell. By a count of three, the door whipped open. Ricky erupted in a white-toothed beam as if Victoria were the most important woman on the planet. "You're here!" he exclaimed, and his eyes glistened appreciatively.

"Well, you said nine-thirty," she said as she shifted her handbag from one sweaty palm to the other. *Good grief! He's just too good looking for his own good.* Her former resolve to keep this encounter brief blurred in the face of his magnetism, a magnetism he seemed oblivious to. That heightened his appeal.

"Yes! Come on in!" Ricky opened the door wide and allowed Victoria to step inside. As she passed him, she picked up a citrus, carefree scent that reminded her of a cologne her kid brother used.

Victoria's open-toed sandals padded against the short pile carpet as she strode into the modest home neatly kept but void of any flair. The smell of cinnamon tea, warm and inviting, wafted from the kitchen. Victoria gazed around a room full of furniture she probably would have passed over at a yard sale.

"See what I mean?" Ricky despaired. "I need help. This place is the pits! Do you think there's any hope?"

"Well . . ." Victoria hedged as she took in the metallic blinds, tweed sofa, and yucky brown carpet. When she observed the petite brick home that sported a neat, cheerful exterior with bushes and ferns, she had wondered if Ricky had been exaggerating. But the place looked more like a college student's pad instead of the home of a young professional.

The room's only salvation was the corner devoted to musical pursuits. A black lacquer electronic piano glistened beneath a brass floor lamp. A guitar propped against the piano gleamed in the lamplight. A saxophone rested on its stand nearby. Above the piano hung a poster-sized print of an ebony grand piano with a rose lying atop the keys.

"Before I bought this house, the people

who lived here had it fixed up." He raised his hand, palm outward. "Okay, it wouldn't have held a candle to your place, but it at least had *something* going for it. Then when I got my stuff in . . ." He shook his head. "All this was fine as long as I was in that tiny apartment in grad school, but now it's the pits."

"Did you just get out of graduate school?" Victoria asked. She scrutinized the tiny crow's feet at the corners of Ricky's eyes.

"Yes. I took a couple of years off between degrees to do some traveling. Then I did a double master's, which took five years." He shrugged. "Some of us are late bloomers, I guess."

"And some of us never completely bloom," Victoria muttered.

"Meaning?"

"Oh, I have an education degree in home economics," she replied. "I taught awhile out of college and toyed around once or twice with going to grad school, but then I wound up getting married. I guess I was trying to say that grad school never happened for me." An old longing, latent and unfulfilled, floated to the surface of her heart. Perhaps if she had pursued her master's degree, she would have

218

met someone else — someone who would have put as much energy into their marriage as Tony put into his fishing.

Ricky inserted his hands into the pockets of his slacks and rolled his eyes. "From the looks of *your* house, I wouldn't say you needed graduate school. Have you ever thought of going into business for yourself?"

"No." Victoria shook her head and smiled. "I'm not much of a businesswoman. I do cohost a home and garden TV show once a week, but that's about the extent of it. I've got a bunch of friends who own their own businesses, but I prefer to be a full-time wife and mom."

"I didn't know you have kids," Ricky commented and crossed his arms.

"Well, I don't . . . yet," she hedged. Victoria set her handbag on the scarred coffee table. Wondering whether she should mention her pregnancy, she noted that Ricky was back to considering the problem at hand. He pinched his bottom lip and gazed around the room as if it were a hopeless cause.

"Like I said yesterday, my mom is coming with her friend — and he's supposed to be some bigwig at a bank. I don't want her to be disappointed." He rubbed

219

his hands together. "She's sacrificed so much for me, the *least* I can do is make a good impression."

"How much money did you say you have?" Victoria dismissed the notion of telling him she was expecting and approached a wooden-based floor lamp that looked like a 1970s reject.

"Five hundred dollars," he said. "And that would barely buy a new couch at a discount house!"

Without further comment, she strolled into the tiny kitchen. The dining room table that seated four looked like a perfect match for the has-been lamp and coffee table. The off-white tile floor lacked as much merit as the carpet. She eyed the chocolate-colored cabinets that did nothing for the blue countertops, and imagined the cabinets in a fresh coat of creamy white.

Ricky hovered in the doorway like an expectant father in a nursery waiting room. She meandered out of the kitchen's other entryway, hung a right, then paused. "Mind if I see your bathroom and bedrooms?"

"No. That's fine. Go ahead by all means. The guest rooms are down the hall. You'll see the bathroom, too. I only have one.

And I hadn't planned to worry much about my bedroom. I'll just keep the door closed if I have to."

Victoria chuckled and wandered toward the restroom. A quick glance answered her suspicions. The room needed nearly as much help as the living room and kitchen. A pair of guest rooms, both empty, were her next area of scrutiny.

"You don't have any bedroom furniture in these rooms at all." She halted and turned to express her concern, only to discover that Ricky was only centimeters behind her. They crashed headlong, and she stumbled backward as a cloud of his alluring cologne enveloped her. Ricky loosely gripped Victoria's upper arms in an attempt to steady her, all the while uttering a plethora of heartfelt apologies. The touch of his gentle fingers upon her skin and the concern spilling from his lips sent a bolt of longing into the center of Victoria's heart. Years had passed since Tony had expressed half as much concern.

"I'm — I'm f–fine," Victoria stammered. Their close proximity afforded her a deeper look into his eyes than she had yet experienced. The effect was beyond mesmerizing, and she was transported into an expanse of a limitless sky the color of exotic blue sapphires.

"Good." Ricky's ingenuous smile assured Victoria that as far as he was concerned she was nothing more than a friend from church, one of his choir members, an acquaintance who was helping him with a domestic problem. He released his hold. Victoria glanced at her manicured toenails, crossed her arms, and rubbed the patch of skin on her forearm that he had touched. A tinge of disappointment over his lack of interest dashed aside her former reaction. Compared to Ricky's dashing good looks, she was nothing more than a plain Jane. A man with his looks and talents wouldn't consider the likes of her.

And well he shouldn't! a stern voice corrected. *You're married!* Like a diver plunging into a frigid ocean, Victoria's doorstep vow to keep this visit short engulfed her in chilling caution. *Not only am I married,* she affirmed, *I'm also pregnant.*

Trying to feign nonchalance, Victoria eased up the hallway and back into the living room.

"So do you think there's any hope at all?" Ricky implored.

"Okay," she paused at the end of the tired sofa and placed a hand on one hip.

"There *is* hope," she began. "There's always hope. The question is, how much time do you have to put into this? One month is not very long to pull off a major overhaul."

"I can give it as much time as I need." He lifted both hands. "I'm free nearly every evening from five until midnight. And I've got a couple of friends in Pensacola who just might come down and help. Just tell me what to do!"

Victoria pivoted and gazed around the room whose paneling was the same shade of yuck brown as the carpet. "Okay, the first thing we need to do is paint." She shook her head. "Problem is . . . I'm expecting," she blurted and faced him. "So I can't help you there. I'm not supposed to breathe any kind of fumes like that."

Ricky slapped his forehead. "Oh no! I didn't know! How could I have even asked your help when . . . when . . ." He waved toward her midsection. "I'm so sorry. I never should have imposed on you." His hands twittered, and Victoria was reminded of a 1920s hero from a black-and-white movie. "You should be at home propping up your feet and — and —"

"It's okay. *Really.*" Victoria managed to smile despite the fact that her betraying heart leaped once more. Tony had been far more low-key about her welfare. "I'm not very far along and I feel fine." She raised her hands to assure him.

"Look . . ." Ricky raced toward the kitchen. "I made tea," his voice rose as he entered the other room, and Victoria was reminded of the honey-smooth solos the high-energy musician bestowed upon their enraptured congregation. "I'll pour some tea, and we can sit down and discuss this at the table. I'm sure you've been on your feet too long now!"

Chuckling, Victoria followed him. *"Really,"* she insisted, *"I'm quite all right.* The early stages often go like a breeze for many. As a matter of fact, I can barely even tell." Victoria, forever sensitive about propriety, stopped short of more commentary. Instead, she settled at the table and reached for the mug of fragrant tea he proffered.

"Now!" Ricky plopped in the chair across from her. "If you'll just tell me what I need to paint, how I do it, and what colors I need to use, then I can take it from there."

Victoria nodded and began stating the instructions. Ricky took a long draw on his tea then held up his hand. "Hold it!" he said through a chortle. "Let me get a notepad. There's one on the piano."

With a smile Victoria nodded and sipped her tea while he whipped out of the kitchen then rushed back in. Ricky thudded back into his chair and with the studious expression of a sixth grader said, "Okay, shoot!"

After detailing the necessary steps, Victoria branched off into some inexpensive options he might consider for decor. "In order to save money, there are a whole bunch of things you can do. For instance, you can buy an attractive throw for your sofa and an inexpensive tablecloth for this table. You could also strip down your dining table and repaint it, if you have time. I'd recommend a blue that would be in the same family as the countertops. That way you'd get a fresh country look."

"Right, right," Ricky muttered and scribbled down another array of notes.

Victoria eyed the weblike script and wondered if he would be able to read it once she left. "Meanwhile," she continued, "I'll visit some resale shops and see about hitting a few garage sales. One thing you need for sure is some bedroom furniture."

"Do you think you can find anything that will look decent? I mean —"

"Just a minute." Victoria deposited the warm mug onto the table, stepped into the living room, and retrieved her Dooney and Bourke handbag. With a smug flourish, she deposited the designer bag on the coffee table. "This purse sells for more than 200 dollars at department stores. Two months ago I got it brand-new at a garage sale for five bucks." She raised one brow and awaited the usual reaction.

"No way!" Ricky's mouth fell open.

"There's no telling what I'll find out there. For instance, if I can spot a couple of sturdy used bed frames, you can sand them down and paint them any color you choose. The last time I scouted out the Goodwill in Pensacola, they had some brand-new mattresses and box springs. Granted, they probably aren't the highest quality in the world, but they'll work for a couple of guests for a couple of nights — and nobody will be worse for wear!"

Ricky's expressive eyes lit up as a thousand possibilities churned across his features. "We really might pull this off!" he marveled.

"I have no doubts," Victoria claimed. "My only concern is the time. One month is not very long." She took a long swallow of the cinnamon tea and recalled the friends he mentioned. "You're going to need your friends' help. Are you sure they'll be willing to come?"

A shrill ring erupted from the living room, and Ricky glanced at his sporty wristwatch. "That might be one of them now." He nodded. "Yes, I really think they'll help. They both owe me big!" A clever smile created twin dimples. "I introduced them to my two cousins who were sisters — and they married them!" he called while rushing toward the phone. "As a matter of fact, all four owe me. I think I'll rope them all into this. We could probably pull it all off by the weekend if we work hard."

Victoria nodded then inspected her French manicure as a tinge of nausea flitted through her tummy. She took several sips of the tea in hopes that the warm liquid would wash away the momentary discomfort. Yet the cinnamon beverage increased the queasiness. She scowled at the tea and marveled that a flavor that once brought her pleasure was now inflicting discomfort. *Could it be my pregnancy?* she wondered as a new awareness of the life within was followed by a hot wave of renewed guilt. *What am I doing? I shouldn't stay here a minute longer,* she scolded herself. She abruptly stood and snatched her purse.

"Hi, Francine!" Ricky's pleasure-filled voice sliced through Victoria's quandary. "Okay . . ." he hesitated. "Well, what about Saturday night, then? Are you available?" The anxious hope in his voice told Victoria more than she wanted to know. This Francine might very well be Ricky's girlfriend. "Great!" he continued on a relieved note as Victoria eased toward the front door.

"Oh, I forgot!" Ricky stopped and slammed his palm against his forehead as an uncertain silence cloaked the room. "My mom is coming for a visit in a month, and I *have* to do some work on my house. This place is a disgrace. I have an interior consultant here right now. I might be up to my eyeballs in paint Saturday night."

Ricky darted a glance toward Victoria, held up his finger, and enveloped her in one of those heart-stopping smiles that Victoria was certain he'd shared with Francine. A splash of jealousy erupted from the pit of her stomach, and a new wave of mortification followed in its wake. *I'm being beyond ridiculous,* she affirmed. Indeed, the potency of these foreign feelings both astonished and appalled her. *I have got to get out of here and get a grip!*

I don't think I have ever experienced any-thing like this!

Her eyes stung as she clutched the doorknob and pondered the fabric of her life. Compared to the excitement of several of her sisters' lives, Victoria's existence had been almost boring. She had been raised and adored by functional parents who loved the Lord, were nuts about each other, and still provided ample support for their three grown sons and daughter. Growing up, Victoria had been the baby and borne the brunt of her brothers' teasing as well as the bounty of her parents' doting. She seldom missed a church service during childhood and continued that habit into her adult years. She had never smoked or drank or even contemplated using drugs. She had guarded her virginity until marriage, and through the years she had thanked the Lord for her choices and His protection. She had even refused to sneak out at church camp and spray whipped cream all over their counselor's car. Victoria had been dubbed goody-two-shoes by her school and church friends, and it didn't even bother her.

They certainly wouldn't think I was a goody-two-shoes today, she thought, and her fingers flexed on the doorknob. The nausea bulged against the back of her throat. A clammy chill burst over her body. Victoria twisted the knob and decided she could call later and explain her hasty departure. Ricky would understand.

"Just a minute, Francine," he said. "Victoria, is everything okay? You don't look so hot."

"I don't feel so hot." Victoria swallowed against the warmth assaulting her mouth. "I think I need to lie down." She stroked her chilled forehead. "When you get all the painting done, call me."

"Okay!" Ricky nodded. "Francine has just agreed to help, too."

"Great," Victoria said and stepped through the doorway onto the petite, railed porch. "You're going to need as many hands as you can get."

"J–just a minute Francine," Ricky rushed. "I'm going to lay down the phone. I think we've got an emergency." His voice seemed to vibrate from a distant canyon. "Are you sure you don't want to lie down here for awhile?" Ricky urged from close behind.

Victoria glanced at Ricky, and the view of him wobbled. "N–no . . ."

"Seriously, Victoria," he continued, his brow wrinkling, "you look gray." Ricky reached to steady her, and Victoria jumped away. The last thing she needed was for him to touch her again. The effects of that, coupled with the nausea, might push her over the edge. "I'm — I'm g–going home," she stammered. "It's only a f–few minutes away. I'll be fine." Victoria swiveled and staggered to her Volkswagen.

Somehow she managed to maneuver the vehicle home, drag herself through the front door, and plop onto the sofa's cool cotton cushions. She closed her eyes and lay perfectly still. The shame that ravaged her soul like a rampaging hurricane made the physical nausea seem minuscule.

Something's got to change in my marriage, Victoria thought. *It's Tony. Tony has got to change.*

She opened her eyes, and the room swirled in an eddy of sea foam and pale blue and taupe. Victoria tightened her lids once more and gripped the side of the cushion until the nauseous wave passed. She cracked open one lid and eyed the fishing photo on the end table. Those had been the good years. The years when Tony had put a lot of energy into romancing her. They had done almost everything together. But now their almost everything had dwindled to nearly nothing. Years had passed since Victoria volunteered to go on one of Tony's fishing excursions.

"I'm not that wild about fishing," she argued with herself.

But you used to be thrilled to just be with him — whatever he did. She frowned against the factual recitation. "Well, he used to go to garage sales with me, too! But I can't remember the last time he agreed to go!"

The fishing photo came into sharper focus, and if not for her nausea, Victoria would have turned it facedown. The thought of the roll and pitch of the fishing boat on rhythmic waves increased her queasiness. A warm wash of saliva coated her mouth, and Victoria gulped against her throat, strained and quivering.

Tony's the one who needs to change! she insisted again and snapped her eyes closed. *It's Tony, not me. He needs to be more sensitive to my needs.*

Fourteen

Dr. Cox stared at Brett as if he had sprouted two heads replete with racks of elk antlers. "Put that down," he commanded. "Where did you find it?" his voice rose with every syllable.

Brett jumped. He looked at his mother and dropped the bag onto the floor. His face crumpled, and a terrified wail erupted from his lungs — the "special Brett wail" Sam was sure people heard six blocks away. She stepped over the puppy, rushed forward, scooped up her son, and retreated back to her spot by the sink. Sam refused to make eye contact with the rude vet whose cigar-odor tainted the room again.

"I–I'm sorry," he coughed out, and a rush of crimson raced from his neck to the top of his shiny, bald head. "That powder is a special medication we make a paste of and use on mange. If your son were to swallow it, he could become extremely ill."

"It's okay, it's okay," Sam crooned into Brett's ear. She never acknowledged the doctor's explanation. *Just give me the dog medicine, and let me get out of here,* she thought.

The vet leaned from side to side as he huffed his way toward the bag of white powder. He stopped and gazed at the open drawer. "Was this where he found it?" Cox pointed toward the drawer and turned those chilling green eyes on Sam.

After nodding, she tried to find some resemblance between him and his Barbie doll daughter. No likeness posed itself. None — except the color of their eyes. Yet while Audry's vibrant gaze hinted at no speck of duplicity, intuition told Sam the vet should never receive her trust.

With a surprised grunt, Cox kicked the drawer shut. It slammed against the table then popped back open. After easing the drawer closed with his sneaker, he doubled his bulging middle and retrieved the bag. "He didn't open it did he?" Cox examined the Ziploc seal.

"Of course not." Sammie stroked Brett's back and encouraged him to rest his head upon her shoulder. "He picked it up just when you walked in." Brett sniffled and rubbed his eyes with a fist. "I was about to tell him to put it down," Sam continued.

"Good." The vet leaned toward Sam,

and the lecherous gleam from earlier had dissipated but a fraction. "I'm taking this to my office before somebody else gets into it." He studied Brett as if the child were the shrewdest of criminals.

Sammie's back went rigid, and her arms tightened around Brett. Purposefully she broke eye contact and glanced down at the languid pup who had crawled next to her loafer to prop her head on the tassels.

Dr. Cox trudged toward the door, placed his hand on the knob, then turned to face Sammie. "Your dog has an intestinal infection that is deadly if the antibiotics aren't started as soon as possible. Even when she's feeling better stick to the prescribed time frame." The veterinarian glanced down at Miss Puppy, and his mouth softened. "We'll be sending a bottle of medication home with you. Just do what it says, and you'll be in good shape. As soon as we get her all well, you'll need to get her back in to begin her shots. Audry will be in with instructions."

"Okay, thanks," Samantha mumbled and felt about as grateful as a vexed mountain lion.

"Where'd you get the puppy, anyway?" Cox tilted his head in query.

"The Pet Shoppe," Sammie responded

and wished the man would just leave. "I got her a couple of days ago."

"Humph, who'd a figured," Cox mumbled enigmatically then plodded out the door.

R.J. plopped the final pair of jeans into his suitcase, zipped the case, then tugged it by the handle. The small bag bumped against his knee then swayed at his side. He gazed around the penthouse bedroom, settling on the antique mantel clock perched on the cherry highboy. Ten o'clock neared, and he wanted to see Sam before he left for Arkansas.

Larry's call this morning had instigated this emergency trip. As if mischievous high school boys weren't enough, a fire had gutted the kitchen in the spacious ranch-style home. Even though Larry insisted he could handle the problem, R.J. refused to allow his partner to bear the burden alone. He and Larry had gone into this endeavor as full partners, and R.J.'s conscience wouldn't allow him to remain in Dallas while his friend and the new assistant handled the repairs without him.

Sam should be in the office by now. R.J. glanced at the clock once more. *I wonder how that mutt of hers is doing. If the pup died, Brett would be heartbroken.* R.J. decided that he would buy a replacement if needed. *And I wasn't exactly Mr. Congeniality on the phone this morning.* The truth was, he woke up still aggravated at Sam. And if R.J. was brutally honest, he'd have to admit that he was still miffed. All he had to do was think about washing those detestable, dirty dishes without so much as one thanks from her and his temperature threatened to boil.

He glanced toward the bed's rumpled comforter and dashed aside the negative thoughts. He hadn't thought of making the bed in days. R.J. had called his parents after talking to Larry and told them he was stepping out of the magazine for several days. They were so confident in the staff that they expressed no concern over R.J.'s absence. And well they shouldn't. He was beginning to suspect his presence was barely noticed.

Meanwhile, the bed begged to be made. If his parents did decide to stop through in his absence, R.J. hated to leave the bed rumpled. His father was the neat freak of the century. With a resigned sigh R.J. stepped toward the bed, gave the covers an obligatory upward yank, and nabbed a couple of decorative pillows that had wedged themselves between the bed and nightstand days ago. He stared at the comforter's swirls of creamy taupe and garnet and clicked off a mental list of the other rooms in his parents' penthouse. *The kitchen's clean,* he thought. *Bathroom clean enough. Formal living room barely touched.* With a nod, he decided that his presence in the penthouse would be hardly noticed.

As R.J. lingered near the bed, a memory from the recent past mingled with the comforter's polished cotton sheen — a memory created here.

The night Sammie left her husband, R.J.'s mother had put her in this room. The next morning he had volunteered to keep Brett while Sammie worked downstairs on the magazine. After lunch, R.J. and Brett had stretched out in a recliner for a doze. When Sammie entered the penthouse and trod into this bedroom, she awoke R.J. Concerned for her well-being, R.J. put Brett in another bedroom and went to check on Sam. . . .

He tapped on the bedroom door and awaited an answer. None came.

"Sam?" he gently beckoned. "May I come in?"

Silence still prevailed. He frowned and

pivoted to check the bathroom. The door stood open; the room was vacant.

"Sam?" R.J. called again. "Are you in there?"

"Yes," she croaked, her voice quivering. "Come in."

He turned the knob, inched open the door, and observed her surrounded by spectacular antiques and sitting amid the folds of the comforter. While she should have looked like a wealthy lady couched in the lap of luxury, the dark circles under her eyes and the wild panic in her gaze revealed her desperate situation. R.J. couldn't stop the wince that told more than he wanted to see. His fingernails bit into his callused palm, and he once again thought of tracking down Adam Jones and doing him more bodily harm than he'd ever inflicted upon Sam.

"You woke me up when you walked through," he said, his steady tones belying his churning emotions. "I just wanted you to know that I'm stepping out for awhile. Dad's home now. Brett's asleep in the room your friend stayed in last night."

"Okay, thanks," Sammie said. Her lips moved as if they were made of wood, her eye twitched, and she pressed the corner of it with her index finger.

"You don't look so hot," R.J. said.

"Would you?"

"No." He shook his head. "No, I wouldn't." He made a special effort to lace his smile with sympathy. Sam's mouth softened. "Okay," he continued, "I should be home for dinner. Jac asked me to keep an eye on you for awhile."

"Oh?"

"Yes. Do you mind?" he drawled, figuring she would protest.

"Do you have anything else to do?" she shot back as her baby-blues flickered with evidence of the temper he remembered all too well.

"No, not really," he said then pondered the innumerable tasks that awaited him at the boys ranch. "I was just stopping through town to meet with my financial planner anyway," he said and decided not to mention the ranch. "Keeping an eye on you for a few days won't alter my schedule too much." His gaze drifted toward the window, and he wondered what Larry would do to him for not returning on schedule. *Perhaps the time has come to hire some additional help,* he thought. "Mom says she wants you to stay here for now," R.J. continued. "If you like, I can go to your home with you while you pack up some of your stuff."

"Adam's restraining order includes our home," Sammie stated.

After a pensive pause, his attention shifted back to Sammie. R.J. crossed his arms and did his best to keep his voice calm. He debated whether her statement about the restraining order was an indicator that she really planned to go home alone or a device to stop him from escorting her home. R.J. couldn't pretend that their past relationship left him cold anymore than she could. But just in case she planned a trip home alone, he decided to plunge forth with a warning she would hopefully heed.

"How do you know he won't violate the order?"

Sammie held his gaze as terror crept across her features then stirred her eyes with a pathetic glint that reminded R.J. of a cornered doe. Her jaw flexed and her lips trembled.

"Sure, you can call the police if he shows up," he continued, despising the necessities of such brutal honesty, "but what's to stop him from breaking in before they get there or hiding inside until you get home one evening?"

"Stop it! Stop it! Stop it!" Sammie cried and slid from the bed. "Just — just stop it!" Her hands clasped tightly, and she shivered as if she had been exposed to zero-degree temperature.

Before R.J. could predict his own moves, he was standing in front of her, gently gripping her upper arm. "Listen, I'm not trying to scare you, but you also need to understand —"

"I understand!" Sammie stumbled away as tears trickled onto her cheeks. "I've lived — lived with him for f–five years! I under–understand!"

"Okay, okay." Regret clawing his gut, R.J. held up his hands, palms facing Sammie, and stayed himself from stroking away her tears. "I just wanted you to know that I'll be back by dinner. Until then, *please* don't go anywhere."

Sammie huffed and scrubbed against the moisture on her cheeks. "If you think I'm going anywhere Butler, you're nuts." She crossed her arms and hugged herself as she focused on his hair.

With a resigned sigh, R.J. pressed his thumb and index finger against his eyes and detected the faint wildflower scent Sam had left in the bathroom that morning. "I'm sorry. I didn't mean to freak you out. I'm really worried here. Mom says Adam threatened to kill you. I don't think you should take his threat lightly."

"What makes you think I do?" she snapped. "I'm not some idiot who —"

"Because you've stayed with him for five years for cryin' out loud!" R.J. raised his hand then dropped it to his leg. The faint snap of skin against denim punctuated his words. He imagined pummeling Adam's face. Never had he loved a woman as he loved Sammie, and every year she was married to that jerk the biker fought his increasing resentment. Now that he knew of Adam's cruelty, every fiber of R.J.'s being craved vengeance.

"The reason I stayed is because . . ." A rush of tears gushed past her lashes. Sammie hiccuped and covered her face. "Because I was afraid he *would* kill me. You don't know what it's like, R.J. I've been terrified!"

At last R.J. gave into the urge that had engulfed him since the moment he saw Sammie that morning. He moved close, draped his arms around her shoulders, and patted her back in an awkward tattoo. Sam, stiff with caution, rested her head against his chest. A warm longing engulfed R.J. in a sea of what-might-have-beens. He rested his cheek against her hair and her wildflower smell danced upon his senses.

"I am so *sorry,*" he breathed. "I know you're scared. I'm worried about you, that's all, and — and I'm worried about Brett, too. That little guy could steal my heart in a New York minute."

And the truth is, Brett has stolen my heart. R.J. rubbed the back of his hand against his beard, snatched up his suitcase, and stomped toward the bedroom door. *Okay, maybe I was too hard on Sammie last night,* he decided as the memory of her escape from Adam, potent and haunting, reminded him of the agonies she must have endured. *No, she didn't thank me for cooking and cleaning up, but then she didn't really invite me either. The whole dinner was my idea.*

As he walked up the hallway, the sagacious logic disintegrated his irritation. *What I need is a patience pill,* he thought, chuckling. "Yeah, about ten of 'em," he added under his breath. *Sammie isn't going to come around overnight. It's going to take time. I can't get all bent out of shape every time she doesn't respond like I want her to. At least I am making some progress,* he continued on an upbeat note. *Two months ago if I had shown up on her porch with spaghetti and a smile, she probably would have thrown me out on my ear.*

He stepped into the living room, and the mint-colored carpet and upscale antiques that reflected his mother's taste reminded him of the Victorian-style homes they were featuring in the next issue of *Romantic Living.* "Who'd have ever thunk I'd be running a magazine," R.J. muttered. He pondered his parents' lack of surprise when he had agreed to their offer. R.J. narrowed his eyes and wondered if they suspected his goals involved Sammie — nothing more, nothing less. *Knowing those two, they probably set this whole thing up then took their hands off and are praying like crazy that Sam and I can make it before I destroy the magazine.* The thought that began in jest took on a credence that he couldn't quite dismiss. Wanda Martin's unending expertise and capable management style increased his suspicions.

During the days after Adam's death, R.J. had sensed his parents' silent scrutiny as he tried his best to help Sammie. He'd been thankful that his mother hadn't reverted back to the old days when she continually attempted to force her son into her mold — the mold his elder, "perfect" sister, Phoebe, had fit so well. R.J. was in his thirties when Colleen Butler finally accepted the fact that her son would never be the slick, executive sort. That was the year R.J. and his mother stopped their perpetual arguing, and Tom Butler breathed a deep sigh of relief. It was also the year R.J. truly heard Jesus Christ calling him. The rest was history.

I wish Sammie could accept the fact that I'm not who I used to be. As he trudged toward the front door, Sam's words from two nights before sliced through his mind. *But you still dress like you did when you were 25 and as wild as a March Hare. And then you expect me to believe you've undergone some sort of metamorphosis?* R.J. stopped in his tracks and looked down at his worn jeans, T-shirt, and boots.

A new concept sprang into being like a tiny cloud on the horizon of his mind. The idea gradually took on shape and eventually became unavoidable. R.J. turned on his heel and marched into the ornate bathroom that smelled of deodorant soap. As he gazed at his reflection, he squinted and thought. *Sam's right. I look about like I did 17 years ago.* The crows' feet had deepened. Some gray had sprung up in his hair and beard. But overall he did look as rough

246

as a member of a pot-smoking motorcycle gang.

At last the new idea would no longer be harbored, and it sprang upon his lips. "If I change the way I look, maybe Sammie will see that I'm not the same person I used to be."

R.J. pondered the high-dollar suits hanging in the closet. In a moment of weakness, he'd worn the suits his mom bought because he knew they pleased her. The marvelous part about his mother's taking her hands off his life was that he actually enjoyed bringing her pleasure now. Still, every time he put on one of those suits he thought, *I'm going soft in my old age.* Just imagining them made him want to scratch all over.

His gaze trailed to his left ear lobe that sported a pierce but no gold. *I quit wearing the earring years ago,* he mused. R.J. rubbed his short beard with the ends of his blunt fingers. The facial hair was an on-again, off-again prospect. This particular round had been accumulating for only two weeks. *This could go,* he thought. Even though Sam had seen him often enough without the beard, maybe the lack of it would give him a more reputable appeal.

R.J. dropped the suitcase onto the turquoise tile, unzipped it, scratched through the contents, and pulled out an electric razor. He plugged it in and attacked the beard. The sharp blades buzzed against his face and cut a path through the growth — a path that expanded with every flick of his wrist. At last he turned off the razor and gazed at himself in the mirror. His dark eyes and brows now appeared more prominent, and his face looked much more narrow — like it always did after a good shave. Rubbing his jaw, R.J. debated whether he liked himself better with or without the beard and voted for "with." Nevertheless, he'd do almost anything at this point to influence Samantha.

As he leaned forward and unplugged the razor, R.J.'s braid fell across his shoulder. He tossed the razor back then dropped the cord. R.J. reached toward his neck and squeezed the spindly ponytail — something he'd worn since he was 20. The thing had driven his father nuts when R.J. came home from college with it trailing down his back. At the time, R.J. had clung to the symbol of independence and refused to cut it. As he matured the braid had simply become a part of him.

Should I cut it off? R.J. winced then wrapped the plug around the electric razor and plunked it back into the open suitcase. He faced the mirror once more and tried to decide whether he'd rather go back to wearing the suits or lose the ponytail. The urge to scratch overtook him once more.

"I think I can live without the braid," he said to his reflection as he tried to remember where he'd put the scissors. R.J. checked his flat-faced wristwatch; Larry and the burned-out kitchen called his name. "Forget the scissors," he grunted and pulled a pocketknife out of his jeans pocket.

With a snap he flipped the largest blade out, grabbed the braid in his right hand, and gingerly felt along the base of his neck. R.J. positioned the blade in his left hand and gave it a short, upward flex. The sound of metal slicing through hair vibrated off the pale walls with a sickening cadence. The strip of hair fell limp in R.J.'s right hand. Another wince overtook him, and he lowered his hand. He gazed at the ponytail lying across his fingers. "Now that hurt!" He dropped the remnant of the past into the trash can then snapped the knife closed, stuffed it into his pocket, and eyed his hairline. A swirl of longer locks, once caught in the braid, now hung limp around a gap where the ponytail had begun. With a dubious grimace R.J. glanced at his wristwatch then pivoted and snatched open the linen cabinet.

"Scissors . . . scissors . . . scissors . . ." he muttered, nudging around the neat rows of linens, bottles of body lotion, and medical supplies. When that venture proved fruitless, he recalled the kitchen scissors in the butcher knife drawer. "Better than nothin'. I just hope it's sharp enough to cut hair."

Within a minute he was back in front of the mirror, scissors in hand. With the swish and snap of metal against hair, he snipped the stray pieces and did his best to even up the hairline. Piece by piece he dropped the disconnected tufts into the sink until there were no stragglers left.

Finally, he stroked a spot that looked as if it had been chewed and decided a trip to the barber was apropos — and soon. "For now, this'll have to do." R.J. scooped the locks of hair out of the sink and dumped them into the trash can. He plopped the scissors into the linen cabinet, slammed the door, zipped his suitcase, then grabbed the handle and marched toward the hallway. Yet as he stepped out of the bathroom, a reminiscent urge seized him. R.J. whirled back into the restroom, retrieved the braid from the trash can and crammed it into his suitcase's outer pocket.

As he stood again, he pondered the state of the black T-shirt he wore. He owned ten of them, all just alike. The brand and style were so comfortable they felt like a second skin. *I've been wearing the same kind of T-shirt all my adult life.* Like a swooping buzzard that refused to be ignored, those fine suits swished into his thoughts again. R.J. rubbed his fingers along his chest, and a rash of aversion raced up his spine.

"I ain't puttin' on another suit," he growled. He dropped his suitcase and strode back to the bedroom. Whipping open the closet door, he flipped up the light switch and glared at the six ensembles in varying shades of basic blue, black, and gray that heralded the finest in gentlemen's wear. Beside the suits hung an array of long-sleeved dress shirts that provided color scheme diversity. R.J. looked down at his T-shirt then snatched one of the shirts — a polished cotton menace in a deep shade of gray. Without removing the T-shirt, he crammed his arms into the shirt sleeves, pulled the shirt over his shoulders, then buttoned it up. He stuffed the tail into his pants.

He shoved the closet door wide open and observed himself in the floor-to-ceiling mirror attached to the inside of the door. The only indicator that he still wore the T-shirt was the snatch of black just above the top button. Other than that, the change in R.J.'s appearance struck him as bordering on drastic. No one had ever wasted any breath on his looks. While he figured he was a long shot from ugly, he'd never been asked to pose for any magazine covers, either. Nevertheless, the lack of beard and semblance of a clean-cut hairline, along with the texture of the expensive shirt, made him look like . . . He paused and narrowed one eye. "Makes me look like a city slicker," he grumbled. "I hope Sam notices all this hard work."

R.J. gave a daredevil wink that made the mischievous glint in his eyes shine. "At least I'm not wanting to scratch all over," he added under his breath. He glanced down at his jeans and boots.

R.J. eyed the suit pants in the closet then shook his head. "Nope. Enough is enough," he decided, remembering Larry's words about sipping tea and wearing suits. *If I show up at the ranch in a suit, Larry will laugh me all the way to South Dakota.* He snapped off the closet light and clicked the door shut. *I'll take off the shirt the minute I leave Dallas.* He touched the

252

back of his neck. Flinching, he wondered how long it would take for the ponytail to grow back.

Fifteen

Subject: Rana!
On Monday, 17 Jan 2002 9:25
Mara O'Connor
<mara@oconnor.hhp> writes:

Colleen,
   You are never going to believe this, but I just got a call from Rana! She's in Oklahoma and wants to come down! I am so excited! She sounded so good — like her old self. She cried a little and said she needed to get her life together. When she asked if she could come visit, I told her that would be fine. She might even move in if she needs to.
   Colleen, I am SO EXCITED! I have been praying for my daughters, praying for reconciliation. Honestly, since Rana got involved in drugs, I didn't even know where she was — and nobody else did either. I figured the first reconciliation would be with Sam. But now Rana is here! She showed up at her father's place

and got my phone number from him.

Oh, no! I was planning on going to Dallas before now. I almost forgot. I was on the phone with Rana for 30 minutes, and I was so addled I forgot about the trip.

Okay, I think I'll wait until the evening to drive over. I'll try to be at the magazine when Sammie gets off work — or I might go to her house later in the evening. Rana is arriving tomorrow. Maybe I can talk Sammie into coming over for the weekend.

Keep praying! God is moving!

Your friend,
Mara

Subject: Rana!
On Wednesday, 17 Jan 2002 9:46
Colleen Butler
<candt@butler.hhp> writes:

Mara,

Wow! It's so amazing to see this answer to prayer. You know, sometimes when we pray it's like we don't really expect the Lord to honor our requests. Then when He does, we're surprised. I admit that I'm guilty this time. My faith wasn't where it needed to be.

Man, oh, man. If only I could see that same kind of miracle with R.J. and Sammie. Let's keep praying!

Hugs!
Colleen

Sammie deposited the puppy cage beside her desk, dropped her canvas bag into her chair, and glanced behind for the sixth time in one minute, to make certain Brett followed in her wake. Sure enough, the toddler padded into the office and headed straight for his playroom.

"Barney!" he proclaimed. "Brett want Barney!"

"Okay, okay," Sam agreed and peered into the puppy's cage. The forlorn canine, chin on paws, stared up at her as if it didn't have a friend in the world. When she decided to bring the cocker spaniel to work, the idea had seemed the only option. Now Sam began to wonder if perhaps she had made the wrong choice. The last thing she needed was having to clean up after a puppy. She drew her brows together and stared at the short-pile, steel-blue carpet only two years old. Sammie glanced toward the playroom as Brett trotted into his haven. She envisioned the room marred by innumerable puppy puddles and thought about the carpet deodorizer. Biting her bottom lip, she stepped around the desk and whipped out the top drawer. Sure enough, the baggy remained where she'd dropped it last week.

Sammie picked up the bag and instantly forgot about her dog dilemma. She recalled a larger bag filled with powder — a bag that the vet nearly had a heart attack over. Samantha frowned. Something about the man's story didn't ring true. She wondered if mange were treated with a topical white cream. Sonsee would know. Until she married Taylor and moved to his Houston ranch, Sonsee had run her own animal hospital in Florida.

"Her number's in my Day Timer," Sammie mumbled to herself. She dropped the deodorizer back into the drawer, retrieved the leather-bound organizer, and flipped it to the address section.

As Sammie ran her finger down the "Ds" a long, slow, wolf whistle meandered up the hallway and through her open office door. Sam dismissed the intrusion until R.J.'s deep voice interrupted the shrill pitch.

"Mind your own business, Wanda."

"Lookin' good there," Wanda shot back with a twinkle in her tone.

Sammie, tempted to observe just how good R.J. *did* look, pressed her lips together and forced herself to concentrate on finding Sonsee's number.

"Don't get any ideas," R.J. teased. "You're too young for me!"

"Too young? Oh, you *do* go on! I'm old enough to be your mother, and you know it." Sam imagined the aging lady with line-free skin the color of teak and a graceful gait that suggested she was royalty.

"No way!" R.J. gasped.

Sam couldn't deny that the conversation was steadily approaching her end of the hallway. Instead of seeing Sonsee's phone number, Sam was assaulted with memories of R.J. standing in her kitchen in that apron . . . of the look in his eyes when she told him to go . . . of his headlights illuminating the darkness as his vehicle puttered away from her home. The names and addresses all mingled together like a bunch of tangled briers.

"Don't stay away too long, now." Wanda's gleeful challenge enticed Sam to peer down the hallway; instead, she tried to focus on the Day Timer.

Footsteps neared and stopped at her door. "Knock, knock," R.J. called.

Sammie forced herself to glance up with as much nonchalance as she could muster. R.J. stood in her office doorway, ebony suitcase in hand. For once he was clean-shaven *and* wearing a dress shirt — all at the same time. Wanda's wolf whistle was the only appropriate reaction. While R.J. had worn suits to work in recent months, he'd never completely accomplished the attractive, professional look. The facial hair and ponytail annulled any aura the semiformal attire might have lent him. But this morning he had pulled it off — even with his faded blue jeans and cowboy boots. The effect of the clean shave coupled with the sheen of his charcoal-colored, polished cotton shirt, added to R.J.'s appeal. And from where Sam was standing, the ponytail wasn't in view at all. Not that she'd mind if it was. The braid had always added an "I refuse to conform" aspect to R.J. that Sam found as fascinating now as she had 17 years ago.

"Hello," he said, raising his brows, "are you with me?"

"Yes, I'm with you," she replied.

"And . . ." One dark brow quirked over his gorgeous, dark eyes, and Sammie remembered the first time she had realized the son of her father's best friend deserved a second, third, and fourth look. They'd just moved back to Dallas. R.J. came strolling down the center aisle of the massive sanctuary, and Sam decided right then and there that he would be her date for the Valentine's Day banquet. While R.J. couldn't be called handsome in the classic sense, he oozed unbridled masculinity that suggested he should be riding a rough range on a spirited stallion. Today, his good looks struck Sam full force. She glanced back at the planner, curled her toes, and decided she must be going soft.

"Whatza matter, Sam?" he teased as his footsteps neared. Out of the corner of her eye she caught a glimpse of blue jeans. The swish of denim against leather announced that R.J. had claimed one of the chairs across from her desk.

"Er . . . nothing . . . nothing's wrong," she stammered as his suitcase plopped onto its side. R.J. reached to right it. Sammie gulped and stiffened her shoulders against the unexpected rush of longing that raced from the center of her soul. She wondered what it would feel like to lose herself in the warmth of his embrace once again . . . but only once. In an attempt at logic, she reminded herself that she wasn't ready for another relationship. But R.J.'s allure prevented Sam from scraping together enough resolve to stop her mind from replaying those tantalizing dreams from the night before. Dreams of motorcycle rides and sunsets, laughter and kisses, joy and contentment. Dreams that R.J. made no qualms about wanting to fulfill in real life.

"I'm sorry I was . . ." R.J. coughed, and Sam's attention riveted upon him. "I'm sorry I was rude this morning," he stated, wincing as if the words tasted like bitter bile.

A soft chuckle escaped Sam, and she shook her head.

"What's so funny?" he demanded, his mouth curling at the corners.

"You never were any good at apologies," she chided.

"Oh, and I guess you're some sort of champ?"

The good-humored challenge hung between them like an unspoken plea. Sam squirmed inwardly as a flautist's rendition of "Yankee Doodle Dandy" floated from the playroom. She glanced toward her son who had successfully plunked in a Barney movie and turned it on. Brett squatted in front of the TV, mesmerized by the purple dinosaur cavorting across the screen.

Of its own accord her gaze traveled back to R.J., and Sam would have vowed that the warmth in his eyes had increased since last night. She grabbed her purse, deposited it near the desk, and sat in her chair. Sam gripped the sides of the planner as if she were on a dangerous mission. This time Sonsee's phone number came into prominent focus.

"What do you know about cocaine?" Sammie asked as she reached for the white packet of carpet deodorizer lying in the top drawer. She lifted it to her desk, rubbed her thumb across the cool package, and peered at R.J.

"Good grief!" he said, leaning forward. "How did you get your hands on *that?*"

"Oh, you noodle-head!" Sammie laughed. The barb sounded more like an endearment. "This is carpet deodorizer." She pulled the sliding lock and the full-bodied smell of Obsession mingled with the faint scent of coffee. "Here, smell." Sam leaned across her desk and extended the package to R.J.

He reached for the plastic baggy, and his fingers brushed the tops of hers. An electric charge raced up Sammie's arm. She yanked her hand away, shocked by the intensity of her feelings. The carpet deodorizer crashed onto her desktop, teetered on the edge, then toppled over the precipice.

"Uh oh," R.J. grunted. He slid from the chair and knelt to retrieve the bag as the designer scent invaded the office. "Whoa!" he croaked. "I'll say this isn't cocaine! Smells like a perfume factory."

Sammie watched R.J. from the side and scrutinized the base of his neck. Her eyes widened. Where a braid once securely hung, nothing remained but an array of gaps along his hairline. Sam's mouth fell open and a horrified gasp exploded from her.

"What is it?" R.J. asked. He swiveled to face the door as if he expected to see a horrid foe poised to devour them.

"Your braid!" Sammie yelped.

"What about it?" R.J. slid back into his chair and put the deodorizer back on the desk.

"It's gone!" Sam sat straight up, and the chair wheels squeaked beneath her.

"So?"

"I . . . what happened to it?"

"I cut it."

"Why?"

He shrugged. "For the same reason I

shaved, I guess, temporary insanity." R.J. averted his gaze, and Sam sensed he wasn't telling her the whole story.

"But . . . but . . . are you going to keep it gone? I mean are you ever going to let it grow back?" Sam gripped the chair's armrests.

"Don't know."

"But . . . but . . ." R.J. without his braid was like a dog without its bark, a plane without wings, a river without water.

"You act like you've lost your best friend or somethin', Sambo."

Sammie blinked and recalled the summer of 1985 when she'd given her tender heart to a man with a braid who called her Sambo. Nobody else had ever called her that — just R.J. — and he hadn't used the name since that summer. Sammie was overwhelmed with a sweet yearning to roll back the years and start over. Start with a clean slate and trusting heart. Begin again and see if they could make it this time around.

"Did you *like* my ponytail?" R.J. asked incredulously.

Yes, I did! Sam caught herself before the words escaped her mouth. "I — it's just so strange to see you without it. I've never known you without it."

"Well, I'm the same man whether I have it or not," he stated evenly.

"Yes, yes, I know," Sammie hedged. "It's just that —" She bit her bottom lip and reached down to boot up her computer. The whirring of the fan and the clicking of the machine mingled with Barney's cheerful rendition of "Pumpernickel Bread."

"Where are you going with that suitcase?" she asked abruptly, pretending to concentrate on the computer screen's changing display.

"Home," R.J. stated.

"And that would be?" Sam asked, suddenly curious about where R.J. lived. During the season surrounding Adam's death, R.J. really hadn't had the time to share personal information. Perhaps he had intended to discuss these issues when he proposed, but Sam had been so quick to refuse that he had precious little time to fill in important details. Furthermore, she and Colleen had exchanged only a few conversations about R.J. during the years of Sam's employment at the magazine. The only time Colleen mentioned her son was when he paid one of his infrequent visits. Sammie had done her best to stay in her office and out of R.J.'s way at those times.

After all, she'd been married, and she'd convinced herself that he was nothing more than a phantom of her past.

As she mused over her lack of knowledge, the puppy's occasional whine was the only forthcoming sound. Finally Sammie turned her full attention toward R.J. and raised both brows in a silent query that urged him to continue.

"Who wants to know where I live?" he drawled as a satisfied smile crawled onto his face, making him look like a lazy lion, fat and full.

Sam shot him a challenging look.

"I do," she said in a neutral voice.

"Why?"

"Well, you know where I live. And . . . you've always been such a wanderer." She shrugged and nonchalantly ran the tips of her fingers along the edge of her desktop calendar. The blast of winter sunshine spilling past the window curtains seemed but a glimmer compared to her glowing curiosity about the location of R.J.'s home and his mysterious partnership with a guy named Larry.

"What'd you think, Sammie?" He stretched his legs in front of him, leaned against the back of the chair, and crossed his arms. "That I'd live on the road my whole life? Everybody has to settle down sometime and, hopefully, become a home-owner. It's inevitable — even for the worst of us."

"I didn't even know you *owned* a home."

"There's a lot about me you don't know."

"Maybe it's time I find out." Sam marveled at the words the second they left her mouth. The last thing she needed to do was give R.J. the wrong impression. Last night's resolve faded in the light of the morning, and she wasn't even sure what the right impression would be.

"Why?" he asked with a clever smirk.

"Why?" she repeated like a mindless parrot.

"Yep. What's your purpose?"

Sam looked up at the ceiling, replete with recessed lighting, and expelled a long breath.

"Last night I slaved away and cooked you dinner, cleaned your kitchen, and then you told me to get lost." R.J.'s voice rang with a twinge of irritation. Sam fixed her gaze upon the corn plant in the corner of her office. "Now you want to know all about me. Excuse me, but I'm a little confused here."

Sam scowled, yanked on the neck of her

turtleneck sweater, and leveled a glare straight into R.J.'s eyes. All the while, she hoped like crazy that the scowl hid the rush of guilt. She *had* been rude to him last night, and he was undoubtedly and justifiably miffed. "Are you trying to be obstinate on purpose, R.J. Butler, or does it just come naturally?"

"You know me, Sambo," he said, his words meandering forth like a lazy Texas river. "Obstinance just comes natural." He scrubbed his knuckles along the side of his jaw and rested his elbow on one of the chair's arms as if he didn't have a care in the world.

"Okay," she snapped. "I'm sorry I was rude last night. Now —"

"What's the deal with the cocaine questions?" he asked.

Sammie tapped her index finger against the edge of her desk, and the puppy's protesting yelp mildly echoed her own internal shriek. "You're still just as pigheaded as you ever were!"

"Of course." Another mild smile suggested he was enjoying his perverse little game to the max. "What else did you expect?"

With a groan Sammie stood and snatched the carpet freshener from the edge of her desk. "What do you know about cocaine?" she demanded.

"Not much. I was bad, but not that bad. I know it's a white powder — looks like that stuff." He pointed to the deodorizer. "And it kills people. I know people who are involved in distributing it can be meaner than the devil himself and would just as soon kill somebody as look at 'em. I've got a friend or two who were once up to their eyeballs in the stuff, but we don't sit around and talk about our former bone-headed eras all that much. What's going on?" The edge to his voice bade her put his mind at ease.

"I was at the vet's this morning, and Brett found a plastic bag full of white powder. I'd say it probably weighed close to half a pound. The vet almost had a stroke over it. He told me it was made into a paste and used as a topical treatment for mange."

"No way." With a swift shake of his head R.J. leaned forward and sat erect. "My dog had mange last year. They dipped her."

"Are you sure?"

"Yes, I'm sure. It was *my* dog, for cryin' out loud." His former obstinance vanished in the wake of a sunny grin that Sam was certain had knocked the socks off of more than one female.

"How do you know they don't mix a white powder to make the dip?" Sam argued, forcing herself not to smile.

"I don't. But didn't he say they made a paste out of it?"

"Yes." Sam narrowed her eyes and nodded. "That's a good point." She eyed R.J. and wondered what kind of canine a man like him might own. "What kind of dog do you have?" she asked.

"Who wants to know?" R.J.'s dark brows rose as if he were immensely enjoying the repeat of their repartee.

"I do."

"Why?"

"None of your beeswax," Sammie said, and her own grin wouldn't be denied. She snagged her lower lip between her teeth and reminded herself she was on the verge of flirting with a man whose proposal she had rejected several months before. Nevertheless, the invigorating sunshine invited her to continue down the slippery verbal slope.

"She's a pug bulldog, if you absolutely *have* to know."

"So your dog's a female?"

"She's my leading lady." R.J. rested back in the chair, and his chin tilted a fraction.

"Whose taking care of her while you're gone?"

"My, my, my, aren't we curious." He shook his head back and forth, and Sammie pressed her lips together.

"That — that Larry person is taking care of her, right?" she guessed with confidence.

A single laugh exploded from R.J. He gripped the back of his neck and said, "Now that's a new one. I've never thought of Larry in that term before."

"What term?"

"As a person!" He slapped his knee and let out another round of chuckles. "That was a good one, even if I have to say so myself. Too bad he had to miss it!"

Sammie released a noisy yet impatient huff and rolled down the top of her turtleneck. The room was quickly getting stuffy.

R.J. stopped laughing long enough to observe Sam's fingers drumming the desk.

"Okay, okay." He lifted his hands, palms outward. "Let me tell you about Maddy. Let's see . . . for starters, she likes to ride my Harley with me."

"Maddy?" Sam raised her brows, and an unexpected dart of jealousy pierced her midsection. She lowered her gaze and rubbed her blunt fingernail against a non-existent spot on the desk.

A silence, long and laden with tension,

swept into the room. A silence broken by the muffled sounds of Barney's boisterous voice, the distant ring of a phone, and the clap of a drawer shoved into place. Sammie cringed. Without so much as a glance at him she knew he saw her momentary flash of jealousy. And if he saw that, he probably perceived more — much more.

"Maddy is actually short for Madeline," he said without a hint of mockery. "That's my dog's name." This time the words oozed the essence of tenderness, patience, and mercy.

Sam diligently scrubbed against that imaginary spot and fought the urge to crawl under her desk and not come out. Yet in the midst of her chagrin, she also imagined R.J. on his motorcycle with a bulldog sitting in front of him. In her mind's eye the dog wore a helmet and a red Snoopy scarf waved in his wake.

"Your dog rides your motorcycle?" she exclaimed. A burst of laughter, spontaneous and unrestrained, erupted from Sam. She forgot about the need to hide and stared at R.J.

"I'm serious!" he chimed in, grinning. "She perches herself right up front. I've made a special harness that holds her in place."

Sam and R.J. shared a round of companionable chortles that filled the office with the kinship of two spirits who never quite lost each other. And Sam's dreams from the night before grew more attractive every passing minute. Yet, without warning, a nightmare, cold and haunting, invaded her mind. A vision that involved merciless blows and a loveless marriage. A dreadful scene still so much a part of Sam's soul that she didn't know if she would ever be free — truly free — to love again. Her laughter died, and Sammie pressed her fingernails against the sides of the baggy. She darted a glance toward her son, who still squatted motionless in front of the TV.

"For whatever it's worth, I think you should forget about the possible cocaine connection," R.J. said, his voice void of mirth.

"But shouldn't I at least call the police?" Sam peered down the hallway and saw Wanda, photos in hand, on her way to some important mission.

"Do you think the vet would leave cocaine lying around? And if it *was* cocaine and you do call the police, when they show up, they most likely won't find anything. He's undoubtedly hidden it by now. And if that man figures out you're the one who called, you just might wake up dead one morning."

"You've always had such a way with words." Sammie pressed the tips of her fingers above her nose and pondered her choices.

"I'm just trying to keep you from getting yourself killed. If I knew beyond doubt that he did have cocaine, and I also knew beyond doubt that a call to the police would get him nabbed, then I'd say call 'em. Problem is, you're stabbing in the dark. I figure you've got enough problems on your hands without askin' for more."

"Like you, for instance?" Sam teased and wondered where in the name of Horace McDugal that taunt came from.

"Am I a problem?" R.J. raised both brows as if he were delighted to be her problem.

"Who wants to know?" Sam returned. She stood and peered into the puppy's carrier.

"I do," he quipped.

A rush of pleasure assaulted Sam, and she stayed herself against expressing even the slightest hint of enjoyment. The longer she interacted with R.J., the more memories she had about the mystique and merriment of their youthful engagement. The more she recalled, the more her injured heart yearned to feel him close again. The more she yearned, the more she ached for the companionship and strength of a man in her life — a doting man, a free-spirited man, a man named R.J. Butler.

In the midst of her momentary reverie, panic exploded in her soul. *Adam's going to kill me! He is . . . he is! I know he is. He's going to kill me!* Roots of nausea sprouted in Sam's midsection, and she began a brief internal lecture that breached no argument. *If I allow R.J. to move closer, he's going to expect marriage. This is not a high school flirtation! This is the grown-up world with grown-up problems.*

Yes, and you're a grown woman with the needs of a woman, a haunting voice suggested. *Deep inside you're longing for the adoration and respect and love and companionship a healthy marriage can offer.*

Samantha gripped the handle on the puppy's cage and clamped her lips tight. "Was there something you needed my help with?" she asked with an attempt at a firm edge that wobbled out. A silent current, unrelenting and irresistible, beckoned her to look at R.J. As her gaze slid to his, she attempted to school her features into a disinterested mask. The effort was lost in the fervor of his adoring appraisal. Sammie felt as if his brown eyes had transformed into a sea of unconditional love, warm, comforting, inviting. A love that blazed from the depths of his soul. A love she had never known.

"I'm supposed to be wrapping up the recipe page for the next issue." The words came out on a breathless rasp. Sam gulped and tried to gather enough grit to pull off the disinterested, matronly approach. But this time she couldn't. R.J.'s silent communication of his heart's desire never wavered. Her cheeks flashed hot. She scrutinized the puppy and panicked for some means to break the riptide that threatened to pull her under. "Seriously, R.J.," she said on a light note. "I've got to get to work." In a last attempt to end the moment, she leaned toward him and whispered as if they were conspirators. "I've got a really mean boss. He cracks the whip and won't give an inch."

"So I understand," R.J. drawled. "But I also hear he makes a mean batch of spaghetti." His gaze roved her features as if searching for a place to lay a kiss on her she would never forget.

Another wave of warmth spread its fingers across her cheeks, and Sammie realized she was enjoying R.J.'s company much too much. By now the poor guy was probably thoroughly confused by her mixed messages. And she was even confusing herself. She wasn't sure she could maintain a safe distance if they enjoyed a kiss or two. And several kisses would undoubtedly open a door Sammie simply wasn't ready to enter — a door labeled involvement and commitment.

"Uncle R.J.!" Brett's elated squeal vibrated over yet another Barney song. The child bounded from his playroom and jumped onto R.J.'s lap with a force that would have put Sam in ICU.

R.J. growled and playfully rubbed Brett's tummy. The child erupted into a chorus of giggles. "Turn me upside down!" Brett pleaded. R.J. wasted no time in obeying the toddler's whims. He stood and lowered Brett's head toward the floor. His red hair spiked downward as if it were reaching to the carpet. R.J. secured a firm grip around Brett's ankles and mildly swung him back and forth like the pendulum on a grandfather clock. A new round of laughter gurgled from Brett's throat — the kind of laughter Sammie had experienced only minutes ago when thinking about Maddy on the motorcycle. Years had passed since Sam had laughed like that.

Her breath caught in her throat; hot tears blurred her vision. Her spirit ached with a renewed awareness that Brett desperately needed a father — a man to teach him to play catch, a man to take him camping, a man to unconditionally love him. While Sam's love for Brett was as high as the heavens above, she never once duped herself into believing she could be a father and a mother. Her son needed both.

Sixteen

R.J. did his best to focus on the elated child in his arms, but all he could think about was the child's mother. The exalted chorus that surged through his mind was, *Yes! After almost six months, I'm finally breaking through!* From the second R.J. stepped into Sam's office he suspected that her resolve to keep up the walls was at last slipping. Every minute that progressed intensified R.J.'s positive impression. For one wrinkle in time, he even suspected she might have fantasized about kissing him. R.J. had to use stringent self-control to keep within the bounds of Sam's comfort level. Instead, he taunted her in a verbal game he figured she secretively enjoyed . . . if the impish gleam in her eyes was anything to go by.

Sometime R.J. would tell her about the ranch. Until then, she could spend some time stewing in her own curiosity juices. A little mystery wouldn't hurt in the least.

As Sam removed the puppy from its

cage, R.J. pointed Brett's head downward for one more round of "pendulum." Brett released another stream of giggles. "Look, mommie!" he exclaimed. "I upside down again!"

Sammie cast a cursory glance toward her son then studied the puppy. R.J. was almost certain a thin mist clouded Sam's eyes.

"Yes, I see!" Sam chirped. "You're a swingin' dude, aren't you!"

"Yeeeeessss!" Brett squealed.

Her shoulders stiff, Sam snuggled the puppy close and then turned and marched toward the playroom.

"Excuse me," Wanda said from the doorway.

R.J. flipped Brett upright. The child plopped right into the crook of R.J.'s strong arm. Brett wrapped his arms around R.J.'s neck, and a strand of straight red hair prickled the end of his nose. R.J. brushed aside the hair, raised his brows, and pivoted to face Wanda. Her dark eyes sparkling, she gave R.J. a white-toothed grin that suggested unspoken predictions might be coming true.

"I'm going to close this door," she proclaimed. "Your little family reunion is disturbing the peace."

"Ah, Wanda," R.J. said, "if I didn't know any better, I'd say you were up to your eyeballs in my mom's schemes."

Wanda's forehead wrinkled. "Excuse me?" she chanted good-naturedly.

"You can act innocent all you like, but I'd stake my last steer that you're the spy in this whole setup."

"Who me?" Wanda placed a flattened hand against the lapel of her fiery red business suit.

"Go ahead, act like you don't know what I'm talkin' about, but you and I both know this magazine needs me to run it like a duck needs a bicycle."

Without another word, Wanda snapped the door shut.

"Just in case you're interested," R.J. bellowed, "I'm headin' home for a week. I hope you can function without me."

The door whipped open. Wanda stuck her tongue out at him and the door clapped shut once more.

"You know I just *love* all that respect!" he hollered at the door. "And when you e-mail mom with your latest report, tell her about your juvenile streak as well."

"Juvenile streak!" Wanda screeched as she shoved the door back open. She placed a pair of narrow reading glasses on the tip

of her nose and glared over the top of them. "Takes one to know one!" she teased, pointing a stack of photos at R.J.'s nose.

They both erupted into a round of laughter seconds before Brett squirmed against R.J.'s grip. "I turn upside down!" Brett declared, hurling himself forward.

"Wait!" R.J. hollered. His heart pounded as he snared Brett's arm. R.J. whisked the child back into the crook of his arm. "Don't do that again! You could have broken your neck!" He looked squarely into Brett's baby-blues and furrowed his brow to better drive home the message.

Brett's bottom lip trembled. His eyes pooled with tears. He crammed his face against R.J.'s neck.

"It's okay," R.J. soothed while his heart slowed to its normal pace. "You just can't do that. Uncle R.J. didn't know you were going to dive down. If I hadn't been quick, you would have gotten a big, big boo-boo."

A remorseful sniffle accompanied Wanda's, "Oh my goodness!"

R.J. jumped and whirled to face the doorway. "I thought you were gone!" he said.

Wanda covered her lips with red-tipped

fingers and shook her head. "I can't believe it!"

"What?"

"I knew there was something different about you besides that shirt and the shave when I saw you coming down the hallway, but I didn't put it together until just now. You cut off your braid!" Wanda gasped as if a national security breach had been discovered.

"That rumor seems to be spreadin' high and low," R.J. dashed a glance to the playroom. Sammie had shut the door, and he caught only a glimpse of her through the narrow window near the door as she knelt beside the sick pup.

"My, oh, my. Just *wait* till your mother hears about this." Wanda sounded like a very pleased spy.

"I'm sure you'll waste no time telling her," R.J. retorted. "Quick! Dash off an e-mail while the news is still hot!"

"That smart mouth of yours is going to get you killed one day." Wanda took the glasses off her nose and allowed them to hang by the chain around her neck.

"Ah, you love me, darlin', and we both know it." He mimed an exaggerated wink, and then he patted Brett on the back.

"It looks like I'm not the only one."

Wanda returned his wink, eyed Brett once more, then cast a last glance toward the playroom before clicking the door shut. This time it stayed shut.

Brett shifted his head onto R.J.'s shoulder.

"I sorry," he whimpered.

With a sigh, R.J. rested his head against the top of Brett's. "It's okay, little champ," he said.

"I not do it again."

"Good. You just about scared me out of a year's growth, that's all." R.J. walked toward the massive window and tugged aside the sheers. The skyscrapers looming nearby produced their usual boxed-in effect. R.J. resisted the urge to bolt. He wondered, as he had a hundred times, if Sammie would consider leaving all this behind. Brett raised his head and pointed toward a lone, silver airliner that soared near a towering building covered in mirrorlike squares.

"See the plane?" Brett asked, his gaze fixed upon the jet.

R.J. peered at the child's profile so like Sammie's. And he was aware that if Sam had agreed to marry him six years ago, Brett might have been his own. A jolt of love blazed through his soul. R.J.'s arm tightened against Brett's waist. An unexpected rush, warm and wet, seeped into his eyes. R.J. swallowed hard and commanded the tears to leave. *Real men don't cry,* he scolded himself. *Yes, they do,* he countered, *they do . . . when little boys steal their hearts.*

"I like planes," Brett said with a firm shake of his head. "I fly one when I grow up."

"*Oh really?*" R.J. asked and did his best to blink away the tears.

"Yes." Brett nodded. "I take you and mom on a ride in my plane."

"That sounds like a good idea to me." R.J. placed an open palm against Brett's chest. Then he held the boy parallel to the floor, blew through his lips to create a motor sound, and spun in a circle.

Brett extended his arms and squealed, "I a plane!"

The playroom door opened and R.J. stopped in midspin as Sammie stepped into the office and snapped the door behind her. Today Sammie wore a vibrant teal sweater and knit pants that complimented everything from her hair color to her curves. As far as R.J. was concerned even the blemish on her chin looked good.

With a scowl, Sam covered her chin with

the tips of her fingers. "Stop looking at it," she snapped.

"What?"

"My chin! And don't tell me you weren't."

"I was just —"

"The pimple popped up somewhere between the house and the vet. The last thing I need is some face inspector sizing it up!"

"Ah, Sammie," R.J. whispered. "I was just thinking that even your zits are good lookin'!" *As far as I'm concerned you're the most beautiful woman on the planet.*

She averted her gaze and stepped toward the portable puppy cage still on her desk. "I'm going to have to find some sheets of plastic," she said yanking the cage up. "I think they probably have some in production. And I need some newspaper, too." Sammie plopped the carrier near the bookshelf behind her desk as a wash of red crept up her cheeks.

A satisfied smile crawled onto R.J.'s lips. "There's a stack of newspapers in my office," he said. "Whatcha need 'em for?"

"The puppy!" she snapped as if he were daft.

"Oh!" R.J. nodded. "That *would* pose a problem all the way up here. Tell ya what, I'll go get them for you." Out of habit R.J.

286

glanced at his wristwatch and frowned. Eleven o'clock was shoving itself upon them, and that burned-out kitchen surged into his mind. "As soon as I get the paper, I've gotta leave for home," he stated as he deposited Brett onto the floor.

"I go home with Uncle R.J." Brett said.

Sam shook her head. "Uncle R.J. is going to an undisclosed destination for an undetermined length of time for an unknown reason," she said as if she were a peeved newsanchor. "You've got to stay here with mom and help take care of the puppy."

R.J. stepped toward the office door.

"I take puppy with me." Brett's determined footfalls neared the playroom.

"Nope," Sammie said. "You go on into your playroom. I need to get to work before I get fired."

"I go with Uncle R.J.," Brett wailed.

As R.J. gripped the office door, he swiveled to face Sammie. "I really wouldn't mind if he wanted to go home with me," he said before he realized the words were coming out.

"Excuse me?" Sam crossed her arms and tapped her foot. "You're crazy as a betsy bug if you think I'm going to let you take my son off into the sunset to who knows where for who knows how long, and —"

"Mena, Arkansas," R.J. said. He imagined Brett snuggled in front of him for a horseback ride across his 50-acre ranch.

"What?" Sammie asked.

"I live in Mena, Arkansas." He pictured a bonfire after sunset and roasting wieners and marshmallows with his little buddy. "I own a ranch there. I've owned it for a little more than three years now. I run a home for troubled teenage boys." R.J. focused upon Brett who stood motionless as if he sensed the fate of the decision rested in the next few minutes. "Larry Tently's my partner. His wife is there, too. They don't have kids, but they want 'em." R.J. wondered how much one of those jungle gym sets he'd seen at the department store cost. There was a perfect place in the backyard. "They would love it if I brought Brett for a visit. I'm going to be gone a week. It would give you time to finish that novella and —"

"No!" Sam exclaimed and raised both hands. "No. And that's final." She marched toward his suitcase, yanked it up, and stomped toward him. Sammie dumped the case at his feet, crossed her arms, and said, "The Sahara Desert will freeze solid before I let you take *my* child anywhere for a week! I'd go nuts!"

"I want ta go home with Uncle R.J." Brett demanded.

"Okay, okay!" R.J. raised his hands, palms outward. "Don't go spastic on me. Whatcha say you let me keep him until the weekend — that's only a few days. Maybe you can drive up Friday evening or Saturday morning to get him. It's only a five-hour drive. We have a couple of extra rooms, and maybe you'd even like to go to church with us Sunday morning. From all I can gather, you haven't been to church in about a year. It'll do you good."

"How do you know about my church attendance?"

"I have my sources."

"Why do I feel like there's this big tangle of underground activity going on here that involves me?" Sammie asked.

"Maybe because there is," R.J. teased. He tilted his head to one side and shamelessly produced one of those smiles that usually got him exactly what he wanted.

Sam's gaze faltered.

"I want ta go home with Uncle R.J." Brett moaned.

"Ah, come on, Sambo," R.J. chided. "It's just for a few nights. Why not indulge the heart of an old man and let me pretend I have a son for awhile. I'll even take the puppy with me. Maddy'll be glad for the company."

Sammie's breath caught in her throat. R.J.'s smile coupled with that earnest plea nearly crumpled her resolve. She whipped around, marched toward the window sheers, and yanked on the rod that flung them open. Sam gripped the edge of the windowsill and gazed onto the vast expanse of downtown Dallas blurring into a distant blue.

The truth was, she'd enjoyed the 24 hours when Brett stayed with R.J. She hadn't been alone at home in so long she'd almost forgotten how it felt. The idea of having a couple more nights to herself certainly held an appealing ring. *I could wrap up the novella!* she thought. *I could clean out my closet! I could also check out that vet.*

The last thought crashed into her mind from nowhere, and Sammie's fingers flexed. Something about that vet bothered her a lot. Sam would never spy on him with Brett in tow, but the temptation posed itself as almost irresistible if she were alone. While R.J. had presented some logical arguments against calling the police now, he had yet to convince her that there wasn't something fishy going on. And if

Sammie acquired enough evidence, her call to the police would probably not be in vain. Those post-college years she beat the pavement as a reporter for the *Dallas Morning News* rose from her past like a thirsty beast panting for the waters of knowledge. And a sprig of the old determination burst from a dormant stem in her soul — a stem that Adam had tried to strip of life.

Sammie prepared to give her permission for Brett to spend the night; then she stopped herself. R.J. said he owned a ranch of some sort — one for troubled boys. That meant her son would be with those troubled boys. All sorts of unpleasant scenarios roared through her mind. Narrowing her eyes, Sam turned to face R.J.

"What's the deal with this boys ranch?" she asked.

"What do you mean?" R.J. looked at her. "There's really nothing to tell. I own a ranch. It has horses and some cattle and, right now, six boys — ages 14 to . . ." He peered up at the ceiling. "Let's see . . . I guess to 17. Yes, Carlos just turned 17. And the way things are going, he might not be with me when he's 18."

"Oh?" Sammie crossed her arms.

"I'm seriously thinking about sending him to Siberia." R.J. placed his hands on his hips as if his decision were made and sealed.

Sam eyed her son, who opened the playroom door and crawled toward the puppy. Her mind buzzed with exactly what evil Carlos might have orchestrated to deserve banishment. With each of Sam's perverse possibilities, every one illegal, Brett's chances of going to the ranch diminished tenfold. "So . . ." Sam hedged, "what exactly has Carlos done?"

R.J. crossed his arms and rocked back on his heels. "You wouldn't believe it if I told you." He shook his head.

"Try me."

"Okay." R.J. ran his fingers through the fringes of his chopped-up hair. "He and two of his cronies — that would be Jake and Dave — who are also at my ranch and who are also facing Siberia for sure . . ." He raised a hand for emphasis, ". . . or at least a life sentence of KP. Anyway, all three of them climbed up on top of our church and nailed to the roof three mannequins dressed in women's lacy underwear."

Sam's mouth fell open. Her eyes bugged. A rush of guffaws exploded from her soul.

"I don't think the pastors would have

minded so much if the bishop hadn't been visiting the next morning. They're a husband-wife ministry team, and, accordin' to Larry, the bishop was consulting with them about doing a seminar for team ministry."

New hilarity drove Sam to another round of laughter. "I love it!" she squeaked through breathless tears.

"Your sense of humor has really gone nuts!" R.J. exclaimed.

"No . . . no . . ." Sammie stumbled to the chair near her desk and collapsed into it as a vision of the mannequins posed on top of the church steadily upped her level of hilarity. "I was just . . . just expecting something like — like a store robbery or drugs or . . . or . . . something illegal."

"Actually, I think this would qualify as illegal, especially when you consider that the ladies' mission auxiliary was meeting that morning as well, and old Mrs. Belomy was forced to use her smelling salts."

A round of musical giggles teetered from Sam. She tossed her head and mopped at her damp eyes. *"That is just too funny!"*

"That's easy for you to say!" R.J. declared. "You're not the one who has to face the pastors this Sunday — unless, of course, you agree to come up like we were discussing."

Sam brushed her fingertips along the edge of the desk before peering at her black flats. "Exactly how troubled are these boys you take care of?" she asked. A root of respect, deep and permanent, sprouted in the center of her soul. R.J. Butler had grown more than she had given him credit for. The next question posed itself before he had the chance to answer the first one. "And why didn't you tell me about the ranch in the first place?" Sam stood and faced him, her close-minded accusation from two nights before taunted her: *But you still dress like you did when you were 25 and were as wild as a March Hare . . . And then you expect me to believe you've undergone some sort of metamorphosis?*

R.J. shoved a hand into his jeans pocket and silently observed Sam.

"How long did you say you've been running this ranch?" she asked.

"Just over three years."

Sammie shook her head. "I had no idea."

"I know." R.J. leaned against the doorframe. His eyes, hooded and wary, shifted toward the window.

Sammie closed her eyes and took a deep breath. "I have really misjudged you, haven't I?"

"I wanted you to decide that without having to see material proof, Sam," R.J. drawled. "I mean I'm the same man whether I own a boys ranch or not or whether I dress a certain way or not or whether —"

"You have a braid or not?" she asked swallowing against the lump in her throat. "You cut your braid off because of me, didn't you?"

He straightened. "Let's not go there." R.J. rubbed his palms together. "Let's see, I think we were trying to decide if Brett could come home with me for a few nights."

"I–I'm sorry." Sammie raised her hand and let it fall at her side. "Really, I really don't exactly know what to say."

R.J.'s gaze roved her features with a nuance of hunger. Hunger and love. Love and hope.

A new round of heat assaulted Sam's cheeks as wave upon wave of longing crashed into her soul. A gateway within her heart flung itself open and beckoned her to run with abandonment down the pathway she had resisted all these months. A pathway upon which R.J. awaited with outstretched arms. A pathway of discovery that would reacquaint her with her first

295

love. Sammie, caught in the tide of what-might-have-beens, tried to remember all the reasons she shouldn't step through that gate. She even attempted to conjure images of her former husband's baleful sneers, but only one man filled her mind. A man who had filled her dreams the night before. A man who stood before her, his heart in his eyes.

R.J. bent over, unzipped the side panel of his suitcase, and retrieved something from within. He neared Sam, stopped mere inches away, and reached for her hand. Mesmerized, Sammie watched as he turned her hand palm-upward then placed a spindly strand of braided hair across her palm. R.J. closed her fingers around the braid then covered her hand in his. The roughened texture of his fingers upon her knuckles contrasted with the feathery strand against her palm. Sammie looked into the eyes of a man whose rough exterior hid a heart of gold.

"One day you're going to wake up and realize that I would give my life for you, Samantha Jones," he whispered. "And when you do, I'll be waiting."

Sammie bit her lip as a sheen of tears sparkled across her vision. Her gaze lowered to the top of his black T-shirt peeking from beneath the cotton dress shirt. R.J.'s thumb caressed her jaw, and Sam's breath caught in her throat. His fingers slipped to the base of her neck, and a cascade of tingles dashed down her spine. She knew what was on his mind because the same thing was on hers. She couldn't remember the last time she had kissed a man and enjoyed it. But the time had come to revel in the nearness of this man who had gently pursued her for months.

R.J.'s lips neared hers, and Sam stepped through the gateway in her heart and into the arms of her first love. Her pulse hammering, she closed her eyes and enjoyed the brush of his lips upon hers. As the kiss deepened, a wash of tenderness and nostalgia and longing bubbled from a soul betrayed and lonely. Lonely and bereft. Bereft and aching to be cherished.

Sam didn't realize she was clinging to R.J. until he pulled back and nudged her shoulders. Her head spinning, she inched away and peered up into half-opened eyes that glittered with masculinity.

"Good grief, woman!" he gasped. "I wasn't expecting . . ." He shook his head to gather a semblance of control.

Through the haze of attraction Sammie was jerked back to reality. *Adam beat me.*

He raped me. He ripped my heart into tiny shreds and left me nothing but an empty shell. I'm not sure I have any love to offer a man. The tantalizing dreams from the night before and the flickering hope were blotted out by the nightmares that had plagued her for months.

Her legs trembling, Sammie broke away from R.J. She rounded her desk, snatched up the carpet deodorizer, and dropped it and the braid into a drawer. She slammed the drawer. In her heart, she raced back through the gate and banged it shut behind her. Samantha ran hard and fast to the vacuum she had fallen into after Adam's death — a dark but familiar cavern in her torn and scarred soul.

After a lengthy pause laden with confusion and tension, R.J.'s voice floated in from miles away. "I promise I won't let Brett out of my sight. And if it's any consolation, none of the boys at my ranch are hardened criminals. They're just misguided and need a firm hand." He continued, his voice deceptively steady, "Honestly, I don't think a one of them would hurt Brett, but I promise I won't leave him for one second. He can even sleep in my room on a cot."

Sammie plopped into her chair and

faced the computer screen. She snatched her mouse and clicked on the MS Word icon. "You'll have to go by my house and pack him a bag," she snapped as the computer chugged through the file-opening routine.

"Yes, I've already thought of that."

"Let me get my house key," Sammie said, her voice wooden.

"No need." R.J. hesitated. "I've got a key."

Sammie's gaze snapped to his face. "You what?"

The eyes that had brimmed with love minutes before warily shifted as R.J. rocked back on his heels. "I was going to return it this morning," he said. "I found it last night under the milk can on your front porch. I used it to lock your front door. Your doorknob lock is broken. Did you know that?"

"Yes, I know." Sammie continued to observe him. Despite her resolve, she peeked from her soul's cave back toward the gate. The hot, sinking, melting feeling from his kiss assaulted her limbs. She tried her best to break free of his appraisal, but to no avail.

"I was going to suggest you find another hiding place for your key anyway," he said.

The wariness vanished in the warmth of a lazy smile that suggested he might be melting too.

Sam blankly stared at him. "Brett's room is at the end of the hallway. Can't miss it. It's full of Barney stuff."

"Who'd ever guess that?" R.J. said, amused.

Sammie peered past him, toward the trash can near the door — a trash can stacked with used Pull-Ups. Sometimes Sam wondered if those things crawled out of her canvas bag and hurled themselves into the garbage. "And don't forget to get plenty of training pants," she added. "There's a new bag on top of his dresser."

"Don't worry. I'm sure that between the two of us we can get all his stuff."

She focused on the computer screen and clicked on the recipe file. "And if you give him *too* much caffeine —"

"I know. He goes crazy. I've already figured that one out. Believe me, I won't give him caffeine."

"Okay, good." The recipe file opened, and Sammie stared at the collection of Tex-Mex contributions from readers and freelance authors. The recipe titles and measurements jumbled together. All Sam could think about was the man in her office and the braid lying in her desk drawer.

"So," R.J. said, "I guess I'll take Brett and go then."

"Okay." Sam swallowed hard. "And the puppy too, if you really don't mind."

"Don't mind a bit."

She gripped the mouse and stared at the recipe page, but it might as well have been written in Greek. Sam clicked the mouse on a recipe for cheese dip and adjusted the margins for no reason whatsoever.

"I assume you'll come up this weekend?"

Sam envisioned a sprawling ranch house nestled in rolling Arkansas hills. Horses and cattle, trees and pasture, a clear, open sky, and R.J. riding a stallion with Brett secured in front of him completed the delightful scene. "Yes, I'll come up Friday evening." She tapped at the keyboard. "Write down your address and phone number, would you? Directions would also be helpful."

"Sure. I'll put my cell number there, too, although I'm not that great about leaving it on. That's why I usually forward my phone calls to wherever I'll be."

"That's fine," Sam said and felt as if he were scrutinizing her every move. She remained riveted to the computer. "Why don't you e-mail me the driving directions once you get home?"

"Of course. No problem."

"And if Brett cries and won't stop, I'll come and get him." Sam inspected the description of how to roll crusts for sopapillas.

"I don't think that will happen," R.J. said. "He seems content with me so far."

"Yes," Sammie said. The word hung between them almost like an admission of the friendship that suspiciously resembled a father–son relationship.

R.J.'s boots scruffed against the carpet and stopped near the playroom. "Hey, li'l buddy, still want to go home with me?" R.J. asked.

"Yes!" Brett exclaimed, and the two began the process of collecting the dog and her cage.

Finally, Brett threw himself into Sam's arms for the goodbyes. He squeezed her hard but released just as abruptly as the hug began.

"We go now," Brett said.

"You be good for Uncle R.J." Sam planted a kiss on his forehead, savored the smells of Pop-Tarts and baby shampoo, then reluctantly released her son.

"I be good," he stated and trotted toward the doorway. "C'mon, Uncle R.J.," he called over his shoulder.

Sam bit her bottom lip. Her motherly instincts kicked in, and a bittersweet longing swept through her. Sammie was elated for the chance at freedom but still worried that Brett wouldn't be okay without her.

"Well, I . . . guess we'll see you Friday, then," R.J. said.

"Yep," Sam whispered. She refocused on the computer. "The puppy's medicine is in the top of my duffel bag. You can't miss it."

"Okay." The rustling sound of fabric filled a strained pause. Finally R.J. said, "There's a small bag of dog food here, too."

"Yes, take that." Sam forced herself not to look at R.J. . . . She wanted to do more than just look at him. Once again, her heart peeked out of the cavern and longingly gazed toward the gateway. R.J. still stood on the other side, his arms outstretched. The recipe blurred as a stinging mist filled her eyes.

His footsteps neared her office door, and Sam sneaked a glimpse of him, the dog cage in one hand and the suitcase in the other. She winced at the hair along his neckline, now mangled and sorely in need of attention. Without a backward glance, R.J. exited her office and called, "Brett, wait up!"

After another cautious glimpse revealed a hallway void of human life, Sam opened a desk drawer and pulled out the braid. She wrapped the length of hair around her finger and held it against her lips as hot, doubtful tears seeped down her cheeks and trickled into the hair.

The telephone's ring jolted Sam, and she stared at the blinking light through three rings before reaching for the receiver. She sniffed hard, picked up the receiver, and did her best to produce a normal "hello."

"Hi, Sam," Victoria's greeting warbled over the line. "I — I need to talk," she continued before breaking into unrestrained tears.

Sammie's fingers curled around the braid as Victoria's baleful crying spilled over the line.

"What's the matter?" Sam asked while a list of tragic scenarios plowed through her mind . . . death, miscarriage, financial ruin.

"Can I come over for a few days?" Victoria wailed.

"To my house?" Sam released the braid, and it fell on the desk calendar with a gentle plop.

"Y–yes. Tony came in early from his fishing trip this morning, and we had a t–terrible fight, and we're just having so many problems. Oh, Sammie, I don't even know if he loves me anymore!" Her words tumbled out like a gushing river held long at bay.

Sam's mouth fell open. "But I thought — I mean, you just found out you're pregnant and we, all the sisters, thought you were so happy!"

"You don't have to have a blissfully happy marriage to get pregnant," Victoria asserted with a disenchanted huff.

Nodding, Sam recalled her own pregnancy. "I know that from personal experience."

"Honestly, I thought that maybe when I got pregnant it might fix some things, b–but I think we're just going downhill faster. And all the other — other sisters are so happy right now, it makes me sick." Her shrill voice broke. "I've got to talk to somebody who can understand or I'm going to absolutely shrivel up and die!"

"Of course," Sam crooned, recalling a time not so long ago when Jac had stood by her. She would do the same for Victoria. Sam rubbed a weary hand over her tense face. This day was really starting to stack up fast. "Are you going to drive?"

"N–no," Victoria stuttered. "I checked into taking a–a shuttle flight. There's a flight this afternoon that isn't booked up. Would you pick me up at the airport this afternoon if I can make it to Dallas/Fort Worth by five o'clock?"

"Sure," Sammie agreed, silently listing all the grandiose plans she had made for the next few days. Maybe Victoria wouldn't mind talking about her marital problems while spying on the vet. As Victoria expressed her thanks, Sammie glanced down at the planner still open on her desk. When she finalized arrangements with Victoria, Sam planned to call Sonsee and confirm R.J.'s comments on the treatment for mange.

Seventeen

Shrill ringing jolted through Terrence like a bolt of lightning streaking to earth. He clawed at the covers over his head as if he were buried alive. As soon as the room came into view he yanked the comforter back up and blotted out the possibility of encountering the phantom who had harassed him through the night. The phone shrieked again. Terrence extended a hand past the covers to the nightstand. He felt across the phone until he gripped the receiver and tugged it under the covers with him.

"Hello," he mumbled into the mouthpiece as the mid-morning light oozed past the covers. His exhausted mind desperately hoped Mallory wasn't still sitting on the end of his bed, yet the prickling hair on his neck verified her presence.

"It's me," Barry bit out.

"Yes," Terrence barked.

"I found the other bag of stuff this morning."

Fear of Mallory's ethereal form evaporated. Terrence flipped the covers off his head and lifted himself up on one elbow. A long stream of oaths flowed forth, then melded into a rigid command, "Where'd you find it?"

"It must have fallen off the examination table and landed in one of the drawers. The drawers on that table are really loose, and we have a hard time keeping them shut. I guess one was open and I scooted the last bag off the table into the drawer." An almost undetectable note of contrition laced Barry's words.

The memory of Barry's false accusations ignited an inferno in Terrence's gut. A charge of heat, blistering and hungry, crept up his body. "Listen, you jerk," he snarled. "If you *ever* handle that stuff when you've been drinking, I'll — I'll . . ." *I'll kill you,* he threatened silently.

"Are you going to strangle my brother like you strangled me?" The accusing feminine voice floated from the end of the bed, and Terrence jerked his legs underneath him.

A voice from within screamed that he shouldn't look at her, but a more potent force tugged his wide-eyed gaze straight to the woman sitting a few feet away. Mallory gazed at him just as she had last night and the night before. Her inky eyes, sunken and haunting, drilled twin points of accusations straight into the center of his soul.

"Killer," she hissed like a serpent. Then she repeated the same mantra she had begun in Barry's office. "You're a murderer." Her thin lips curled away from teeth that gnashed in accusation. "You strangled me. You killed me. Murderer!"

"Are you still there?" Cox barked.

"Y–yes," Terrence stuttered as Mallory lifted her hair, heavy and red, away from her shoulders. Scarlet streaks and black bruises marred her neck. Terrence's heart raced, and he groped for every breath. Gooseflesh erupted along his spine.

"Tell him!" Mallory challenged. Her eyes glowed with a fiendish red light. "Tell Barry you killed me, you chicken-hearted fool. Tell him!" Her upper lip twisted in disdain as she repeated the challenge she had tormented him with most of the night.

"What's the matter with you?" Barry demanded.

Terrence slammed the telephone into its cradle and shoved aside the covers. Arms flailing he stepped over a pile of dirt-crusted clothing and stumbled toward the bathroom. A desperate moan erupted from his soul as he rammed open the bathroom door, raced inside, and closed it behind him. Hands trembling, he twisted the lock as a terrified chorus of "no, no, no, no, no" ricocheted off the white-tiled room. In frenzied heat Terrence searched the bathroom, suddenly realizing *his* voice was the source of the horrified screams.

He turned to face the locked door, backed against the sink, and gripped the edge with hands damp and hot. The coolness of the cabinet wood seeped through his boxer shorts as Terrence stared at the doorknob, fully expecting it to jiggle beneath the pressure of Mallory's attempted entry. The knob remained unmoved.

With a broken cry, Terrence turned toward the sink, twisted the cold water handle, and dashed the icy liquid into his face. He stared in disbelief at his hands caked in dark earth. The water streamed from between his parted fingers like rivulets of muddy testimony to his nocturnal wanderings. "Oh, help me. Somebody please help me," he moaned as he relived the fervid clawing at packed earth in the corner of his barn. "I thought it was a dream," he groaned. A horrific thought pierced his mind, *Am I going insane? How do I know what's real?*

He reached for the bar of soap in the dish and twisted on the hot water handle until a warm flow cascaded into the sink. Terrence lathered the soap with frenzied resolve and scrubbed his soil-caked fingernails. After the dirt dissolved down the drain, he lathered his hands once more and rubbed shaking fingers across his tense face. He groped for the hot water handle, reduced the temperature, and splashed away the layer of soap. But the cooler water couldn't peel the guilt from his soul.

Terrence gripped the sides of the sink and peered at the folds of foam the gushing water shoved down the drain.

"Stay away from me, Mallory!" he screamed as fat droplets of water dripped from his nose and chin into the basin. "Do you hear me?" He swiveled to face the door. "Stop it, stop it, stop it!" Terrence lurched at the door and pounded both fists against the center. "You're dead! You aren't real! You can't be!" he bellowed, struggling to hang on to his sanity. The pounding continued until one fist sank into the door and the loud crack of wood breaking accompanied the sting of splinters against the sides of his hand.

The ensuing silence was broken only by Terrence's shallow panting and the continued swish of flowing water. The telephone's demanding ring sent a zip of panic through him. He jumped, stilled, then forced himself to take several deep breaths. *That's Barry,* he thought. Terrence rubbed an open palm across his upper torso, now covered in a thin film of sweat. "He'll just have to talk to the machine," he muttered before pivoting to stare at himself in the bathroom mirror. The haggard man who stared back looked as if he had lived on the street for ten years. The dark bags under his eyes, the red darts across his eyeballs, the sag of his mouth, the ashen lines on weathered skin testified to the powerful presence of Mallory. Six months had lapsed since Mallory's influence had driven him to the brink of insanity.

"Why now?" he growled at his reflection. Finally the phone ceased its noise. Terrence snapped off the running water and waited as Barry's muffled voice floated from the bedside machine.

"Terrence, I know you're there, and I know you're listening!" Terrence imagined Cox's fleshy jaws flapping like the jowls of a bulldog. "I want to take care of the shipment tonight. That way we can keep on schedule next week. Be at the clinic by six o'clock," he commanded. "Everybody should be cleared out by then, so we won't be interrupted. Bye." The phone clicked.

"I'm really sick of you ordering me around," Terrence snarled. He glowered at his own reflection and wondered if Barry even suspected who he was dealing with. "A killer!" His eye twitched. "I *am* a killer." *And Mallory wants me to tell Barry. She's wanted me to tell him for years.* "But I'll never tell. *Never!*" he vowed as he clenched his fists. Mallory's forceful presence pierced his mind, and self-doubt overtook him. *Will Mallory torment me so much that I'll one day blurt out the truth?*

Terrence rubbed his damp fingers against the back of his skull and tugged at his hair, short and stiff. A tremor of panic zipped through his gut.

If Barry were dead, I couldn't tell him. The thought exploded through his being and became a sensible option to a horrid predicament. "That would stop Mallory nagging at me," he whispered as a band of shimmers started in his knees and radiated up his torso.

Terrence lowered the toilet lid and eased onto it. *I could also keep the money from the present deal.* Thoughts of doubling his profit ignited a flicker of greed that swooshed into full flame and devoured his mind. He recalled the night before when his anger spewed forth and there was a glimmer of fear in Barry's eyes. The corners of Terrence's mouth tilted upward, and a surge of power made him feel invincible. A heated, prickling sensation needled his eyes and ushered in the image of the copper-colored necktie he had crammed into the back of his closet 13 years ago. The slip of silk had ended Mallory's life — and it would work on Barry. *That should make Mallory shut up and leave me alone,* he thought as a satisfied smile slithered across his mouth.

Sammie stood by the luggage carousel belt and scanned the crowd for any sign of Victoria. Numerous passengers meandered around the belt awaiting its chugging delivery of their suitcases. Sam glanced over each new face and strained to look down the never-ending hallway that stretched to the airport escalator. The faint smells of hot pretzels and tile cleaner mingled with the chatter of passengers and the bustle of moving baggage.

In the midst of her searching for Victoria, Sam reached for Brett's hand. It wasn't there! Panic grabbed her stomach. Her heart pounded. She searched the crowd, and a startled cry shoved up her throat. Suddenly she remembered Brett was with R.J. She expelled a long sigh, placed her palm over her racing heart, and hunched her shoulders. To underscore her realization, Sam reiterated R.J.'s voice mail message that announced he and Brett had made it to his ranch without a hitch. Thankfully, Sammie was in a meeting and couldn't talk with him. Even the subtle undertones in his voice had rattled Sam's heart. She couldn't imagine what talking to the man would have done. A delicious tendril of expectation flowed through her. *Get a grip!* she admonished herself as she tried to recall all the reasons why she wasn't ready for a relationship. Sammie placed her hand into the side pocket of her black leather bag and stroked R.J.'s braid. Before placing the piece in her purse, she had taken the time to rebraid it and slip another rubber band on the other end so it wouldn't unravel.

I'm acting like a lovesick teenager, she chided herself. She could almost hear R.J.'s satisfied snicker if he found out she carried the braid around.

Her cell phone nestled in her purse played the "charge chant" she had chosen as the designated ring for all the six sisters.

Wonder if that's Victoria? she thought, hoping it would be a teary yet joyful report that Victoria and Tony had kissed and made up.

"Howdy," Sammie said into the receiver.

"Howdy yourself," Sonsee responded. "I can do Texas as good as you can now."

Sammie chuckled. "You're learning, but you're still not quite there. You need to spend a couple more years in Houston before you get it down to a fine art. Keep tryin' though, girlfriend. Your effort is commendable."

"Yeah, yeah, yeah," Sonsee teased. "You're just jealous because you're afraid I'm going to be able to do Texas better than you!"

"In your dreams!" Sammie playfully replied.

The two fell into a round of companionable snickers. "So, you rang?" Sonsee finally asked.

"Yes, as a matter of fact, I did." Sammie eyed a long-legged businessman plowing forward while talking on his cell phone. She hoped he realized she was smack in the middle of his path. "Where have you been?" Sam asked. "I called and left two voice mails."

"Taylor took the afternoon off, and we

took Donny on a little family outing that included a trip to the zoo and a picnic. Donny was absolutely fascinated by the birds. He and Taylor are sound asleep right now." A stifled yawn meandered over the line.

"Sounds like you're headin' that way, too," Sam commented, sidestepping the businessman. He whipped past Sam as if he hadn't seen her.

"I would but I've fooled around here so long that if I go to sleep now I'll be awake half the night. I'm about to wake up those two sleepyheads. What's up?" she added.

"I wanted to ask you how to treat mange."

"What's the matter? Did Brett contract it or something?"

"You're just too funny, aren't you?" Sammie asked through a dry chuckle.

"Well, I try," Sonsee said over another yawn.

Sam instinctively reached for Brett's hand but curled her fingers into her palm instead. "I took my new puppy to the vet this morning —"

"You got a new puppy?"

"Yep! She's a cocker."

"Great! I love cockers."

Sammie rolled her eyes toward the

lighted panels overhead. "It would appear everybody does. She cost me nearly $500."

"If you got her for under five, you got a good deal."

"Actually, I traded in the birds —"

"Birds?"

"It's a long, long story. Anyway, I was at the vet and I saw some white powder in a plastic bag. The vet told me it was a powder used to make a paste for treating mange."

"Hmmm . . . I've never heard of anything like that," Sonsee said.

"Oh?"

"No. As a matter of fact, mange is usually treated with a dip you buy prebottled. What I always carried is called Paramite. You just sponge it on the dogs. It's the same medicine used for ticks and fleas. You can buy it at most any animal clinic."

"R.J. mentioned a dip as well." Sammie nodded and noted a familiar figure striding around a knot of elated Asians hugging each other. Victoria's petite frame and fine-boned features nearly affected Sammie like the Barbie-vet-helper did. She was once again reminded of her increasing collection of fat cells.

"Hello? Have I lost you?" Sonsee's voice cut in on Sam's musings.

"No, I'm still here," she responded.

"So you're saying a *vet* told you this white powder was to treat mange?" Sonsee asked.

"Yes," Sammie agreed.

"What did it look like?"

"Baking soda. About a half pound of it."

A contemplative silence permeated the line.

"I don't feel good about it, Sonsee," Sam admitted. "Something in my gut tells me the man is dealing cocaine. R.J. thinks I shouldn't call the police unless I'm sure. He's also afraid that if the guy *is* dealing cocaine and finds out I'm the one who reported it, then, in his immortal words, I might 'wake up dead.'" Sammie stroked the side of the cell phone.

"Why don't you consult Jac? She'd probably be the best person to give you advice."

"Good idea," Sam said. She waved toward Victoria who responded with a weary smile and a quick wave of her own. "I think I just might do that. But right now, I'm also thinking I'll drive over to the parking lot next to the animal clinic and watch for awhile. You know, see what I can see and all that."

"Will Brett sit still long enough to do that?"

"R.J. took Brett home with him." Sammie eyed Victoria as she stepped toward the lurching luggage belt. "Come to find out, he owns a 50-acre ranch and has a home for troubled boys. The kitchen burned up and he went back to Arkansas for a week to help get everything back in order." She walked toward her friend and stopped inches away. Sammie squeezed Victoria's hand, smiled, and noted her friend smelled like she just stepped out of the Saks perfume department.

"You let Brett go for a week?" Sonsee yelped.

"No, you doofus. I'm going to drive up Friday evening to get Brett. I'll spend a couple of nights in the guest house and come back home on Sunday."

"Sounds really cozy," Sonsee teased.

Sammie thought of the feel of R.J.'s braid against her palm and wondered how cozy it might get. She bit her bottom lip. "Victoria's here," she said instead, winking at her friend.

"She is? Where are you?"

"She came for a visit, and I'm at the airport picking her up."

"Who is that?" Victoria whispered.

"Sonsee," Sammie said and noted that Victoria's precise application of eye

320

makeup didn't hide all the puffiness. "Hey, we'll e-mail you later," Sam continued. She wondered if Victoria knew her days of precise makeup and upscale perfume would probably end when she landed in the maternity ward.

"Okay. Don't have too much fun," Sonsee said through another yawn.

"We'll try not to," Samantha agreed impishly. "We'll make sure to talk about you, though!"

"Please do!" Sonsee exclaimed. "I need all the attention I can get right now."

"Sounds like you need to get out a little more."

"Sounds like you're getting too sassy for your own good. Hey, tell Victoria I said to keep an eye on you!"

"Not on your life!" Sam said.

"Okay, then just try to stay out of trouble."

"Sure thing," Sammie replied. She bid a cheerful adieu, and disconnected the call. Phone still in hand she wrapped her arms around Victoria, who clung to Samantha as if she were drowning. The hug lengthened into a gentle rock that communicated Sam's support like no words could. Victoria sniffled. Sammie gripped her shoulders, backed away, and stared into her hazel eyes.

"Everything is going to be okay," she said without reserve. "You're going to get through this."

Victoria bit her lips and nodded as tears trickled down the sides of her nose.

They moved toward the luggage conveyer belt. Victoria attempted to snag a small black bag that whizzed right past them.

"Wait! I've got it," Sammie crowed. She whipped around a line of people poised to snatch their luggage, cruised down the length of the belt, then grabbed the bag's handle and hauled it to the floor with a swoosh and click. Sammie snapped the handle out, dropped her cell phone back into her purse, and walked toward Victoria.

"Are you having trouble with morning sickness or afternoon sickness or are you —"

"Actually, I'm feeling normal today — *physically.*" Victoria tucked a strand of wayward, curly hair into the weave of her French braid. "I'm just emotionally on low, that's all."

"Hmm . . ." Sammie said. She debated whether to take Victoria on a sightseeing expedition past the vet's office or go straight home. Suddenly she recalled that the parking lot next to the vet's clinic belonged to a burger joint. Perhaps she could buy Victoria dinner while keeping an eye on the clinic. "Want to get a burger on the way home?" she asked.

"Sure. That sounds fine." Victoria fell in beside Sam as they headed toward the escalator that would take them to the parking lot. After walking only a few feet, Victoria gripped Sam's arm and halted.

Sammie raised questioning brows toward her friend, who scrutinized Sam through a speculative squint.

"What?" Samantha asked.

"It's good to see you back," Victoria said with a slow smile.

"Excuse me?"

"You've got the old spark back," Victoria claimed.

"The spark?" Sam thought of the sparks that flew in her office that very morning.

"I don't know. We'll just call it quality X. It's the old Sam — the way you were before you got married. And I've missed her! You're looking great, Sammie!" Victoria's hazel eyes glistened with love and admiration.

Samantha broke into an immediate grin that reflected the warm rush of appreciation gurgling from her soul. Then she rolled her eyes and drawled, "Oh puullleeeze, let's don't exaggerate here. You're starting to sound like R.J. You two ought to start a fan club — I'm sure you could attract all of two members!"

"Now we're getting to the bottom of all this. I know why you've got that spark!" Victoria teased. "Is there something you'd like to share with everyone?"

Sammie paused and looked squarely into her friend's eyes. "Did R.J. call you and give you those lines or what? He says that *all* the time!"

"No!" Victoria said through a sunny smile that momentarily chased away the shadows in her eyes. "But it sounds like you've been talking to him — *a lot!* Maybe even up close and personal?"

"Oh get *outta* here!" Sammie called. She rushed to the escalator and hopped onto the top step. "Last one down's a rotten egg!" she called over her shoulder and maneuvered the suitcase onto the step behind her.

"First one has to eat it!" Victoria responded before claiming a spot six steps above her friend. The two fell into a chorus of laughter that reflected their carefree college days. The time when dreams were still enchanting and promises were yet to be spoken . . . or broken.

Eighteen

Subject: Waiting on Samantha
On Wednesday, 17 Jan 2002 5:53
Mara O'Connor
<mara@oconnor.hhp> writes:

Hi, Colleen! I'm at Samantha's house. Now it's my turn . . . I'm on my Palm Pilot. You aren't the only senior citizen with high-tech equipment. :-)
Are you online? If so, please pray for me. I'm terribly nervous. I've been waiting for Samantha to come home for about an hour. I tried calling the magazine, but all I got was the recording saying it was closed. I wonder if she's working late. Is there a private number that bypasses the answering service? Do you know where she is?

Yours,
M.O.

On Wednesday, 17 Jan 2002 6:17
Colleen Butler
<candt@butler.hhp> writes:

Dear MO,
   I just got your "e." Hopefully by now Sammie's home. I called Rhett in case he might know. He said she called from the airport just after five to talk to Brett. She was there picking up one of her friends — you know, one of the "sassy seven." They've had a girlfriend connection going since college. Rhett said she mentioned stopping for a burger on the way home. Be patient. She's around and will hopefully be home soon.
   There is an after-hours number given to a select few. The number is 214-555-2929.
   Are you sitting down? Sam let Rhett take Brett home with him for a few nights! Can you believe it?! Also, Rhett sounded a little too enthused for something not to be brewing between those two. According to Wanda, Rhett stayed in Sam's office for quite awhile this morning before taking Brett home with him. Wanda also said Rhett cut off his braid and put on a dress shirt. Glory be! Tom is almost as excited as the day Rhett stopped wearing his earring.

Honestly, I still scratch my head and wonder what the two of us did to produce such a wild child. But I think he's settling down now.

Mara, I'm breathing a prayer for you and hoping everything goes well during your visit.

Hugs,
C.B.

Terrence stepped out the back of the clinic and closed the door. He leaned against the doorjamb and took in deep gulps of air. The city smells of car exhaust and hamburgers were a welcome reprieve to the animal odors inside the clinic. He swallowed against his tight throat as his stomach threatened to unload the light supper he'd managed to choke down. Terrence observed his glove-covered hands. Smudges, wet and red, marred the latex and attested to his recent assistance in surgery. Barry had implanted the final bag of cocaine into a German shepherd's abdominal wall. Now all that was left was to wait for the incision to heal so Barry could remove the sutures. After that the entire shipment would be ready to go.

Terrence eyed a lone red bird hopping

along the empty lot that spanned to the busy intersection. A balmy wisp of a breeze mocked the remaining patches of snow that still dotted the city. For the most part, only the spongy earth, damp and oozing, bore witness to their recent kiss with an arctic front.

Swallowing against the bulge in his throat, Terrence tried to erase the images of surgery from his mind. He never had been the iron-stomached sort, especially not after one of his spells with Mallory. Thankfully, she had left him alone the rest of the day, and Terrence had slept peacefully until late afternoon. Rest, coupled with Mallory's absence, made Terrence feel more balanced than he had in weeks . . . Until he watched Barry cut open the German shepherd. While the vet hadn't so much as flinched, Terrence's nausea had increased tenfold with every passing minute. All he could think of was Mallory's reddened neck, her choked cries, the bruises deep and ugly. As soon as Barry tied the last suture, Terrence escaped.

He ripped off the blood-stained gloves, slammed them into the green garbage bin, closed his eyes, and awaited the relaxed state that held the promise of easing his revulsion. He stroked his forehead, beaded in sweat, and rubbed both hands across his rigid features. At last he pushed away from the clinic and meandered around the side. A few more minutes in the cool air would undoubtedly relieve his discomfort. Then he would step back in long enough to grab his jacket and say goodbye.

After his heavy sleep, Terrence decided that getting rid of Barry wasn't the most logical of choices. After all, he was the major contact in the cocaine operation. While getting 100 percent of the profit from the current shipment would be nice, Terrence figured that the most sane choice would be to continue as they had been.

For the first time in 48 hours, Terrence glimpsed the return of his strength of will. He yawned, stretched, and thought about the soft folds of his king-sized bed. Given the wild ride Mallory had taken him on the last couple of nights, he would welcome an early night. Maybe, just maybe, this spell was over for a while and the demon would disappear forever. He gazed up at the sky, darkening from sapphire to blue-black as night crept from one horizon to the other. He peered at his scoured fingernails, and the morning's frenzy seemed as far removed from his psyche now as peace had seemed this morning.

The final fibers of nausea seeped from his gut, and Terrence cut a last cursory glance over the Plano traffic whizzing from one intersection to the next. Yesterday he had cautiously looked for Mallory everywhere he went. With a flash of relief, Terrence realized he hadn't even thought in those terms today.

"It's over," he whispered and reveled in the freedom that swept over him like a refreshing evening breeze. "This spell is finally over." No more crawling skin. No more needing to look over his shoulder. No more sensing that Mallory was hovering nearby, ready to appear at any moment. Terrence shoved wiry fingers into his jeans pockets and hoped he would never endure another episode. The last couple of days had almost cost him his sanity.

Planning to reenter the clinic, Terrence pivoted on his heel but stopped midturn. The first thing that caught his eye was a flash of red hair gleaming under fluorescent lights. Hair the color of Mallory's. As soon as this acknowledgment entered his consciousness, gooseflesh raced up his spine. Terrence, shoulders hunched, searched the burger joint's shadowed parking lot and the lighted intersection in front of the restaurant. The last frontier proved to be the restaurant window — a window where two women sat. One of them, pale yet pretty, had a cloud of curly brown hair that hung loosely from a braid of sorts. The other one had straight locks as red as the flames of Hades.

Terrence's serenity fled as he slipped toward the rim of the jagged cliffs lining a dark sea of confusion. Drawn into a whirlpool and pulled into the unrelenting fathoms, the rev and honks of vehicles blended with the bustle of stores and service buildings to create a mind-numbing cacophony of hissing accusations: *Murderer! You killed me! Did you think you got rid of me for good? Ha!*

As the words beat a relentless tattoo in his pounding chest, Terrence fixed his gaze upon the redhead. The play of the bright lights against evening shadows coated her hair with hazy radiance. His eyes bugged as she flipped her hair over her shoulder. For a wrinkle in time Terrence detected streaks of crimson around a milky-white neck.

After nodding to her companion, the woman nonchalantly glanced toward the clinic and studied the building as if she were memorizing the structure's every crevice. In the seconds that followed, the parking lot lights flickered on and reduced the contrast of brilliance and shadow. Nevertheless, her image remained before Terrence as if she were inches away. Following a lengthy evaluation of the clinic, the woman swept her attention across the parking lot. Finally her gaze flitted to Terrence and stopped.

Air burst from his tight lungs. Terrence held her gaze as silent communication flashed between them. *Mallory . . . Mallory . . . Mallory,* his whirling mind chanted the name as he fell over the edge and tumbled into the cold, dark waters of an unrelenting sea.

While their gaze lengthened, the woman's eyes widened just as Mallory's had the night before. Her lips tightened. She jerked away, then looked back at Terrence. This time those haunting orbs glowed scarlet.

"Oh no, no, no," Terrence begged as the ground pulled him down. Only when the sidewalk ate into his knees did he comprehend he had actually collapsed.

Mallory spoke to her companion, turned her back upon him, and the two bustled from their window vantage. Terrence stared at their vacant booth and heeded the urgent, inward call to swim toward a nearby beach of shifting sand. Reaching the beach, he forced himself to reconnect with the present. Placing trembling hands on taut thighs, he stared at the parking lot's bumpy texture.

"That's not Mallory," he whispered. "It can't be. She's — she's dead." The claim had barely left his lips when a movement from the neighboring lot snared his attention. The redhead and her companion dashed toward a blue Honda parked near the restaurant exit. Mallory tossed a glimpse his way before fumbling with the door lock and sinking inside. Her companion was seconds behind her. The bang of car doors preceded the engine's rev by seconds.

A voice rising from the frothy waves of the illusory sea insisted on one course of action: *Follow her!* Without another thought, Terrence sprang to his feet and raced toward his pickup. Only when he slid across the cool leather did he remember his jacket, but Mallory was pulling him into her wake — Mallory with splendid red hair, eyes that mesmerized and terrified, and a slender neck awaiting his caress. Terrence cranked the engine and leaned over to pop open the glove compartment.

A striped tie in muted hues of rust tumbled forth and plopped onto the floor mat.

He snatched up the strip of silk, wrapped it around his hand, slammed the vehicle into drive, and rolled across the parking lot. As he eased into traffic, he crossed to the lane the blue Honda claimed.

Mallory's taunts, her accusations, her rantings tore through his tormented soul. The emotional tornado whirled up memories of the reasons he'd killed her in the first place. *Mallory hadn't been able to stop the insidious carping then, and now she's stalking me all over town!* His eye twitched. "I almost made a mistake. I almost made a mistake," he muttered with fervid certainty. The traffic moved through a series of green lights, and Terrence kept the Honda in sight. "Barry isn't the one I need to kill — it's Mallory." His hands squeezed the steering wheel while he wiped his other hand on his jeans-clad thigh. *Yes, yes, if I kill her, if I kill her, she'll stop — stop haunting me. Then she'll stop telling me to tell Barry and I can get back to my life.* The sudden roar of the sea's ravenous waves filled his ears and blotted out his connection with reality. He sank into the folds of the inky water's swift tide. The tainted liquid warped every nuance of perception. This time he welcomed the unending rush of tingles that assaulted his senses.

Nineteen

"Do you think he's following us?" Victoria squawked.

"I don't know." Sammie's fingers tightened around the steering wheel. She glanced into the rearview mirror, and encountered a collection of headlights, all of which appeared nearly identical.

Victoria swiveled in her seat and peered behind the car. "I vaguely remember a truck in the parking lot he was in, but I don't know what color it was."

"Blue. It was blue," Sammie snapped, her spine stiff. "And there was a black car too — some kind of luxury model. Maybe a Cadillac or a Lincoln. I'm not sure."

"Why don't we take the scenic route home?" Victoria suggested, her voice unsteady.

"Good idea." Sam cut across traffic to get into the far right lane. Amid angry honking, she hollered, "Hang on!" Sam hung a sharp right and whizzed from the commercial intersection into a lush residential area. Breathless silence filled the cool interior when she pressed the accelerator past her comfort level.

As the houses clicked by, Victoria remained riveted to the view behind. After spanning one long block, Sammie dared glance into the rearview mirror. No vehicle followed. Her fingers relaxed a fraction. She took a deep breath of air laden with the scent of Victoria's delicious perfume. Sam's attention flicked back to the road illuminated by her headlights and the city lamps.

"There's a vehicle behind us!" Victoria yelped.

Sammie's eyes widened. Her foot pressed the accelerator another centimeter closer to the floor. She bit down on her bottom lip. The image of that man in the parking lot swamped her mind. His eyes, wide and glazed, seemed to bore into her as if he knew her, as if she were the bane of his existence, as if she were Medusa with serpents flailing from her scalp.

"Ahh!" Victoria shrieked. "It's a truck!"

"Is it blue?" Sammie insisted.

"He's getting closer!"

Her heart pounding, Sammie already knew the answer to her question. "Hold tight!" she yelled and orchestrated a hard left. Before the vehicle behind had the chance to follow, Sammie took the first right she spotted and found herself in an alley separating two rows of elegant, two-story homes from decades past. She sped past several homes then whirled up one of the open driveways and slammed on the brakes. The tires squealed as she lurched against the seatbelt. She rammed the Honda into park, turned off the engine, and held her breath.

"Duck down, Victoria!"

Silence, chilled and terrified, descended upon the friends — a silence marred only by the distant rev and roar of traffic.

As one, Sam and Victoria lifted their heads to look out the back window for what seemed an eternity. No vehicle entered the secluded alley. At long last Sammie gazed across the shadows toward her friend's pallid features.

"You all right?" she queried.

"Yes," Victoria whispered, her eyes wide.

"And the baby?"

"Everything's okay as far as I can tell. I didn't get jostled all that much. What do you think that was all about?"

"I have no idea. But it was like that man thought I was somebody he knew." Sammie swiveled to face the closed two-car garage.

"It was so weird," Victoria added. "Did you see him fall to his knees?"

"Yes." Sam swallowed against a throat dry and tight. "Victoria . . ." she hedged, "uh . . . there's something I didn't tell you. I —" She clasped the front of her neck as the white powder teetered through her mind. "I put you smack into the middle of a mystery that could be very dangerous."

"Oh no," Victoria breathed. "What are you up to now?"

"The reason I chose that restaurant is because I wanted to spy on the vet clinic in the building that man came out of. I took my puppy there this morning and I think — I think I saw a bag of cocaine. The vet tried to cover it up by telling me it was powder used to make a paste for treating mange." Sammie rested her forehead on the center of the leather-covered steering wheel and closed her eyes. "That's what I was talking to Sonsee about when I picked you up."

"Are you assuming he lied?" Victoria asked.

"That's what I was checking on with Sonsee. I think he did." She started the engine and turned the heater on low.

"Do you think you should call the authorities?"

"R.J. seems to think there's not much they can do right now. And he's worried I'll get into something that might get me hurt. He was once on the edges of the drug scene so he thinks I ought to leave well enough alone. Sonsee suggested I talk with Jac when we get home," Sammie added as the heater's whirring ushered in ample warm air.

"Good idea."

"Let's go home," Sammie said and sat straight.

"Sounds good to me."

Sam flicked on the headlights, put the vehicle into reverse, and eased back into the alley. Soon they were cruising across Plano toward Sam's modest home. Every few seconds Sammie glanced in the rear-view mirror and was increasingly eased by the continued absence of the truck.

"You never asked about Tony and me," Victoria commented when they turned onto Sam's street.

"Yes, I know," Sammie said, reaching to squeeze her friend's cool hand. "I decided you could use some time to relax and enjoy your meal. I also figured you'd talk when you got ready. Obviously I didn't count on that bit of excitement back there."

"Well, I think I'm ready," Victoria said with a sigh.

"Why don't we go inside and make a cup of hot cocoa. We can curl up on the couch and flap our jaws half the night if you'd like."

"You always did have a way with words, Sammie." Victoria giggled.

"I'm a writer. That's what we do best," Sam responded with a grin as she slowed and turned into her driveway. Her headlights illuminated a vehicle next to her house. Sam slammed on the brakes.

"What is it?" Victoria gasped.

"There's a car in my driveway!"

"Yes, I saw it. I just thought . . . I'm not sure I thought anything. I guess it's not supposed to be there?"

"No, it's not!" Sammie prepared to ram the gearshift into reverse, but a tall, lanky woman with auburn hair and glasses emerged from the driver's seat and looked toward her. A woman who appeared lonely and listless in the brightness of Sam's headlights.

"Oh no . . . it's my mother . . ."

"Mallory . . . it's Mallory! I know it is!" Terrence wadded and rewadded the tie in his damp palm as he cruised down Elmwood Avenue. He scanned the row of humble homes in search of a royal-blue

Honda. Even though he'd made the mistake of trailing Mallory too close the first time, fate had smiled upon him. Terrence had spotted Mallory pulling from a street lined with majestic older homes. He had managed to follow at a greater distance, and this time his diligence paid off. He slowed as he neared a small brick home with a Honda parked in the driveway.

Terrence's teeth clamped together and shifted from side to side as he maneuvered past the Honda. "So this is where she's staying when she's not harassing me," he snarled. A knot of fury burned deep within him, a fury Mallory had invoked often in the miserable years they'd been married. The more Terrence contemplated her recent visits, the angrier he became. "You've got a lot of guts, Mal!" he raged. "You'll pay for how you've treated me. Never again will you sit on the end of my bed, follow me around, or disrupt my dates with other women!" He scrutinized the home's entryway and peered beyond the porch's twin rockers. The blinds in the window obliterated any chance for a glimpse inside the home. The silky tie moved beneath the pressure of his fingers as he cruised to the end of the street. Elmwood Avenue eventually came to a "T." After halting at the stop sign, Terrence glanced one way, then the other. The left view offered a cul-de-sac that bordered an empty lot. Terrence steered toward the left, past three houses, and bumped his truck over the curb and into the vacant lot.

His cell phone emitted an annoying chirp, and Terrence stared at the lit up instrument lying in the seat's center. A disturbing scene sneaked onto the edge of his turbulent thoughts . . . a flash of a floppy-jowled man, a blood-smeared canine fast asleep, and a man racing from the room without any explanation. The vision of a red-haired woman sitting near a restaurant's window brought him back to the task at hand. With a flick of his wrist, Terrence yanked up the phone and ended the shrieking. He threw the phone onto the passenger floorboard, put the vehicle into park, and wrapped the tie around his opened hand. As his fist closed upon the silken strands, his spastic lips curved upward.

Twenty

Sammie hovered over the teakettle sitting on her stove top. She stared at the steam billowing from the spout and wondered how long she could stay in the kitchen making tea. Her mother and Victoria sat in the living room exchanging meaningless chitchat. After greeting her mom in the driveway, Sam had given the obligatory hug and fabricated enough surprised delight to be polite. Even though she was caught off guard, Sammie was able to maintain the wall she had erected 22 years before. As far as Sam was concerned, the barrier was there to stay.

Upon entering the house, Sam had asked to be momentarily excused in order to place a call to Jac Lightfoot. She had decided to share everything that had happened regarding the vet and that lunatic in the parking lot to her friend and do whatever the private eye recommended. Although her first gut instinct had been to call the police, she wasn't sure they could do anything about the man in the parking lot or the vet. All she really knew was that the vet had a bag of white powder that looked like a large package of carpet deodorizer. *That will really impress them,* she thought sarcastically.

The phone rang twice before the "leave a message" direction clicked on. Sam left a message and hoped Jac would call back soon.

The man in the parking lot had looked at Sam and fallen to his knees. She could only conjecture that it was he who had followed them. But there was no solid proof they had been tailed. Samantha had learned enough from her experience with filing the restraining order against Adam that the man in the parking lot had done nothing illegal, even if he *had* followed her in his truck.

After leaving the message for Jac, Samantha flitted here and there, straightening cushions, picking up toys, moving breakfast dishes from the table, inventing a million unnecessary tasks — anything other than sitting and having a direct talk with her mom.

She reached for the teapot's handle and moved the kettle to the cabinet where three emerald-colored mugs waited. Sammie filled each mug with water and watched as the bags of herbal tea turned the water raspberry red. She moved each warm mug to the service tray and wondered how long her mother planned to stay.

Mara had been disappointed that Brett wasn't around — disappointed, but not surprised. *It was like she already knew he wouldn't be here.* Sam grabbed a handful of sugar packets from a box sitting near her flour canister and narrowed her eyes. Once again she experienced the uncanny sensation that there was an underground communication network with her as the primary subject. *Somehow my mother always knows my phone number, and obviously she has acquired my address as well.* Tossing the sugar packets onto the brass tray, Sam nabbed three spoons from the silverware drawer, plopped them near the sugar, and picked up the tray.

If I didn't know any better, I'd say Colleen was the culprit. Sammie immediately dismissed the idea. Colleen understood how Sam felt about her mother. "She wouldn't betray me," Sam stated, ignoring the niggling doubt. That very morning she had overheard R.J. teasing Wanda about being a spy for Colleen. The possibility that Colleen would ask Wanda to report to her about R.J. had been gaining credence with every work-related thought. Sam had observed enough of the relationship between R.J. and his parents to figure out that Colleen would never completely stop trying to arrange R.J.'s life for him — despite her claims otherwise. *So, if Colleen would spy on her son, she wouldn't stop at serving as a spy for my mother.* With a frown Sam decided to think about those possibilities at a later date. Right now she needed to gather her energies to get through this visit.

Sam meandered out of the kitchen, stepped onto the edge of the living room carpet, and eyed her mother. When Victoria mentioned her pregnancy, Mara clapped her elegant hands and squealed in delight. Her bulky sweater, woven with silver threads, glimmered in the low lamplight. She leaned toward Victoria as if they were the greatest of friends. Mara's auburn hair emitted a vital glow that framed her creamy complexion in an attractive cloud Sam figured had caused more than one man to do a double take. As she had all her life, Sam wondered how she wound up with such a bright shade of red hair and the scattering of freckles that had obviously skipped a generation.

I wonder if she's dying her hair? Sam thought. The last few times she had seen her mother, she'd debated whether Mara's hair color seemed a bit off compared to what it had been years ago. The mother Sammie remembered used to wear her hair straight, much like the shoulder-length style Sammie now chose. During the summer she'd snatch her hair up in a ponytail and go for a bike ride with her daughters or take them swimming or go on a picnic. Why the mother who had so freely manifested her love had betrayed Sam and Rana was still a great source of mystery. A mystery Sammie didn't even want to delve into.

Sam's eyes watered; her hands trembled. The spoons clinked upon the tray as she blinked against the unshed tears and marched forward. The sooner they got this over with, the better.

"Ah, there's Samantha!" Mara exclaimed, and her straight denim skirt shifted as she leaned forward. "Victoria and I were wondering if we should send out a search party," she teased.

"No . . . I . . . was just waiting for the water to boil." Sammie glanced toward her mother's vivid blue eyes and wondered if others were as awed by her own azure orbs as she was by her mother's. Sammie purposefully broke eye contact and glanced toward one of Brett's green balls lying beside the recliner where Mara relaxed. Images of the ball ushered in thoughts of Brett. Sammie strained to get a glimpse of her watch. Only a couple of hours had lapsed since she'd chatted with her son. But still Sam wondered how he and R.J. were faring.

She set the tea tray on the magazine-laden coffee table, passed a mug to her mother, then one to Victoria who snuggled into one corner of the striped Midwest sofa. Sam picked up a mug and settled into the couch's other corner, the farthest from Mara. She wrapped her fingers around the warm cup, inhaled the aroma of raspberries, and sipped the fragrant liquid.

"This hits the spot!" Mara exclaimed.

"Yes, it's nice for me, too," Victoria said. "This has been a long day." She extended her feet in front of her and rested her head against the back of the sofa.

"Anybody want sugar?" Sammie offered as she retrieved a packet of sugar and a spoon from the tray.

"No, oh no," Mara said with a gentle shake of her head. Her modest hoop earrings glimmered with golden glee as they swayed near her face.

"I'm fine, too," Victoria agreed.

"Okay." Sammie touched her earlobe; she hadn't even remembered to put her earrings on this morning. She set her mug on the coffee table, tore the packet of sugar, dumped it into the tea, and began stirring.

"So, you guys got some snow a few days ago I hear," Mara said.

"Yes, it was quite bad for a while, but it melted soon. You know how the weather is around here," Sammie replied, wincing at her brittle tone.

"We didn't get any snow," Mara said as Victoria cut Sammie a look that said, *Are you going to be okay?*

No! Sammie wanted to scream. *No, I'm not going to be okay!* Instead, she peered into the tea and brainstormed ways to bring the present situation to a close. No inspiration came. Instead, the smell of Victoria's exotic perfume mixed with Mara's lifelong favorite, Opium. Sammie used to beg her mother to let her place a few drops on her wrist when she was a child. Now the fragrance only ushered in nausea and pain. The two perfumes to-gether created a cloying bouquet that made it difficult for Sam to breathe.

As the awkward silence stretched into an ache, Sammie pinched the side seam of her comfortable knit pants and recalled her initial elation over having a few days to herself. She thought of her manuscript, rumpled and stained with chocolate milk. The book, still crammed in her canvas tote, had been dragged from home to office to home so many times Sammie hoped all the pages were still there. She gulped down some tea and eyed the short stack of books in the middle of the coffee table — six novels with her name on them.

Squinting, Sammie tried to remember placing the books on the table. She glanced toward the bookcase, next to the wood-burning stove, and noted the empty slots where her books had been. She stopped herself from dashing a searching glance toward her mother, and then she recalled R.J.'s presence the night before. Perhaps he had perused her bookshelf at some point. The thought of him thumbing through some of her work sent an unexpected warmth through her midsection. A gentle longing urged her to hope R.J. had been proud of her accomplishments.

The telephone's abrupt peal jolted

Sammie, and she struggled not to slosh her tea. Sammie glanced toward Victoria and her mother prepared to apologize for the interruption. Yet the pleading pain oozing from Mara's eyes stopped Sam's words before they spilled from her tongue. For the first time, Sammie caught a glimpse of her mom's heart, bleeding and overcome with regrets. Regrets and agony. Agony and fear. Sammie's breath caught in her throat.

Could the choices Mara made have been as tragic to her soul as they were to Rana's and mine?

The phone rang again, and Sammie tore her attention from her mother to the cordless instrument. Blinking against an unexpected shroud of tears, Sammie clutched her mug, grabbed the receiver, and spoke a hollow "hello" into the receiver.

"Sambo?" R.J.'s voice floated over the line. "Is that you?"

A wave of relief washed over Sammie as she welcomed R.J.'s voice. This phone call would give her a legitimate excuse to step into the other room.

"Oh, hi!" Sammie said with more enthusiasm than she intended. She dashed aside the painful issues that hung between her and her mother and focused upon the call. "Of course it's me, you doofus!" she teased. "I was just wondering how you and Brett were doing." Darting another glimpse toward the stack of her books, she scooted to the edge of the sofa and prepared to stand.

"Wow! I figured it was too much to hope you'd been thinking of me." The ardor in R.J.'s voice reminded Sam of one of those heart-stopping smiles — a smile that usually unleashed a warm comfort, which she could certainly use right now. Sammie longed for R.J.'s presence, for his arms around her, for his strength she could draw from during the stressful visit at hand. Sammie peered toward the kitchen and refused to look back at her mother.

"Hey! Are you still there?" R.J. asked.

"Yes," Sammie said, "just a minute." She covered the mouthpiece and darted a glance toward her mom's hoop earring. She settled her attention on Victoria. "This is R.J. I don't know what's up. Might be something with Brett. Mind if I take the call in my room?"

"No, go ahead," Victoria said. As Mara echoed the agreement, Sammie detected an unexpected glint in her friend's hazel eyes. A glimmer of sympathy, impatience, and mercy.

Sammie broke eye contact, grabbed her mug, and headed for the hallway. Apparently she wasn't the only one who detected Mara's despair.

Terrence crept from the empty lot and back up Elmwood Avenue. The warming temperature that had built all day recessed in the face of the night's chilly arms. Mallory's presence was almost palpable, and Terrence imagined the cold embrace of death. A relentless, forbidding shiver spun around his spine and shimmered to his limbs. As he neared the house, every crunch of his boots brought the promises of freedom and warmth closer.

"Just as soon as I find a window to crawl through . . ." He caressed the tie between his fingers. Yet with every whisper of the silk against his skin, Mallory's baleful wail echoed in his mind. *Murderer. Murderer. Confess or you'll never be rid of me.* The collection of cars and houses and streetlights began a slow spin as a familiar shroud enveloped Terrence's senses. He re-lived those haunting hours when Mallory's piercing eyes filled him with the terror that she was still alive. He compulsively flexed his hands and supressed the compulsion to claw at the yard as he'd assaulted the barn's floor. A chill shook his body, and Terrence was sure he heard Mallory's caustic whispers behind him. He glanced over his shoulder before spinning to face the opposite direction. Knees bent, he waited, rigid and ready.

"I'm sick of you!" he hissed. Raw hatred sent delicious tingles through his heart.

The swoosh of traffic, a distant dog's bark, and the rustle of bare branches beneath a frigid breeze were the only responses. Slowly Terrence realized that Mallory must be watching him from the house. He turned to face the small home with the blue Honda in the driveway. Gritting his teeth, he stalked along the edge of the yard, just inside the shadows, until he neared the side of the house where darkness ruled. He gazed into the shadows and crept to a window. Touching the brick ledge, cold and rough, Terrence peered through the window. A light snapped on. He blinked against the slices of brightness that cut past half-opened blinds; he panted like a winded dog. When his eyes adjusted, he spotted Mallory's slender form entering the room, phone in hand, as if she didn't have a care in the world.

Twenty-One

"Okay, I'm back," Sammie said into the receiver.

"Good. Listen, I'm sorry to bother you again, Sam, but I started thinking about that whole drug business."

"Yes?" The wild chase from the burger joint into the alley crashed upon her, and a rash of gooseflesh broke out along her arms. She frowned at the half-opened blinds covering one of the windows.

"I think I told you wrong on that."

"Oh?" Sammie neared the window, fumbled beneath the polished cotton drapes, gripped the blind's rod, and twisted until the blinds were tight. On an afterthought, Sam inserted her fingers through the blinds and double-checked the swivel lock. All was secure.

"I talked with Larry about it, and we think you should call the police."

"You don't think the vet will discover who I am and come after me?" Sammie asked.

"Larry said that in a criminal investigation, the officers have access to records. If he's involved in trafficking cocaine, there will be electronic transfers that should be enough for probable cause. From there they can issue a search warrant and whatever else they do."

Sammie moved to the other window near her bed, tightened the blinds, then made sure that lock was secure as well.

"Larry says the vet might never link a thing to you. If he's up to his eyeballs in drug trades, there's going to be all sorts of people he could suspect of turning him in. And once the cops have a starting point, they have ways of tracking the whole shebang. If there's a regular record of transactions going down with a source country —"

"Source country?" Sammie lowered herself onto the bed and covered herself with a floral comforter. She felt like an undercover agent in a late-night spy thriller.

"The country where the coke is processed and imported into the U.S."

"I see. And if there's evidence that he's doing financial hokeypokey with somebody from say, uh, Turkey —"

"Yes, you're on."

"How does Larry know all this?" Sam

asked and absently grabbed a tube of apple-scented hand cream from her nightstand. "Was he in law enforcement or something?" She secured the phone between her ear and shoulder, unscrewed the lid, and squeezed a blob into the center of her palm.

"No," R.J. said through a cough. A meaningful silence permeated the line.

The smell of sour apples assaulted her senses as abruptly as R.J.'s silent message invaded her mind. Sammie fumbled with the tube and lid. They slipped from her grip and collided with the taupe carpet. She scrubbed her palms together as she slid down the side of the bed and landed on the floor with a plop. The phone slid from her shoulder, but Sammie managed to catch it and get it back in position. "Are you telling me that I sent my son home with you and your partner in this — this boys ranch is a —"

"That would be a *former* —"

"Drug dealer of sorts?"

"Yes, I guess you could say that," R.J. hedged.

"It's worse than that, isn't it?" Sam demanded.

"Sammie, listen to me!" R.J. commanded. "Larry Tently is a man of God now. I would trust my life with him. Yes, he has done his share of producing and importing cocaine, but —"

"Production of it!"

A long sigh of resignation hissed across the miles. "He was an illegal in Mexico for ten years and was involved in processing the coke."

"They make cocaine in Mexico?"

"They make it in places you've probably never heard of and use people to transport it you'd never suspect. Larry says one of the popular ways they ship cocaine from Mexico to the U.S. now is to hire senior citizens with travel trailers to carry the stuff across the border."

"People like your parents?"

"Exactly — except my parents would never —"

"You can say that again!" Sammie interrupted, imagining the fate of the poor soul who asked Colleen to do anything illegal. Sammie stared at the door of her cherry jewelry case sitting atop her oak dresser. That vet was probably ten years younger than R.J.'s parents. "So what did Larry think about the possibilities of the vet being involved in something like this?"

"He says that some people use dogs to transport drugs all over the place. They can implant it in the animals in all sorts of ways — some of which you do not want to know."

"So it makes sense for a vet to be involved in something like this?"

"Yep. The reason I told you not to call the police this morning is because my gut instinct is to do whatever I can to make sure you stay safe. But the more I thought about it and talked it over with Larry, the more I think that you should call the police. The vet already knows you saw the powder. If it is cocaine, he could get paranoid and check you out."

An ominous silence radiated over the line. Sam's eyes closed as she rubbed her slightly damp palm on the short-piled carpet.

"I wonder if that's why one of the men acted like he knew me."

"Excuse me?" R.J. asked.

"There was a man in the vet's parking lot this evening," Sam said. "I took my friend Victoria to the burger joint nearby because I wanted to see if there was anything peculiar at the clinic. This man came out to the parking lot and looked at me as if he'd seen a ghost. He even fell to his knees —"

"Humph," R.J. grunted. "Maybe that's not so odd."

Sam, caught in the intensity of her predicament, knitted her brows and attempted to decipher R.J.'s meaning. Like the morning dawn creeping upon the horizon, his full meaning illuminated her heart and highlighted the memory of their kiss. Sammie pressed her fingertips between her brows, propped her elbow on her knee, closed her eyes, and imagined R.J. standing inside the gate beckoning for her to come back into the circle of his embrace. She moved deeper into the cavern in her soul, afraid that if she stepped into the open she would hurl herself straight into R.J.'s arms.

"R.J.," Sammie whispered, "I . . ."

"So," R.J. said, his voice thick with satisfaction, "the man was in the parking lot, and —"

"I — I think he tried to follow us home."

"What!" The exclamation boomed against her eardrum.

Wincing, Sammie tilted the phone away from her ear. "I'm not sure, but there was a truck in the clinic's parking lot, and a similar truck followed us down a residential section. I was able to lose him, but —"

"Did you call the police?" R.J. demanded.

"N–no." Sammie shook her head. "I

don't think there's anything they can do, R.J." She raised her hand and leaned her head against the side of the bed. The gold sparkles in the ceiling's textured surface reminded Sammie of the thousands of stars blazing against the magnificent sky the night R.J. first proposed. She gave herself a firm inward shake and forced her mind to focus on the subject at hand. "It's not illegal to look at someone from a parking lot," she continued, "or even to follow them. Really, I'm not even sure he *did* follow us. If it makes you feel any better, I left a voice mail for my friend Jac Lightfoot asking her to give me a call. I thought I'd ask her advice on all this."

"Okay . . . okay," R.J. said absently, "but I don't like you being home by yourself."

"Right now I'm not. Victoria is here. She's spending the night. I think you met her at Adam's funeral. She was the petite one with curly hair. If you put her in a long dress with frills and gave her a lacy umbrella, you'd vow she plopped in straight from 1890."

"Ah, yes. The one who was so ladylike."

"Sometimes she makes me sick," Sammie drawled in teasing timbre.

R.J. chuckled.

"And my mom's here," Sam continued.

"Really?" His one word held a wealth of understanding that brought tears to Sam's eyes. "How are you handling that?"

"Well, I'm sitting in my bedroom talking to you, so I guess we could say I'm not." Sammie reached for the brass alarm clock and cradled the oversized timepiece against her palm. She eyed the motionless second hand and shook her head. The clock had obviously ticked its last hour. She nestled the timepiece against her chest. In emotional terms, the instrument was a priceless heirloom because it was one of the Christmas gifts from her mother a few months before she ran off with O'Connor.

"Sam?"

"Hmm?"

"Is there any way you'd consider driving up here tomorrow morning?" The protectiveness in R.J.'s voice brought Sammie back to her predicament.

"Well," Sam hesitated, "Victoria is here. I can't just ride off and leave her. She flew in all the way from Florida."

"Why did she decide to come tonight anyway?" R.J. huffed.

"She called after you left. She and her husband are . . ." Sammie placed the alarm clock back on the nightstand, picked up the hand lotion, screwed the lid back on, and dropped it next to the clock.

"I see," R.J. responded. "Well, I'm really uneasy here. If I were there I'd probably pitch a tent in your front yard tonight."

Sammie stood and ambled toward the jewelry case. The contrast of R.J.'s sheltering concern to Adam's destructive abuse struck an aching dart of appreciation through Sam's heart. She clambered to the entrance of the dark hole in her heart and teetered between falling back into the shadows and racing forth into the light. Sam tugged on the jewelry case's door, pulled out the bottom drawer, and dug to the very bottom. Beneath a mound of chains she extracted a thin gold band with a tiny solitaire mounted atop it. She hooped the ring over the end of her index finger, curled her hand into a fist, and pressed her fist against her chest. The ring, like the clock, represented heartache and loss. Loss and loneliness. Loneliness and betrayal.

Oh, Jesus, help me! The plea resounded from the depths of the cavern and echoed through the ebony crevices carved into Sammie's soul in more years than she dared even guess.

"Sambo?" R.J. prompted.

"Yes," she rasped and squeezed her eyes tight. "I'm still here."

"Why don't you go ahead and call the police?" he suggested as if he were afraid she might not agree. "At the very least they should be patroling your neighborhood tonight."

"Yes. Okay. That sounds l–like the best thing to do." She opened her eyes and observed the diamond that winked at her from the tip of her finger.

"And, if you don't mind, please call me before you go to bed and first thing in the morning."

"Sure, no problem," Sam agreed. She stroked the top of the diamond. R.J. had told her he had cashed in some savings bonds his grandfather had given him in order to buy the ring. He and Grandpa Butler had been "two peas in a pod," according to Colleen. To listen to Colleen talk, Sam wondered if Grandpa Butler had grown a braid. He had died just before Sammie married Adam, and she figured R.J.'s ability to fund a boys ranch came through an inheritance.

Sammie reached for her black leather purse sitting on the end of her dresser. She extracted the braid from the side pocket, slipped the ring over it, and looped the strand of hair until the ends touched. She tucked the ring and braid into a drawer in her jewelry box. Sam pondered the location of her child, now on a ranch with troubled teenagers and a former drug lord.

"R.J.," she said without a trace of leniency, "are you *sure* Larry isn't —"

"He's now an ordained minister, Sammie," R.J. stated. "He's been straight for more than 15 years. Will you trust me this once?"

Sammie sighed and rubbed her forehead.

"Trust isn't something that comes naturally with me — not any more. And we're talkin' about the person I love more than I love my own life. I'm a mom, R.J., let me act like one, okay?" she challenged softly as a thread of anxiety plagued her heart.

"Okay, okay," he agreed.

"Brett's doing okay?"

"He and that puppy are connected at the hip, and he doesn't have a care in the world."

"Good. Is the puppy much better?"

"Yes. She's perking up a little and showing some improvement."

Sammie became aware of how her house seemed unnaturally quiet. No kiddy videos blaring from the living room. No wild parakeets squawking and swooping. No puppy yaps into the wee hours.

"I guess I miss Brett more than he misses me," she said through a wobbly grin.

"That's what they always say."

"Well, okay, well . . . I–I probably should go now," Sammie said, trying to sound much braver than her mamma's heart felt. "I'm sure Victoria and my mother are wondering if I got swallowed up or something." Sammie slid the jewelry drawer closed and tapped the cabinet's door in place.

"Right. I understand. Oh and Sammie?"

"Yes."

"I love you." The words stretched out like a treasure long hidden from human eye but untarnished by time.

The unexpected proclamation wrapped around Sam's heart like golden twine, revealing R.J.'s longing to join their hearts. She pressed her lips together and steeled herself against the inevitable sting in her eyes.

"And I love Brett!" R.J. added with equal fervency.

Sam sniffled and her hand tightened on the phone.

"I've loved you for years, Sambo." The

endearment caressed her mind and promised to ease her tattered heart. "I never stopped loving you. Even — even when . . ." The obvious words remained unsaid as his next calm but firm proclamation came. "And nothing's going to change my love for you."

"You said n–no pressure," Sammie warbled, as if they were still on last night's terms.

"This isn't about pressure," R.J. said quietly. "It's about my heart."

The phone clicked in Sammie's ear. She pressed the off button, laid the receiver on her dresser, and covered her face with both hands. "Oh, Lord, please help me," she breathed against the palms that still smelled of tart apples. "I'm not ready. I know I'm not. But Brett . . . there's Brett to consider." The last several months replayed in Sam's mind like a movie in slow motion that highlighted every hint of adoration cloaking her son's countenance the minute R.J. Butler stepped into a room or affirmed Brett.

"This isn't just about me — not by a long shot," Sammie whispered. "Brett needs a father so much." Sam uncovered her face and stared into the mirror. Her eyes were so much like her son's. "And, little tiger," she continued as if she were talking to Brett, "I *do* love you more than I love my own self. *I really do.* I'd do anything for you, even if it means . . ." Sammie's voice trailed off. She examined her bloodshot eyes in the dresser mirror and dotted at the corners until all signs of tears were erased.

Sammie reopened the jewelry case, tugged on the bottom drawer, and extracted the braid. Absently she dug a rubber band from her purse and tied the braid ends together. Samantha chuckled under her breath as she recalled R.J.'s chewed-up hair. But the laughter died in the face of his sacrifice.

"You really chopped this off for me, didn't you?" she whispered, shaking her head in amazement. The upcoming weekend loomed both promising and daunting. A delicious thread of anticipation wove around her heart, and a mild tightness followed in its wake. *I wonder if he'll kiss me again?* she mused, then giggled. Sam pressed the braid against her lips. In the wake of the giggles, a wave of nausea washed over her. More kisses would lead to a request for commitment. A commitment would lead to marriage. Marriage would lead to physical intimacy.

Her throat tightening, Sammie shoved the braid back into the drawer, slammed it shut, and crashed the door into place.

"All I need to worry about right now is getting through this evening," she reminded herself. *R.J. isn't until this weekend. My mom is now. I'll worry about R.J. when I see him.* Samantha squared her shoulders, schooled her features into a disinterested mask, picked up the phone, and headed back to the living room.

Terrence stuffed the necktie into his jeans pocket and crept to the back of the house. He attempted to open every window he encountered. So far, none budged. Winter's frigid breeze mocked the earlier warmth and sent an icy stab straight down his back. His boots created a mild crunch and swish as they settled against spongy earth covered by dried grass. The tantalizing smell of grilling meat was evidence that somebody in the neighborhood would soon enjoy a feast.

As Terrence approached a glassed-in room that protruded off the back of the house, he narrowed his eyes and tried to detect exactly where the door was or if there were windows that opened. He stopped within inches of the sunroom and peered inside. A soft glow radiated from within the house and illuminated the room decorated in wicker and plants and frills. He inched back from his perusal as his unsteady fingers trailed a window ledge. Terrence discovered the affixed storm windows didn't slide up.

Smothering a growl, he stepped around the back of the sunroom and approached a glass door. Terrence sidestepped a shovel propped against the house then wrapped taut fingers around the screen door handle. He pressed the button; the door remained steadfast. He eyed the shovel and considered prying the door open with the garden tool. While mulling over his next move, Terrence cupped his hands around his eyes and gazed into the sunroom.

This time he noticed someone sitting in one of the wicker chairs. Someone with fiery red hair and pale skin. Someone whose glowing eyes, livid as burning coals, stared at him in raging accusation. *Murderer!* Her bluish lips flexed around the word, spitting it out hard and low. *You murdering swine.*

The roar of crashing waves filled Terrence's mind. He clutched the sides of his head, opened his mouth, and let out a gurgling protest. Mallory stood and approached the window in front of her husband, and peered down at him. The blazing heat from her eyes sent a firebrand deep into his soul.

"No . . . no . . . no," he whispered. Terrence tried to run but Mallory's hatred formed a barrier he couldn't cross. Like a man caught in an electrical surge, he wobbled and thrashed and struggled for control in the maze of terror. The only constant was the deliverance promised by Mallory's demise.

With a determined grunt, Terrence broke Mallory's invisible grip. He lurched backward, stumbled, and crashed to the cold earth. His shoulders and elbows mashed into the spongy ground as a swoosh of air burst from his lips.

Terrence's eyes popped open and he scrambled to sit up. He scrutinized the sunroom. Mallory had disappeared. He pulled his legs to his chest, wrapped his arms around them, and rested his forehead on his knees. As he rocked back and forth, a groaning chant spilled from his icy lips: "She's never going to leave me alone. She's never going to leave me alone." Terrence wadded a clump of earth in his hand; he scrubbed his palm against the grit. He thought about the phone call this morning, about Mallory taunting him to tell his brother-in-law, about his pounding on the door and demanding that she leave him be. "I can't take any more of this. I've got to do something!"

His own words pierced his psyche and his desperation became determination. Terrence raised his head and stared toward the sunroom as the last vestiges of the storm-tossed sea ebbed from his mind. Molten lava coursed through his veins, radiating from his midsection to his extremities in a rush of fury that invaded his senses. The night's chill no longer held him fast. He sank both hands into the spongy soil, and the dirt caked beneath his fingernails. He swallowed against a tongue thick and dry. Sweat, warm and profuse, dotted his upper lip and forehead as he glared at the sunroom door.

"I have to get in there," he vowed. "I've got to stop Mallory before Barry finds out. I've got to!" Terrence eyed the shovel propped next to the back door.

Twenty-Two

Samantha eased down the hallway, cordless phone in hand. She racked her brain for another chore to perform that would appear appropriate yet keep her away from the living room. The last thing she wanted to do was sit in the corner of the couch again and chat about the weather with the woman who had betrayed her. Sam neared the edge of the living room, eyed her tea mug cooling on the coffee table, and decided it probably needed a microwave zap. *Maybe Mom and Victoria would enjoy a warm up too,* she rationalized. Taking another step, Sam encountered a scene that shocked her. Victoria, hands twined, was leaning toward Mara, sharing teary-eyed confessions. Mara, engrossed, gripped Victoria's tense fingers and nodded. The lamplight's ethereal beams cast a gauzy glow upon the cozy setting, and the faint scent of raspberry tea hung in the air. Sammie halted in the shadows and strained to hear Victoria's tremulous voice.

"I'm so ashamed," Victoria said, her voice low and quiet. "I — I don't know what came over me. It's just that —" She swallowed and gazed at the floor. "Th–there he was and there I was and — and —" She covered her face. "It's so awful. I've always played by the rules. . . ."

"Has there been an affair?" Mara prompted.

Sammie swallowed the gasp that bulged up her throat. She tried to imagine Victoria "the perfect" Roberts involved in an illicit affair. She could only arrive at one conclusion: *That is ludicrous! Victoria would never —*

"No, oh no." Victoria shook her head so adamantly that Sam wondered if her French braid would come undone. "No . . . we . . . we've never even kissed."

"But there has been somebody else?" Mara asked, her voice gentle but knowing. A hint of grief filled her eyes.

"J–just somebody — somebody I've —" Victoria hesitated. "Someone I seem to be finding myself attracted to." Victoria's cheeks flushed crimson and her eyes grew glassy. She covered her face with her hands; then she looked back at Mara. "He's — he's actually . . . I'm pretty sure he doesn't suspect that I'm having this problem." Victoria groped for her purse and pulled out a packet of Kleenex. "He's a single man at our church. He's actually the choir director," Victoria continued. "And I think he has a girlfriend. It's just that my husband, Tony, doesn't seem to really care anymore, and I — I — here I am pregnant, and —" Victoria touched her abdomen, and a broken wail ripped from her throat. She hunched forward as if trying to disappear. "This is so shameful," she squeaked out. "I don't even know what possessed me to tell you. I — I — if my friends found out they'd think I was the most wanton woman on the planet."

Sammie almost rushed forward to reassure Victoria that that comment was leagues from the truth, but she was stopped in midstride when Mara spoke.

"I know exactly how you feel," Mara soothed. "I've been there." She lifted a strand of Victoria's hair away from her tear-dampened cheek and caressed the side of her face.

Discomfort twisted through Sam's heart — a discomfort that suggested she didn't like her mother bestowing such attention upon Victoria. *I'm jealous!* Sammie thought, and her fingers flexed against the cordless phone. *But Mom never offers me that kind of affection!* she defended, and then looked at the floor as the years unrolled in her mind. Years when her mother had attempted to move in closer. Years when Sammie had purposefully kept her at a distance.

"Do you have any other children?" Mara prompted. Sam's attention snapped back to the living room.

"N–no." Victoria dabbed at her cheeks. "This is going to be our first." Victoria hiccuped then cried, "Oh, what am I going to do?"

Mara's auburn hair, cropped in feathery fullness, glistened as she continued to nod. "My advice to you is to do the best you can to make your marriage work. I'm talking from experience here. When I left my first husband, he had so closed me out that I thought I was going to shrivel up and die. Then a man came along who made me feel like a million bucks. I — I thought I had met the man of my dreams." Mara lifted her hand as if she were announcing royalty. "I lost my head to the point that I even abandoned my own daughters." A mask of despair and self-contempt settled on Mara's expertly made-up face. She seemed to age ten years in 30 seconds.

Sammie raised trembling fingers to her compressed lips and realized that the tears pooling in her eyes were cascading down her cheeks.

"My lover told me that once we settled into his mansion in Australia we could send for my girls. I really thought that would happen." Mara's voice broke, and Victoria riveted her gaze upon the elder woman. Her own tears ceased, and her delicate sniffles mingled with Mara's stifled sobs.

Sam bit down on her lip and swallowed against her quivering throat. All these years she had been so caught up in her own pain she hadn't even considered that her mother might have also suffered pain and regret.

"Now it's been more than 20 years, and no matter what I do I can't seem to get through to Sam. And — and Rana — Rana got involved in the wrong crowd and no one knew where she was for years." Mara lifted both hands, obviously overwrought to the point of breaking. Her diamond rings flashed in the dim light. Diamonds that Sam's dad could have never given her. Diamonds that were a cheap trade for the treasure of a family that stayed together regardless of life's storms.

Silence engulfed the room like a gloomy mist rolling inland through the valleys of heartache. Sammie stifled her rapid breathing that she was sure could be heard for miles. The emotions from wretched, dreary nights when she sobbed into her pillow burst forth from her scarred heart. Like a stream of scalding water traveling a vein in the earth's hardened crust, the pent-up emotions snaked their way to the surface. Sam clutched her midsection, tightened her facial muscles, and clamped down her spirit to rein in the surge that demanded liberation. But Sammie's self-control, fragile and bruised, was no match for the might of the emotional geyser that began to spew forth with ferocious force.

A cacophony of sobs exploded from Sam so fiercely that she barely recognized her own voice. She dropped the cordless phone, slammed into the wall, and slid down until she crashed to the floor. The years peeled away, and Sammie was once again 12 — 12 and in desperate need of her mother.

"Why did you do this to us?" she wailed. "How could you? We need you, mommy! We need you! Where are you?" And mingled with her own weeping were the memories of Rana's wails. Rana, a little girl cast off by her own mother. Rana, a soul still lost at sea. Sammie covered her face as her sobs turned to moans of a spirit bereft and alone . . . alone and tormented . . . tormented and tattered.

Warm arms descended around Sammie. Arms that were loving and caring and created for hugging Sam. Arms whose touch she hadn't enjoyed since she was a child. Comforting arms of a mother who loves her child.

"Oh, Sammie," Mara groaned, coughing over a bucketful of sobs. "Oh my sweet, sweet little Sam. I am so sorry. I was such a fool — a total fool. I . . . oh, Jesus, help — help her know how much I love her!"

And for the first time since Mara had walked out, Sammie reached for her mother. She clung to the one who had given her life. Mara's torrent of tears mingled with Sam's. Breathing in great gulps of air, Sam was whisked to a scene from the closet of reminiscence — an elegant, auburn-haired lady indulgently dabbed costly perfume on the wrist of a delighted little girl, who twirled around the room as if she were a princess. For the first time in years, the smell of Opium didn't invoke nausea.

As the mother–daughter storm abated, Mara stroked Sammie's hair just as Sam had stroked Brett's thousands of times. "Oh, Samantha," Mara soothed. "I — I love you so, so much. Is there any way you can even begin to forgive me?"

The ready nod posed itself before Sammie even had the chance to resist. In response, Mara bestowed a light kiss atop her daughter's head.

"Rana called today," Mara whispered.

"Rana?" Sammie pulled back and looked her mother squarely in the eyes. Mopping her drenched cheeks, Sam asked, "Is she okay?"

Mara, her eyes glistening like exquisite blue sapphires, nodded and laughed. "She's going to come for a visit tomorrow. I — I was wondering if you would like to join us as soon as you can get away?"

A new flood of tears accosted Sammie, and she propped her head upon her mother's shoulder. "You know I'll come," she whimpered. "I've prayed for Rana so much."

"I know. I know. And I — I've prayed for both of you. We'll have our own little reunion, okay?" Mara bestowed another kiss along Sam's hairline.

Sam pulled away, dabbed at her eyes, and wished for one of Victoria's tissues. "Yes, that would be good," she agreed. "Very good," she added with a smile.

★ ★ ★

Victoria dumped the remainder of her herbal tea down the kitchen sink. Through a curtain of tears she watched as the drain gulped the red liquid with one great slurp. Hands trembling, she glanced toward the other two mugs she'd retrieved from the coffee table. She decided to save the tea in case Sam and her mother wanted some for later.

As the low mother–daughter conversation filtered from the nearby hallway, Victoria shook her head in wonder. "It's just so beautiful," she whispered, grabbing a kitchen towel and shoving it against her lips. The towel's sour odor and stiff folds assaulted her senses. "Yuck!" Victoria exclaimed, yanking the towel away. She eyed a pile of soiled dishcloths not far from the place she'd snagged this one. *Sam really needs a housekeeper or something,* she thought and shook her head. *She's so behind.* Victoria slapped the offensive scrap of cloth on top of the others and looked at the breakfast dishes piled on the kitchen counter.

She checked the dishwasher, which was full of clean dishes. Without another thought, Victoria turned on the water, adjusted it one level lower than scorching, plugged in the stopper, and squirted a generous dollop of dish soap under the hissing stream. She glanced toward the plates and cups and bowls, replete with caked-on food, then turned the bottle upside down again and squeezed hard and long. Satisfied, Victoria plopped the soap bottle on the sink ledge next to a large yellow sponge and filled the basin half full of dirty dishes. When the water neared full, she snapped off the tap, snatched up the sponge, and plunged her hands into the hot depths.

As she washed, her own problems rose to the surface. Victoria pressed her tongue against the inside of her top teeth and forbade herself to cry. She started crying anyway. The tears, warm and salty, dripped into the suds with the pitter-patter of a gentle rain. *Did Sam hear my confession to Mara?* The instant she had realized Sam was present, Victoria nearly melted in embarrassment. When Mara rushed to Sam's side, Victoria had jumped to her feet, wrung her hands, and wobbled on the precipice of mortification.

"I wish I could just disappear," Victoria whispered. "I know Sam must have heard me. What is she going to think?" Victoria rolled her eyes toward the fluorescent light and allowed the teardrops to stream down her neck. She thought of Tony and her hands stilled as she relived the fight they had gotten into this morning. When he arrived home his first thoughts were for physical intimacy. Victoria, piping hot with resentment, had wanted anything but sex. With her back stiff she had coldly rejected his advances and slammed into the bathroom. Tony, frustrated and confused, pounded on the door and demanded an explanation. From there everything had gone downhill. They both exploded and hurled insults and voiced their disillusionments. Victoria had been shocked. She never imagined that Tony was as disenchanted with her as she was with him.

After several minutes of yelling through the bathroom door, Victoria had thrown open the door for the showdown.

"All you ever think about is sex!" she accused.

"Well, I've about decided you never think about it," he returned, his gray eyes crackling. "Or me!" he added. "Or the fact that I have needs here, too!" Tony shook both hands toward the ceiling. "What's the deal with women, anyway? It's like — like you scorn men for having sexual needs. Do you think men have a choice regarding their sex drive?" He placed his hands on his hips and leaned forward as if he were preparing to lunge into battle.

Flinching, Victoria stumbled back. "Well, I've got needs, too! You never even talk to me, Tony. And the only time you show any affection is when you want me to perform for you. It's like I'm equipment you only use when *you* feel like it. You are living in your own world now, and I don't feel welcome anymore!"

"I tried to get you to go fishing with me, but you wouldn't!" he challenged, his fair hair a stark contrast to his reddening face.

"But I'm pregnant!"

"You weren't last year," he hollered. "Or the year before that — or even the year before that. How many years has it been since you graced *me* with *your* presence?" He jabbed his index finger into the center of his chest.

"Well, how long has it been since *you* bothered to even think about buying me flowers or taking me to a movie or —" Her weeping increased and sobs tumbled out like rocks on a slippery slope. Victoria covered her face and stumbled backward until she bumped into the wall.

"This is just great!" Tony growled.

Victoria's head snapped up.

"Just great!" Tony stuffed his T-shirt into

the waistband of his jeans. "Now you're going to start bawling and try to make me feel bad for being a man."

"That's *not* what I'm doing!" Victoria groaned. She tried to stay the tears, but they refused abeyance.

"Whatever!" Tony snarled, and he marched toward the front door.

"Where are you going?" she demanded.

"It's none of your business," he barked.

The door slammed with a resounding boom.

By five o'clock Victoria had arrived in Dallas. And now she was scrubbing Sam's dishes with fierce determination. Victoria wiped at her tears with the sleeve of her sweater and wished she could stop her interminable crying. She flipped up the water lever in the next sink and began rinsing the soapy dishes. With every plate she stacked in the dish drainer, Victoria's fury mounted. *I don't know why I ever married that man in the first place!*

Then she remembered their baby. Victoria snatched a clean dish towel from one of the drawers, dried her hands, blotted her face, then settled her fingers against her abdomen. A helpless, innocent life had begun inside her. A life that needed a mother and a father.

What am I going to do?

A faint bumping at the back of the house sliced through her internal turmoil. Victoria frowned and wondered if it might be an animal. The longer she listened, the more purposeful the sound became — as if someone were trying to get in. Victoria gripped the side of the sink and held her breath. *Surely not,* she thought. But her denial didn't dissipate the thudding. In fact, it grew more intense, more determined, more persistent. Until, at last, a huge bang reverberated throughout the house.

Twenty-Three

Sammie jumped and stared at her mother.

"That must be Victoria," she said. *Why would she be beating around in the sunroom? She is pregnant,* Sammie reminded herself. *Yeah, but pregnant women do weird things.* She stroked away her tears, stood, and offered a hand to Mara, who gripped Sam's hand and rose to her feet.

"Sammie?" Victoria's voice, quivering and panicked, beckoned from around the corner.

"What's up?" Sammie stepped out of the hallway and faced her friend, whose wide eyes and pale cheeks signaled panic. "What's the matter? Did you knock something over in the sunroom?"

"I haven't *been* in the sunroom," Victoria hissed. She leaned closer to Sammie and gripped her hands. "I've been doing the dishes."

Sam and Mara exchanged a momentary glance. Samantha scrutinized the open doorway that led to the back of the house.

Heavy footfalls barely drowned out the echo of her heart's fierce pounding. The tall, thin man who had watched her in the parking lot burst into the room and halted. In one breathless moment, he glared at Sammie with malicious intent. His crazed, green eyes bore into hers, daring her to make one false move.

A cry of protest gurgled up Samantha's throat.

Mara took several steps forward. "Get out of here!" she demanded, her trembling voice belying her bravado.

Victoria ran in place as if she were stomping a mouse. She belted out a blood-curdling scream that made Sam's ears ring.

The intruder focused on Sammie and pulled a necktie from his pants pocket. He lunged forward shrieking, *"I've got you now, Mallory! You've hounded me for the last time!"*

Another screech erupted from Victoria, and a jolting scream scraped along Sam's throat and ricocheted off the walls. A wave of heat roved her body as fear took over and hurled her into a surreal nightmare. Her shocked mind conjured up memories of Adam chasing her down a hallway and cornering her in the bathroom. But this was no dream. The man racing forward was the weirdo from the parking lot. In a flash Sam recalled the time last summer when Jac had knocked her abusive husband flat with a couple of TaeKwonDo kicks. Sam thought about trying a move or two, and then dismissed the idea as ludicrous. She'd probably fall flat on her backside.

Run! a practical voice urged. Sam whirled around and raced down the hallway. Her heart hammering, she hurled herself toward the bathroom. The short corridor stretched like a warped passage in a mirror maze. As the man's footfalls slammed behind her, a wail burst from her lungs. This man's ragged breathing raked along Sam's spine. Her lips quivering, she swallowed against the terror bulging up her throat.

"Stop, Mallory! You can't get away from me now!"

Cold sweat covered Sam from head to toe. She coughed and drew a panicked breath into burning lungs.

Footsteps pounded closer and fingernails left a burning trail along her shoulder. Sam screamed as she slammed into the bathroom and tried to close the door. But the psycho was too close. The door smashed against the bathroom wall as he lunged inside. Samantha stumbled backward, and her scream ricocheted off the tile. She was cornered and beyond hope.

"I've gotcha now!" the man snarled. He raised the copper-colored necktie, and his eyes glittered with insanity.

"I'm not Mallory!" Sammie yelled, and the power of her voice burned her throat.

A war cry erupted from the bathroom doorway, and Mara raced in holding an iron skillet over her head. Mouth gaping, the man began to pivot. Mara didn't give him time to face her. She pressed her lips together, sucked in a deep breath, and crashed the iron skillet smack against his temple! The resulting thud, dull yet forceful, sounded like the impact of rock on watermelon. The intruder's eyes rolled back in his head. He emitted a garbled cry and collapsed to the floor in an unconscious heap.

Sammie held her breath and stared at her mother, whose face was drawn into a furious mask. Mara raised the skillet over her head again as if preparing to pummel him whether he stirred or not.

"I called the police!" Victoria yelled from the hallway.

"Good! He's down." Mara bent over and snatched the tie from his limp hands. "Let's tie him up before he wakes up!"

Mara dropped the skillet atop a clump of rumpled towels sprawled on the floor. "Help me roll him over. We'll get him face down, and tie his hands behind his back."

"S–sure," Sam agreed as a band of tremors wobbled from her legs, up her torso, and overtook her arms. She smacked down the toilet lid, collapsed onto the fuzzy cover, and laid her face in her hands. Sammie took in several deep breaths and tightened her gut as the real-life nightmare replayed in her mind. No tears came this time — only a wave of gratefulness to her mother. While Mara might have walked out on Sam during her adolescence, she had certainly been there tonight when Sammie might have very easily been killed. She raised her head and eyed the unconscious man who lay near her feet. Her momentary repose was overcome by a new onslaught of fear. *What if he wakes up?* Goosebumps burst across her body and she shuddered.

Mara cut a sharp glance at her daughter.

"Are you okay?"

"Just scared half crazy, that's all," Sammie said.

"Here, let me help," Victoria offered as she whisked into the room.

"But you're pregnant," Sammie protested.

"Maybe if we all pitch in . . ." Mara left the rest unsaid as the man moaned. The three exchanged intense glances, then jumped to the task. In minutes, they bound the man's hands and secured his feet with an extension cord Sam scrounged up.

"That ought to hold him tight until the police come," Mara declared as she tested the knots for one last time.

On the heels of her words, a faint siren penetrated the night.

The man stirred against his bonds and groaned out a faint, "Mallory . . . Mallory . . . no . . . no!"

"Let's get out of here," Victoria declared as she stumbled toward the door.

Sammie wasted no time following her, and Mara was close behind. As the three women moved into the hallway, the invader thrashed against the floor and released a protesting cry as wild and hair-raising as a panther's scream.

The three women huddled in the hallway as the man's protests grew louder.

"Stop it! Stop it! No! I won't tell! I won't! Barry, where are you? Tell your sister to leave me alone!"

Sammie's blood chilled, and a tight knot of tension claimed her chest. She peered at

Victoria and then at her mother. "He's crazy," she whispered as the siren grew so loud it sounded as if the police car was in the living room.

All three lurched up the hallway, and Sammie raced to the front door. Snatches of red lights flashed through the pencil-thin gap in the drapes, and the deafening siren came to an abrupt halt. Sammie wrestled with the deadbolt, and then hurled the door open. A knot of police officers were deploying around the house.

"We caught him!" Sammie yelled. "He's tied up in the bathroom down the hall!"

"Mallory! . . . I'll tell him, Mallory!" Terrence's shrill raving pierced the air.

"Sounds like we've got ourselves a live one," a stout policeman drawled as five officers rushed toward the bathroom.

"Are you ladies okay?" the first cop on the scene asked. His kind, dark eyes and capable hands, the color of sepia, radiated security and assurance.

The knot eased in Sam's chest. "Yes, we're fine considering all that's happened," she answered.

"Not sure how our visitor will be, though," Mara added with a wry smile. "I whacked him over the head with an iron skillet."

"I guess you're a 'bad news' mamma!" Victoria quipped over a stressed giggle.

"No, she's a *good* news' mamma!" Sammie corrected. She reached for her mother's hand. Mara squeezed Sam's hand as pools of unshed tears filled her eyes.

The poignant moment was swept away by the loud crashes coming from the bathroom. The ranting paused for only a moment, and then continued with a desperate edge. "I killed her! Barry, I strangled Mallory. Barry, I killed your sister. You understand though, right? She was always causing trouble. I had to do it, Barry. I had to!"

Terrence's belligerent rants echoed across the living room. Sammie crossed her arms and tried to resist the shiver that danced along her nerves. The police officer asked the women to step to the side and strode toward the commotion in the hallway. Surrounded by officers, the intruder soon appeared. He squirmed against the handcuffs and fought every step; his wild gaze darted around the room. His glazed eyes focused on midair. He stopped, pointed toward the fireplace, and shrieked, "It's her! It's her!"

The determined cops shoved him toward the front door. Terrence turned his attention to one of the officers.

"Can't you make her go away? It's her fault! Mallory, leave me alone!" His words bounced off the living room walls as his haunted stare penetrated Sam's defenses.

The blood slowly drained from Sam's face. Her lips grew cold and stiff. Her knees locked. She couldn't tear her gaze from his.

"There she is again!" he yelled, his eye twitching and a thin stream of sweat trickling down his temple. "I hate you, Mallory!" he hollered one last time. His lips flexed against yellowed teeth, but no sound came out.

Sammie, numb yet trembling, stumbled backward but was steadied by the strength of Mara's grip. The officers maneuvered the protesting man outside. A car door banged shut a few minutes later.

The policeman with dark eyes tugged Sam toward the edge of the living room and nudged her onto the sofa. She crossed her arms and rocked with the jerky rhythm of the terrified. Victoria, her face drawn, closed the door. Mara sank onto the couch beside Sam.

"That man he mentioned, B–Barry . . ." Sammie stuttered and ceased her rocking.

"Yes?" the officer prompted.

"I — I think I saw cocaine in his office this morning."

"Pardon me?"

Sammie fixed her attention on the officer's name tag. The metallic pin proclaimed he was P. Wilson. "I'm almost positive I saw cocaine in his office. It's the Cox Veterinarian Clinic," Sammie explained. "The vet told me it was a white powder used to make a paste to treat mange, but mange is usually treated with a dip."

"Yes, I know," Wilson said with a nod. "How did this fruitcake play into it?" He asked, jerking his head toward the front door.

Sammie, overtaken by an onslaught of chills, resumed her rocking and grappled with where to start.

"We went to the restaurant next door to the Cox Clinic," Victoria supplied as she sat down on the other side of Sam and reached for her hand. "Sam said she wanted to watch the clinic to see if she could spot anything strange. Th–that man," Victoria pointed toward the door, "came out of the clinic and saw Sammie sitting in the restaurant. He stopped and stared at her. We both got the creeps and decided to leave. We were afraid he was following us, but then we thought we lost him. Apparently we didn't lose him for long."

The officer nodded. "I'm not any kind of a shrink," Wilson claimed, "but it sounds like he killed some lady who must look like you."

"Someone named Mallory," Mara interrupted.

"I hate that name," Sam muttered.

". . . and his mind's playing tricks on him. He's going nuts, and you were in the wrong place at the wrong time."

"This is just too weird," Victoria said with a shiver.

"Tell you what," Wilson said as he stood, "we'll figure out what this Cox fellow is up to. We'll need all three of you to come to the station to sign statements tomorrow."

"Yes, of course," Sam stammered. She recalled the night when she'd pressed charges against Adam and had to sign a statement. *I guess I'm getting to be a pro at this,* she whispered to herself. A forlorn ache settled in the center of her heart.

Twenty-Four

R.J. waited as the florist's website loaded. He moved the cursor from one blank to another as he filled in the appropriate information for sending roses. Two dozen red roses, to be exact, for Samantha Jones. A smug smile claimed him as he applauded his own ingenuity. When the time came for him to fill in the signature line, he simply typed, "Looking forward to the weekend. Your not-so-secret admirer." He nodded, imagining her thrill when the flowers arrived in her office in the morning.

"The Internet is a wonderful thing," he said. The screen announced his order had been accepted and would arrive at Sam's office tomorrow morning by ten. "Yes, I am *so good!*" he claimed, producing a hacking laugh that bounced off the utilitarian office walls.

"What are you up to in here?" Larry's bass voice floated from the doorway. "The last time you were laughing like that you were planning to overthrow the government."

"Ah, shut up," R.J. chided and grinned toward his haggard friend whose resounding voice didn't match his compact size. The dark circles under his eyes and the smudge of soot on his cheek attested to the day's hard work. R.J. felt about as exhausted as Larry looked. After the drive, he had immediately pitched in to clean out as much of the kitchen as possible before the remodeling team arrived in the morning. Finally their crew of teenage boys had begged off to go play a round of basketball on the lighted court out back. The distant cheers and calls confirmed that they were enjoying the game despite winter's chill.

"Don't tell me . . ." Larry walked into the austere room, halted in front of the desk, and crossed his arms. The smell of soot trailed him as he strained his neck to read the computer screen.

Scowling, R.J. covered the screen with both hands and said, "Hey, mind your own business!"

"Oh, isn't that just all so tweet?" Larry teased in a falsetto voice. "Rhett is sending flowers to Scarlet."

R.J. narrowed his eyes and stared at his partner. Frankly, he didn't know whether to burst out laughing or pummel the man.

After the end of a short mental debate, R.J. decided Larry had gone too far. "Listen you," he snarled before coughing over a chuckle. R.J. sprang from the chair, rounded the desk, and charged at Larry, whose thin frame and modest height made him about half R.J.'s size. "I told you once already you were dead meat."

"Okay, okay, okay," Larry yelped, holding up his hands. "I give! I promise I won't do it again."

"You better not." R.J. grabbed a fistful of Larry's Western shirt and grinned. "Otherwise, in a loving and Christlike manner, I'll toss you out the window."

"In the name of Jesus, I am sure," Larry quipped and knocked R.J.'s hand from his shirt. "Stop messin' with me, man." Larry smoothed the front of his shirt. "I've got an image to uphold."

R.J. rolled his eyes. "Right. You look like a refugee camp reject right now." R.J. crossed his arms, rested his backside against the edge of the desk, and extended his legs in front of him.

"Well, I love you, too," Larry replied.

"Glad to finally hear it." R.J. tucked his fingers under his arms and allowed his thumbs to rest on his chest. "I guess you've finally realized I'm a real loveable kinda guy." Truth was, the two friends had formed a bond long ago that some siblings never enjoyed.

Larry rolled his eyes and pointed to the computer.

"Looks like maybe I'm not the only one."

"Oh, get outta here." R.J. waved his hand. "You've sent enough flowers to Emily to fill this house. And the way you moped around here for a year before the two of you got married — you don't have any room to talk."

"One thing's for sure, you ain't moped since you got home." Larry stroked his jaw, covered in dark stubble. "The only thing worse than cleaning out a burned kitchen is cleaning it out with somebody who is singing. What'd Sammie do? Lay one on you before you left?"

"Well, as a matter of fact . . ." R.J. cocked his head to one side, but the bells of caution warned him that this was not the time or place to be bragging about his progress with Sam. His guess was that she wouldn't quite appreciate it.

Larry raised his brows and waited.

"Let's just say things are looking up," R.J. responded.

Larry glanced around the room, quirked

one eyebrow, then peered back at R.J. "Are you, by chance, *missing* something in here? Something besides your braid? Or should I say *someone?*" The corners of his mouth curved downward, and his brows rose as if he already knew the answer.

R.J. stiffened and tingles assaulted his cheeks. His panicked gaze darted across the room's every inch, from the bookcase to his worn leather jacket lying near the door. He whipped around and stared out the oversized window behind his desk. He caught sight of six teenage boys, of various sizes and races, hammering away at the ball court — but no Brett.

"I — I totally forgot about Brett!" he croaked. "He was here just a minute ago! Brett!" he hollered. He held his breath as the room vibrated with deafening silence, a silence broken only by the whir of the computer.

"I'd try the dining room first, if I were you," Larry said with a twisted smile. "By the boxes where we put all the salvageable food," he continued. "And if I were you, I'd take some paper towels — both wet and dry."

"Oh no," R.J. groaned, glowering at his friend. "I'm going to knock you flat one day, and nobody's going to ask why. Don't ever scare me like that again!" he commanded as he swept toward the doorway.

"For a cool thousand bucks I won't report this to Sammie. . . ."

"Ah, stick a sock in it," R.J. muttered. Not waiting for further remarks, he bounded up the hallway, past the charred kitchen, and into the massive dining room with a rustic table capable of seating 12. There sat Brett, perfectly at home beside the scattering of cardboard boxes that held the ranch's food supply. One hand was crammed into his mouth. The other hand held a peanut butter jar. Peanut butter dotted his face and the edges of his hair. Miss Puppy, chin on paws, dozed blissfully by his legs.

"What do you think you're doing?" R.J. asked as he neared the child.

"I hungry," Brett stated. He jabbed his hand back into the jar.

"But we just ate an hour ago," R.J. said, eyeing the empty pizza box still claiming the end of the table.

"Make that three hours and counting," Larry said from behind. R.J. frowned at his partner who tapped the face of his watch.

"What time is it, anyway?" R.J. asked.

"Nine o'clock, lover boy," Larry called

over his shoulder as he moved toward the kitchen. "Can't wait until tomorrow night!"

"You've got a really big mouth for such a short guy," R.J. shot back.

"Oops! Couldn't hear a word you said," Larry answered, and the back door slammed shut behind him.

R.J. scooped Brett up into his arms. "What if we fix you a sandwich?" he asked.

"Okay," Brett said. "Puppy wants one, too."

"Oh, she does?" R.J. said and bestowed a tender kiss on the child's forehead. When he pulled away, peanut butter was on his lips. "You've got this stuff all over you, don't you?"

In answer Brett scraped out another dollop and crammed it into his mouth. Shaking his head, R.J. spotted a loaf of bread atop one of the boxes overflowing with food. He deposited Brett on a bench and nabbed it.

"Okay," R.J. began, "there's one thing you need to understand before your mom and I get married and I officially adopt you — Butlers always eat their peanut butter on wheat bread with home-grown honey, along with a glass of cold milk."

"Coke! Brett want Coke!" Brett exclaimed. His red brows furrowed with the intensity of his desire.

"Nice try, champ." R.J. shook his head. "Coke is bad for you. Uncle R.J. is having milk," he added as an enticement.

After careful consideration, Brett nodded and then concentrated on licking his fingers.

R.J. shoved his hand into the side of another box and pulled out a bucket of honey he'd bought from a local farmer. "I think I'll have a sandwich, too," he said and scrounged through the paper supplies on one end of the table until he produced a couple of knives, plates, and some disposable cups. "But first we need to get your face clean." R.J. removed the peanut butter from Brett's grasp and swung the child upward.

"I ride your shoulders!" Brett insisted.

"No, not now, buddy. You'll get peanut butter all over me. Let's wait until we get you cleaned up."

A shrill ring emanated from the den. R.J. rolled his eyes. "Oh brother," he groused. "I'm just going to let the answering machine get it."

"Might be mommy!" Brett said with a sage nod.

"I doubt it." R.J. stepped into the blue-tiled spacious bathroom and plopped Brett on the sink side. The aroma of peanut butter mingled with the smell of tile cleaner and soap. "Your mommy said she'd call again in the morning." R.J. grabbed a washcloth and barely acknowledged the machine's beep.

Sam's hesitant voice floated from the den. "R.J.? Are you there?"

"Mommy!" Brett squealed.

R.J. snatched up Brett and hurried into the den that housed boy-worn recliners, high-topped sneakers, and a big screen TV. He orchestrated a moderate dive for the phone perched atop a solid table between two recliners. The recliner scraped along the linoleum floor before halting with a jar. R.J. grabbed the receiver as Brett declared, "Whoa, Uncle R.J.!"

"Hello," he gasped into the receiver. Other than the child's lopsided position in R.J.'s lap, Brett appeared unaffected by their crash landing.

"R.J.?" Sammie's wobbly voice carried an undercurrent of trouble and turmoil.

"What's wrong?" R.J. sat straight up, braced Brett against his sudden movement, and listened in gaping silence as Sammie related the events of her harried evening.

A deranged invader! An old murder! Sam's attempted murder! Police!

As Sammie wrapped up her recitation, R.J. deposited Brett onto the area rug and began pacing. "I could kick myself for leaving today!" Frustration twisted his stomach.

"I'm just glad Brett was with you!" Sammie said.

"Right. If he'd been there, he could have been —"

"Don't even say it!" Sammie commanded.

R.J. could almost see the glint in her eyes that brooked no argument.

"Okay, then, I'll say I wish *you'd* been with me, too!"

Taut silence permeated the line, and R.J. wondered if it were a good silence . . . or a bad silence . . . or a strained silence. *Darned if I know,* he thought. *I'm tired of trying to figure out her moods.*

"I'm not really cozy-comfy with you bein' there tonight, either," he continued. "What about that vet? Do the police think he might show up for a visit, too?"

"The police are patroling my neighborhood all night. As a matter of fact, they've got a car parked at the end of the road right now. And as far as Barry Cox goes, when the police officer who took my statement called to confirm that we'd be there in the morning to press charges, he mentioned that Terrence Blackwood has started talking about cocaine dealing. So . . ."

R.J. released a slow sigh. "Okay, okay," he acquiesced. "And your friend is still there?"

"Yes. And my mom is staying awhile longer, but then she has to get back home. Rana is supposed to be coming to her house tomorrow and —"

R.J. whistled. "Rana? No way!"

"I know," Sammie said hopefully. "We're praying she's making a turn for the better."

"Sounds like positive things are finally happening in your family."

"God is answering prayers," Sam claimed.

"And you and your mom?"

"God is answering prayers," she repeated.

"Good," he said. If ever a family needed healing, he figured Sam's did. And R.J. hoped the healing would usher in progress for Sam in other areas as well.

He stroked the side of his face and a sticky blob stuck to his hand. He pulled his fingers away, observed the glob of peanut butter, and then noticed several streaks on his T-shirt. An indulgent chuckle wove its way up his throat.

"What is it?" Sammie asked.

"Oh, Brett found a jar of peanut butter and got it all over himself. I was in the middle of trying to clean him up when you called. I just discovered I've got peanut butter on my face and all over my shirt."

"Oh no, not the 'drobe!" Sammie giggled and R.J. figured a little comedy was just what she needed about now. "Serves you right for not watching him any closer than you were."

"Excuse me?" R.J. protested, not daring to acknowledge she was nearer to the truth than he wanted to admit.

"Don't sweat it, Butler," she teased. "He does that sort of stuff to me all the time."

R.J. stopped pacing, rocked back on his heels, and observed the ceiling fan as it rotated in counterclockwise rhythm. The kiss from this morning burst into his mind, and R.J. wasn't certain whether the whole room was spinning or just his head.

"Are you saying it's time for me to get used to it?"

After a breathless pause, the reception was interrupted by a brief click. "Oops!" Sam said, relief oozing from her voice, "that's my other line. I think it's my friend, Jac. Gotta go!"

"Coward!" R.J. called and laughed out loud as she ended the call.

Twenty-Five

Subject: Samantha and Rana
On Friday, 19 Jan 2002 8:15
Mara O'Connor
<mara@oconnor.hhp> writes:

Hi, Colleen!

You are never going to believe this! The Lord is really at work in our family! Finally, after years of prayer, I am seeing huge breakthroughs. Two nights ago Sammie let me past that wall she's had up all these years! We cried together and laughed together and even knocked out a deranged intruder together. (Call me and I'll give you the rundown!)

I got home late that night and, would you believe it? Rana had left a note on my door. She wasn't supposed to be here until yesterday, but she drove in early. She checked into a local hotel then called and left her number on my voice mail. I called her. Guess what! She's here for good — or at least for a long while.

She's very thin, Colleen, and I suspect she's been using drugs and alcohol. I don't know the extent of it all, but for now, she's home. My baby is home! Please pray that I can create a bond with her and help her find healing and get stable.

I'm so excited I can hardly stand it!

Love,
Mara

Subject: Samantha and Rana
On Friday, 19 Jan 2002 9:03
Colleen Butler
<candt@butler.hhp> writes:

Mara!
Wooooo Hoooooo! Praising the Lord! (About Sammie and Rana, NOT that crazy man!) I'll be calling later for the rest of that story so get ready. I want details, details!

Re: Rhett and Sammie. I had an e-mail from Rhett this morning. He told me about the break-in. He said Sam pressed charges yesterday. She also worked late last night ... because she had to get a little ahead at work so she could leave for Arkansas mid-afternoon today! That should put her at

Rhett's ranch in time for dinner. Keep your fingers crossed!

Yours,
Colleen

Sammie set her plate of waffles and fruit on the dining table, then sat down beside Victoria who silently toyed with her food. Wasting no time Sam dove into the morning meal and savored the taste of crisp waffles and maple syrup mixed with an occasional snatch of thawing strawberries. After several bites Sam paused to cut up Brett's waffle, only to have to remind herself that he was with R.J. For two days, Sammie had reveled in actually being able to get dressed without her son's constant interruptions. Now the lack of his laughter and Barney videos and cheerful chatter was beginning to weave a longing in her heart.

"The house is really quiet without Brett," she mused, sipping her coffee.

Victoria nodded and stared at her barely touched plate of waffles and fruit. Her downcast eyes and flushed cheeks reminded Sam of a small child who had been caught robbing the cookie jar. Ever since Wednesday night, Victoria had remained reticent and thoughtful. Sammie hadn't pushed for information, because she had been highly distracted ever since the phone call with R.J. two nights ago. Somehow they had fallen into loaded banter that left her reeling in memory of that kiss. She had briefly spoken with him yesterday, but they were brief calls to see how Brett was doing. She also figured Victoria was preoccupied with her marital problems. Finally, Victoria blurted, "Sammie, how — how much of my conversation with your mom did you hear the night before last?"

"Well . . ." Sam hedged. She aimlessly toyed with the pepper shaker and groped for comforting words. She had wondered if her "sister" would bring up the subject. Victoria's problems, while certainly valid, had taken second consideration to her own.

"You heard me, didn't you?" Victoria prompted. Her hazel eyes appeared haunted and sunken against her translucent skin.

Sammie rubbed her chin. She nodded. "Yes, but it's okay." She gripped Victoria's hand. "Really. I — I've been through so much myself. There were times in my marriage when I'd fight attractions for other men — especially when Adam was being a world-class jerk. Has — has Tony started acting like Adam?" Sammie asked on a snatch of breath.

"No, oh no!" Victoria waved her hand. "Nothing like what you went through at all." She shook her head and stared into her coffee cup.

The smells of the amaretto brew mingled with the aroma of waffles, and Sammie grabbed a bite of her syrup-laden delicacy.

"It's just that —" Victoria shrugged. "We've grown apart. Part of the reason we had that big fight was because he'd been out of town and came back home and immediately wanted to, well, you know." She shrugged again. "And I didn't — not in the least. He walked out and wouldn't tell me where he was going, so I decided I could do the same. That's when I called you."

Sammie toyed with a strawberry on the edge of her plate.

"I see," she said. "And, he's not trying to be forceful or . . . or abusive in any way or . . ."

"Not in the least," Victoria said. She swallowed a gulp of coffee. "We just . . . he just . . . he seems to have lost interest in me except when he wants sex. And — and it's getting really old, that's all." She gazed toward the sunroom and smiled apologetically. "Really, in light of what you've gone through with Adam, I guess my problems seem petty." She tugged the end of her French braid across her shoulder and toyed with the mesh band holding the end.

A thought bubbled from deep inside Sammie — one she dared not voice. *Sounds like Tony's not the only one to blame here.* Instead, she said, "Do you feel like you're putting as much energy into your relationship as you would like him to?"

Victoria dropped the braid and stared straight at Sam.

"Why are you asking that?" she snapped like a feisty Chihuahua.

Feeling as if she'd been verbally slapped, Sammie groped for a response. "Well, I . . ." She shrugged. "I . . . I just . . ." She grabbed her hot coffee and drank a mouthful. One slurp traveled down the wrong channel, and she sputtered and coughed.

"I'm — I'm sorry," Victoria said, patting Sammie's back. "I shouldn't have snapped at you. I just — I —"

As the coughs dissipated, Samantha observed her friend through watery eyes. Tears trickled down Victoria's cheeks. She pressed her lips together and shook her head. "Maybe — maybe it's just that you were too close to the truth for my own comfort. After I yelled at Tony for not giving me any attention, he shoved my complaints right back at me. The truth is, I haven't been fishing with him in years, and I used to go all the time."

"Maybe it's time to buy a fishing pole," Sammie suggested through a final cough.

"Maybe," Victoria said with a tinge of dubiety. "I'm just wondering if we're too far gone."

Sammie carefully sipped her coffee and savored the taste of heavy cream and extra sugar. "Well, you've got someone else to think about now," she coaxed.

Victoria touched her abdomen. "Yes, I know."

"I think you're probably talking to the wrong sister this time." Sam's chuckle hobbled out in uncertain rhythm. She methodically folded and unfolded the edge of her paper napkin and grappled for the most diplomatic means to deliver her message. "I mean, I'm the one whose guts were ripped out when my mother left and my parents divorced. And — and — well, it's just that —"

"Well, you're just a really loyal friend, aren't you?" Victoria said through a sad smile. "What I really wanted you to say is that Tony's a jerk and the whole situation has to be his fault. I hoped you'd say I should just go back home and let him have it." Victoria swayed her shoulders from side to side as if she were a prizefighter.

"Maybe you need to go home and do some serious praying to find out what you can do to start mending the fences." The words came out in a quiet cadence that was packed with the power of indisputable truth. Only the sounds of the refrigerator and the drip of the faucet interrupted the silence. "Don't get me wrong, Victoria." Sammie covered her friend's hand and looked squarely into her eyes. "I am not saying Tony isn't to blame here. I figure he's up to his eyeballs in it just like you are. What I am saying is —"

"What your mom said last night," Victoria finished with a wobbly grin. "To do everything in my power to make my first marriage work."

"Yep." Sam nodded. "Please don't misunderstand me. I mean, if Tony were beating you half to death like Adam was me, or if he was out sleeping with so many women you were afraid you were going to get AIDS or another STD, then I'd say to get out and do it without a backward glance. But that's not what's going on here, the best I can tell. Like you said, it just sounds like the two of you have grown apart."

"More like fallen out of love, I think." Victoria crossed her arms and rubbed her shoulders. "I can hardly remember the last time I really felt anything for Tony — other than irritation of course!" She grimaced.

Sammie debated whether to continue her honest probing but decided that perhaps God was using her to help Victoria sort things out.

"Do you think he feels the same things about you?" Sam prompted. She braced herself as she rubbed her thigh.

Victoria cut her a sideways glance that held a brief spark of ire. She examined her waffles, and the sound of a distant siren ushered in the ambiance of the former night's terror. On impulse, Sammie glanced toward the sunroom door and reassured herself that it was still wired shut. Mara had refused to leave last night until she was sure all doors and windows were impenetrable.

"Well, I — I guess you need to get to work," Victoria said. She stood, her spine stiff, and checked her wristwatch. "It's already after nine. Aren't you supposed to be there by nine?"

Sammie scrutinized her own watch and

wondered where the morning went. "Yes, I am," she said and shook her head. "Looks like I can't even make it on time when Brett isn't here. I guess I need to get a move on it."

"Okay, well, I'm already packed," Victoria said. "Since you're going to be driving to Arkansas today, I was thinking I'd just head on to the airport this morning and see if I can buy a ticket home. I can —"

"Why don't you drive up to Arkansas with me?" Sammie stood and extended her hand with the intent of squeezing Victoria's arm in friendship.

"No, that's okay." Victoria grabbed her plate and cup, sidestepped Sam's show of affection, and marched toward the kitchen sink. "I'll just call a cab to take me to the airport. Really, I'll be fine here until the cab arrives." She set the dishes on the counter and kept her back to Sammie. The fluorescent lights illuminated the red highlights in her mellow brown hair. Victoria shoved the stopper into the bottom of the sink, turned on the water, and squeezed the detergent bottle until Sam was sure the thing would squeal.

Grappling for something to say, Samantha scooped up her own plate, cup, and silverware and put them next to the sink.

"Thanks for doing the dishes so much," she finally said.

"Sure," Victoria mumbled.

Sammie hovered near her friend, not knowing exactly what to say next. "I — I'm sorry," she finally stammered. "I didn't mean to upset you."

Victoria's shoulders shook, a broken sob sprang forth, and she gripped the edge of the sink until her knuckles shone white.

"Ah, Victoria," Sammie said. She placed a loving arm around her friend.

Without a word, Victoria hurled her arms around Sammie. "I'm sorry," she choked out. "I shouldn't have gotten aggravated at you. It's just that — that — I thought you'd take *my* side. And I'm already so embarrassed over — over that other. It's all so shameful."

Sammie didn't say anything. Instead, she shut off the flowing water and simply hugged her friend and allowed her to get her cry out.

"It's okay. Really," Sammie eventually said. "And just for the record, I'm not taking Tony's side any more than I'm taking your side. It's just that I can see two sides here, and —"

"Promise me you won't tell the other sisters, Sammie. Promise me!" Victoria inched away then grasped for Sam's hands. "I would die of embarrassment if any of them found out I've been flirting with the danger of adultery." Splashes of red marred her cheeks.

Sam gripped her friend's shoulders. "I promise I won't tell any of them. But Victoria . . ." she shook her head, "I *also promise* not one of them would think any less of you. Just think about them. Between the six of us, we've experienced divorce, an affair, a near-murder, grudges, and abuse. And you know what I've been through, girlfriend." Sammie stabbed the center of her chest with her index finger.

"I don't for one second want you to think that I am in any way judging you because I'm not. During all that torment Adam put me through, you better believe there were times when I'd look at other men who seemed, well, together, and sigh about my own fate."

"But — but — I've always been so . . . I don't know." Victoria pulled away, snatched a tissue from her sweater pocket, and scrubbed at her blotchy cheeks.

"You're the epitome of everything I've ever wanted to be, actually," Sammie said and shook her head.

"What?"

"You come from a solid Christian family that was functional." Sam raised her hand; then she yanked the front of her blazer. "You guys get together for every holiday and actually *enjoy* each other. Imagine that! And you're so ladylike and proper it just seems to ooze out of every pore. You're petite, and I'd stake my last laser jet cartridge that you don't have one trace of cellulite. And look at your complexion! Oh please! It's flawless. Me? I've got freckles all over the place — and zits for cryin' out loud!"

"And blue eyes most women would *kill* for," Victoria interjected. "Plus, you've got a man of gold who'd die for you." The words hung in the air, encouraging both women with the promise of tomorrow.

Sammie blinked and scrutinized her friend. R.J.'s admission from two days before echoed through her heart. *One day you're going to wake up and realize that I would give my life for you, Samantha Jones. And when you do, I'll be waiting.* The visit to R.J.'s ranch loomed. Sam's heart skipped a beat and a shroud of misgivings followed in the wake of the thrill.

"How do you know that?" she asked.

"It's as plain as the nose on your face." Victoria's brow wrinkled with certainty. "I saw it at Adam's funeral and at Jac's wedding. The man worships the ground you walk on, Sam." Victoria pressed the tissue against one eye and then another. "And really, I don't know if I've ever felt that from Tony. Maybe — maybe when we were first married, I don't know. It's been so long that I can barely remember what those first couple of years were like. And now . . . now I've hauled off and offered to help Ricky decorate his house!" she bleated like a desperate lamb.

"Excuse me?" Sammie asked.

"Ricky!" Victoria explained, her eyes frantic. "Ricky Christopher, the church's choir director!"

At last Victoria's meaning became clear.

"Oh!" Sam gasped. "You offered to help him decorate his house?"

"Yes! He came over to pay a courtesy call about choir. He saw what I've done to my house and said he was desperate for some help with his. His mom is coming for a visit and —" She waved her hand.

"Do you think he was making a play for you?"

"No!" Victoria's brows arched toward her hairline. "He *does* need help with his house! The place is the pits!"

"So you're committed to helping him?"

"*Yessss,*" Victoria hissed as if she were scandalized by the admission. "And I don't need to be working that close to him. He's just too — I'm just too —" She pressed her lips together as she grappled for the best euphemisms for the whole horrid ordeal.

"Well, why can't you bow out?"

"Because he *does* need help. He doesn't have the money to hire a professional, and I feel sorry for him. He's in a lurch. He's got his heart set on my helping him." She rubbed her forehead and leaned against the kitchen counter. "I also think he's clueless about how I'm feeling. He's so upbeat and carefree and unsuspecting, he'd probably fall over in a dead faint if he ever suspected how I've been feeling."

Sammie ran the tip of her finger over the towering suds and watched as the tiny bubbles popped in quick succession. An idea, like a wisp of a cloud on the horizon, appeared and gradually gained credence. "Would it help if I came to Florida for a few days and helped? I could be a buffer so you don't have to be with him alone."

"You'd do that?" Victoria asked.

"Of course." Sammie resumed her bubble popping. "I've got some vacation time coming, and Brett and I would enjoy the break." She packed bucketsful of assurance into her smile.

Victoria covered her lips and shook her head. "If you would do that, Sam, I'd be indebted to you for life!"

"Nah," Sammie said with a quick shake of her head. "That's what friends are for. Jacquelyn got me out of a tough spot; I'll do the same for you. End of discussion."

"Thanks!" Victoria grabbed Sammie for another tight hug. "You're the greatest," she said as the hug ended.

Sammie was transported to several days before when R.J. had said the same thing to Brett. The glow in Brett's eyes that evening surely matched the warmth now in Sam's soul.

"Some days, it's just good to hear that," she wobbled out.

"Don't ever forget it, Sammie!" Victoria declared. "You are a wonderful woman, and all the sisters were ready to come after Adam themselves when they found out . . ." She trailed off and gazed out the window that ushered in a cascade of morning sunshine.

Sammie didn't elaborate on Victoria's unspoken thought. And for once the mention of her past didn't provoke any trace of tears.

"I'm sorry. I didn't mean to drag all that up," Victoria mumbled.

"It's okay," Sammie assured her. "Actually, I really think I'm starting to heal." She blinked as her admission took her off guard.

"That's good to hear," Victoria said. "We've all been praying for you." She approached the sink and plopped the breakfast dishes into the suds. "I wonder if I'll ever say the same thing about my marriage."

"I'm sure it's all going to work out," Sammie assured. She squeezed her friend's arm. Doubt glimmered in Victoria's eyes, and Sam wondered how God was going to handle this situation.

"Meanwhile, I'm thinking about dropping out of choir altogether. What do you think?"

Sammie chuckled. "I think that's probably a smart move. You're going to have to do that anyway. Once the baby gets here, everything else will be put on hold."

The telephone's impetuous ringing cut off their conversation. Sammie glanced at her watch and noted that another 15 minutes had lapsed. "That's probably Wanda," Sam said. She walked to the end table where the cordless phone resided. "A lot of times she'll call to check on me if I'm late and haven't called in."

"Are you ever on time, Sammie?" Victoria teased.

"Seldom!" Her hand on the phone, Sammie shot her friend a mischievous grin. "If I ever were, I'm not sure Wanda's heart could take it." She picked up the receiver and gave a cheerful greeting.

"Great to hear you're not *dead*," R.J.'s voice boomed over the line. "I was beginning to get worried."

"Oh, no!" Sammie slapped her palm against her forehead. "I told you I'd call this morning, didn't I? I totally forgot! How's Brett?"

"He's fine! Want to talk to him?"

Sammie glanced at her watch. "Does he want to talk to me right now?"

"Nope. I think he's forgotten all about you, actually," R.J. teased.

"Well, just make me feel important, why don't you?"

"Aren't you sassy all of a sudden? Feeling your oats this morning?"

Sammie smirked. "Actually, I guess I'm feeling my waffles."

A groan chorused across the line. "That was *so* bad."

"Look," she said, "I need to get to work. Can I call you back as soon as I get a chance? I do want to talk to Brett."

"Sure. And . . . you might want to call Wanda before you leave. I called the magazine first, and she was wondering where you were. After all that's happened, she was starting to get worried."

"Sure. I . . . I've been distracted." Sammie eyed Victoria who scrubbed the dishes as if they were coated with something contagious.

"Okay, I guess I'll see you tonight then?" The nuance of his voice suggested they were new lovers planning a balcony tryst on a star-studded night.

"Yes," Sammie agreed and swallowed. "Tonight."

"Don't forget to bring church clothes for Sunday morning. I want to introduce you to the Ingrams."

"The Ingrams?"

"Yes, they're our pastoral team at church. I've told you about them. I think you'll really like them."

"Okay." Sensing the Ingrams were important, Sammie nudged her toe against a parakeet feather lodged near the sofa's skirt. *I'm still not sure I'm ready for all this,* she thought. But whether she was ready or not, Sammie knew beyond any doubt that Brett was more than ready for a father.

Twenty-Six

Late Saturday afternoon Sammie sat straight up in the middle of the poster bed and gazed around the unfamiliar room. For a startled second she couldn't remember where she was or how she got there. Cold sweat beaded on her upper lip, and she wondered if Adam had forced her into a reclusive existence in a secret cabin. Her heart pounded hard, and her temple throbbed. Darting a panicked gaze around the simple room, Sam kneaded the covers with taut hands as she gulped against a helpless whimper.

No, no — Adam's dead, her disoriented mind reminded her. *It's that crazy man who broke into your house.* Memories of his fiendish screaming seared through her. *Mallory! . . . Mallory! . . . I hate you, Mallory!*

A pathetic yelp escaped her quivering lips. She shoved aside the covers and tumbled from the bed with one goal in mind: *Escape!* With a muted thud her sock-clad feet collided against the hardwood floor. The shafts of evening sunlight spilling past the striped curtains whisked in the glow of truth. In a flash, Sammie recalled where she was, why she was there, and how she got there. R.J. had invited her to his ranch for the weekend, and she had grabbed a nap after lunch. She took a deep breath and reveled in the faint scent of lavender that radiated from the potpourri basket on the antique highboy.

Finally her legs no longer felt like cooked pasta, and Sammie stretched and glanced toward the digital clock perched atop the nightstand. Four-thirty glared back at her, and Sam's eyes bugged. She'd been asleep since one! She had yawned all through the chips-and-sandwich lunch, and R.J. had insisted she take a nap. Brett, declaring he was staying awake with Uncle R.J., hadn't minded in the least. After her recent escapades and stress level, Sam desperately needed a time of rest.

Sammie rubbed her eyes and straightened the striped comforter and covers. She padded around the cot where Brett spent the night and approached the broad window that offered a breathtaking view of R.J.'s ranch. Nudging aside the bold, striped curtains, she peered down from the two-story vantage. Acres and acres of rolling pastures stretched toward a plethora of Ozark mountains covered in pines and cedars, oaks, elms, and maples — now barren in winter's chill. Three barns claimed the countryside. A scattering of cattle meandered across one pasture while a group of horses grazed in another.

Yesterday when she drove up the winding lane, the sun was blasting its final rays across the horizon and christening the ranch in a golden glow tinged with pink. The sprawling ranchhouse, surrounded by acreage and livestock, had taken Sam's breath just as the scene before her now inspired and soothed. The last 24 hours replayed in her mind, and she smiled when she thought of meeting Larry and his wife, Emily. Neither of them had even hinted that they suspected a thing between her and R.J. Nevertheless, their dancing eyes had silently teased R.J. — especially Larry's. Emily, on the other hand, had declared herself Sam's confidante from the moment she entered the rambling home. And the crew of six brawny boys, along with the assistant, Steve, had treated Sam with a quiet respect that both reassured and impressed her.

Certainly R.J. and Larry were proving a powerful influence in the lives of these young men. The one named Carlos even jokingly called R.J. "dad." Eventually Sam gleaned that Carlos had been the driving force behind the mannequins-on-the-church escapade. She also noted that he and R.J. had a lot in common — including the braid. Sammie winced and wondered if Carlos or Larry had given R.J. a bad time about cutting off that length of hair. She had noticed upon arrival that R.J.'s hairline had been clipped.

Sammie almost dropped the curtains, but caught herself when a movement in the nearest pasture snared her attention. R.J. trotted across the field on an oversized beast-of-a-horse the color of chestnuts. In the horse's wake, a short-legged, pug-nosed bulldog pattered along as if she didn't have a care in the world. All yesterday evening R.J.'s pet had suspiciously eyed Sam as if she were a rival. With a smile, Sammie noticed that R.J. had another occupant with him — his own little buddy. A buddy with red hair and freckles and a delightful smile that hadn't tired the whole weekend. One of R.J.'s strong arms held Brett snugly in front of him while the other gripped the reins. Sam's throat constricted, and she knew that R.J. had managed to topple her defenses through her son.

Shifting her focus back to R.J., Samantha noted that he rode with the confidence of a man who spent his life in the saddle. Sammie couldn't imagine what had possessed him to agree to stifle himself at *Romantic Living*.

You did! a strong thought demanded. Sammie pressed her knuckles against her lips. When she arrived yesterday she had barely stepped from her car when R.J. enveloped her in a brief, tight hug. He'd then looked her in the eyes and said, "I've been worried sick about your safety." Sammie, taken aback by his unbridled concern, had focused upon Brett and attempted to smother her growing admiration for her ex-fiancé. But it wouldn't be denied.

"Relationships still scare me," she moaned. She contemplated the silent communication that had coursed between them all weekend. They hadn't even had so much as one conversation alone, but the undercurrents were so strong Sam wondered how he could breathe. Her breathing had certainly become difficult.

Samantha dropped the curtain as if it were hot and jolted from the window.

"Okay," she whispered. "Okay. This is it. I know he's going to ask me again this weekend. And — and this time, I guess I'll say yes. I've got to . . . for Brett." She scrubbed her damp palms along the front of her sweat pants; then she eyed the matching shirt, now rumpled from her nap. "I need to change," she muttered, then gazed into the antique dresser's ornate mirror. "Yuck." She took in her crumpled hair and the smudged makeup that had started out fresh that morning. At least the blemish on her chin had receded to a small dot.

She glanced at the clock once more and figured she had a little more than an hour until dinner. They all agreed that a takeout dinner was in order since the kitchen was in the midst of repairs. Emily said she'd have dinner available by six. Samantha reached for her makeup case lying on the edge of the dresser, and a lone red rose plopped to the floor. She scooped up the slightly wilted member of the bouquet of 24 that had arrived at her office yesterday morning. On a sentimental whim Sam had plucked this lone bloom and carried it with her all the way from Texas to Arkansas. She held the petals to her nose, inhaled the sweet scent, and smiled. Any time Adam sent her roses it had been as a token apology for his abuse. The roses, always accompanied by "I'll do betters," had eventually grown meaningless. Indeed, Sammie even developed an aversion for red roses. But R.J.'s "not-so-secret-admirer" tag dashed negativity aside.

As she laid the single bloom upon the dresser, Sam hoped R.J.'s ardent love could reach beyond the scars Adam had left upon her soul. Yet copious doubts sprang from the dark cavern inside and stifled the flutter of hope. Sam, blocking out her misgivings, busied herself with repairing her appearance. This was undoubtedly going to be a pivotal evening — an evening when she would trade herself to receive a father for her son.

R.J. followed Samantha up the stairs and down the hallway that led to her room. Brett stirred in his arms and rubbed a hand across the top of his head. R.J. slowed his gait and eyed the sleeping child. Shortly after their takeout dinner of steaks and baked potatoes, Brett had followed R.J. to the den and crawled into his lap. By seven, the toddler was fast asleep, which fit perfectly into R.J.'s plans. He'd given Larry and Emily the word that he'd like to have some time alone with Sam tonight. The two had vowed to keep the back deck off limits for their entourage of teens.

Sammie entered the bedroom, snapped on the brass lamp to its lowest setting, turned back the covers on the cot, and stepped aside while R.J. snuggled Brett between the sheets. "Sleep tight, champ," R.J. breathed and bestowed a kiss upon his forehead. Brett clutched the covers, rolled onto his side, and sighed.

Rising from his task, R.J. gave the thumbs-up sign to Sam and hoped his smile would qualify as the knock-'em-dead variety. She responded with a smile and thumbs-up of her own. The two crept from the room, and R.J. tugged the door nearly closed before turning to face Sammie. R.J. almost gasped. Sam looked so good. Better than he remembered seeing her look since before she married Adam. For once she appeared rested. And she'd managed to pull off something special with her makeup and hair — nothing R.J. could put his finger on, other than maybe she'd taken a little extra time here and there.

Sammie returned his observation with a determined glint in her eyes that R.J. wasn't sure he'd seen before — a glint that gave him the extra courage to make his request. "Emily said she left a pot of decaf brewing on the back deck. Feel like watching the stars with me?"

"Won't it be cold outside?" she asked.

"The deck's glassed in," R.J. explained as they fell in side-by-side to stroll the length of the hallway. "Kind of like your sunroom, only —"

"What? Four times as big?" Sam asked.

"No, not quite." R.J. chuckled.

"I'm surprised. This place is *huge*. I had no idea it was so big."

"Like it?" As they came to the top of the stairway, R.J. paused and cast a searching glance into her eyes.

"Of course! Who wouldn't?" she responded without reserve.

A warmth settled into the center of his being. Now all he had to do was convince Samantha she needed to marry him and move up here.

"Actually, I could have never afforded any of it on my own," he admitted as they descended the stairs. "When Grandfather Butler died a few years ago he gave me a huge chunk of his estate."

"Ouch! How did that sit with your father?"

"Dad? Oh, Dad was just fine with it. He still got a good inheritance by anybody's standards. He even offered to pitch in on the ranch if I needed extra help. My sister Phoebe was the one who was fit to be tied. She's always been the family star of sorts — of course, she is perfect in every way," he added sourly. "And it didn't sit too well with her that somebody in the family actually had the audacity to show favoritism to her rebel brother."

Sammie grinned. "Do I detect a hint of sarcasm?" she teased.

"From moi?" R.J. laid a hand over his chest and produced the most innocent expression he could muster.

A faint snicker echoed off the pine walls, and R.J. resisted the temptation to snare Sammie's hand in his. They stepped into the hallway that led to the den where the teenagers sprawled across recliners and couches, with their attention riveted to a televised basketball game.

"This way," R.J. said as he nudged Sammie through a doorway leading to a glassed-in deck that housed a pool table, hot tub, jukebox, and a couple of pinball machines. He stopped long enough to close the door, snap on the lights, and turn the knob that dimmed the glare. "Mmmm, Emily was as good as her word. I smell the coffee."

"I'll pour," Sammie offered. She approached the padded refreshment bar in the far corner. Her back to R.J., she made use of the cups Emily had already prepared. To the accompaniment of clinks and gurgles, she filled each mug with steaming coffee. "Let's see if I remember right — you like yours black as night." Sammie extended the mug to R.J.

"You got it," he answered and wondered if she even began to comprehend how deep his love was for her. He took the warm cup, cradled it in his hands, and watched as she stirred an abundance of cream and sugar into her coffee. Samantha looked at him and took an appreciative sip of her coffee.

"You look great, Sambo," he said.

She gulped and averted her gaze as if the compliment had taken her off guard.

"I mean *really* good," R.J. added. He wondered how well he hid the hunger in his voice.

"Th–thanks. Part of it could be the color of this blazer." She tweaked the lapel of the bronze-toned jacket. "Earth tones always seem to fit me."

R.J. hooked a thumb through his belt loop and tried to act casual. No sense in scaring her off. "Well then, it's a nice fit by anybody's standards," he agreed. "Want to sit by the window?" R.J. pointed toward a couple of wooden chairs in the far corner. "If it wouldn't make you uncomfortable, I could turn off the lights so we can really see the stars."

She took a sip of her blond coffee and eyed him over the rim with a cautious glint in her eyes.

"No, I'm not planning on making any moves," he said with an indulgent grin. "I promise. There really are stars out there, and you can see them for 'bout a million miles. We might even see a falling star, if we're lucky."

"Okay," she agreed and nodded, yet R.J. detected a wave of hesitancy.

All the more reason to be a perfect gentleman, he reminded himself. He prayed he could pull it off. R.J. had never claimed to be a perfect anything. "Go ahead, turn one of the chairs to face the window and sit down," he said as he walked toward the light switch. "I'll get the lights." R.J. made certain Sammie had settled in before flipping the switch. A great black wave of darkness splashed into the room and obliterated all traces of light. As his eyes adjusted, the moonlight gradually appeared brighter and brighter. By the time R.J.

turned his chair around and sat across from Sam, the room was bathed in a warm luminescence that created the perfect glow for star gazing.

"Wow!" Sam's voice radiated with awe. "It looks like a bazillion diamond clusters tossed across the sky."

"I thought you'd like it," R.J. said. "This is where I come for my quiet time. I try to sit out here every evening when I'm home. I feel . . . I don't know . . . so close to God here. It's almost unreal."

"Yes, I think I know what you mean," Sammie agreed. She sipped her coffee.

A silence, companionable and peaceful, settled between them. R.J. reveled in Sam's field-of-flowers scent he'd enjoyed the day after she purchased the puppy. Certainly star-gazing had its advantages. He eyed her hand, lying upon the chair's arm, and forced himself not to reach for it. Something exciting and unexpected was finally unfolding between them, and R.J. didn't want to blow it by being pushy. All weekend he'd watched her and never once offered to do anything but love her son and show her kindness. Larry had even admitted that he was impressed with R.J.'s restraint — and that itself was a miracle. The guys, all six of them, had given R.J.

ample grief when he'd assigned them barn-cleaning duties that afternoon. He hadn't even responded to their wolf whistles and catcalls. Instead, he'd threatened them all within an inch of their lives if they wiggled one toe in the wrong direction while in Sam and Brett's presence. They'd seen through R.J.'s tough performance and teased him all the more.

Now R.J. had Sam right where he wanted her — right where he'd hoped to have her all weekend — in the majesty of the night, in the silence of his soul.

"So . . ." he began. He didn't quite know what else to say.

She turned her pensive gaze toward him, and R.J. suppressed the urge to move closer. "How are you feeling now? I mean, since that man broke into your house. Are you —"

"I'm still kind of wigged out," Sam said. "This afternoon when I woke up from my nap, I was so confused I thought the creep had kidnapped me." Cradling the coffee mug, Sammie propped her head against the back of the chair.

R.J. nodded and took a tiny swallow of his steaming coffee. The mellow brew slipped down his throat and left behind a trail of fire that settled into his stomach before dissipating.

"Have you thought of installing a security system on your house?"

"Yes. Wanda suggested the same thing. Problem is, I really need more than a security system. I also need somebody to come in and put in new windows and better locks — and certainly a better door on that sunroom."

"Works for me," R.J. agreed. "The lock on your front door doesn't even work, Sammie. If you ever forget to turn the deadbolt, anybody could walk right in."

"I know . . . I know," she sighed. "Up until now I was a little skeptical that anything like that would happen. I mean, I've lived in the city my whole life and never once has anyone broken into my home."

Her soft voice floated across R.J. like a rhythmic sea, smooth and inviting. He forced himself to focus upon the stars shimmering like silver glitter upon a child's black construction paper. But they weren't glitter, and this moment was galaxies removed from child's play. Indeed, an urge powerful and untainted overtook R.J. — an urge to protect Sammie for the rest of her life. In the path of his gallant desires a latent tremor, forbidden yet irresistible, bubbled along his veins. R.J. prayed for more control. If ever a man was ready to get married, it was he. *Tonight! Yes, I'd like to be married tonight!* He gripped the armrest and forced himself to stare at the barn, a hundred feet or so from the house.

"So . . ." Sammie hedged, then added a question R.J. never expected, "what exactly is your take on a healthy marriage, R.J.?"

Twenty-Seven

"What?" R.J. shifted in his chair, riveted his gaze upon her, and spilled hot coffee all over his hand. *"Yikes!"* he exclaimed as the liquid scorched his skin.

With a soft chuckle, Sammie stood. "There's a towel over here on the bar. I'll get it for you."

"Oh, uh, sure," R.J. agreed. He tried to gather his scattered senses. By the time Sam arrived with the towel, he was certain he had imagined her question. He was also sure this gazing-at-the-stars business wasn't the best of plans. As the towel absorbed the coffee off his hand, R.J. figured he'd probably do better to turn on the lights and find some blaring music. Anything to break the moment. If things progressed much further, he feared he might pull Sam into his arms. *Why not?* a dissident voice urged. *You kissed her a few days ago and hugged her when she got here yesterday. What's wrong with a repeat?*

R.J. tossed the towel onto the table between them and reminded himself that he promised Sam he wasn't going to make any moves. He put the coffee cup against his lips and gulped down a huge swallow of the rich liquid. It impacted the back of his throat with scalding punishment.

"So, what do you think?" Sammie's gentle query invaded his internal struggle.

"About what?" R.J. croaked.

"Marriage."

He hacked against his stinging throat.

"As in, what makes one healthy?" she continued.

"Well, I figure if I ever found a woman who'd have me," R.J. started with a hopeful lilt, "I'd want my marriage to be, well, biblical, I guess." His words sounded as awkward as that of a 12-year-old, and he wondered where every vestige of his confidence had gone.

"Explain that," Sammie stated, a suspicious shadow in her words.

"You know, the Bible," R.J. replied and peered toward her thoughtful profile. "That big black book that says men aren't supposed to act like I've acted the majority of my adult life. You know, Sammie," he continued, his voice teasing yet strained, "that book we all study at church."

"No, I mean define what you mean by a biblical marriage."

"I mean . . . I figure I'm supposed to love my wife so much I'd die for her."

"And do you also figure she's supposed to be blissfully subservient to you for the rest of her life?" she queried.

Finally sensing where she was heading, R.J. set his coffee on the table, placed his elbows on his knees, peered at the short-piled carpet, and took several deep breaths.

"Actually, no," he said, and his voice's stability suggested his self-confidence was back. "Basically because that whole take on Scripture violates the Golden Rule — Do to others what you would have them do to you.

"I'd hate to think my wife thought of me as some sort of — of underling. As a matter of fact, I'd feel about as respected and appreciated as an earthworm if she tried something like that."

Sammie plopped her coffee cup next to R.J.'s. "Exactly."

"Furthermore, I think that any time a man insists on forcing his wife to follow six feet behind him, he's more interested in himself than in her. It's hard to cherish a woman when you've got your back to her."

"Right!" Sammie asserted with a vigorous nod.

"Glad you agree," R.J. said, chuckling.

"How can somebody say he loves a woman so much he'd die for her and then turn around and force her into a position he'd hate if it was forced upon him?" Sam raised her hand as if she were arguing before a grand jury.

"Preach it, sister," R.J. encouraged.

"Submit to one another out of reverence for Christ," she added.

"Hey, I can do submissive, if that's what you want," R.J. said on impulse. "I can even roll over and speak. I'll do anything but play dead — I'm a long way from dead!"

Sammie continued as if she hadn't heard his joke. "You know, I've been thinking a lot about this lately," she said. "I've come to the conclusion that submission is *unconditional* love in action. How can a person say he or she loves somebody but won't submit? That's like taking the heart out of love."

"It's like saying you're going to eat, but you're not going to chew," R.J. said. He fixed his attention upon the farthest star on the horizon.

"Exactly! You're right," Sam encouraged.

"All I know, Sam, is that I love you," R.J. stated in deliberate tones, and the lone star sparkled all the brighter. *"Really. All the way. It's the real deal.* And — and I know —" R.J. turned to observe the woman he wanted by his side, "I know you've been through a lot. I know from what you've already told me that your old church played a big part in the mess."

He paused and weighed his next words. "Since I've gotten back into church, I've begun to realize that sometimes people decide what they want to teach on a specific subject, then they approach Scripture and pick out the passages that fit their concepts. They turn a blind eye to the passages that don't line up with their supposition." R.J. nudged the toe of his boot against the wall, shifted his position, and picked up his coffee mug. "This submission business is one of the prime areas where that's done more often than not. And it's a cryin' shame because I think it produces a one-sided setup that actually creates bondage."

"You're right," Sammie agreed pensively.

Her doleful tenor sent a twist through R.J.'s gut. He gripped the hot mug until he was sure it would shatter. The coffee's heat was but a mere flicker compared to the angry inferno blazing through his soul. The stars, once sharp and brilliant, blurred together as he fought the images of what Sam had experienced with Adam. But Adam was no longer alive, and it was time for a new beginning. R.J.'s grip on the mug relaxed. The stars once again became pinpoints of light amid a sea of ebony velvet.

"I've decided our sinful minds don't want to submit to anyone." R.J. continued, "not to God, and certainly not to other people, consistently anyway." His even tones belied his momentary turbulence. "When we approach God's Word on our own strength and with our own wisdom, we end up going around the heart of Christ, around His message of sacrifice and love and servanthood and lifting each other up. When people elevate themselves and consider others less than themselves, they're doing the opposite of what Jesus Christ taught." He shook his head, then enjoyed a generous swallow of the cooling coffee.

"My stomach twists when I hear men talk about their wives as if they were one step below men in God's order. I cringe when I hear a husband or wife treating the other like a child or a subordinate or an underling."

"You aren't the only one," Sammie agreed. She rested her elbow on the chair's arm and leaned toward him.

R.J. resisted the urge to get rid of the mug and show her exactly how much he loved her with a kiss that would rock the stars. Instead, he hung onto the cup and feigned a casual shift in the opposite direction. *You promised to be patient,* he reminded himself, wondering if he'd been daft when he'd said "no moves."

"What I think is even sadder is when women really believe God made them as a second-best creation and that His perfect will is for them to lose their individuality and authority the minute they say 'I do.' " The sorrow oozing from Sam's voice rang with hollow hopelessness. "And during all that time with Adam, it was hard for me not to start believing it."

R.J. stared into the raven sky, silken and glistening, and the lustrous night held the promise of romance. Despite the bells of discretion that began a faint jingle on the horizon of his mind, R.J. chose to go ahead and take her hand. He deposited the mug onto the table and laid his hand on top of Sam's in a gesture meant for comforting. Her fingers, tense and chilled, flexed against the chair's wooden arm, then relaxed. Like a flower unfolding in the newness of spring, she turned her palm up and their fingers entwined.

R.J.'s stomach tightened. A strong tremor laced his spine. He forced himself to remember that taking Sam's hand was to offer support.

The words that tumbled from his lips rang with the sincerity of a soul bound by love, "Well, you aren't inferior in my books, Sambo. And you never will be. I don't think I could claim to know Christ — I mean, *really know* Christ — then treat my wife like she's second-best or is my slave. Those kinds of attitudes, no matter how subtle they are or how sugar-coated people want to make them, are the opposite of God's love. From the time I encountered Christ, He's done nothing but lift me up and better me and give me a love that's so strong, some days I can hardly believe it. And never once — *never even once* — has He made me feel like I'm of secondary importance in His eyes or limited in any area of my life. I figure if He's done that for me, and I'm supposed to love like He loves, then I need to do the same for my wife."

Sam's fingers grew rigid and tension radiated from her. "But Genesis 3 says the husband is to rule the wife, doesn't it?" Her swift claim challenged him to refute her.

"Playing devil's advocate, are we?" R.J. teased and stroked the inside of her palm with his thumb. Her fingers eased under his caress, and he reveled in the feel of his thumb against her skin. *Hmm, soft,* he thought and tried his best to remember the question at hand.

"Well . . ." he began, then grappled to refocus. "The Bible doesn't say that Adam ruled *over* Eve until the fall. I figure Adam didn't want to rule Eve before sin entered his heart, so his wanting to rule her is a direct consequence of sin. This is my opinion, of course, but I think the best thing to ask is, Do I want my marriage to be based on sin or on the love of Christ? You really can't have it both ways, ya know. I mean, look at all the non-Christian nations where women are shoved to the bottom of society and treated like slaves in their marriages. Seems to me that a radical encounter with Jesus Christ stops that kind of disrespect — no matter how subtle — in its tracks."

R.J. paused and debated whether to trot out the other side of sinful attitudes. *Well, what's good for the goose is good for the gander,* he thought, and plunged forth. "I also believe a real encounter with Christ would stop women from disparaging men, too. Frankly, I've met up with a few of those women as well. Christ's love doesn't do that. It doesn't demean other people for *any* reason. The kind of love God gives us doesn't ask, 'How can I bend you to my will or make you look bad?' It asks, 'How may I serve you?' Like I said before, you can take that Scripture in Genesis and several others and build a case for a husband to elevate himself and insist his wife follow six feet behind him, but you have to trample over a host of Scripture passages and the love of Christ to do it."

"Good." Sammie peered through the shadows with a hint of respect, even though her nod of agreement took on the nuance of a teacher who is applauding a student for a correct response to a tough question.

R.J. knitted his brows and cast her a curious, yet intense, glance. For a flicker in time he wondered if they were having a conversation or if he was being tested. Her guileless gaze suggested that he must have read more into her one-word comment than she intended. *Best to stay with the subject at hand,* he thought. "Did you know that before the Civil War people used to use the Bible to prove that it was God's will for them to own slaves?"

"I . . . I think I've heard that somewhere," Sammie said.

"Well, it's true," R.J. said. "Slave owners used to say that because Ephesians 6 tells slaves to submit to their masters, that was God's way of saying He approved of owning slaves. Today most Christians think that's way off base, but then some of them turn around and use the same kind of logic when it comes to principles of marriage."

"So, then," Sammie said with a deceptively mild tone, "would you agree that an interpretation of Scripture — or any attitude for that matter — that devalues a person violates Christ's teachings on selfless love?"

"Of course," R.J. agreed. "That's what I've been saying all along."

"And do you agree that distorting or pulling God's Word out of context can lead to repression and abuse in marriage?"

"Sure. I figure it's sometimes subtle and —"

"Sometimes it's very blatant," Sam cut in.

"We're on the same page, babe," R.J. said. He winced. The last time he called her babe, she'd given him a drop-dead look and told him not to call her that. He avoided eye contact and rushed on, "I haven't ever met a man who teaches that stuff who wants to be subjugated to his wife. And I'll bet there wasn't one slave owner who wanted to be a slave. Just like we already said, Sambo, the whole thought process is a violation of the Golden Rule."

"I've known some Christian women who were really down on men," Sam said with candid diplomacy.

"Like I said, that stinks just as bad."

Sam's fingers tightened around his hand, and R.J. eyed their entwined fingers. He rubbed the knuckles of his free hand along the side of his freshly shaven jaw. An odd restlessness jittered along the edge of his nerves. Something about this conversation wasn't sounding as genuine as it appeared.

"Have you thought about writing articles on this stuff?" Sam asked.

"I already have," he stated, and an inner voice suggested he should be wary of her motives. He drew his brows together and dismissed the stray thought.

"Really? When?"

"I did a paper on the subject when I wrapped up my second bachelor's degree last year. I majored in biblical studies," he mumbled, turning his gaze toward the barn. He cast a tentative glance back at her.

"No way!" Eyes wide, Sammie covered the top of his hand with her free hand and leaned toward him.

"Yes way! I did!" he replied with a saucy grin. Inwardly, however, his attention once again settled on their entwined hands. *Something is wrong,* he thought, *and I don't know what.*

"Do your parents know?"

"What?" He focused back on her.

"About your second bachelor's, you doofus," she said with an endearing undertone.

"Oh that." He shook his head. "I haven't gotten around to telling them."

"Why not?"

"Oh, I don't know." R.J. stretched out his legs, leaned into the chair, and disentangled his hand from hers. He crossed his arms and said the first thing that came to his mind, "I guess I'm afraid it'll mess up my image."

"You and your image," she teased. "You're like a pit bulldog with the heart of a teddy bear."

"Oh?" He raised one brow and directed a penetrating gaze straight into her eyes.

Even in the starlight, her baby-blues shone back with an intensity that riveted. Nonetheless, the sirens of caution continued their clamor. A sickening knot in the pit of his stomach replaced his masculine musings. Suddenly he knew what was wrong. Their conversation about marriage had the aura of a job interview. He narrowed his eyes, broke eye contact, and scrutinized the crescent moon that peeked over the eastern horizon. If he and Sam ever did get married, he wanted to know that she loved him as much as he loved her. And it would be a cold day at the equator before R.J. ever married someone who wanted to fill a "position" — as if he were a commodity that could be hired or traded. The idea insulted his love and sent a simmering heat through his veins. The part of his heart that loved Sam with fierce abandon scolded him for thinking anything negative about her. His practical side vowed that something was amiss. Something he'd rather not admit. Something he really wouldn't appreciate.

"So," R.J. mused, and his voice sounded steely even to his own ears, "why all these questions about marriage, Sammie? Thinking about proposing or something?"

Twenty-Eight

Sam's tongue stuck to the roof of her mouth. She grabbed her coffee mug and clutched it close as if the cup could offer some stability. After the warmth of R.J.'s hand upon hers, the backs of Sam's fingers now cooled, and she missed his touch. She peered at the slip of a moon creeping across the star-studded canvas and decided the best answer to R.J.'s question was to avoid answering. Sammie had expected the discussion about marriage to naturally lead into R.J. repeating the proposal; instead, he had thrown her into a tailspin.

"I — I think my coffee needs a warm up. What about yours?"

"No thanks," R.J. said, his voice flat.

Disconcerted, Sammie wrestled with how to respond.

"Okay," she agreed as she stood and walked toward the coffeepot. Out of habit she inserted her hand into her blazer pocket and encountered the braid she'd slipped into her pocket right before dinner.

The strands of hair still served as a hoop for the engagement ring R.J. had given her years ago. When she had followed the whim to place the braid and ring in her pocket, she'd told herself she was acting like a sentimental old fool. Now she wondered if that was closer to the truth than she'd first anticipated.

The squeak of R.J.'s wooden chair suggested he also was rising. His boots produced faint thuds as he walked across the room. Wondering if he were leaving without an explanation, Sammie gripped the coffee carafe and glanced over her shoulder as the lights flickered on. She squinted against the brilliance; then she refocused on her task. The coffeepot trembled in her hand as she poured a generous measure into her depleted brew. From the corner of her eye she noticed that R.J. had neared the end of the refreshment bar. She replaced the pot with the clatter of glass on metal and made a monumental task of adding an abundance of creamer and sugar to the fragrant liquid.

"Why the sudden change, Sam?" R.J. asked, and this time nothing but pain dripped from his words. Sammie snapped her gaze to his. In the stark lighting, his dark eyes revealed the agony that matched his voice.

"Excuse me?" she asked as her heart pounded at an uncomfortable rate. *He knows why I've decided to marry him,* she thought, *and he doesn't like it.* Her gaze faltered back to her coffee.

"Forgive me if I'm being paranoid here." He paused, rubbed the back of his neck, then trailed his palm down the front of his T-shirt. "But it's a little odd to me that earlier this week you were claiming you had nothing to give. And tonight you're nearly begging me to propose again."

Sam's mouth fell open as an appalled gasp escaped her. She said the first thing that popped into her mind, "Of all the arrogant —"

R.J. raised his hand and the disenchanted wilt of his lips repudiated any hint of arrogance. "You know, Sam, I've never claimed to be the most subtle guy on the planet. I've always lived by the rule that the best thing in most cases is to get everything out in the open. So here goes — I think I just underwent some kind of interrogation over there." He pointed toward their chairs.

Sammie looked toward them. She then stared at the floor-to-ceiling windows that now masked the majesty of the stars.

"It almost feels like you've decided to grit your teeth and marry me, but before you do you've got to make sure my attitudes fit your job description . . . that way you can at least endure my presence."

A gnawing heat, slow and persistent, crept from Sammie's abdomen, up her neck, and straight to her hairline.

"How dare you!" She plopped her coffee cup atop the bar, and the hot liquid splattered across her fingers.

"Then tell me you love me, Sammie," R.J. entreated. The torment in his words sent a spear through Sam's heart. "Tell me that — that — the reason you asked me all those questions is because you've somehow reconnected with what we used to have. Tell me you just wanted to make sure we understand each other. Tell me you can't imagine life without me. Tell me that you need me." Leaning forward he jabbed his fingers against his chest.

"But we — we *do* need you," Sammie defended. Her head spun with the force of his outburst, and she wasn't sure of what she was saying or even what she *should* say.

"*We?*" He shook his head and gripped her upper arms. For what felt like an eternity R.J. peered straight into her soul — and Sam didn't have the will to even so much as flinch. The powerful love pouring from his heart hit Sam full force. For the first time since her mother walked out, a wisp of hope arose that another human being really was capable of loving her . . . all the way . . . forever . . . without selfish intent.

After her parents split up, Sammie doubted if true love really existed. Then R.J. came along and Sammie's belief in love returned. She fell for him — and fell hard. But he left. Then there had been Adam. After him, she was convinced she didn't want to love again. Then R.J. came back, and she wondered if she could even receive love, much less give it. Now here she was standing in front of her first love. Looking back, she'd never seen the depth of love in his eyes that she was now drowning in. A wash of hot tears blurred R.J.'s image, and Sammie floundered with the realization that she'd truly hurt him.

"This is about Brett, isn't it?" he finally asked, and a pair of frown lines formed between his dark brows.

Sammie opened her mouth but no words came. She'd been so certain R.J. would take her on any terms that she'd never even considered he'd question her change of mind.

"You finally saw how much Brett loves

me, so you decided you'd just — just —"
he shook his head again, "that you'd sacrifice yourself for a father for Brett."

With a twist of trembling lips, Sammie
stumbled out of R.J.'s grasp and bumped
into the wall. "If all of that was so infer-
nally important to you, then why'd you ask
me to marry you right after Adam died?"
Sammie cried. She leaned against the wall
lest her quivering legs collapsed beneath
her.

His eyes, once blazing and intense, reddened with a hint of moisture. "Because I
— I thought that somehow maybe you'd
never really stopped loving me, even after
all I did and after all you've been through.
I hoped that since the chemistry is still
there between us it must mean . . ." R.J.
swallowed, blinked hard, then turned his
back to her. He strode to the chairs,
stopped, snatched up his mug, and took a
long swallow. "I guess I was acting like a
sentimental old fool," he finally ground
out, not bothering to turn around.

Sammie swiped at the lone tear that
seeped from her eye and commanded herself not to cry another drop. She doubled
her fists and prepared to march to her
room so she could dissolve into a heap of
humiliation. Then R.J.'s words slammed

her right between the eyes. He'd called himself a sentimental old fool — the exact same thing she thought about herself when she put his braid into her pocket. She crammed her hand into the blazer and grimaced with the feel of prickly wool against her coffee-dampened fingers. She stroked the braid with her index finger and wondered if she'd ever feel whole — so whole she could once again relinquish her heart with abandon.

A quiet thought from the depths of her soul whispered, *Maybe you really never stopped loving R.J. Butler, with his motorcycles, his black leathers, and that ever-present braid.* She eyed his hairline, clipped and tidy, and was once again stricken by the power of his love.

Sam climbed to the front of the cave in her forlorn soul and gazed at R.J., who still stood on the other side of the gate, his arms outstretched, his eyes beseeching her to embrace him as he so wanted to embrace her. Her pulse hammering, her breathing shallow, Sammie stumbled from the cave. She took several steps toward the gate, but the chains of her past bound her to the cavernous darkness. A blackness that thrived in a fog of fear — a fear that warned her to never again give her heart to a man.

R.J. pivoted to face her, and his shadowed eyes, tired and disillusioned, barely acknowledged her presence. Sammie hovered near the refreshment bar and stayed the impulse to fling herself into his arms. She bit down on her bottom lip, then bolted from the room. Halfway expecting R.J. to follow, Sammie bounded past the den without so much as a glimpse at the lanky boys and their TV. She hustled up the stairs, down the hallway, and paused outside her door long enough to glance up the hallway. Despite her expectations, R.J. wasn't following.

Panting, Sammie gripped the chilly doorknob and eased into the room. Closing the door behind her, she turned toward Brett snoozing in his cot. She locked the door, kicked off her loafers, crawled into the center of the bed, and wrapped her arms around her knees. Sammie rocked back and forth while biting back the tears.

And so she sat alone in the dank cavern. Where she had hidden after her mother's desertion. Where she had run after R.J. jilted her. Where she had escaped when Adam became abusive. And somewhere near the mouth of that gaping cave a soft, masculine voice called her name. A voice of love. Love and compassion. Compassion and regret. *One day you're going to wake up and realize that I would give my life for you. . . . And when you do, I'll be waiting. . . . I'll be waiting. . . . I'll be waiting.*

"Oh, Jesus, help me. I am so confused." Sammie prayed until she was so spent she stretched out on the bed. Tortured by invisible arrows of pain, she lost all awareness of time. At last sleep overtook her, and she lapsed into a fitful doze.

The next morning R.J. neared Sam's room and hesitated outside the door. He checked his wristwatch and wrinkled his brow. Already dressed in his Sunday boots and jeans and the corduroy blazer he begrudgingly donned for church, he wondered if Sam and Brett were dressing. Church started in just over 40 minutes, but there were no signs of life within the room. When Sam and Brett didn't come down for their makeshift breakfast of cereal and doughnuts, he'd decided to let them sleep. Now he rubbed his gritty eyes with an unsteady hand and debated about asking Emily to check on the two. But Emily was busy getting ready herself.

He balled his fist for a tap on the door

and then stopped. A quiver shimmered through his gut, and he gritted his teeth. Last night had been weird to say the least. And he wondered if the morning light would ease the tension between Sam and him. He rubbed his temples and paced the hallway. As he'd wondered a thousand times during the night, R.J. debated if he'd overreacted. His earlier vows to exercise ample patience with Sam mocked him. He had been anything but patient last night. Indeed, he'd shoved her advances back down her throat because they didn't quite fit his idealistic schemes.

"I just hoped you'd say you loved me as much as I love you," he whispered to the mute door. *But now I wonder if that's too much to ask so soon after . . .*

R.J. pressed his lips together and tapped on the door. Frowning, he took a deep breath. The air, crisp and cold, was tinged with a hint of his aftershave. R.J. listened for any signs of life, but none came. Oddly, Brett hadn't made one peep all morning. Cold suspicion snaked its way through the bottom of his gut. R.J. knocked on the door.

"Sammie?" he called. He was rewarded with another dose of eery silence.

He rattled the knob and cautiously

inched open the door to encounter a neatly made bed. His fear became fact. R.J. flung open the door. His boots scruffed against the hardwood floor as he rushed into the room. Brett's cot, like the bed, was made to perfection. He perused the room's every corner and discovered not one piece of luggage or toy. R.J. whipped around and rushed into the vacant bedroom across the hallway. He shoved back the floral curtains, gripped the sides of the window, and stared at the front driveway where Sammie had parked her Honda. The car had vanished.

Doubling his fists, R.J. propped them against the windowsill, and lowered his head. *She must've left in the night,* he thought. *And it's because of me.* His stomach clenching, R.J. stared at the barren trees that covered the countryside and wondered if he could have blown last night any worse than he had. His answer was a resounding no. He shook his head; his shoulders drooped. He pondered the irony that after he had proclaimed the glory of Christ's selfless love, he had promptly railed about what *he* expected from a potential union with Sam.

But it would be nice to know she at least thinks she might love me one day, he argued with himself. *Isn't love what healthy marriages are all about?* Shaking his head, R.J. felt as if he were on the edge of a paradoxical abyss. While sorting out his thoughts, R.J. whirled around and headed into her room. A tiny hunch suggested that maybe — just maybe — Sammie might have left a note. "Probably just wishful thinking," he mumbled. He glanced across the top of the antique dresser and matching nightstand. At last his attention settled upon the highboy covered by one of Emily's lace doilies. A small envelope, propped against the clock, bore his name. Without a breath, R.J. grabbed the bulky envelope, ripped it open, and plunged his fingers inside. Fully expecting a note he frowned when he encountered a rope-like object. R.J. extracted the contents and realized he was holding his braid — a braid looped together by a rubber band that held both ends fast. A wisp of gold slid along the length of hair, then stopped in the center. R.J. turned the ring over and gazed at the tiny diamond sparkling on the engagement ring he'd purchased for her 16 years ago.

His eyes went misty for the third time in a week, and R.J. wanted to blast himself for his weakness. He pulled apart the envelope for a final inspection. That's when he saw her simple note of six whole words: *I'm really sorry about everything. Sam* And her vow of needing him seared a path of regret smack down the middle of R.J.'s heart. Last night he'd been so focused on his own disillusionment he'd trampled her claim that she and Brett needed him.

"Oh, man," he groaned.

R.J. pressed his fingers against his forehead. In his mind's eye he saw Sammie driving half the night to arrive at her weathered home, which featured the latest in dysfunctional locks and the memories of being attacked. Panic heated his veins, and R.J. wondered how soon she could get the doors and windows inspected. *Certainly not by tonight,* he reasoned. If by some wild chance that veterinarian discovered Sam had talked to the police . . . R.J. didn't allow himself to finish the thought. He decided he'd be the one who would fix her doors and windows — today!

He crumpled the envelope and hurled it onto the bed.

"You idiot!" He shoved the braid and ring into his jacket pocket, stomped from the room, and walked straight to his bedroom in the east wing. In minutes, he emerged with his overnight bag packed tight. R.J. raced down the stairs and straight to the office where he'd left Larry.

His partner, dressed in Sunday best, slumped in front of the computer. He looked up from the monitor, glanced at R.J.'s luggage, and lifted a speculative brow.

"Sam left in the night. I need to go back to Texas for a day or two," R.J. explained.

"Thanks for letting me know," Larry quipped, then swiveled and glanced out the window where six teenage boys were shooting hoops despite their church attire. "Don't forget to tell the guys," he added. "They're missing you lately — as in *a lot.*"

"So why don't you just put a guilt trip on me?" R.J.'s lips twisted in a tense smile as he gripped the doorframe.

"No guilt here, bro," Larry said, his kind gray eyes alight with assurance. "A man's gotta do what a man's gotta do."

"But . . ." R.J. knew Larry well enough to perceive when he was preparing to make a point.

"But on the other hand," Larry supplied without missing a beat, "I'm beginnin' to think part of the reason Carlos headed up that mannequin business is to remind you that he's still alive." Larry pivoted to face R.J. "I've never claimed to be a child psychologist, but I see a little more than I think Carlos wants me to see."

"Meaning?"

"He misses you, man. Considerin' he hasn't seen his dad since he was three, you're the closest thing he's got. And you know as well as I do that I don't have the bond with that kid the way you do."

R.J. expelled a long sigh and rubbed a callused hand over his tense face. Squinting against the blinding winter sunlight, he peered out the window and observed Carlos orchestrating a slam dunk. When he landed, his shirt tail flapped outside his baggy jeans as his black ponytail rattled against his back. The truth was that R.J. also missed the guys, probably as much as they missed him — especially Carlos. Even though his visits during this magazine stint had been frequent, it wasn't the same as being a full-time resident, which was the ultimate fulfillment of R.J.'s calling. A conviction, strong and irrefutable, settled upon his shoulders. A conviction he couldn't shake. A conviction that he had sensed for a few weeks. The time had come to return to the ranch for good.

"I guess my little vacation should come to an end," he said, wondering if there was any way Samantha would fit into that decision.

Larry smiled and propped his elbows on the desktop. "Whoa!" he said. "I must be some kind of persuasive. Maybe I missed my calling, and I should become a lawyer or somethin'."

"Nah . . ." R.J. curled his upper lip and shook his head. "You ain't smart enough."

"Get outta here," Larry quipped.

"Consider me gone!" R.J. shot back as he turned into the hall. Yet a new thought barged upon his mind. *What if Sam wants to come back?* He whipped around to face his partner. "Think we can make room for a couple more round here?" he asked.

"As in boys?" Larry faced the computer again and clicked the mouse.

"You know what I mean," R.J. growled.

"Sure. But you gotta tell the short guy to stay out of the peanut butter. Emily gets grumpy when we run out." Although Larry didn't look up, the corners of his mouth tilted up.

"Humph," R.J. grunted as he started walking down the hallway, "I don't think she's the grump around here."

"That's right! The chief grump is headin' south!"

"I can't hear a word you're sayin'," R.J.

replied as he left the hallway and strode toward the living room.

"Then you're getting old! Buy a hearing aid!"

R.J. spanned the massive living room decorated with Western flair and approached the front door. He gripped the knob and hollered his final shot, "Why? When I can borrow yours?" Before Larry had a chance to retort, R.J. stepped into the frigid morn. He slammed the door hard enough to punctuate the fact that *he* got the final word in this time.

With a satisfied smirk, R.J. realized he should have taken the back exit. He still needed to let Carlos and the other guys know he'd be home really soon — this time for good. A playful breeze, cold as ice, cavorted along the porch's pine rails. The brilliant sunshine shone forth as if it were celebrating the height of summer, but the barren oak whispering in the breeze testified that summer was still a forgotten mystery.

As R.J. neared the short flight of steps, a blue Honda turned from the country lane and purred up the sloping driveway. He stopped in his tracks. After his hopes rocketed, his common sense suggested that the vehicle must belong to someone besides

Sam. He walked to the edge of the steps, gripped the cedar porch post, and stared at the nearing vehicle as if it were a mirage. But the purr of the engine proved this was more than a wishful vision. At last the vehicle pulled to a stop, the engine ceased droning, and the driver's door snapped open. Out tumbled a little redheaded tyke whose chubby legs churned across the front yard and carried him straight toward R.J.

"Uncle R.J.!" Brett wailed, tears streaming down his cheeks. "I miss you!"

R.J. dropped the overnight bag, pounded down the steps, and met Brett halfway. He scooped the child into his arms and held him close. Brett's tears turned to gurgles of laughter as he squeezed R.J.'s neck past the comfort zone.

"I miss you! I miss you!" Brett repeated then pulled back.

With eyes that threatened to go misty again, R.J. brushed away his little buddy's tears. "And I missed you," he said then glanced toward the Honda. Sammie, still in the driver's seat, silently observed R.J. An aching question cloaked her features — a question R.J. wanted to be the answer to.

Sammie unlatched her seatbelt and told herself to get out of the car, but her legs wouldn't cooperate. Instead, she sat and stared at R.J. as he smiled into her son's face before tugging him closer for another hug. He delivered one of his heart-melting gazes, and Sam's vision faltered to his boots.

Within her heart Sammie had crawled outside the dark cave and stood in the stream of morning sunshine spilling across the terrain. R.J. still waited inside the gate, one arm reaching for her, the other arm holding Brett. A soft voice within urged her to race forward, fling open the gate, fall into R.J.'s waiting arms, and never return to that sorrow. But she couldn't. Sam thought she was doing well to hang on outside the cave, to resist the pull of the shadows that demanded she return to the depths of despair.

Sam simply sat in the car and allowed the winter's breeze to nip her nose until the end grew numb. While one unsteady hand gripped and regripped the floor gearshift, the other pinched the inside of the steering wheel. Instead of focusing on R.J.'s boots, she gazed downward at the folds of her overcoat bunched in her lap. Her breathing, shallow and swift, matched the rapid tattoo of her pounding pulse. The smell of her floral perfume mingling with the musty smell of wintry pines nearly suffocated her.

At last the crunch of R.J.'s boots neared, and Sammie's hands stilled. She scratched at an invisible mar on the center of her steering wheel, tugged her top lip between her teeth, and didn't dare look up. R.J. stopped inches from her open door.

"Hi," he said with a low, unsteady rumble.

Sammie's gaze roved from the steering wheel to a pair of long-legged jeans, to Brett's cobalt blue sweat suit, and, ultimately, to R.J.'s loving eyes. At that moment, Sammie knew he had stopped expecting her to meet him behind the gate. Instead, he had left the gate behind and now stood with her beside the cave of desperation and fear. He understood. He accepted. And he no longer expected her to do more than she was capable of doing.

Without a word, R.J. extended his hand to hers, and the love in his eyes promised he'd hold her until she could stand on her own. Sam gulped against the frigid air and clutched the side of that cave until her fingers ached. Then she reached forth and plunged her hand into his. R.J.'s fingers tightened over hers and urged Sammie to step from the car. Her square-heeled shoes touched the earth, she stood, and R.J. tugged her into the circle of his embrace. While Brett laid his head on one of R.J.'s shoulders, Sam nestled her head on the other and reveled in the warmth of his unconditional love.

"I drove to DeQueen after midnight and checked into a hotel," she mumbled against his corduroy jacket. "I was planning on getting up this morning and driving home, but when Brett woke up he wouldn't stop screaming for his puppy and for you. I forgot all about Miss Puppy."

"And what about me?" R.J. whispered while stroking Sammie's hair.

"I can't seem to forget about you," she whispered. A cow's lonely lowing matched the cry in her heart.

"Mmmm." R.J. bestowed a trio of kisses along her temple.

"All I could think was that I was going to drive to Dallas with Brett screaming all the way. And — and I just don't think I've got the will power to take much more of that. Finally, I decided we'd just have to come back."

Brett began to squirm in R.J.'s hold. The boy proclaimed, "I want down!" Sammie moved out of the embrace as R.J. deposited Brett on the frozen grass and adjusted his jacket.

"Don't you run off now," R.J. admonished.

"I go see Miss Puppy." Brett pointed toward Maddy and his puppy who had just trotted around the house.

"Okay, go on," R.J. said and gave him a reassuring tap on his bottom. "I let Miss Puppy out this morning with Maddy," R.J. explained. "Those two are gettin' along like two peas in a pod."

Brett ran toward the dogs who greeted him with ample licks and grunts.

"I — I'm sorry about last night." Sammie focused upon R.J.'s chin that sported a razor knick. "I didn't mean to hurt you. I really didn't. It's just that —"

"It's okay," he said and slipped the tips of his fingers into his jeans pockets. "And I already decided that I'm the one who needs to apologize. The way I acted wasn't exactly selfless love in motion. It's just that —"

"We really *do* need you." Sam settled her chilled hands on either side of R.J.'s face and peered into his eyes. She encountered a shadow of last night's agony. "Some days it's all I can do to handle the house and Brett and work. I'm tired of carrying all the burdens alone. B–but — I'm just so —"

"You're scared," he said. He tugged her hand to his lips and bestowed a tender kiss in the center of her palm then closed his eyes. "I think I finally understand," he added. "Looking back, I crowded you and expected too much too soon. It's just that —"

"You love me?" Sam asked with a wobbly smile.

"Yes." R.J. nodded and his eyes glistened with intensity. "With all my heart." Hope blazed in his eyes — a hope that Sam might someday return his love.

She swallowed against her tightening throat. "Well, I — I don't think I ever completely stopped loving you, R.J."

The tense lines around his eyes relaxed, his mouth softened, and the flame brightened.

"But I've been through an awful lot, and right now nothing is going to be the same as it would have been 16 years ago. I've been through too much." Sammie raised her hands in a desperate plea for him to understand. "In a lot of ways I'm not even sure if I can . . . I mean . . . what I can even offer you."

"Ah, Sam." R.J. pulled her into the circle of his arms and swayed to a silent rhythm. "I'm not asking for a thing except to love you."

Twenty-Nine

Subject: THEY'RE MARRIED!!!!!!!!
On Friday, 26 Jan 2002 3:13
Colleen Butler
<candt@butler.hhp> writes:

Mara!
AAAAAAAAAAAAHHHHHHHHHHHHHHH
HH!!!!!!!!!!!!!!!!!!!!!!!
I just got a call from Rhett! He and Sammie are in Florida and, believe it or not, they're married! Can you believe it? Somebody pass the smelling salts. I am fainting. *YES!!!!!!* I'd be aggravated that they did this without us, but I'm toooooo thrilled to worry about how they pulled it off.
The bad news is that Sammie has turned in her resignation at the magazine. We're going to stay on the road awhile longer then head on home. Meanwhile, Wanda is doing fine without us.

Yours,
Colleen

Subject: THEY'RE MARRIED!!!!!!!!
On Friday, 26 Jan 2002 4:30
Mara O'Connor
<mara@oconnor.hhp> writes:

Colleen,
Sammie just called me, too! Did R.J. tell you they're at her friend's house — at Victoria Roberts? I met her when I was at Sam's. Sammie mentioned having promised to help Victoria on a short remodeling job. (By the way, pray for Victoria's marriage. I can't say more.) In exchange for Sam's help, Victoria is going to keep Brett for the newlyweds while they take a honeymoon cruise. Sammie sounded ecstatic. I'm so happy! What a joy!

Please pray for Rana. I found a bottle of whiskey in her room. I think she's got a serious drinking problem, but I've decided I'm in this for the long haul. With God on our side we'll conquer this problem.

One more thing . . . Sammie said they arrested that veterinarian for dealing cocaine. Can you get a copy of the *Dallas Morning News*? It's plastered all over the front page, I guess. He and his brother-in-law are both in jail now. Am I glad or what!

Blessings!
Mara

★ ★ ★

Sammie toyed with her cell phone and inhaled the crisp ocean breeze as the ship sliced toward the Caribbean Islands. The sun sank toward the western horizon like a great ball of fire ensconced in a sea of blue. She tugged on her sweater for a snugger fit but still reveled in the moderate temperature. This was certainly a pleasant break from the cold front that had assaulted Dallas a few days ago. She observed the infinite water curling away from the ship in foaming wavelettes that splashed and frolicked in the vessel's wake.

Soon the water blurred, as Sam's thoughts focused on the approaching evening. This was their second night on the cruise. So far R.J. had treated Sammie as if they were courting, despite the fact that their marriage was five days old. Their first three nights together were spent in a hotel room and at Victoria's. Every night Brett had insisted upon having Sammie in the same room in which he slept. At first Sam tried to carve out some privacy out of respect for her new husband, but he had insisted that she not rock Brett's world any more than necessary. Then last night, the first night of their cruise, Sammie had anticipated R.J.'s desire for a physical relationship. In fact, she had dreaded it so much that she stalled in the bathroom until R.J. finally got worried and asked if she was ill. When Sammie emerged, she couldn't stop the cringing she desperately attempted to hide. The battle for restraint in R.J.'s eyes heightened Sam's respect for him. At last he turned his back upon Sammie and muttered an edict against every man like Adam Jones. Then he'd crawled into bed beside her, wrapped his arms around her, and sang love songs while the ship's rhythm rocked her to sleep.

But this morning had started with a slow simmer Sammie sensed would find full expression once the sun disappeared. Indeed, when Sam left R.J. in the cabin he had been preparing to shower and had bid her farewell with a kiss that begged for the courtship to be over. Yet the caution in his eyes promised Sam he wouldn't push until she was ready. Sammie's palms oozed sweat, and she shifted the cell phone in order to rub them against her slacks one at a time. The smell of salt and sea mingled with the waft of coffee they were serving in the nearby open lounge. Sammie pondered whether she should order a cup of the strong, black brew — maybe two. A quiver knotted her stomach, and she wondered if she had lost her mind when she accepted R.J.'s proposal. The last time she experienced Adam's brutality, she'd vowed that if she ever got out of that marriage she would never put herself in the hands of another man.

"Now here I am," she said, amazed. She gripped the cell phone until she was sure it would break. Then her mind flew to the rapture on Brett's face when she'd told him he could call R.J. "daddy." A shiver danced in her heart as she relived R.J.'s chaste kiss and the security of his embrace after their brief wedding ceremony in her home. Once again a heavenly peace invaded Sam's heart — the same peace that had prompted her to accept R.J.'s offer of marriage. Samantha sensed that God was with her, just as He had been with her during all her life's heartaches. He would sustain her and empower her during this new phase of life, too. Her grip on the phone momentarily lessened. A rippling wind stirred her hair around her shoulders, and a wave of nerves assaulted her again. A strip of gooseflesh started at her neckline and crept down her spine. The sun continued its steady approach toward the horizon while Sam was accosted by a dozen doubts circling her mind like buzzards bent on devouring any chance of happiness.

The cell phone's "charge chant" sent a startled zip through Sam's midsection and she jumped. She fumbled with the phone through two more rings until her unsteady fingers finally pushed the answer button and she said, "Hello."

"We're all so excited! . . . You go, girl! . . . What a great surprise!" A chorus of encouragement tumbled across the line so swiftly Sam could barely decipher which sister said what.

"Hey, hey, hey, how are the newlyweds?" Melissa's encouraging question penetrated through the others.

"Great!" Sammie said, but her voice sounded hollow, even to her ears.

The dead silence coursing over the line revealed the sisters' hesitation.

"Okay, I'm nervous," Sammie said gulping. "Really nervous. I — I know getting married was God's will, and R.J. has been just wonderful but we still haven't . . . you know."

"What?" Melissa gasped. "But this is the fifth night!"

"And the mouth of the south speaks again," Jac drawled with a hint of humor.

"Well, don't tell me everybody on this line wasn't thinking that," Mel challenged.

Sammie curled her toes as heat rose into her cheeks. "It's just that — I — I —" she stammered.

"You don't have to explain," Victoria said in a matronly tone. "I'd probably be just as hesitant."

"It's okay, Sam," Marilyn piped up. "This is my second marriage, too, you know. And even though I didn't live through what you did, I was just as nervous that first night. It was as if I'd never been married."

The sun-kissed ocean glistened toward the horizon sparkling like a sea of crushed rhinestones. And the gently lapping water seemed to whisper that everything would be okay. "You guys need to pray for me tonight," Sam croaked. "R.J. has been nothing but patient and kind. He has spent the last few days wooing me, but it looks like tonight's the night."

"I really believe everything's going to be fine," Kim Lan soothed, and Sammie imagined her Oriental eyes, dark and encouraging. "Really, I was nervous when Mick and I got married. I hated having to tell him about that awful affair I had all those years ago. But he was so understanding and . . ." her voice grew husky with emotion, "and it's just so cool to have a man love me so much that he's just glad to have the present with me."

"All this sounds so romantic and sweet," Sonsee drawled on a sarcastic note. "But right now, all Taylor and I want to do is get some sleep. Donny still has colic half the night, and right now our love life is almost nonexistent — and neither of us even cares!"

Sammie laughed and turned her back to the ocean. She propped an elbow on the rail and peered across the deck, dotted by numerous couples enjoying the spectacular sunset while wrapped in each other's arms.

"I have been there, Sonsee," Marilyn encouraged. "Just wait. Things will improve before much longer."

"Yes," Sam agreed. "Donny will learn how to walk, and then invade your bed in the middle of the night."

"Actually, Brett crawled into bed with *me* last night," Victoria said.

"Is everything still okay with him?" Sammie asked. "I know we just talked a few hours ago, but —"

"Yes, you mother hen," Victoria teased. "He's fine. Buying that puppy was a stroke of genius."

"R.J. says they're connected at the hip," Sammie mused. "The good thing is that he never missed those annoying birds."

"So did Brett bring the puppy to bed with him?" Marilyn asked.

Victoria giggled. "Actually, he did!"

"And how did that sit with Tony?" Melissa asked as the sisters joined together in a round of chuckles.

"Uh . . ." Victoria hedged, and Sam winced for her. When she and R.J. left Victoria's house to take the cruise, Tony still had not returned. Victoria said he was sleeping at the fire station, whether he was on duty or not. "Has Sammie mentioned my situation to any of you?" she asked, her voice drifting away.

"No, I haven't," Samantha said. "You asked me not to say anything, remember?"

"Thanks." Victoria's voice floated over the line with a generous scoop of heartfelt appreciation. "Well, guys, Tony and I are . . . having some problems."

"No!" Kim Lan gasped.

"But you just found out you're expecting," Sonsee said, and Sammie was certain she detected an honest hint of Texas creeping into the vet's speech.

"And you've wanted to be a mom for so long," Jacquelyn added.

"Well, I still do," Victoria said. "But Tony and I just aren't getting along right now. It's all so —" She stopped in midsentence while a movement from the end of the deck snagged Sam's attention.

The sisters' consoling conversation blurred into the background as Sam watched R.J. amble toward her. With an apprehensive smile, she wiggled her fingers at him. In turn he shared a white-toothed grin that stirred Sam's pulse despite her misgivings. Sam never knew when the man would appear dressed in his usual jeans and T-shirt or when he'd go on a tear and dress up a bit. Tonight he had chosen one of the dress shirts she'd seen in his luggage. And something inside her hinted that he was doing everything in his power to please her. Sammie's knees wobbled, and her heart almost burst with a deepening love that refused to relent.

At last R.J. stopped beside her, draped an arm around her waist, and nudged his lips against her free ear.

"Miss me?" he asked in a seductive voice.

Sammie swallowed hard and nodded. As the sisters continued their conversation, R.J.'s fingers trailed up Sam's back and stopped on her shoulder.

"You're nervous, aren't you?" he whispered.

She lowered the phone a fraction, looked straight at him, and didn't try to hide the misgivings plaguing her heart.

"It's okay," R.J. soothed. "As much as I want this part of our marriage, I'll wait until you're ready."

"No," Sammie replied, and a new trickle of love flowed from the center of her spirit. A love that focused on R.J. just as he focused on her. A love that suggested she should do the best she could to please him. "That isn't fair to you."

"What isn't fair?" Marilyn's faint query reminded Sam she was supposed to be talking to her six closest friends.

She clamped the telephone to her ear. With an embarrassed giggle, Sam announced, "R.J.'s here now."

The immediate round of wolf whistles made Sam wince. "You people are merciless," she accused through a smile.

"Yeah, but we love ya, sis," Kim Lan replied.

"And we'll be praying for you." Jac's gentle voice, warm and loving, hugged Sammie. "You know I've been there," Jacquelyn continued, "so I know what you're going through. But believe me when

I tell you, it's going to be okay, Sammie. *Really.*"

"Thanks," Sam whispered then bid her farewells to the group of women who had stood by her through life's most horrid moments. At last she disconnected the call, dropped her cell phone into her sweater pocket, and leaned into R.J.'s embrace.

"I think you're the most wonderful man alive," she breathed.

"Mmmm," R.J. responded as he nuzzled her neck. The smell of his fresh aftershave teased Sam's senses. She pulled away and cradled his face in her hands.

"When are you going to stop this?" she asked through a shaky grin.

"What?"

"All this shaving," she said as she stroked the sides of his lips with her thumbs.

"I don't know," he said and snagged her thumb between his teeth, then released it.

A delicious warmth invaded Sam's body, and she began to think that maybe Jac was right. Maybe it really would be okay.

"I've just been thinking," R.J. continued, "I've got a son now. I need to give him the best image possible. And, well, I'm starting to like the feel of a clean shave."

"Miracles will never cease!"

"I hope not." R.J. propped his forehead against hers, and the fire in his eyes alluded to another miracle he'd been praying for.

A burst of bravado instigated Sam's next words. "Want to skip dinner?" she asked and silently prayed that the miracle would indeed happen. If only she could get through the coming evening with even a small measure of enjoyment she would know prayer was being answered.

"Hmmm . . . I'll skip dinner tonight . . . and breakfast tomorrow morning . . . and lunch, and . . ." R.J. lowered his lips to hers for a kiss that started out chaste but threatened fireworks.

Sam and R.J. simultaneously pulled apart, then cast guilty glances across the deck's various occupants. "I guess we need to take this into the cabin," R.J. said huskily.

With a silent nod, Sammie slipped her hand into his as the embers in her stomach swept a fire through her veins — an unexpected hunger she hadn't experienced in years. A vibrant, healthy desire to express her budding love to her new husband surged through her. They walked hand-in-hand across the deck while the sun's final rays bathed Sam's cheeks in a warm glow that sent God's blessing to her heart. She squeezed R.J.'s broad hand, smiled into his shiny eyes, and knew beyond doubt that Jacquelyn was indeed right. Sammie couldn't fool herself into believing all her wounds were completely healed or all her struggles were over, but she knew, finally, that life with R.J. was truly going to be fine.

Author's Note

Dear Friend,

If you were moved by R.J.'s love for Sammie, realize that it's far from a fairy tale. This selfless love is what my husband and I see every time we look into each other's eyes. After nearly 20 years of marriage we are best friends, lovers, confidants, and spiritual journey-mates. Our home is filled with so much laughter and love we are sometimes left breathless! Indeed, our first goal is to fulfill Christ's commandment, "Love one another as I have loved you" (John 15:12). This kind of love stems from a servant's heart that focuses on uplifting and empowering. Sadly, I've come to realize that the relationship my husband and I share is the exception to the rule, even in parts of the Christian community.

During my growing up years, my pastor father taught me that I was valuable in God's eyes. I was never told that God viewed me as a "lesser" person because of my gender. As an adult I have phoned my father and gasped, "Daddy! You're never going to believe this, but some Christians use the Word of God to demean women and treat them like spiritual inferiors. And some women even support this!" My father replied, "Debra, I have wondered if I prepared you for the real world by not telling you that these wrong attitudes exist in the church. But I was determined you wouldn't believe that because you are female you have less standing with God in your home, church, or community."

When some people read Holy Scripture, they look for ways to confirm that God favors them so they can be in control. Even the disciples exhibited self-elevating attitudes by repeatedly asking Jesus, "Who is the greatest among us?" But Jesus, forever patient, washed the disciples' feet and taught "the greatest in the kingdom is the one who serves" (Matthew 22:24–27) and "do unto others as you'd have them do unto you" (Matthew 7:12). The selective use of God's Word to prove superiority or "exalted" status breeds suppression, abuse, and dysfunction in churches, marriages, and homes. This error also drives unbelievers away from Christ because they believe the repression comes from God. But using the Bible to subjugate a group of people requires overlooking major passages of Scripture, such as: "Then God said, 'Let us make man in our image, in our likeness.' . . . So God created man in his own image . . . male and female he created them" (Genesis 1:26–27); "God does not show favoritism" (Acts 10:34); "there is neither Jew nor Greek, slave nor free, male nor female, for you are all one in Christ Jesus (Galatians 3:28); and "submit to one another out of reverence for Christ" (Ephesians 5:21).

The Lord does not condone oppression in any form. If you are in an abusive marriage, please know that God loves you and values you as a woman. The abuse you have endured makes Him weep. Pray for the Lord's wisdom and strength as you seek help. Nearly every city has a shelter, and there are numerous nationwide hot lines for battered and abused women. Make the call. It will be one of the healthiest decisions you have ever made.

If your marriage is mildly dysfunctional or blasé, remember that God didn't give you spiritual gifts and insights to be suppressed. Set aside enough time every day to seriously seek God with your whole heart; then, be still before Him and listen for His voice. Also, never underestimate the power of thinking about your marriage in the presence of God. Turning mental energy toward your marriage in God's presence will unleash a wealth of insights and ideas that will transform your union. No matter what problems you see in your husband's approach to marriage, be prepared for changes in your own heart and actions. God loves you and wants the best for you!

In His service and yours,
Debra White Smith

About the Author

Debra White Smith continues to impact and entertain readers with her life-changing books, including *Romancing Your Husband*; *The Harder I Laugh, the Deeper I Hurt*; *More than Rubies: Becoming a Woman of Godly Influence*; and the popular *Seven Sisters* fiction series. She has 29 book sales to her credit and, since 1997, has more than 500,000 books in print. The founder of Real Life Ministries, Debra touches lives through the written and spoken word by presenting real truth for real life and ministering to people where they are. Debra speaks for events across the nation and sings with her husband and children. She has been featured on TV and radio shows, including "The 700 Club," "At Home Live," "Getting Together," "Moody Broadcasting Network," "USA Radio Network News," and "Midday Connection." Debra holds an M.A. in English and is working on a master of divinity through Trinity Seminary. She lives in small-town America with her husband of 19 years, two children, and a herd of cats.

To write Debra or contact her for speaking engagements, check out her website:

www.debrawhitesmith.com

or send mail to:

Real Life Ministries
Debra White Smith
P.O. Box 1482
Jacksonville, TX 75766

The employees of Thorndike Press hope you have enjoyed this Large Print book. All our Thorndike and Wheeler Large Print titles are designed for easy reading, and all our books are made to last. Other Thorndike Press Large Print books are available at your library, through selected bookstores, or directly from us.

For information about titles, please call:

(800) 223-1244

or visit our Web site at:

www.gale.com/thorndike
www.gale.com/wheeler

To share your comments, please write:

Publisher
Thorndike Press
295 Kennedy Memorial Drive
Waterville, ME   04901